One Distant Summer

SERENA CLARKE

FREE
BIRD
BOOKS

Copyright © 2017 Serena Clarke
www.serenaclarke.com

One Distant Summer
Free Bird Books
ISBN 978-0-473-36626-1

Cover design by Elizabeth Mackey

This is a work of fiction. Names, characters, brands, media,
and incidents are either the product of the author's
imagination or are used fictitiously. The author
acknowledges the trademarked status and trademark
owners of various products referenced in this book.

For Dee…
my favorite peninsula girl, wherever you roam.

Praise for *All Over the Place*

"Filled with rich, deep emotion, engaging characters and dialogue, and plenty of intrigue that kept me turning the pages...Ms. Clarke is certainly an author to keep an eye out for!"
– Storm Goddess Book Reviews

"This book reminded me of a great chick-flick kind of movie, only in book form. And everyone knows the book is always better!"
– SMI Book Club

"One of the best, most romantic, awe-inspiring and awwwww-inspiring happily ever afters I've read in a long time. Brava, Serena Clarke! I plan to read more by you."
– Random Book Muses

Praise for *The Same But Different*

"You can't help but want to keep reading. It's not just romance literature, but also a story about sisterhood, loss and finding yourself. Extremely glad I found this book and *All Over The Place!*"
– Amazon reader

"Plenty of steamy tension...a recommended fun, feel-good story with some unexpected twists and surprises."
– WiLoveBooks

"A beautiful story about one woman's adventure of a lifetime."
– Written Love

Chapter One

You never know what your last straw will be, until it's right in front of you.

Over the years, Jacinda Prescott had put up with enough to send most people running for the exit, or the vodka bottle, or a little plastic bag of something uplifting. She'd avoided all those excesses...mostly. But now, she was literally staring her last straw in the face. He was over-tanned and over-confident, smug with his own power, slick enough to oil a grill. And he had no idea how far he'd pushed her this time.

She leaned back, resting her butt against the dressing room counter, and looked him in the eye. He was one of a sadly not-dying breed: a record label exec who still believed in the power of the casting couch, and counted on the silence of the female artists who felt dependent on him. Behind her, the bulbs around the mirror framed them in a square of warm light, and flowers sent by her friend Hannah before the show sat on the countertop. He thought he had the better of her, one hand on the curve of her waist in its black sequined bustier, the other hand pushing her cropped jacket aside to grab at her breast.

"I understand exactly, Greg," she said, in answer to his question.

His face lit up as he leaned toward her, but there was uncertainty there too, as if he couldn't quite believe her change of attitude.

"You should have done this long ago." He pulled her closer, grinding his hard-on against her, and murmured, "A tour like this could take you to the next level. A lot of people will be glad to hear it."

Did she dare? His beard scratched her skin, and this close she could practically see the dollar signs in his eyes, along with whatever dirty thoughts he was fermenting.

Yes, apparently she did dare.

She smiled sweetly. "Will your wife and kids be glad to hear it?"

As his face changed, she hesitated only for a moment. Her stage heels brought her to just the right height, and she used every inch of it, lifting one knee with violent force. As he crumpled, she turned abruptly and opened the door he'd locked behind him when he came in.

"I don't want your tour if it comes packaged up with you, Greg. Go home to your wife. And every time the phone rings, wonder if it's me calling to tell her what a cheating asshole her husband is."

She grabbed up her bag and the flowers and strode out, heart pounding, leaving her last straw doubled over and groaning behind her.

Out in the corridor, the first thing she saw was her manager, Todd Sheehan, looking determinedly casual.

"Oh, have you guys finished?" he asked.

She stared at him, realization dawning. He looked shifty. There was no other word for it.

"Are you kidding me? Did you send him in?"

He looked anywhere but at her. "Well, he wanted to talk business, so..."

"Yeah, the business of me sleeping with him in return for a national tour. I told you he'd still been hitting on me. Isn't my manager supposed to protect me from all that?"

At that moment Greg came out of the dressing room, still holding a hand against his groin. When he saw Todd there with her, he stood straighter, pulling his ego around him again.

"You need to think about what you're doing," he told

her. "You're not getting any younger. There are plenty of kids coming through who'd take your place in a heartbeat."

He turned and walked away, and she resisted the urge to give his back the finger.

"I hope you're not trying to screw them, too," she called after him, well aware of the other people in the corridor. He didn't reply, but she had the satisfaction of seeing his back stiffen.

Not getting any younger. She'd got her start later than most, after years living the cliché of waiting tables by day and playing dives and dead-ends at night. Now, at twenty-seven, she was a good decade older than some of the girls he threatened her with. Girls who found themselves going along with being dressed up and sexed up in the name of marketing and promotion, especially when they were told it was non-negotiable. And guys like Greg—making the most of his job in the artists and repertoire division—were more than ready to trade on that willingness, promising them breaks in return for sexual favors. She'd had plenty of offers herself, but so far, her guitar playing and songwriting had been enough to open doors. She knew the serious boobage she carried right there above her guitar didn't hurt her appeal any. But she never tried to purposefully shift the attention upward to those assets, despite the increasing pressure from her management team at Altitude Records.

Todd shifted into placating mode. "Listen, I know that guy's an ass. Everyone knows it. But they just want you to be successful. And I think you deserve a bigger audience than you have, too."

"I don't want a bigger audience if I have to be half naked to get it, no matter what some A&R guy dangles in front of me."

He sighed. "Jesus, Cin, loosen up, why don't you? You're a beautiful woman, what's the problem? You should make the most of it."

His eyes fell to her chest, where her double Ds—her blessing, her curse—swelled from the bustier.

She looked down at them herself, then back at him, pointedly. "Seriously?"

He had the grace to look sheepish, but only slightly. "I'm only human."

"You're married to my best friend."

Hannah McBride—now Hannah Sheehan—wasn't just Jacinda's friend. She was also her assistant, and her sanity in a crazy world. They'd met when Jacinda arrived in Pleasanton in sophomore year, the start of her longest stint anywhere since her dad left. Hannah had seen her through some tough times, so if anyone commented that Hannah was lucky to go along on this ride, she set them straight— Jacinda was the lucky one.

"Yeah, well..." Todd shrugged. "You wouldn't have me."

His tone was joking, but she hated that he'd even go there, because she knew there was truth behind the lightly spoken words.

"Todd, stop." She pulled the little jacket closed, but it wouldn't fasten across the front. Damn.

He grinned. "It's a selling point, is all I'm saying. Use what God gave you. Hourglass Reverb got its name for a reason." He made an hourglass shape in the air with both hands, raising an eyebrow.

She put her hands on her hips, where the curves angled in to her waist. "There's a difference between a selling point and selling out. The music is the selling point."

Hourglass Reverb. It was one of the first songs she'd ever written, and the title had seemed so perfect that it became the name of her band. Except the band was her—or her alter ego, Cin Scott, a name she'd agreed to when she was more pliable than she was now—with an occasionally changing lineup of musicians. When it was finally released, Hourglass Reverb had been her breakout song, hitting the Billboard Hot 100, and now they were trying to build on that success. Her brand of feisty, melodic rock, studded with poignant moments, had brought her a core base of loyal fans, even if she hadn't gone stratospheric.

But she wasn't about stratospheric—for her, there was more to it than fame and money. As a teenager, she'd learned that her own strength was the only thing she should

4

expect to rely on (apart from Hannah). With her father gone, and her mother battling depression and anxiety as they moved from town to town, music was her refuge—her safe place from the world. When a high school music teacher recognized her passion, and gave her an old electric guitar and a cheap amp, she knew she was holding something that would never let her down. And it hadn't...unlike some of the people it had led her to.

Todd persisted with his cause. "Music and sexiness aren't mutually exclusive, you know. Sex and drugs and rock 'n' roll, hello."

"Go find Hannah, and go home," she told him. "God only knows how she puts up with you."

"It's your fault," he said. "You introduced us."

"Yeah, I really should apologize to her again for that."

He laughed, good-natured. "There's a car waiting for you." After a pause, he added, "Just think about it, okay? I hate to say it, but Greg's right. The new kids are upping the ante. You're hot, Cin—shit, you and that guitar would give a monk a hard-on. But there's no harm in dialing up your image. Sexy sells."

She rolled her eyes. "Go."

If other women wanted to take that path, and they did it knowingly and willingly and in control, good luck to them. She wished them giant royalty checks, and Grammys, and their own perfumes, and platinum records, and whatever else. She and her double Ds had other plans.

★

Back home, she kicked off her boots, put Hannah's flowers in a vase, and grabbed a Diet Coke from the fridge. The rambling loft, on the top floor of a character building tucked into a Los Feliz hillside, had a killer view. But she couldn't settle in her usual spot on the deck, where the city lights sparkled below. On top of the performance buzz—a natural high she still loved—the extra adrenaline rush of her encounter with Greg had left her antsy, edgy, pent up.

She went into the bathroom and had a hot shower, scrubbing the stage makeup off her face and washing all the product out of her long hair. Wet, it reached all the way to the small of her back, a pale blonde testimony to the talent of her very expensive hairdresser. Sometimes she got tired of all the work involved in keeping it from breaking off in bleached pieces, but it was her signature look. Cutting it would probably buy her even more drama with Altitude.

With her makeup off and her hair hanging damp down her back, she looked like a completely different person. She slathered her face with moisturizer, noticing the tiredness in her blue eyes. Without makeup, she looked way younger, but she always went out fully made up. It was a small protection from the critical gaze of the world, a little bit of preservation. Sometimes it seemed like for every fan, there was a hater—which was why she held her distance a little. No Instagram bathroom selfies, no attention-seeking tweets, no are-they-aren't-they paparazzi shots with basketball players.

No wonder her management were tearing their hair out—she was terrible at playing the game.

Although...she sometimes thought that a little more are-they-aren't-they with someone would be nice. Specifically, the *are*-they. For all the propositions from dodgy record label execs, and the eager (and sometimes disturbing) messages from fans, she was sadly under-served in that department. But she just hadn't met anyone she *wanted* to get involved with lately—not even on a temporary, horizontal basis. She turned sideways, and then front on again, considering herself in the mirror. Yep, still the hourglass. Not getting any younger, maybe, but not going to seed yet either.

She finished moisturizing the rest of her body, then pulled on yoga pants and a loose sweatshirt. Sitting cross-legged on the sofa, she turned on the TV and flicked through a few channels. On MTV, a lineup of girls who looked like they should still be in high school were shaking their booties behind some guy in a hoodie and chains. Okay, compared to them, she probably was old. She switched the TV off and threw the remote on the sofa, sighing.

How many more times would she have to fend Greg off? Supposedly, one of the perks of being in the entertainment biz was being surrounded by yes men—so where were hers? She'd gotten tough over the years, by necessity, but sometimes, keeping on her toes was exhausting.

Tonight's show was the last one for a while, but earlier in the year she'd signed a publishing contract to contribute to a book, and the deadline was drawing near. The book was supposed to be a guide for girls who wanted to break into the music industry. Her brief had been to write two chapters, drawing on her own personal experience—one on developing your skills and being prepared, one on what to expect once you're in the door. Both with an *uplifting* tone. Italics not hers. Knowing what she did now, what the hell would she say? The antsy feeling grew, and she got up and headed for the one place she knew would settle her.

Her music room was soundproofed and plushly carpeted, the walls were lined with guitars, and there was a piano in one corner. She didn't play it very well, but it was nice to pick out a tune sometimes, especially when she was composing. Now she walked along the wall, letting her fingers trail across the guitars as she went: Fender, Gretsch, Gibson...she didn't make enough to invest in tech startups or restaurant chains, but she did believe in the value of a great guitar.

Eventually she lifted down her favorite, a slightly scuffed black Gibson, and took it to the sofa. Felt the peace settle on her as she held the instrument, as curvy as herself, and picked out a few notes. She leaned her head back for a moment and closed her eyes, letting the weight of the guitar anchor her. Then she opened her eyes again. Above the piano, a stylized silver fern hung on the wall, the elegant swoop of the frond a memory of a different time and place in her life.

For a while, an idea had been hovering in the back of her mind. And now, it was suddenly more than a vague maybe—it felt like a certainty. Before she had time to second-guess herself, without stopping to figure out the time difference, she pulled out her phone.

Within a few rings, a faraway voice answered, bringing a rush of familiarity and longing to Jacinda's heart.

"Nana Mac, it's me. Can I come back?"

Chapter Two

Sweet Breeze Bay, New Zealand. In the ten years since she'd been there, it had reverted to a mythical place in her mind. The gentle sweetness of the air, the beautiful light, the beaches and hills and sky...sometimes she wasn't even sure that it was a real place at all.

Except for the memories that lingered. All these years later, recollections still woke her in the night sometimes, breaking into her dreams even though she should be free of them by now. At least she wouldn't have to be face to face with the guy at their center—Nana Mac had said his whole family moved to Australia. An ocean between them should be enough, even if she still didn't have that much emotional distance. She'd made herself so tough in other ways, but that tiny chink in her armor seemed to always be there. Maybe, as well as giving her a desperately needed break, going back to the bay would finally clear away the last remnants of the past.

With her newly cut and colored hair pulled back into a ponytail, wearing oversized sunglasses and a baseball cap pulled down low, she took a taxi to LAX, hoping to slip out of the country undetected. It wasn't a long drive, but crossing the city with only a single suitcase in the trunk felt like a rite of transition—shucking off her old life, clearing the way for something new. It didn't seem to matter that she had no idea what the new might be.

Her first week in LA, she'd gone up to Griffith Park and looked out at the sprawling city, wondering, hoping, imagining. Since then, she'd barely stopped for breath—the relentless effort of trying to support herself while building a music career from nothing didn't leave much time for leisure. The reward was achieving so much of what she'd wanted, including an ever-increasing distance from her past. But the price was realizing that what she'd wanted might not be worth it. The flip side of her fledgling success was being under the spotlight—critiqued, judged, and scrutinized by the media and the public for more than just her music. She knew it was just part of the game, but it took a thicker skin than hers to be unaffected by it all. She'd proved some things to herself though...and to her father, who'd left her and her mom to manage without him, and never looked back.

She tipped the taxi driver and wheeled her own suitcase inside, just another traveler checking in. Now she'd made the break, she was almost thankful for the pressure she'd been under, and even for the Greg-shaped last straw that broke her back and forced her to strike out. She planned to do things on *her* terms now, and that meant not giving head space to people who didn't deserve it—including record label execs, mean-spirited reporters, and her so-called father. She found a quiet seat in a corner, and called her mom, Trina, in Florida one last time to say goodbye. Her mom was surprised, but she promised not to tell anyone where Jacinda was going, and Jacinda promised to keep in touch.

Her plan to go incognito worked—with her new hair and a makeup-free face behind her sunglasses, she made it on board without anyone giving her a second glance. And if the cabin crew recognized her as they ushered her into business class (a splurge that should increase her chances of staying anonymous), they were professional enough not to say anything.

The minute she was on the plane, she felt like she was halfway there already. The flight attendants had accents that instantly transported her to her other, neglected home in the South Pacific—the place that was her childhood retreat, but her teenage downfall.

She'd already talked to Hannah, but now, while she waited for the plane to take off, she wrote a quick message to her band members, telling them just enough without giving anything away. She didn't know exactly how long she'd be gone, but with the latest string of small gigs finished, they all had other work lined up anyway. She hit 'send' on the message, then turned off her phone and leaned back in the soft leather seat, feeling some of her long-held tension start to recede. Twelve, or maybe thirteen, hours in the air stretched ahead—more than half a day of suspended animation from which, hopefully, she'd emerge into some peace.

★

At Auckland airport, she made a quick stop to buy a prepaid phone, then headed for the taxi stand, eager to get to the house. Nana Mac wouldn't be there—she'd just left for a long-planned trip to Europe. Her last gasp, she'd pronounced in her lingering Scottish accent, a last hoorah now that she was in her eighth decade. But Jacinda doubted that. Her grandmother was one of the most vibrant characters she'd ever known, and being in her seventies had hardly slowed her down. If anything, she'd seemed even more vigorous and determined in their phone calls. They'd talked regularly since Jacinda had last been in New Zealand, through her slow rise in the music biz, and through the family dramas that occasionally sprang up. Even though Nana Mac was far away, she could sometimes see things more clearly than Jacinda or her mom could.

Although she wouldn't be there herself, she'd said Jacinda's timing was perfect. Her cat Velvet was expecting kittens, so Jacinda could mind the house and be on kitten watch. Her neighbor, Nadia, would feed Velvet until then. Jacinda had no idea what was involved when a cat had kittens (apart from the obvious mechanics of it all), but Nana Mac sounded confident that she could manage, and Jacinda figured there'd be a local vet if anything went wrong.

Now the taxi made its way via a winding route toward the center of the city. It felt weird to be on the wrong side of the road again, taking in the quaint wooden houses, the lushness of the landscape, and the grassy volcanic cones that dotted the city. Eventually the driver turned onto the freeway, and they skirted the city, then started up the bridge that spanned the harbor. She watched the city spread out before her as they rose higher: yachts and gin palaces in the marina, a jumble of buildings, the Sky Tower topping them all. Then over the sparkling water to the North Shore, green and suburban and homely. And beyond that, Rangitoto, Auckland's king of volcanoes, keeping guard in the gulf just as she remembered it.

On the northern coast, directly opposite Rangitoto, waited Sweet Breeze Bay. The little neighborhood was tucked away at the end of the road, a nook carved into a steeply forested peninsula. It was the kind of place where kids played barefoot in the street, the tang of salt was in the air, and whole families swam in the shallow bay on summer evenings. It was a tiny village retreat on the edge of the city, as though a small country town had been picked up and popped down on the suburban coast, only separated from the 'real' world by the tree-clad peaks of the peninsula.

That was how she remembered it, anyway. The world was only getting tougher, and ten years was a long time, even in this idyllic part of the planet. She hoped that all her better memories of the bay would hold true, and that she could make some new ones—just herself, quietly in the sun, with a little cat family for company. And maybe then, the bad memories would lose their power.

As the taxi turned into Tui Street—named for a native songbird—she realized she was holding her breath. When they stopped outside number ten, she let it out in a long release. It looked just the same. She paid the driver, and he looked surprised when she gave him a tip; she'd forgotten that people didn't tip here. God, so civilized.

She got out and stood on the sidewalk, staring up at the house. The trees were bigger, and there was a new gate, but otherwise, nothing had changed. Clematis tumbled over the porch roof, the camellia hedge was neatly trimmed, and a cluster of tree ferns still stood in one corner of the garden, the spiral of each new frond just like the one over her piano. She looked back along the little cul-de-sac. Same thing. Even the tire swing was still hanging from the gnarly old tree a few doors down. She breathed in the salty-sweet sea air, still cool this early in the morning. The clean goodness of it flooded through her, and she could practically feel every cell in her body perk up. No more city fumes or stress, for a while at least.

The driver took her suitcase up the path to the front door, and left her to it with a cheery goodbye. Then, for the first time in ten years, she turned the key in the lock and stepped forward...into her past, and maybe her future.

Chapter Three

L iam Ward turned over in bed, the sheet tangling around his legs. Slowly surfacing from the depths of a blank sleep, he groaned and rubbed his forehead. The neighborhood was usually quiet during the day, letting him catch up on the sleep he missed at night. But today there was music, loud enough to wake him in his upstairs bedroom. He cursed, heavy-headed, and unwound himself from the sheet, then swung his legs out of bed. The music changed to something hard rock. What the hell...was that Wolfmother? He got up to investigate, irritation joined by curiosity. Who around here would listen to anything so grunty?

He threw the sash window open wider, and stood for a moment with his hands high on the top rim, letting the breeze glide over his bare torso. The summer days were getting hotter, and—like many of the character homes in Sweet Breeze Bay—the old house didn't have any air conditioning. Then he leaned out. From this vantage point, he could see some of number eleven across the road, where Mrs. Marsh lived. At eighty-something, she seemed sprightly enough, but he couldn't imagine her knitting along to Wolfmother. Over the back hedge was the beach, which wasn't usually noisy, apart from the occasional gang of kids partying at night. And he knew that number ten would be quiet, because Nana Mac, as everyone called her, was away. She'd dropped a note in his letterbox to let him know, even though he'd never gone over to say hello when he came back.

Wait a second. He caught a glimpse of someone on the back deck at number ten. A woman—a *curvy* woman—was moving in time to the music, her body freely swaying and arching in the sun. She was wearing a short, short denim mini skirt and a black bikini top, which was barely doing its job under the strain of her ample bust.

Then an electric guitar solo kicked in, and she cut loose into wild head-banging moves, her dark hair flying and her full breasts bouncing as she lost herself in the rhythm. Despite his interrupted sleep, he laughed. Couldn't complain too much about being woken for a show like that. Damn, she was hot, and obviously kind of wild. *Luscious* was the word that sprang to mind, luscious in an old-school pinup kind of way. Who wouldn't watch that, given the chance?

Then she gave a sinuous twist as the chorus kicked in again, and the bikini top suddenly gave out. The strings tied around her neck came undone, and—thank you God—the little scraps of fabric fell down completely. She grabbed at her chest, covering herself up—but not before he had a glorious view of creamy flesh and generous curves. His lazily stirring interest was suddenly fully awake, and he breathed out in a hot rush. The neighborhood had gone from sleepy to sexy in one short song.

But as she turned and made for the doors, arms wrapped around herself, he got his first clear view of her face...and his heart constricted in his chest.

No.

Shit, no.

What the hell was she doing here?

★

Safely inside, Jacinda retied the bikini strings as her heart settled. No one would have seen, anyway—the hedge around the back yard meant that the deck was totally private, apart from being overlooked by the second story of number twelve. And Nana Mac had told her that the Ward family had moved to Australia, leaving the house untenanted.

But what was that noise she'd heard as she came in—a kind of slam? Was there someone next door after all? Presentable again, she walked back out to the edge of the deck and looked up at number twelve. There was no way she'd have come back to stay right next door if they were there. She stood on tiptoe and looked again, but there was nothing to see—the upstairs windows were closed, and all was quiet. Maybe the noise had come from the beach.

She shook her head and went to rummage in the fridge for something cold. The ghosts of summers past were all in her imagination—and the real people were on the other side of an ocean, in the Australian sun. She couldn't be jumping at the smallest thing if she wanted to get any kind of relaxation.

Velvet came into the kitchen, meowing as she wound around Jacinda's ankles. She was slow on her feet, obviously feeling the heat and the weight of her kitten-full belly, and Jacinda felt sorry for her. They sat together on the cool tiled floor, and Jacinda sipped a Diet Coke as she stroked the little black cat.

"Us girls will have to stick together," she told Velvet, who purred in agreement. "We don't need any guys, right? This is our summer."

Sitting on the floor, barefoot and makeup-free, she almost felt like the girl she'd been when she arrived in Sweet Breeze Bay at seventeen. And despite the years that had passed, she now looked more like that girl than like Cin Scott, thanks to the home makeover she'd done on herself. She smiled, remembering how Hannah had reeled back in shock at her first sight of the transformation.

"What have you done?" she'd exclaimed, standing slack-jawed on Jacinda's doorstep.

Jacinda had run a hand through her hair. "Can you check that it's even? I had to use the kitchen scissors." She pulled Hannah inside and shut the door, dragging her through to the bathroom, where shanks of blonde hair still lay where she'd swept them into the corner.

"Oh. My. God." Hannah couldn't tear her eyes away. "I have to sit down. When you phoned to say you wanted to talk about something, I didn't expect this." She plunked down onto the side of the bath, one hand on her head as if protecting her own blonde locks.

Jacinda had to laugh. "Sorry. I should've warned you."

"You should have! What's going on? Are you okay?"

"I'm fine. I'm not having some diva breakdown, if that's what you mean."

"Well, good." She leaned back against the tiled wall. "That's not your style, anyway."

"I do have to tell you something though." Jacinda cleared her throat. "I'm going away for a while."

Hannah stared at her. "What? Why?"

She sat on a leather-topped stool and propped her feet up on the bath, next to Hannah. How could she explain it? "It's just...I've worked so hard to get this far, and I love that I get to do this. I especially love that we get to work together. But everything that comes along with it—being under the lens all the time—it's sucking the joy out of it. And if one more person looks at my boobs and tells me to sex up my act..." She grimaced, and told Hannah the gist of what Greg had done.

"Oh, gross. But Todd looks after that for you, right? He wouldn't let anyone push you into something you're not happy with, or take advantage of you."

She hesitated, thinking back to that conversation in the corridor, then looked at Hannah's concerned, open face. "No, of course he wouldn't. I guess I'm just tired of being perpetually 'on'. You know me, music is like...my oxygen. I need it. And I know that sounds like such a stupid cliché. But all this peripheral stuff..." She shook her head. "Sometimes I just want a regular personal life. Know what I mean?"

"Yeah, I wanted to smack Eli Tyler in the head." Hannah powered her fist into her opposite palm, demonstrating what she'd do to the singer who'd dated

Jacinda in the full glare of the media, then dumped her equally publicly when his publicist came up with a more famous movie starlet. "But I don't want you to go."

Jacinda smiled. "I know. And I don't care about Eli anymore, but I need some time out—time away—and I won't get it here. I'm getting out of town, and I'm going Snapchat-free, Insta-free, email-free...like, everything-free."

Hannah rubbed her chin, still processing the bombshell. "What will I tell Todd? He'll want to know where you are."

"Tell him you don't know, because you won't." She nudged Hannah with one foot. "I'm not going to tell you where I'm going."

She knew Hannah adored Todd, and it wasn't fair to ask her to keep a secret from him. She only wished that Todd was worthy of the adoration. Yes, she'd introduced them—but that was because when they finally got her record deal, and things started happening, the only person she'd wanted as her assistant was Hannah.

She'd known from the start that Todd was creatively brutal in his approach to getting things done—which was great in a manager, who needed to be clear-eyed, ruthless, and scrappy, but not so great in a love interest. He'd first spotted her playing in yet another shady bar, on a night when she wasn't waiting tables (a common enough occupation for a music major, she'd learned). And although he had no track record to speak of as a manager, she was ready to take a chance on him too. From the beginning, he'd made it clear that she only had to give the word, and he'd be in. In her panties, that is. Not wanting to jeopardize the income that she provided, though, he never pushed it beyond suggestion, innuendo, and the occasional drunk-on-the-road proposition.

Given all that, it was beyond awkward when he took an immediate liking to Hannah. She never in a million years expected sweet, principled Hannah to fall for him so hard and fast. All she saw of him—all she wanted to see—was the model boyfriend and then husband he played for her. Now that he had a growing list of successful acts, Jacinda hoped he was man enough to be what Hannah needed and deserved, but she wasn't convinced that he could keep it up. In the meantime there was no concrete reason to upset her friend's happiness, so she kept quiet.

Hannah frowned. "How will I get in touch with you then? What if I have to reach you, for business? Plus...I don't want us to be completely cut off."

Even without that sad face, she had a point. The truth was, Jacinda wouldn't be able to go long without talking to Hannah either. There was no one else who'd been there through everything, the way she had. And if there was some kind of emergency, she had to be contactable.

"I don't want that either. I'll get a new phone when I arrive, and send you the number. Keep it to yourself though, okay?"

"Okay." They stood up, and Hannah reached out to feel a lock of Jacinda's newly transformed hair. "I still can't believe this."

They both considered her reflection in the mirror. In place of the ethereal white-blonde lengths was a mane of rich dark hair. Now that it was a little shorter, and less weighed down, it had a natural wave, and the dark brown was glossy against her skin. She wore no makeup apart from tinted moisturizer, mascara and lip gloss.

"It's really shocking how different you look," Hannah said.

Jacinda snorted. "Shocking? Thanks."

"No, in a good way," she insisted. "I don't think anyone would recognize you if they saw you in the street...but they'd still think you were beautiful."

Jacinda turned and pulled her friend into a hug, suddenly swamped with a love rush for the girl who'd seen her through so much. "Thank you." She gave her an extra squeeze. "I'll miss you."

"I'll miss you too," she replied, her voice breaking a little as they separated. "But it won't be too long, right?"

"I'm not making a plan...I just have to take myself back for a while. And I don't have any gigs coming up."

Also, the likelihood of a national tour had probably lessened considerably after that knee to Greg's groin...but it was worth it. She grinned. Shame she couldn't include *that* in the book.

They went out to the living room, where a half-packed suitcase waited on the sofa.

"What about the book?" Hannah asked, as if reading her mind. "Are you still going to do that?"

"Yeah, I have to. I did sign the contract. But it can be my project while I'm away."

She wished she hadn't signed anything now. What honest advice could she give all those aspiring tweens and teens, dreaming of stardom? Be ready to fight off the very people who're supposed to be looking out for you. Be careful who you trust. Hold onto your love of music, your dream, and your clothes…

Hannah's voice broke into her thoughts. "There's that interview with Lainey Kingsley too, next week. Do you want me to cancel with her, or just postpone it?"

Jacinda's heart sank at the reminder. Some music journalists seemed to specialize in being even tougher on women performers than on men, and Lainey Kingsley was Jacinda's personal nemesis. They'd never met, so this interview was meant to be a chance to bring her around, in person. Pulling out would probably only add fuel to her fire of disdain.

"Shit, I forgot about that. She's going to love this."

"Don't worry, I'm sure she has other musicians to torment," Hannah said. "I'll just put her off—she doesn't need to know you're not here." Then she smiled. "I think I can guess where you're going."

Jacinda held up her hands. "In this, I'm the CIA. I can neither confirm nor deny."

Hannah laughed. "Just take care of yourself, okay?"

"I will," Jacinda promised. "And you too."

"I'll be fine. I have Todd."

Jacinda made herself smile too. "Of course you do. Tell him he'd better look after you, or I'll come back and kick his ass."

Behind the joke, she'd been totally serious.

And now, far away in Sweet Breeze Bay, her escape

was complete. Suddenly aware that her butt was numb, she got up from the kitchen floor and stretched. Then she yawned. She felt too lazy to figure out the time difference, but it was probably bedtime in LA, and the jet lag was kicking in. She closed the French doors, and carefully gathered Velvet in her arms.

"I don't know about you, but I need a nap."

The cat gave a little *chir-rup* and leaned in, her fur soft against Jacinda's bare skin. And with that mutual understanding, they headed for bed.

Chapter Four

Nana Mac had told her to choose any room as her own, and there was only one she wanted. It was right up under the eaves, a little attic retreat that she'd loved as a kid when they came visiting. It had been her mom Trina's room, right up until Doug Prescott blew into town with a rally car team and swept her heart away. Jacinda guessed he must have been quite something, to a girl who'd grown up in sleepy Sweet Breeze Bay—the accent, the confidence, and the whole testosterone-fueled rallying thing. He was a mechanic rather than a driver, but the glamour of the whole scene was undeniable.

She could count her childhood visits 'home' to Sweet Breeze Bay on one hand—only three times. One time she couldn't remember because she was too little, but she'd seen the photos. Once again when she was about eight. And then that one summer she was here as a teenager, without her mom. *That* summer. Trina had abruptly decided that Jacinda should finish school in New Zealand, so she'd left halfway through her junior year. She'd desperately wished Hannah could come too, but guiltily, secretly, she was relieved to be getting away from her mom's struggles with her mental health, and the dramas she didn't really know how to handle. Maybe Jacinda living with Nana Mac meant one less worry for her mom too. The plan was to have a summer Christmas with her grandmother, then start high school in February, in the new southern hemisphere year.

That had been the idea, anyway.

Now she shook her head and pushed back the feather duvet. The whole day had passed by while she and Velvet napped. It was still light outside, but through the window she could see that the sky held the softening glow of a coastal evening. Her stomach growled, and Velvet gave her a reproachful look.

"I know. We both need to eat. And you're eating for...well, how many *are* you eating for, I wonder?"

Downstairs, she gave Velvet the contents of one of the little tins in the cupboard. Whatever it was, it was stinky, but Velvet purred as she gobbled it up.

Then she got herself ready—a much quicker job now that she was wearing so little makeup. In skinny jeans and a black and white striped tee, finished off with plain ballet flats, she could be any girl in the world. She smiled at her reflection in the mirror as she put on some lip gloss. Hannah was right—her appearance was so different from just a few days ago, surely no one would recognize her as Cin Scott.

Nana Mac had left three handwritten pages of instructions on the kitchen counter, covering every possible eventuality, good and bad. There was a contact number for the local plumber, should she have any water-related problems (apparently the plumbing was getting old and unreliable). In her squiggly handwriting, Nana Mac had noted *Handsome and single!* alongside. The after-hours medical center and pharmacy was on the opposite side of the peninsula, heading back toward the city. The wi-fi password was 'TomSelleck10'. (Nana Mac had no time for any of those 'new guys', as she called them. Forget Tom Hardy or Zac Efron or Scott Eastwood—anyone who came after Tom was unworthy of consideration.) In the event of a tsunami warning, she should go up Mount Clarion, the nearest volcanic cone. However, in the event of a volcanic eruption, she was to get in the old Volkswagen and *drive,* north or south didn't matter, just away. Amongst it all were some suggestions for local food. She recommended pizza from Tony and Marie's—*Get the meatball!*—but the Chinese takeout was a big *NO*. It was nice to see that Nana Mac was still a woman of clear opinions.

But Jacinda knew where she was going tonight. On the list was a café, Clarion Call—apparently an organic eatery featuring comfort food with a twist, and lots of comfortable armchairs. It sounded exactly like the low-key kind of place she wanted. Plus, she was keen to see if it might be somewhere she could hole up with a bottomless coffee and work on her contribution for the book. That damn book. She'd have to get started on it soon, but for tonight—only her first night, after all—she planned to eat and drink without feeling guilty about the possible extra poundage, or any of the things she usually had on her mind. She wondered if they'd have cheesecake.

It was only a short walk from Tui Street to the little cluster of local shops. Sweet Breeze Bay was no metropolis, but there was enough for day to day. The center sat at a crossroads where Bay Road came over the hill from the other side of the peninsula, and continued to the main beach entrance, with the dilapidated boat club and the ice cream and coffee kiosk. Intersecting that was Fife Street, the main thoroughfare that ran from one end of Sweet Breeze Bay to the other. In the center of the crossroads stood a huge pohutukawa tree, its gnarly branches stretching out toward all four corners of the little settlement. Its roots lifted and buckled the tarmac below, making bumps in the road, but as a protected species, and the country's most iconic tree, it was safe from any ax or chainsaw. It was nice to see it again, grand and steady.

She took everything in as she walked down the main street, amazed at how little it had all changed in ten years. Tony and Marie's was new, as were the twinkly fairy lights strung along the front of every storefront. But she remembered the rest. The corner store, its shelves crammed with everything from candy to clothespins, still open in the evening. The store that only sold fresh fruit and vegetables, spices and nuts. The tiny shop selling magazines, books, lottery tickets, and stamps. The Golden Horse, where you could order fish and chips or Chinese takeout. And the pub, of course. Even on a Sunday night, there was a hum of music and voices from inside—the Kelp and King was obviously still the center of the community's social life.

She remembered how much she'd wanted to go in that summer, at only-just-seventeen, and have a drink. Ethan from next door had turned eighteen right before she arrived—the legal drinking age—and sometimes he and his friends would go in for beers, full of importance, before coming out later to hang with the rest of the bay's teenagers at the beach.

She paused on the corner outside the pub, remembering how his brother Liam would get jealous too, that Ethan was a step ahead of him. It was clear to her, and probably to everyone, that whatever Ethan did, Liam wanted to do too. It was more than big brother adulation, though. Everyone wanted to be like Ethan. Or be *with* Ethan.

Ethan Ward. She pressed her hand to her stomach, feeling a sickish flutter. How ridiculous, really. All that time ago...

She looked up to the spreading pohutukawa, and breathed out a sigh. At this time of year the red blossoms made it look like a native Christmas tree, especially with its branches strung with fairy lights, just starting to glow in the fading light. She'd had a quiet Christmas with her mom in Florida—not very festive, just the two of them at home, but it was all Trina had wanted. Maybe she could talk her mom into coming here for Christmas one year. Stepping back in time to this place might make her feel better...if she'd only give it a try.

Anyway! She hadn't come halfway across the world to stand around on the street being morose. Plus, she was hungry. She mentally hitched up her pants, and carried on down the street to Clarion Call.

★

"I recognize you." The waitress stood with hands on hips, tapping her pencil against her chin. "I'm sure I do."

Jacinda looked up from the menu, her heart sinking. Maybe she didn't look as different as she thought, if her cover was already blown.

"You're Jacinda, right?" the girl said. "Nana Mac's granddaughter."

Or maybe not blown.

"I am," she replied cautiously.

"I knew it!" She slipped onto the bench opposite, and leaned her elbows on the table. "She told us you were coming, and that we should look after you. Do you remember me? We used to hang out that summer. I looked kind of different then. Glasses and braces and the rest, you know." She rolled her eyes, as though her younger self was too embarrassing for words.

Jacinda remembered her then. She'd been a perky-plump, guileless kid, one foot still in childhood, and thus a lot more fun than some of the others, who'd crossed into self-consciously cool territory. "Riley Dawson."

She grinned. "You got it. Pretty different, right?"

"Yeah, but you were always cute."

Riley blushed, tickled by the compliment, but rolled her eyes again in denial. "I don't know about that...but thanks. Okay, now I'd better do what I'm here for. We're supposed to be looking after you, not making you wait for dinner." She stood back up and assumed an efficient waitress pose, notepad in hand. "What would you like?"

Jacinda ordered the vegetarian lasagna (pasta! to hell with all that no carbs BS) and salad, with a glass of organic lemonade, and Riley bustled off, full of purpose.

Normally she would have used the waiting time to check her email or Facebook messages, or return a phone call, but she'd turned her old phone off on the tarmac in LA, and left it in the nightstand in her attic room. And the prepaid phone she'd bought at the airport was in the drawer with it. As promised, she'd messaged her mom, and Hannah—who signed off with a New Zealand flag and a wink, having correctly guessed her location—and Nana

Mac too, living it up on the Spanish leg of her trip. But right now, being unplugged felt really good.

Pretty soon Riley brought her food, and offered her a magazine from an old oak sideboard that was also home to a collection of cool art deco lamps. But she had no desire to look at the fashion tips, movie star breakups, and celebrity gossip. No, thank you. She guessed there was a small chance she might see herself in one of them, but it wasn't just about that. It was pleasantly surreal to be sitting here, miles from LA—like, six or seven *thousand* miles away— alone in a café, detached from her real (unreal) life, completely unrecognized as her alter ego. She might not be stratospheric, but after Hourglass Reverb, Cin Scott couldn't walk down the street in LA on a summer evening and eat lasagna in peace.

Maybe she could get used to this.

When Riley came to clear her plate, Jacinda complimented her on the lasagna. "That was so good."

She smiled. "Thank you. Caro and I came up with all the recipes for the cafe. Caro's my cousin," she explained. "She's kind of pedantic about everything, but the end result is worth it."

"Is this your place, then? It's really nice. I like the artsy vintage thing you've got going on."

Riley sat down again. "Thanks. Everything in here came from the peninsula. We trawled the garage sales for like a year. Some of the things came from the other side, but they were too good to pass up."

She scrunched up her nose, and Jacinda remembered the ongoing rivalry between the communities on opposite sides of the peninsula. They were united in preserving the green peaks that separated them, but beyond that there was a healthy competition that could sometimes get a little *un*-healthy. The Sweet Breeze Bay side looked out toward Rangitoto and the South Pacific beyond, and was so removed from the nearby city that it could be on its own island. The inhabitants were arty, often slightly rumpled, frequently eccentric, and determinedly parochial. The Other Side—Lancet Bay—looked over the water to the high-rises and wharves of the city. Even though they shared the same jutting finger of land, the perspectives of each side were literally and philosophically opposite.

"It's all great stuff," Jacinda offered, her tone suggesting that it was great despite coming from the wrong side of the hill. "I love the lamps, especially that tall one."

"Oh, me too!" They both looked at the floor lamp with its carved stand and woven flax shade. It was Pacific retro at its cheesiest, but it was perfect in here. "I got that from Mrs. Ward when she came back from Australia one time. My mum told her we were setting up here and looking for cool lights, and she said we could have it."

At the mention of the Ward name, Jacinda's heart did a little skip.

Riley's voice lowered, and she leaned in. "Wasn't that so awful? That poor family."

A tightness began to spread in her chest. What was Riley talking about? It couldn't have anything to do with her—according to Nana Mac, she and Mrs. Ward had agreed never to talk about the events of that summer with anyone else in the bay.

Seeing her face, Riley gasped. "Oh God, I'm sorry! I just remembered you had a...thing with Ethan, right? That summer?"

A thing. You could say that. "We...yeah."

Riley looked sympathetic. "So hard. So awful."

There was a moment's silence while she waited for Jacinda to say something, and Jacinda tried to figure out whether she was talking about her, or something else. Just as she decided to come right out and ask Riley what she meant, there was a *ding-ding-ding-ding* from the kitchen, and she sprang to her feet.

"She's so violent with that bell!" She sighed. "I'd better go. See you soon though, okay?"

"Okay."

"And no charge for tonight—this one's on us," she added over her shoulder, as Caro pounded on the bell again. "I'm *coming!*"

"Thank you," Jacinda said, but she was already on her

way to another table with two big bowls of spaghetti, the bell dinging behind her again. The dinner rush had begun.

She'd come back tomorrow, when it was quieter, Jacinda decided as she went back out into the street, the evening air fragrant around her. And she'd ask Riley what exactly it was that had been so awful.

Chapter Five

B each time, finally. Jacinda threw sun lotion and a book into her bag, then paused in front of the old mahogany dresser with its beveled glass mirror, and pulled her hair into a high ponytail. It still felt weird to see herself as a brunette, after so many years as an ever-lightening blonde.

Standing in her mom's old bedroom, she suddenly realized that while this version of herself was closer to the teenage Jacinda who'd been here so long ago, it was also closer to her mom. Clean-faced and without adornment, she looked a lot like that 1980s girl in the family photos on Nana Mac's mantelpiece. The shy, beautiful Sweet Breeze Bay girl who fell for a visiting American loaded with charisma and promises, and went around the world for him…only to find that the dark side of charisma is ego, and that promises easily made are easily broken. From him, Jacinda had learned the same lessons, but she was tougher than her mom. Well, she was *now*, anyway. She smoothed the flyaway strands around her hairline, wondering if a young Trina had looked into the same mirror, into eyes the same shade of blue, and tied her own hair into a ponytail as she daydreamed about her tall, dark, and handsome American. What was the saying? Handsome is as handsome does. Doug Prescott knew exactly what to do with his handsome. He just didn't know what to do with her mother's beauty once he had it.

She shook aside the rising memories of her father's unfounded jealousy and unpredictable anger, which had scarred her childhood with fear and drama. He didn't have any power over her, not anymore—unlike her mom, whose own memories and scars still held so much power. Maybe she'd phone her again today.

But not yet. She'd slept in, and now there was a hungry, furry, expectant mother winding around her ankles, her own stomach was grumbling, the sun was shining, and the beach was calling. It was time to get started on the relaxing she'd come here for.

★

Liam Ward was unimpressed. Since he'd been woken by the unexpected arrival next door, his routine had gone out the window. In fact, he couldn't even think about his routine—all he could think about was Jacinda Prescott. And considering he'd spent the last decade specifically *not* thinking about her, that pissed him off.

Admittedly, his routine was completely screwed anyway, compared to most people. But he operated best that way. And the internet was a 24/7 deal, with half the world online when everyone in this time zone was asleep, so it made sense to get his work done then. He'd forgotten when it was that he'd finally given in and flipped day into night. It was just easier—easier than spending his nights fighting, and losing, the battle to sleep like a regular person.

But after Jacinda had woken him the day before with her music, and her dancing, and her wardrobe malfunction, he couldn't get back to sleep. He'd closed the window and pulled down the blind, trying to block out the brightness of the day, and got back into bed. But the image of her wouldn't leave his head—curves, tousled hair, flexible body moving to the rhythm…and then, those breasts. Damn it. What he'd never seen as a teenager—what was off limits, even if he'd been bold enough to try—was now burned into his brain. As he lay there, eyes squeezed shut, she swayed and turned in his imagination, and the idea of her made him harden even more, just like it used to.

At that, he got up and took himself to the shower—a cold shower. There was no way he'd let her have that effect on him. Maybe he could have rationalized it then, as a horny teenager full of newly brewed testosterone, even though it was his brother who'd had her attention.

But now, after everything...no.

So here he was, the day after, sitting at the kitchen table before noon, feeling like he'd landed up in a foreign country. His laptop was open in front of him, with the website he was working on, but his mind was not on HTML or anchor text or fixed width layouts. It was on the woman who'd once been the girl who loved and left his brother—and left disaster in her wake.

He ran his hand through his hair and blew out a gale of air. Eleven thirty, and the summer heat was building along with his thoughts. A beer wouldn't hurt. He went and grabbed a cold one from the fridge, then wandered out to the living room where, years ago, his parents had replaced one whole wall with a bank of folding glass doors. They'd had some amazing parties here, most of Sweet Breeze Bay's teenagers hanging out long into the summer nights, he and Ethan playing guitar with the other guys. That one summer Jacinda had been here, she'd sat out with them too, still a bit shy, but embraced into the group. As Nana Mac's granddaughter she was an honorary local, after all, and in their teenage minds, her American accent gave her an extra point of coolness. He knew she could play guitar too, but she never played in front of anyone. He remembered her throwing a Frisbee like a pro, braiding Riley Dawson's hair, and laughing with the other girls when the boys goofed around, which was pretty much all the time.

And he remembered her listening, her eyes soft, the night he and Ethan played her the song they'd written. She had no idea that the lyrics were his, not his brother's. Ethan sang, and she soaked it up, mesmerized, hypnotized. Ethan was the singer, the consummate performer, and the boyfriend. As the little brother, Liam wasn't in any position to steal that thunder.

He glanced at Ethan's guitar, sitting on a stand in the corner of the room, and took another slug of beer. He couldn't remember the last time he'd played, or even wanted to play. And he hadn't even had those doors open in the two weeks since he came back from Australia. But it did look kind of nice out there...

He undid the latches top and bottom, and flicked up the lock in the handle. As he pulled the door, it grated a little on its runner, but slid open easily enough. The smell of a flowering vine gone wild hit him as he stepped out onto the deck, and he realized that things were getting overgrown. Before, his parents had been paying for someone to come and do yard work once a month, but he'd promised to do it while he was staying here. At this time of year, everything grew by inches and feet—he'd have to make good on that promise before long.

His eyes went to the entertaining area. Weeds were springing up through the paving stones, and long tendrils of the vine were winding themselves around the stacked outdoor furniture and up the legs of his dad's pride and joy, a huge stainless steel barbecue that grilled, roasted, rotisseried, and made his father's face light up with joy whenever he talked about it. The small kettle barbecue they had in Australia was no comparison, apparently.

He put his beer down on the deck, and went to deal with the leafy marauders. Once the barbecue and furniture were cleared, and the paving stones weeded, he set to uncovering the narrow gate that led to the beach path. With the sun warm on his back, his mind started to feel clearer than it had in a long time, filled up with nothing but the work. The pile of pulled weeds and cut greenery grew pleasingly large, and soon he got too hot. He stopped and bent to wipe his forehead with the hem of his shirt. He'd almost forgotten the satisfaction of honest sweat through honest labor. In Australia, he'd helped out a contractor friend a couple of times a week—building houses was a perfect way to offset the time he spent sitting on his ass all night for his own web design business. He'd had too much computer time lately.

Then he lifted the shirt off, leaning forward to pull it over his head...and as he stood up again, there she was. Frozen still, looking at him over the newly cleared gate.

Even with her eyes covered by sunglasses, her shocked expression was obvious. It was probably a reflection of his own. For a moment she hesitated, maybe weighing up whether to just keep walking, but it was too late for that. Then she broke the silence.

"Hi."

All the things he was going to say, all the words he'd done battle with over the years—good and bad—clogged his head and made him stupid. Shit. He cleared his throat.

"Hi."

Her eyes flicked along the path, toward the beach, then back to him. Her face was pink, and he wondered if she felt ashamed about what she'd done, now that she was faced with a Ward after all this time. Why would she even come back here? He could only see her top half over the gate, but she was wearing a light cotton cover-up over her bikini, and she carried a beach bag over her shoulder.

"Going to the beach?"

At the sound of the inane words, he could have slapped himself around the head. Especially because he knew it wasn't just the sun that had addled his brain. Where was the anger that had sustained him through the toughest times?

But she didn't laugh at him, just smiled. "Yeah. It's such a beautiful day. I thought I'd soak up some sun."

The small talk made him feel itchy. *Why are you here?* he wanted to ask. *Don't you have anything to say to me?* Instead, he frowned.

"I hope you've got sunscreen. And you should have a hat."

She looked surprised, as well she might, with him sounding like someone's disapproving aunt.

"I guess so..."

"The sun's brutal here," he said, trying to backtrack and justify himself at the same time. "You might have forgotten since you were here last time."

At that—*last time*—she looked right at him, and something passed between them. For a second it seemed like she might be going to acknowledge the past, say something about the not-so-distant history that they shared. But then the moment passed.

"Yeah, well. Thanks for the advice, but I don't need it. I'm a big girl now."

He willed himself not to look at her chest, like a complete jerk. On the other hand...was she glancing at *his* chest? Despite himself, he stood straighter, and threw the shirt onto the outdoor table.

"Okay, then." She could look if she wanted.

She glared at him. "Okay."

"Right."

She made a little *pfft* of disdain, then turned and walked away.

You idiot, he told himself. That was your chance to say your piece, tell her everything you planned to, if you ever saw her again. Nice work getting distracted by the thought of what's under that cover-up.

But he stepped to the gate, unable to resist watching her go. She stalked down the path, the cover-up only just skimming the top of her legs. Maybe she had looked at his chest...but she'd never need to know he was looking at her. That he'd been looking way back then, and it had only taken one bikini-string failure to spiral him back into that teenage longing.

As she reached the beach, she turned to look back down the path, and he ducked behind the hedge, like the fool he'd suddenly become.

Maybe coming home hadn't been the smartest idea after all.

★

Jacinda walked a little way along the beach until she found a sheltered spot in the lee of someone's stone wall, took off the cover-up, and spread her beach towel on the sand. As she stretched out on her stomach in the full sun, her heart was still pounding. She hadn't expected to see one of the Wards. If Liam was at the house, was Ethan there too?

She looked farther along to the end of the beach, where Mount Clarion rose abruptly from the shore, its base circled with evergreen forest. Nothing had changed. She remembered how the trees provided a shady retreat from the glare of the day...and, at night-time, from the eyes of the other Sweet Breeze Bay teenagers.

She was still shy that summer, a hopelessly unsophisticated seventeen despite her adult curves. All the moving around with her mom had never given her a chance to hone her social skills, and she was horribly aware of the attention her bust attracted. Ethan was tall, funny, handsome, and good at everything, the star of his little town and of the high school over the hill. She'd had no idea why he chose her, out of all the girls who admired his every move and hung on his every word. Every morning that summer, she woke up convinced this would be the last day of Ethan Ward liking her best. But the days went by, and he kept liking her. And then, that night, he sang her the song, looking at her so intently as he strummed the chords that she felt like the only woman on earth. A woman, not a gauche teenager. Caught in his orbit, she hardly noticed his brother playing harmony on a battered acoustic guitar. And later, when he pulled her away from the beach bonfire and the hum of the party...she went.

That song, with its perfect, cut-to-her-heart lyrics, still played in her head some nights.

She sighed and turned her head in the other direction, resting her cheek on her folded arms. If Liam hadn't been such an ass, she would have asked him about the rest of the family, about why they'd moved away, and what had happened. Now she felt bad—if something terrible had happened, like Riley said, she should have said something appropriate to him. There were things she didn't want to talk to him about—his brother, for example—but she wasn't completely hard-hearted.

Well, if he hadn't distracted her by being such an old

woman about sun hats. And, unexpectedly, by being so...shirtless. She didn't remember him being so cute. But then, they'd all grown up. Herself, and Riley, and Liam, and all of them. She wondered what Ethan looked like now.

It had been forever since she just lay on the sand, letting the sea breeze and the sound of the waves flow over her. Last time she went to the beach, on a rare outing with a couple of the guys from her band, Hannah had spotted photos online within hours. She was grateful that she made a good living from her music—enough to look after her mom, too. But it was annoying to be in a sort of middle zone. Famous enough to have paparazzi shots turn up on the internet, but not successful enough to afford private islands and personal jets and the kind of peace that only big money could buy.

Well, that was in some other life, anyway. And look, here she was, anonymous after all. She only had to go to the ends of the earth to achieve it, but hey—it was worth it. And despite the memories, and Liam Ward's bad attitude, it felt surprisingly like home.

Now, with the sun on her back, she felt too lazy to even get out her book. She let her eyes close, just for a moment. Everything could wait.

Chapter Six

Hot.
Oh God, so hot.

She started to lift her head from where one cheek rested on the pillow of her folded arms…and pain rippled across the back of her body. Every square inch of her skin felt like it was on fire, every pore and follicle screaming.

She let her head fall again, wincing as the tender skin on the side of her neck flexed with the small motion. Oh, no. Lulled by the warmth of the sun in her soft, sandy hideaway, and probably by jet lag too, she'd fallen asleep. And slept, and slept, as the ultraviolet, ultra-*violent* rays baked her to a scarlet crisp.

With a mighty effort, she pushed herself up off her stomach and turned to sit upright. The foamy breakers and blue horizon tipped out of alignment, and her head spun. For one literally sickening moment, she was sure she'd throw up, but she rested her head on her knees until the feeling passed.

Home. She needed to get back to the house, out of the sun, and into a cold shower, followed by a vat of after-sun lotion.

She gritted her teeth and winced as she slowly, carefully got to her feet. From there, the distance she had to bend to pick up her things seemed too great to contemplate. The backs of her legs would surely split right open if she bent down that far. Somehow though, moving in miniscule increments, she gathered up her towel and beach bag. Inside it, under her cover-up, was the sunscreen lotion that she'd fully intended to apply once she got to the beach. She wasn't stupid, and she wasn't going to *not* sunscreen just to defy Liam. But the encounter with him, along with her memories of this beach, had been a distraction.

And now she was paying the price. Wouldn't he love that, after his lecture? Well, he didn't need to know. She gave up on the idea of struggling into the cover-up, and started cautiously back down the beach. There was no way to avoid going past the front of his house, but she'd sneak down the little alley, then hightail it to the safety of number ten. Assuming 'hightail' was a speed she could achieve in this state.

She made it to the path, shuffling like an old woman. The sun on her head and her frazzled skin was like a blowtorch. Yes, she wished she had a hat. But she kept on, grim determination compelling one foot in front of the other...until, damn it, the next foot wouldn't go quite where she was aiming it...and wait, now her legs weren't working right either...and then the world skewed, and her knees buckled...and there was nothingness.

★

Liam looked at his watch again, even as he willed himself not to. He didn't care, of course. But...how long had it been? Maybe three hours? He rattled the space bar with his thumbs. From the other side of the table, where he'd switched to, he had a view out the kitchen window to the little gate. He hadn't seen her go past—but then he hadn't been looking every second. Nope, not every second. Only every *other* second. He sighed. She'd probably gone farther along the beach and come back to Fife Street via the surf club, or maybe in the opposite direction, through the bush walk down by Mount Clarion. She knew *that* spot well enough.

He pushed the thought aside, and slapped the laptop closed. He wasn't achieving anything here—might as well get some fresh air.

Two doses of fresh air in one day? Revolutionary. Most of the Sweet Breeze Bay air he'd had since he came back was night air, shared only with the occasional mosquito. So far, he'd successfully avoided seeing anyone. He waited until night fell to go to the twenty-four hour supermarket on the Other Side, only buying enough to fit in the saddlebags of his dad's motorbike, and parking it back in the garage when he got home. The people he knew before—which included everyone in town, pretty much—didn't seem to have realized he was here. Or if they had, they'd let him be. It couldn't last, he supposed. But while it did, it was just simpler.

Although...he kept thinking about Connor and Dane. It had always been simple with those guys. Messing around, up to nothing half the time, but cracking each other up non-stop. God, they had so much to laugh about in those days. Gangly, wild-haired philosopher Connor, and sporty, outdoorsy Dane. On the surface, the three of them should've had nothing in common. Liam was a computer geek even then, and a music aficionado (like Ethan), boring the other two to death with facts about this band and that label. He'd got over his teenage obsessiveness about it all, but he still loved how the patterns in music were somehow reflected in coding, an unexpected symmetry between his two loves.

Yeah, he was still a geek.

He knew that Connor and Dane had both left Sweet Breeze Bay to go to university—engineering for Connor, at the other end of the country, and sport and exercise science for Dane, in Melbourne. He didn't know if they'd come back when they finished...but then, why would you? There was nothing here.

An accusing voice barged into his head: *Why are you here, then?*

He shoved it away and stepped out through the folding glass doors onto the deck. The chirping of a hundred thousand cicadas merged into a roar in the late afternoon sun, and the salt-tang in the air was the essence of his childhood. Suddenly he remembered playing with Jacinda when they were kids, one summer when she came to visit just with her mom. He didn't think he'd ever met her dad, now that he thought of it. That must have been the summer he turned nine, because his 'big' bike was brand new, and his mother had lent Jacinda his old one. The gap in the hedge they used to squeeze through to visit each other had grown over long ago, but he remembered how they'd found a space inside big enough to make a hut. On hot afternoons they whispered jokes to each other in the shady hideout, hung shells on the branches and threaded leaves onto twigs, and ate their way through his mom's homemade chocolate chip cookies.

Ethan was a whole year older than him, too cool to play with someone who was still only eight. And a *girl*.

That had sure changed.

He turned away from the hedge and the past, and went to look over the gate, trying to appear casual. But—*shit*. There she was. In a flash he swung the gate open and was in the alley, gathering up her crumpled form. Her crumpled, *bikini-clad* form, in the top that had come undone yesterday. He ignored the part of his brain that zeroed in on that, and concentrated on getting her to safety. As he maneuvered back through the gate, trying not to bang her head on the gatepost or let her beach bag get caught on the latch, his mind was tossing up what to do. Where should he take her? He could hardly squash her through the non-existent gap in the hedge, and he didn't want to carry her along the street like this. It would have to be his house.

He carried her inside, set her down gently on the big sofa, and stepped back as she started to come to. She was a mess. One side of her face was scarlet, and although her front was a regular color, he could see that the entire back of her body was sunburned. Well, he'd tried to tell her. But he winced in sympathy as she rolled to her side, revealing the angry redness. That had to really, really hurt.

She looked up at him then, confusion and pain in her

blue eyes. "Liam? What happened?"

"You must have passed out. In the alley."

She groaned. "Oh yeah." Then she sucked in her breath. "Oh God, it hurts. Everything. And my head..." She squeezed her eyes closed, and pressed a hand to her forehead.

"You probably have sun stroke."

"Do you..." Then she stopped, her face suddenly taking on an urgent expression. "Oh no." She struggled to her feet, her hand over her mouth, and swayed precariously. "Bathroom..."

He nodded, and helped her to the guest bathroom in the hallway. Thankfully, she shooed him away and slammed the door, leaving him standing on the other side. He wasn't enough of a gentleman to want to help with that, unless he had to. But he hovered around, trying not to listen. After a few minutes, he called out, "Are you okay?"

"Ungh."

Was that a yes or a no? He'd assume yes. "Okay, then." He retreated to the safety of the living room.

Ten minutes later, she emerged, gingerly hanging onto the door frame. "I'm really sorry," she whispered. "I'll go now. Did you bring my...?" She gestured to her bikini, and he looked, then tore his eyes away.

"Oh, right. Yeah, I got it."

"Thanks."

He could feel the heat in her skin as he helped get the cover-up over her head. When his fingers brushed the back of her arm, she flinched away. "Ow!"

"Sorry," he said.

There was some half-hearted debate about whether he should walk her back to Nana Mac's place, which was settled by her still-wobbly knees as she tried to leave without him. So he walked with her down his own path, along to number ten, and up to the front door. She rummaged in the beach bag and found the key, and got the door open.

"Thank you." She took one step inside.

"You're welcome." He cleared his throat. "We should really talk about—"

She stepped right in, her hand over her mouth again. "Sorry, I—"

And the door shut.

He was left standing on the porch, uncomfortably exposed in the bright sunshine after his weeks of being a recluse inside number twelve. He turned and headed for home, only encountering a flock of boys on skateboards on the way back. They barely gave him a glance as they passed, joking and hassling each other as they headed off on some mission. The noise they made seemed to hang in the air after they'd gone.

Back inside, with the doors closed again against the heat and the cicadas, the quiet felt...wrong. He remembered how the house used to resonate with exactly that kind of boy noise, day in and day out, overlaid with music from the stereo or their guitars. Their amps must have been the menace of the neighborhood, but he didn't recall anyone ever complaining, not even Nana Mac right next door, or Mrs. Marsh over the road.

He looked at Ethan's electric acoustic guitar, resting on its stand in the corner. For a moment his fingers tingled, tempted by the elegant instrument...but it was Ethan's, always would be. Unlike the girl next door.

He took another cold beer from the fridge, sat back at the table, and opened the laptop. A hefty dose of PHP and CDATA and WYSIWYG should erase the image of her in that bikini, the memory of how she felt in his arms, skin hot, sand in her hair, a grown woman, so different from that teenage summer...and yet so familiar.

The nagging suspicion he'd avoided for years rose again, but this time, he was listening. He looked back to the guitar.

WYSIWYG. What you see is what you get.

Not always.

He entered a name into Google, and hit enter.

Chapter Seven

R iley Dawson grimaced, her sweetly round face full of sympathy as she looked at Jacinda lying incapacitated on the sofa. "Oh my God. You poor thing."

Jacinda made a small, tragic sound. "It's so sore."

"It must be."

She tried to hold herself still as she continued recounting her disaster. "It gets even more glamorous. After he brought me inside I was all shaky, and my heart was racing...and then I threw up in his bathroom."

Riley put her hands to her face. "*No.*"

"Yes. So embarrassing." She stuck out her tongue. "And now I'm getting more and more stiff, like my skin's a size too small."

"Horrible! Have you had plenty to drink? You need to rehydrate."

"I don't know...I had a bit of water." She waved a finger toward a glass on the coffee table, unable to bear moving any more of her body.

"Right, I'll get you a refill." Riley stood up and went over to the open-plan kitchen, full of purpose. "I'm glad I stopped by. I came to invite you to dessert night at Clarion Call, but I don't suppose you'll be up to it." Back with the tall glass of water, she paused. "Have you looked in the mirror?"

"Ugh, no." All she'd done was shut the door—kind of in Liam's face, now she thought of it, but she was afraid she'd throw up again—grab a glass of water, and collapse on the couch. Velvet had tried to snuggle in, but even the cat's soft fur had felt like sandpaper against her scorched skin.

"Stay hydrated." Riley put the glass down where Jacinda could reach it, and sat in an old wingback chair. Velvet took advantage of the available lap, and climbed up, her growing belly making her less agile. "Foof, you're heavy, Velvet. When is she due?"

"Any time now, I think," Jacinda said.

"Oh, you're a beautiful girl," she crooned, tickling Velvet under the chin. "Yes, you are. When are you going to show us your babies? When oh when?"

Jacinda carefully adjusted her position on the couch. "Would you like to have one of her kittens?"

Riley smiled. "Maybe. I'd love a black cat like her. But I suppose their coloring will depend on who the dad is." Then she looked at Jacinda. "You know, you're kind of multicolored. I read that color blocking is a trend this season, but maybe not like this." She stroked Velvet, obviously trying not to laugh.

Jacinda put a hand on each cheek. One felt more or less normal, but the other—the one that had been exposed to the sun—was scalding hot. She groaned. "I'm such an idiot. This is going to peel, right?"

"Probably." She screwed up her nose. "I hope not, though. It was lucky Liam found you."

Jacinda squeezed her eyes shut, trying not to think about how she'd woken in his house, wearing only her bikini, all sandy and disheveled and...vomity. She wasn't convinced that counted as lucky. "I guess."

"I didn't even know he was here. No one does, or I'm sure I would have heard. Did you talk to him?"

"Kind of..." She thought back to their conversation over the gate. "I think we sort of had a disagreement."

Riley frowned. "Why would you have a disagreement?"

"It's...I don't know, really."

45

That wasn't completely true. He'd seemed mad at her right off—which she could understand. Okay, she'd left in a hurry, that summer. But after her last talk with Ethan, and what happened after that, her only choice was to leave. Go back to her mom, who, for all her faults, was still the only person she wanted to retreat to. At seventeen, that was all she knew to do. Nana Mac had been here, as much a mother as a grandmother...but staying wasn't an option. She couldn't deal with what had happened, with Ethan right next door.

The sharp nugget of what she probably should have done was still lodged in her conscience. If there were things she'd never told Ethan in person, that she should have...well. What did he care anyway? He'd made that clear. And she didn't want to go into it all with Riley.

"I guess there were some things that happened that summer," she said.

Riley nodded. "I remember. You know, I always wondered if Liam secretly liked you himself. But Ethan was *such* a babe." She sighed in wistful reminiscence. "I wouldn't have stepped on your territory, though! Not that he would ever have looked at *me*."

"Well, I never thought he'd look at me, either. And I don't think Liam felt that way."

He'd always been in the background, but she'd never gotten any kind of vibe from him. She'd probably been too caught up in Ethan to notice anyone else, anyway.

"*And*, for the record, you're super cute yourself," she added. With her cherubic face, trim and curvy figure, and sunshiny disposition, Riley was the definition of cute.

She blushed. "I wasn't fishing for compliments. But thank you." She sighed again. "It's just so wrong that Ethan's not here."

With Liam next door, it did feel like a whole portion of that summer was missing. But it was the portion she didn't want to face. "When I saw Liam, I wondered if Ethan might be here too. I guess he's still in Australia? Do you know where they moved to, exactly? Sydney, or...?"

Riley looked at her, an unreadable expression clouding

her face. "They moved to the Sunshine Coast. Just up and left everything here. Mrs. Ward has only been back that one time, when her sister was sick. I think Liam was staying with them over there, but Ethan…"

She hesitated, and the weight of things unspoken gathered around them.

In the silence, Jacinda could feel her heartbeat in her chest.

Thud. Thud. Thud.

"Ethan what?"

"You don't *know*?" Her voice was practically a whisper.

Jacinda shook her head, her own voice stuck in her throat as she waited.

"I'm so sorry. I don't know how to say it." Riley's eyes brimmed with tears. "He died."

★

Jacinda stood in the shower and let the water run over her burned back, the physical pain a proxy for the pain in her heart. The tears that should have run down her face were arrested by shock, waiting unshed as her brain tried to make sense of something that made no sense at all.

Riley had been beside herself over having to break the news—Jacinda had to comfort her more than the other way around. She'd been reluctant to leave, but finally said she had to go back to Clarion Call to help Caro get ready for dessert night. It had become a weekly institution in Sweet Breeze Bay, apparently, even attracting customers from the Other Side and farther afield. Before she left, she'd taken Jacinda's number, sent a text so that Jacinda had hers, and made her promise to text or call if she felt unwell again. Then, with final instructions to shower and moisturize, and keep drinking water, she tore herself away.

On autopilot, Jacinda followed her instructions and made her way gingerly upstairs to the bathroom. She winced as she reached behind her back to undo her bikini top, but forced herself to keep going. All the years she'd spent being mad at him, justifying her resentment and her actions…he'd been dead. And—at the next thought, her heart clenched even more—his family. His lovely mom, his gruff policeman dad, and Liam, who'd admired and emulated his big brother, even as he grew up in his shadow. All that time, they'd been dealing with their own terrible loss.

And what had happened? That was the one thing Riley couldn't tell her, because she didn't know. No one knew. In a tiny place like Sweet Breeze Bay, something like that should be impossible to keep hidden. And yet, no one knew exactly how Ethan had died. Was there something more to it, even worse than the fact of his death?

Despite herself, her mind went there.

Had he done it himself?

And…was it her fault?

She turned and let the water run over her face, holding her breath as she tried to wash away the thought. No. For starters, he was Ethan Ward, home town hero. Sure, she'd made something of herself since then, but it was ridiculous to even imagine that someone as unspectacular as the teenage her could have affected him enough to do anything so tragic.

She turned out of the water and exhaled a huge breath. The water on her back was a thousand tiny needles, and she was grateful for the pain. Standing in the steam, she pressed a hand against her belly—flat, unstretched—and let herself remember.

That summer night. A bonfire on the beach. The Sweet Breeze Bay teenagers laughing, drinking, flirting. Riley and the younger ones alternately giggling and playing it cool, the older kids, just finished their last year of high school, cruising on their inherent superiority. Liam and his two friends hanging around in the background, the three slightly geeky musketeers, as always.

And the song. Oh, that song. When Ethan sang it to her, there in the firelight, he didn't care who else was listening. She remembered Liam playing harmony, the other kids quietening down, the crackle of the flames, the rush and retreat of the waves...but above all, she remembered Ethan watching her as he sang. And the words—the kind of tender, heartfelt words no one had ever aimed her way—well, they soaked right into her soul, left her heart bare naked. And when he finished, and leaned on his guitar with that look in his eye, and gave her a grin...she knew there was nothing she wouldn't do.

He'd been drinking more as the summer went on, and that night was no exception. She'd had plenty too, the kind of over-sweet mixer she couldn't stomach now. After the song, he finished the last of the bourbon the guys had been handing around, and grabbed her up.

"Come on, American girl." He was a Tom Petty fan, just like her.

He dropped the empty bottle in the sand, and pulled a blanket from around someone's shoulders. They made a token protest, but this was Ethan. He had the run of the place.

She followed him away from the warmth of the fire, her hand in his. In the half dark, she stumbled a little on the uneven sand, but he held her hand tightly, and soon they were deep in the trees, hidden way up under the base of the mountain.

"Take it easy, baby," he murmured as he kissed her, a new intensity to his mouth and hands. "Make it last all night," he breathed, as he lowered her to the blanket spread under the moon-dappled foliage.

Yeah, she was his American girl.

She'd always wondered what the first time would be like. She'd left it later than most girls she knew at high school (apart from Hannah, who was waiting for *the one*). It turned out that the first time was blurry and hurried, her feet cold, leaves in her hair, rocks in her back through the blanket. He was half apologetic afterward about the speed of it all, but he was so tipsy-charming and handsome, she pushed aside the scary fact that they hadn't used any protection, and kissed him into silence. He liked her best.

And the subsequent times were all kinds of eye-opening. They'd stolen three more chances, all at Nana Mac's place while she was out at her quilting group, or poker game, or salsa dancing class. Three times of closing the blinds, undressing in the dimly shuttered light, watching his expression change as her breasts came free from her bra, his hands and mouth doing things that left her breathless, the hot afternoon air getting even more heated in the little attic room.

But it was that first time—her star-struck, unprotected first time—that made the baby.

Where was the luck in that?

More than just a line on a pregnancy test, the baby was the real result of that one night, making her physically nauseous even as she felt heartsick about her poor judgment. A month after that moment on the mountain, with the start of the school year drawing near, she had to face it. She gathered her courage and told Nana Mac, who was pragmatic, unflustered, and just sympathetic enough as they went to the doctor on the Other Side to have it confirmed.

But then, she had to tell Ethan. He'd be leaving before long, heading to college in Sydney. What would they do?

She met him at the beach, took the deepest breath of her life, and blurted it out. And he went into insta-shock. Now, she could understand it better—the well-charted path to success that he'd taken for granted was suddenly, horrifyingly, impeded by a massive hurdle. A Jacinda-shaped hurdle, that would soon become a Jacinda-and-baby-shaped hurdle. At the time, though, all she felt was the rejection, the instant stepping back, the immediate distance that scared the hell out of her. Straight away, she knew she couldn't stay.

But what happened next—was that luck, or bad luck?

Three days later, only the night before her flight home to the States, the spotting started. Then the cramps. And then the bleeding, red and heavy and final, as she clutched her belly and cried for her mistake, and her loss. Thank God her grandmother had been there.

The next day, despite Nana Mac's protests, she got on the plane with a backpack stuffed full of sanitary pads, and left without a word to anyone. Not even Ethan. He hadn't wanted to know about the baby anyway, her teenage self said. After she'd told him, she'd waited, hoping, but he hadn't even come to see her. He'd be pleased she was gone.

And now they'd never have the chance to see the truth from each other's side.

She turned off the water and stepped out of the shower. A brief glance at her reflection was enough. Riley was right—she was multicolored, with wedges of red on her face, neck and arms. The entire back of her body was the same shade, the only white the outline of her bikini. She carefully blotted herself dry with a towel, then searched in the cabinet for after-sun lotion. Finding a green bottle of aloe balm, she applied it to all the parts she could reach without tearing apart. All the while, she thought about Ethan. And the guilt crept back in. She should have told him she'd lost the baby.

All these years, she'd had no idea about Ethan's death, and yet she'd never been able to shake the experiences of that summer. A total of four times. That was all. She'd done it countless times since then, with plenty of guys. Okay, there was the baby, Ethan's blunt let-down, then the conflicted sadness and relief of the loss. But it was long over, done with. It wasn't like she was still in love with him, beyond the knee-wobbling, butterfly rush of her teenage crush. This wasn't one of those slept-together-in-high-school-never-got-over-him stories.

She'd done plenty of living since then. *Plenty.* She was Cin Scott, for God's sake, tough enough to fight in a rock world that chewed up and spat out countless wannabes and pretenders. Sure, sometimes she felt like she was clinging on by her fingernails, but didn't everyone, unless they were rock royalty? She'd made it into the Billboard Hot 100 with Hourglass Reverb, a song she wrote herself. She'd dated Eli Tyler, who went on to become one of the music industry's hottest, edgiest guys. It was only after they split up that she realized his publicist had suggested the whole thing—but she assured Hannah she was fine, toughened up a little more, took the publicity, and used it to climb another rung of the ladder. She'd learned to take an audience with her through an entire performance, leading them from the rebellious high of a power anthem, to the sweet melancholy of a heartfelt love song, and back again. She'd bought the place in Los Feliz, her loft that was the closest thing to home she'd had since forever. Plus, she'd set her mom up in her own little house in Florida—finally got her settled in the right climate and on the right medication.

But somehow, Jacinda Prescott, that naïve, pregnant, lost teenager, wouldn't quite let her go. Or, maybe, Cin couldn't let Jacinda go. No matter how far behind her that girl was in time, she still seemed to be right over her shoulder, or turning up in her dreams.

Maybe, if Ethan was gone—even unspoken, the word was a stab in the guts—she could leave that Jacinda and the baby in the past, where they belonged.

If that was where they belonged.

And if she really wanted to.

Chapter Eight

"Hello love! It's me."

Jacinda winced as the bright voice blasted out of the phone, her headache still gripping her skull as she emerged from sleep. The heat in her skin brought tearing pain with every move. She lay as still as she could, wondering how long this would last, and dragged a few words from her brain.

"Unh. Hi, Nana Mac."

"That took a while, I thought you must be out." Her voice was lively over the music and hubbub in the background.

"Uh, no." She held a hand over her eyes, blocking out the morning light. "I was sleeping."

"Good girl! Getting plenty of rest."

"Mmm." She didn't mention her self-inflicted medical issue. "How's Spain?"

"Marvelous! Just gorgeous. And the men on this salsa course! I tell you, they *certainly* beat Dennis and Bruce down at the village hall. It's a bit pricey, but it's the best money I've spent in ages. You can't take it with you, after all!" Her laughter danced down the line, and Jacinda had to smile through her pain. "But how's my darling Velvet? Any kittens yet?"

"No, not yet." She looked around, expecting to see the

cat curled up on the end of the bed, in the sun that was slanting through the shutters and striping the bed with golden warmth. But there was no sign of her. Maybe she was cuddled up in her luxury cat bed, under the bay window in the living room. It looked like a cozy place to mother a litter of kittens, when they arrived. "Riley said she might want to take one."

"Oh you've seen her then! Wonderful. I knew she'd look after you. Any other news?"

Jacinda hesitated. She didn't want to ruin her grandmother's mood, but she did have questions about Ethan, and about finding Liam next door. "Well..."

Then Nana Mac said loudly, "I'm coming Vicente, I'll be right there! No, no, wait for me!" She lowered her voice. "I'd better go—someone else will grab him if I don't stake my claim. He's the best dancer in the place."

Who'd have the heart to keep her from Vicente? "Okay, have fun. Everything's fine here."

"That's good. Enjoy yourself, and I'll phone you again soon. Ooh, wait! I almost forgot. Danielle and her little one Sam are coming to stay at the house too."

Danielle was Jacinda's second cousin, one of Nana Mac's great-nephews and nieces—just one of the gang of eleven grandchildren her sister Morag had been blessed with. Jacinda always felt sorry that poor Nana Mac had to settle for only her, while Morag luxuriated in an abundance of grandchildren, and now great-grandchildren too. Her three kids had all settled into houses on the huge family farm a few hours south of Auckland, and some of the grandkids had stayed on too, while others came and went. It was a rural idyll that contrasted sharply with the unsettled, hard-edged urban existence that Trina and Jacinda had led after her dad left, moving to a new town every time her mom felt the walls closing in. Well, it would be nice to see Danielle, and she'd never even met Sam...but so much for her peace.

"I haven't seen her since we were kids. Are they taking a vacation?"

"No, Danielle has left her hopeless husband. Sounds

like the best decision she's ever made. She'll explain everything when they get there, next Monday I think." Before Jacinda had a chance to ask anything else, she said, "Have to go...I'll call again soon!"

"Okay. Bye." But she was gone already, whisked away to steam up the dance floor with Vicente. Well, good for her.

She tossed the phone on the bed and looked around for Velvet, then called for her. Both mornings so far, she'd been in the bedroom demanding attention by now. Then she remembered Riley scooping kibble into the paw-print decorated bowl yesterday, enthusing to Velvet about her kittens in a sing-song voice as she filled it to the brim. She was clearly a cat person through and through. There would still be enough food left that Velvet didn't need to come begging for breakfast today.

She rolled over slowly, aware of every frazzled pore. The sun had made its mark on her yesterday...but so had Riley's bombshell. And now she knew that she owed Liam some kind of proper communication, to give her condolences at least. It was unavoidable—she'd have to go over there and talk to him again.

Tuesday today—just under a week until family descended. Then they could take over looking after Velvet, and she'd leave.

But today, she'd lie low and keep still, until the sunburn started to settle. Maybe later, when she felt better, she'd prop herself up and start work on those damn chapters she'd signed a contract to write. But for now, she was staying right where she was—horizontal, and out of trouble.

★

By the time the sun went down, she'd dozed long enough that she couldn't sleep anymore. Plus, she was starving— the banana and pretzels she'd grabbed on her only trip downstairs had hardly touched the sides, and now her stomach was grumbling loudly.

She went down to the kitchen in the silky little slip she'd been sleeping in, the softest, smallest thing she had with her. She'd contemplated sleeping naked, but somehow couldn't do it, knowing Liam was just across the hedge. Despite the warm evening, the cooler air downstairs gave her goose bumps—with half her skin aflame, her temperature control was all awry. She grabbed a throw from the wingback chair and put it carefully around her shoulders. The hum of the fridge was the only sound inside, but when she opened one of the French doors, the chirp of crickets and the deep whooshing sound of waves joined the night-time refrain. She took a breath of sweet, salty, night air, and looked over toward the Ward house. What was he doing over there? And what would she say to him now?

A dog barked in the distance, jolting her out of her thoughts, and she called for Velvet, the 'puss, puss, puss' that all cats were supposed to answer to. Nothing. She pursed her lips and made an array of bird noises, clucked her tongue, and called again.

"Puss, puss, puss. Velll-vet…here, puss, puss."

Nothing.

Damn.

Well, she couldn't go searching around in the dark. And maybe this was part of Velvet's usual routine, anyway. She knew that cats loved to roam at night, and Velvet had the whole of Sweet Breeze Bay to explore. She'd be back in the morning, stepping on Jacinda's stomach with her poky paws, meowing plaintively about the poor breakfast service. She shivered and stepped back in, pulling the door closed behind her. There was a cat flap in the back door, so Velvet could come in when she was done with her adventures.

She went into the kitchen and put together some sandwiches with the ingredients she'd bought on her way home from Clarion Call two nights before. That seemed an age ago. She dipped into the packet of chocolate covered cookies too, and put a couple on her plate. Then she took a Diet Coke from the fridge, and carried it all back upstairs on a tray. She'd better start on those chapters.

At the top of the stairs, she paused for a moment, then set her tray carefully on the floor and went into the other upstairs bedroom. She pulled back the curtain, just a whisker, so that she could see down into the Wards' yard. And yes, there was the glow of a light on, somewhere in the house that she'd been in so many times that summer. She tried to remember the layout. Maybe he was in the study nook tucked into the landing halfway up the stairs. His old bedroom looked in this direction, so he couldn't be in there. Or maybe he was in there, in the dark, and he'd just left the stairwell light on. At this thought, she dropped the curtain, suddenly imagining him looking back at her through a crack in his own curtains.

Except he wasn't—she was the one behaving like a stalker.

She collected the tray and got herself set up on the bed with her laptop. Tomorrow, if he was home, she'd have to go see him, and tell him how sorry she was for their loss. Exactly what she'd say other than that, she wasn't sure. For now, though, the stupid book was a welcome distraction. Easier to figure out advice for girls wanting to throw themselves into the shark cage of the music biz, than to find the right words for the brother of the guy she'd loved and lost, right before he lost him too.

Chapter Nine

At first, Liam wasn't sure he'd heard anything. He turned off the fan in the bathroom and listened, and there it was—the last notes of the ridiculous musical doorbell his mom had installed. For a second he considered ignoring it, pretending there was no one here...but it was too late for that, childish as it was. Jacinda knew he was here, and once she knew, the rest of town probably would too. Especially since he'd seen Riley Dawson go into number ten—if she talked like she used to, Clarion Call would be second only to the Kelp and King as a source of gossip.

He sighed and dried the last droplets from his body, ran his fingers through his damp hair, then pulled on boxer briefs and cargo shorts. His t-shirts were all in the dryer, which meant going past the front door and down the hall to the laundry. He jogged down the stairs, intending to grab a shirt before answering the door, but as he went through the entranceway the musical bell rang again. Through the frosted glass, he could see a figure that looked like Jacinda...turning to walk away.

Without thinking, he flipped the lock and yanked the door open, and she spun around. Instantly, her eyes went from his face to his chest, and he watched with unexpected satisfaction as her expression changed, before she carefully refocused somewhere around the top of his head.

"Hi." She cleared her throat, shifted her weight from one foot to the other. Her face was still sunburned on one side, but he could clearly see the other side blush pink, too. Yep, she was off-balance. He let her wait just a moment longer than was polite before he answered.

"Hi."

"Um, I'm sorry to interrupt." She glanced at his chest again. "But I wanted to say...I mean, Riley just told me..." She paused, taking a breath. "I'm really, really sorry to hear about Ethan. I had no idea."

He tensed as the words hit him. Hearing his brother's name spoken aloud still had the power to throw him off-center. Especially spoken by her. He looked into the blue sky over her shoulder, then back at her face. Maybe it was time to say a few things after all. He stood back, holding the door open. "Come in."

He could smell her light, sweet fragrance as she passed by, almost close enough to brush against his bare skin.

"Take a seat," he said. "I'll just be a second."

He left her in the big living room and went along to the laundry, grabbed a t-shirt from the dryer—wrinkled, but too bad—and tugged it over his head. Focus, he told himself. This girl is trouble. She was trouble then, but now...multiply it by the factors of her life since, and you've got dynamite. Or kryptonite. Just have this conversation and be done with it, and done with her. She surely wouldn't be staying for long—but if she was, a ticket back to Australia was only the click of a mouse away. There was nothing to keep him here. Coming home was meant to be time to clear out the demons of the past, not get pulled back down by the rip tide that was this girl.

He went back out to the living room, and found her standing in the corner looking down at Ethan's guitar. His first instinct was to tell her to get the hell away from it. No one had played it since Ethan died—sitting quietly in the house, it was more of a memorial to him than the stone they'd placed on his grave. But when she turned to him, there was something in her eyes that made him hesitate.

"This guitar…" There was a break in her voice.

"I know," he said gruffly. For a moment they looked at each other, back in time to those carefree summer days. And nights. At this thought, he snapped back into clarity. "So. You were saying?"

She seemed to shake herself into the present too. "If I'd known, I would have said something the other day. I would have said something long ago. I'm so sorry. Ethan was…amazing."

A storm of reactions flooded through him. The long-held anger at the way she'd left, without a word to anyone, leaving Ethan gutted. Never even acknowledging his death, which had been a drawn-out, long-distance slap in the face to his family. How could he believe that she never knew? And once again, underlying everything else, he felt the unwelcome, unworthy stab of jealousy. He couldn't face it then, and he sure as hell didn't want to revisit it now. He couldn't compete with the amazing Ethan when he was alive, and there was no competing with a dead man. But he'd loved his brother to death…until death. A death he could have prevented, if only he hadn't let himself get caught up in his own unwanted feelings for his brother's girlfriend. You don't get much more screwed up than that.

He realized she was watching him, waiting for his reply. Shit, say something—you've thought about it enough times. He fired off the first thing that came into his head.

"If he was so amazing, why did you leave?"

She shut her eyes for a second as the arrow struck, the pain obvious on her face, but he didn't regret it. Well, not much. She *should* feel bad. It was only a fraction of what they went through in her aftermath.

She went and sat on the sofa, where she'd lain in her bikini the day before yesterday. As the image rose in his memory, he scrubbed it away, but his brain betrayed him by recalling how she'd felt in his arms. The softness of her hair under his chin as he carried her, the warmth of her skin, her full breasts pressed together in her bikini top as he held her close against him. He rubbed his eyes, and looked at her now, making himself remember who she was. The girl who'd come out of nowhere and ruined his brother's life, and divided his own life in two—before and after. And he remembered who she *really* was, as confirmed on Google.

"I couldn't deal with everything. I just had to go home." She looked at him. "You knew about the baby, right?"

He stayed standing, his arms crossed. "He told me you were pregnant, yeah."

That was a conversation he'd never forget. It was probably the only time he'd known his brother truly lost, the usual bravado and confidence replaced with something raw and uncertain. He was Ethan Ward, after all—young, smart, and destined for big things. Liam knew he'd been drinking more to smother his nerves about leaving the bay to study music in Sydney, where he'd be a small fish in a big pond for the first time in his life. But the baby bombshell, and Jacinda's exit, were the aces that brought down his house of cards. Despite the hero worship of his little brother, and the admiration of most of the kids in town, Ethan obviously wasn't as untouchable as he seemed.

Jacinda sighed. "I asked Nana Mac to talk to your mom after I left, just in case. I didn't know if Ethan had told her about the baby to start with, but I couldn't let you all think I'd gone away with his baby. With her grandchild."

"Well, it was too late. He died thinking that was exactly what you'd done. He never knew you lost it." He knew each word was a dagger, but he couldn't stop. "You left him broken."

She pressed a hand to her temple. "I don't even know what happened. Are you saying it's my fault he died?"

He could see her emotion rising, but he didn't let her off the hook. This was the girl who'd cut and run, without looking back. If he forced everything into the open now, maybe he'd be free of it, free of the memories...and yeah, free of the power she still had over him. It was worse now than it was then, when he was flush with teenage hormones and fraternal competitiveness. Now, he had no excuse. All he could do was drive it away, ruin any possible connection they might have. He forged on.

"Didn't you notice that he'd been drinking more than

usual? Didn't you think something might be going on?"

"How would I know?" There was an edge to her voice. "I didn't have anything to compare it with. And anyway, all you guys were obsessed with getting hold of beer."

Fair point. He'd still been underage that summer, and it had pissed him off to rely on Ethan and his mates to supply them with drinks. He and Connor and Dane were on the cusp of manhood, or so they'd thought—their toes right on the line, ready to play with the grown-ups. They had no idea that they were about to get a lesson in the realities of life.

But that wasn't the point of this conversation.

"He was going to come and see you. But then we saw you get in the car with Nana Mac, with all your things, and leave."

He saw a flare of something in her eyes then, as if she was recalculating. Disbelief, maybe, and confusion. "Really?"

He ignored the question, and the turmoil on her face. "You expected more from him than from yourself. You told him something so huge, and expected him to deal with it instantly. He was only a kid. Couldn't you have given him more time to get his head around it?"

"I was only a kid too." She stood up. "He was the first guy I ever slept with, and suddenly I had a baby to think about. And then, right when I was trying to get *my* head around that, without him, I had a miscarriage. Can you imagine what that was like?"

"No. But at least you're still alive to tell the tale."

She visibly drew herself together, and steel came into her demeanor.

"I am."

Even as he realized that he'd done what he set out to do—brought down a wall between them, severing any chance of finding comfort in their shared past—an unexpected regret washed over him.

She regarded him for a moment, composed again. "I'll see myself out." But after a few steps, she turned around. "Think whatever you like about me, but I *am* sorry about

Ethan. I'm sorry for your loss." She paused. "And I'm sorry you blame me."

When he didn't say anything, she turned her back and left the room. He heard the front door open, then close quietly behind her. In the silence left behind, he wondered if this was what closure felt like.

Chapter Ten

G ritting her teeth, Jacinda walked the short distance back to number ten, her emotions smoldering hotter than her sunburn. She'd gone to see him with the best intentions, and for a moment there, she'd been willing to lay it on the line, tell him her truth and listen to what he told her in return. But he soon cured her of that. What an ass. A self-righteous, shirtless, self-absorbed…

But her indignation couldn't sustain itself. His words had hit home, and there was only one person she wanted to talk to now. Upstairs, she found her phone, and hit Hannah's name.

"Hey, runaway." Her friend's voice was a ray of sunshine cutting into her overcast mood. "Tell me I guessed right."

"Hey," Jacinda said, remembering the New Zealand flag in Hannah's last text. "Yeah, you were right."

"I knew it. So, what's happening in paradise?"

She flopped down on the bed, wincing as her sunburned skin hit the quilted bedcover. "It's less, um…paradisiacal than I'd hoped."

"Oh, no. What's happened? Did someone track you down already? No one here has questioned it yet—I just keep saying you're taking a short break."

"Thanks. No, no one has tracked me down. It's more that someone was here already."

"Who?"

"Liam Ward."

"Wait...Ethan's brother?"

Hannah was the only person who knew the whole story. Not just the facts of what had happened, but how it had really been for Jacinda, here in Sweet Breeze Bay, and when she got home and had to face the music.

"Yeah. He's staying at their house, next door."

She didn't mention anything about the perpetually shirtless state he seemed to be in, or the unexpectedly distracting effect that had on her. It was so many kinds of wrong to even notice his broad chest, sculpted shoulders, and well-formed biceps, one of which was inked with the sweeping curves of a Pacific-style tattoo. So, so wrong. Okay, little brothers grew up...but that didn't mean this one was a suitable candidate for her attention. Not that he showed any sign of interest in her—only anger and resentment. "We kind of had a confrontation."

"A confrontation? But wait, go back a step. I thought they were in Australia."

"He was, but now he's here. And I can't spend the summer with him right next door glowering every time he sees me, making me feel guilty about everything."

As she said it, she realized just how guilty she was really feeling. Admit it—what riled her more than anything was the fact that Liam was right. She'd expected Ethan to rise to the occasion, tell her everything would be fine, and make everything okay, when she was incapable of doing that herself. Most likely it would have turned out all right—girls have babies every day, and it wasn't like she'd been completely alone in the world. But at that point, it felt like total disaster...and it probably had to Ethan, too.

But Hannah was staunchly on her side.

"Why should you feel guilty? Ethan was the one who let you down. If anything, you let him off the hook."

"Maybe..."

The silence that followed was loaded, and Hannah knew her well enough to guess that something was up.

"What? What is it?"

Her voice came out in a whisper, as if saying it aloud would drive the truth even farther home. "He's dead, Han. He died right after I left."

There was a strangled gasp at the end of the line as Hannah registered what she was saying. Then she came right out with the question that had been tormenting Jacinda.

"Oh my God. Did he kill himself?"

"I don't know. I don't think so..." It sounded more like a question than a statement. The idea was unthinkable.

But Hannah had regrouped. "No, I'm sure he didn't. He had everything going for him. Even if there'd been a baby, you guys would have worked it out somehow."

If there'd been a baby. "He never knew I'd lost it. He thought I flew back to the States pregnant."

"Well, if he didn't want it, then what was the problem anyway?"

"I guess..." She knew it was more complicated than that, but she had no clue what could have been in his mind, or what he would have said if he'd come to see her before she left. "I can't believe Nana Mac never told me."

"She was probably trying to protect you. And your mom. I'm really sorry, Cin. You must be heartsick."

"I feel like I've been knocked sideways." She paused. "But I have no right to be."

"Yes, you do. It was huge. And it was the thing that finished everything with your dad."

"Yeah, well..." That was a topic for another day. "Probably better that way, in the end."

"Maybe. But listen, don't let him drive you away from there. You need this break, and it's the only time you're going to get. When you come home, we'll have you working your butt off. You still have a tour to do, you know."

"I do? Even after I kneed Greg in the...ego?"

She laughed. "Todd told me. Only you, Cin. But all is not lost. Todd's still negotiating, and he's aiming for a ten-city tour at least."

"Shit."

"Aren't you happy about it?"

She looked down the length of her legs to her blue-painted toenails, incongruous against the sweet floral bedcover. "Sorry, I am happy. Of course. I just wonder whose terms it'll be on."

"We'll iron out the details. It'll be fine. No, it'll be more than fine—it'll be amazing."

From this distance, she had to remind herself: it was what she'd always wanted. A springboard to the next level, that they'd all been working for. She had doubts, but she'd have to find a way to deal with them...and with Greg and co.

"Okay. Thanks. And tell your no-good husband thanks too."

"You're welcome. You'll have to talk to him yourself soon, though—I can hold off the Lainey Kingsleys of the world, but I can't hold your manager off indefinitely."

"I know. He's pretty determined." She avoided thinking of the ways in which she'd held Todd off herself, until Hannah had come on the scene.

Now her friend's voice took on a sadder tone.

"He's away again, checking out some new talent in Austin, he said. He'll be back in a few days though, hopefully."

Jacinda hated to hear her sounding so downcast. "Okay, I'll talk to him then."

"Good. You know, now that you guys have *both* abandoned me, I've been training every day."

Hannah had ruled the pool in high school, but given it up, discouraged, when she didn't get a swim scholarship for college. Lately, though, she'd been swimming more again, and even got herself a coach, who was encouraging her to compete.

"That's great! You should enter that swim contest, your times have been so good."

But she made a *pfft* sound. "I'm too old for that."

"Like I'm too old for the music biz?"

There was a pause at Hannah's end. "Okay, I hear you. I'll think about it."

"Good. And take care of yourself."

"I will. Oh, have you got any kittens to snuggle with yet?"

She eyed the empty end of the bed. "No, and I can't find Velvet. I'm starting to get worried."

"Don't cats go off and find a secret place to have their kittens? Maybe she's made a baby nest somewhere."

Jacinda thought of the expensive faux-suede cat bed in the living room, unused. "Oh no. I'd better look harder for her."

"She'll be fine, I bet. Cats have been doing it by themselves forever."

"Not this cat. Nana Mac will be beside herself if Velvet doesn't give birth in luxury. She adores her."

Hannah laughed. "Okay, do what you gotta do. Love you. And I am really sorry about Ethan. But don't let Liam get under your skin."

Jacinda remembered the way the hairs on her arm had practically stood on end as she walked past him into the house, the warmth of his slightly damp skin just a whisper away.

"I won't."

No way would she let that happen. Hannah didn't mean *that* kind of under her skin, but her badly-behaved body was threatening to take it in exactly that direction—and that would only be one more way to complicate an already complicated situation. One more way for him to think badly of her. She wasn't about to let some inappropriate thoughts—*unrequited* inappropriate thoughts—make a bad situation worse. She put him out of her mind, said goodbye to Hannah, and went to look for Velvet.

Chapter Eleven

E ven in Nana Mac's rambling house, full of nooks and crannies, there were only so many places to look for a small black cat.

Jacinda had gone into every room, peered into every closet, cupboard, and corner, and called "puss, puss, puss" until her tongue was tied. Every now and then she stopped and listened, tipping her head and holding her breath, in case she could hear an answering meow, or the sound of tiny mewling kittens. But there was no sign of Velvet anywhere in the house.

Next stop, the yard. She did a circuit of the perimeter, looking under the neatly clipped hedge that ran around the boundary. Then she checked in the garden shed, and carefully got down and looked under the deck. Nothing. There was no basement under the house, but there was a big enough space in the foundations, between the bare dirt of the ground and the wooden floorboards, for a grown person to crawl. Not that she was going in there, amongst the spiders and bugs and God only knew what else. She went back into the house and found a torch in the kitchen, then shone it into the gloom, calling again for Velvet. But there was no flash of iridescent eyes reflecting the torch beam in the dark, no answering *chirrup*. She sighed and closed the creaky access door, then stood up, brushing dirt and grass from her knees. Where could she be?

Her eyes were drawn over the hedge to the Ward house, at number twelve. It would be just her luck. First, though, she'd rule out the other most likely possibility.

The woman who opened the door at number eight looked frazzled, with a preschooler hanging onto her leg and a baby on her hip. But when Jacinda introduced herself, and said why she'd come, her face brightened.

"Oh, of course, Nana Mac said you'd be house-sitting, and Velvet-sitting. We were feeding her until you arrived. I'm Nadia. It's nice to meet you."

"You too." And it was. At least she had a nice neighbor on *one* side.

"I'm sorry, I haven't seen Velvet around our place. She used to come visiting sometimes, but since Izzy and Oliver came along it's been a bit hectic for her, I think."

Izzy, dressed in a pink tutu, a Peppa Pig pajama top, and red gumboots, tugged at her mother's shirt. "I want to see the pussy cat."

"Me too," Jacinda said to her.

At this, Izzy hid behind Nadia's leg, but peeped out with a little smile. "I like Velvet."

"Yes, well, I'm sure she likes you too, Izz." Out of Izzy's sight, Nadia rolled her eyes and grinned at Jacinda. "Izzy is a very...*enthusiastic* animal person. Very hands-on, if you know what I mean."

Jacinda laughed. "I see. Well, thank you." Baby Oliver started to cry as Izzy decided to force a small plastic teapot onto his foot. "I'll leave you to it, but it'd be great to know if you do see Velvet."

"We'll definitely let you know." Nadia jigged Oliver on her hip, unfazed by his escalating volume. "And come any time for a cuppa. My other half goes away all the time for work, so it's nice to have adult company. Not that *our* company is much of a drawcard."

She pulled the teapot off Oliver's foot and threw it into the corner, where it joined what looked like the aftermath of a toy tsunami.

"No, that'd be great, thank you." Jacinda smiled at

Izzy. "Maybe you could make me a cup of tea then?"

Izzy's face lit up. "Okay! I make decaf soy lattes too," she said proudly.

"That's very sophisticated," Jacinda said.

Nadia smiled. "I'm dairy-free at the moment, because of this guy's delicate system, so our tea parties are a bit alternative these days, aren't they Izz?" She switched Oliver to her other hip and his cry settled to a grizzle. "Dairy-free, caffeine-free, Indian-food-free, alcohol-free...fun-free. The joys of motherhood."

Jacinda had no idea about that, but the kids looked sweet to her. "It must be worth it though—they're lovely."

Nadia looked pleased and proud. "Thank you. They are. It's easy to forget sometimes."

There was a pause while Jacinda pushed memories back into the depths of her mind.

"Well, I'd better go and hunt for these kittens," she said. "It was great to meet you."

"And you. Good luck."

"Bye," Izzy said, bold now. "Byeeee!"

Jacinda returned her continuous wave all the way down the path, only stopping when she went around the corner of the fence onto the sidewalk. Then she sighed. So cute. Countless times over the years, she'd wondered whether her baby would have been a boy or a girl. By now, he or she would be in middle school. The ghost of that little person who never was still hovered near, drawing closer in unguarded moments, keeping company with the Jacinda she left behind.

Anyway. Cin Scott was too busy for babies. There never would have been a Cin Scott, if Jacinda's baby had been born. One birth in place of another. Sometimes, she still woke in the night from a surreal dream, in which she traded Cin and her success for the baby, a deal not with the devil, but with the fates. In the dark, half waking, she felt the bargain slip from reach every time.

But in the light of day, she held tight to practicalities. This way, she was free, and her mom was free. Still troubled, and managing her depression and anxiety as well

71

as she could, but free from having to rely on the vagaries of Doug Prescott's moods and finances. On top of that, Cin Scott was proof that Jacinda refused to be diminished by her father's opinions.

By the time she hit puberty—agonizingly early, compared to most of the girls she knew—he'd officially left them. He'd swing back into their lives from whatever rally team he was with at the time, full of loaded comments and back-handed compliments, and make her head spin with uncertainty. Once, she'd been his princess. But when she started to become a woman—a curvy reflection of her mother, her body years ahead of her emotions—he must have felt her starting to grow away from him.

His strategy was a combination of pressure to be amazing, disparagement for what she did achieve, and criticism for the God-given attributes he admired in every pretty girl who passed him on the street (breasts, hair, general womanliness). His attitude—when he graced them with his presence—implied that she specifically looked the way she did in order to have men look at her, and aggravate her father. But she would *much* rather have been without the burden of those breasts, and the unwanted attention they drew.

And when she returned devastated from Sweet Breeze Bay that summer, and he found out about her pregnancy, he was derisive: there, for him, was evidence that he was right all along. Anyone who looked like her was good for only one thing.

At that point, she could so easily have slipped into the same downward spiral that had claimed her mom.

But some small part of her knew better. From that lowest low point, she had something to raise her up again. A branch to grab onto, and pull herself out of the quicksand. Her musical skills were her escape—which was exactly why she refused to be defined by her body now. She was more than the curvy figure and striking cleavage that drew attention she hadn't known how to handle. Todd and Greg and whoever else could push her to sex up her act, but she wasn't going there. She'd walk away before she capitulated to that. The truth was, sometimes the American dream looked better from the outside.

She stopped halfway up the path to number ten, struck by her train of thought. Would she really give it up? Maybe music was her oxygen, but there was more than one way to pursue it. She'd only been out of the industry whirlwind for a few days, but it was already starting to seem unreal. Right then, she remembered the strength it had taken to get where she was so far, and the strength it had taken to stand up for what she believed in and step away, even temporarily.

She looked toward the Ward house. She wasn't going to hide from him.

She went back down the path, and along to number twelve. It looked completely closed up, even on this hot day. He must've gone out after their conversation. She hesitated, then peered down the side of the house. About three-quarters of the way along, it looked like there was a door in the vertical wooden sidings that skirted the base of the house. It was open just a crack, but wide enough to let a cat through.

She went along the grassy width between the hedge and the house, knelt by the door, and peered in through the gap. It took a moment for her eyes to adjust to the dim light. But there, in the seat of an old child's kayak, on top of a worn plaid rug, snuggled Velvet and a litter of three—wait, four—kittens. She looked at Jacinda, newly serious in her role as mama.

"Hey, you," Jacinda said softly. "I've been looking everywhere."

Velvet blinked, unmoved, and then started to wash the nearest fuzzy kitten. She obviously had more important things to think about.

"You can't stay under here, you know."

She tried to push the door farther in. She could gather them all up in the rug, probably, and carry them back to Nana Mac's luxury cat nest. But the metal hinge was stiff with age and salt air, and the door itself had warped. She shoved harder, turned her shoulders sideways, and angled herself through. There! Halfway in. Now the rest of her.

But having allowed her top half through, the door settled back to its original spot, pressing tightly against her waist. She gritted her teeth as it scraped against her sunburned back, the thin fabric of her t-shirt no protection at all. Hell, that hurt. But, no big deal—all she had to do was shuffle back out again. She reached around, intending to shove the door open the way she had before, but from this angle she couldn't get a proper grip of it, let alone any kind of leverage. She struggled for a few minutes, fighting the panicky feeling rising in her chest. The air was cool and dank in her lungs, but behind her the sun was hot on her bare legs, still red from her accidental beach nap. The last thing she needed was more sunburn. She resumed wriggling and struggling—she *had* to get out.

Then there was a drift of a breeze, and for a second, she appreciated the cool relief on her legs…until she realized how far *up* that cool breeze was traveling. She instantly stopped still. Oh, God—her denim mini had ridden up, exposing her underwear to the light of day. And with her front half trapped, there was no way to reach behind and pull it down.

She rested her elbows on the cold dirt, defeated, and tried not to think about spiders, or whether she'd starve to death before she was discovered, or who would be the person to do the discovering. There was no joy in knowing that Liam Ward would probably be that person. And that she was wearing bright red, lacy panties.

"This is your fault," she told Velvet, who'd been watching the show with interest. But the cat stretched in the rug bed and closed her eyes, blissing out as her kittens nursed. Jacinda closed her eyes too. She might be here a while, and she didn't want to see what other company she might have in the half-dark. The only thing left to do was wait…

"Lost something?"

She jolted up at the sound of his voice, half relieved, half awash with embarrassment.

"Yes. But I found it."

There was silence from behind her. He'd better not be

looking at her butt...but she'd bet good money that he was.

"I wonder how many retweets this photo would get."

He was.

"Don't. Even." Her own voice held the chill of death, which right now she'd happily administer with her bare hands....if she ever got out of here. But he laughed. And yes, there was a ring of satisfaction in the sound.

She gritted her teeth. "Just help me." When he said nothing, she begrudgingly added, "Please."

She felt him kneel behind her, so close to the red lace panties and her raised bottom...and despite the circumstances, a shock of lust darted through her body.

"Not like that!" She flinched away as far as she could—which wasn't far. No way was she letting *that* sensation get a hold.

"I can't reach otherwise," he said. "You're in the way."

Damn, he was right. "Fine."

He reached over the top of her back to push at the door, his hips pressing against her raised bottom, and she closed her eyes again. Thank God he couldn't see her face right now—she was pretty sure it would totally give away her body's betrayal. She tried to twist away from him, but at the same time he gave the door a powerful push-and-pull, and their combined movement only made them grind together in a spectacularly inappropriate way.

"Okay, maybe not," he said, pulling back sharply.

There was a moment's silence, during which she was acutely aware of the view he must have.

"This is awkward," she said, stating the painfully obvious.

"Yeah." She heard him stand up. "I'll get a screwdriver and take the hinges off."

"That'd be good."

Within a minute or two he was back, and within five minutes he had the rusty old hinges unscrewed, and the door off. She backed out, tugging down her skirt and dusting off the dirt as she stood up. Mercifully, he had a shirt on this time.

"Thank you."

75

He nodded. "You're welcome."

As they stood on the grass, Velvet came wandering out and wound around Jacinda's ankles, unaware of the fuss she'd caused and the tension that surged between them.

"That's what you lost?" Liam asked.

"Yeah. Her kittens are in there. I'll take them back to Nana Mac's place."

Velvet went to rub against him, and he bent to pat her, his face passing close to Jacinda's bare legs in the mini. As if suddenly realizing it, he stood up abruptly. "Okay."

"Okay," she echoed.

She ran a hand through her hair, feeling a spiderweb tangle in her fingers. Just get the kittens, get back over the fence, and be done with it. It was only a couple of hours ago that they'd slammed into their past, and at this point there was nothing more she wanted to say, or hear.

But neither of them moved.

The rays of the sun were making her skin tingle with heat, but that other kind of heat was making her tingle in an entirely different way. Below the sound of the cicadas singing, the silence between them was palpable.

She cleared her throat. "Well, I'm sorry about the interruption," she said, aiming for briskness to counteract her rising desire. "And thanks again. I'll let you get back to...whatever you were doing." She had no idea *what* he was doing here in Sweet Breeze Bay.

But still he stood there, looking at her. She shifted her weight and bit her lip, thrown. She hadn't bargained on any of this—on him being here, or the effect he had on her. And back in the physical territory of the past, with the shock of Ethan's death still fresh, she was in danger of slipping into the old doubts she'd worked so hard to leave behind...

Realizing what was happening gave her the clarity to remember anew. She wasn't that teenager anymore. She was Jacinda, a grown woman, and she was also Cin Scott, strong enough to build a career in one of the toughest businesses around. What had happened here was terrible, but even though her actions were tangled up in Liam's pain, she couldn't let him bring her back down. The guilt and regret and what-ifs would have to be faced, but she couldn't go back. She stood taller, ready to make a move.

But then his expression changed—the blue of his eyes seeming to intensify, a frown creasing his brow—and in that second, she thought she knew what was going to happen.

He wouldn't, surely.

Oh, but he would.

He stepped forward...and she didn't step away.

The rush of the ocean, just over the hedge, was nothing compared to the rush of sensation that hit her as their lips met. All the wrongness of it was swamped by an irresistible charge of lust and exhilaration. For a few moments she lost all her bearings, any thoughts of who she was, or had been, or might be, gone. There was only him, his mouth insistent against hers, his fingers holding her chin, his body so close, but not quite touching. She let her lips part, and as the kiss crossed that line into blurry, desperate need, their tongues found each other, and he pressed his body to hers. With her back against the house, and her front against the hard, hot length of him, she couldn't stop a moan from escaping.

At that sound, he seemed to snap out of it. He broke away and took a step back, looking at her now as though she'd sprung from some alternate reality. Which, in a way, she had. She put her fingertips to her lips, and blinked in what felt like slow motion as her mind refocused. He'd kissed her. And she'd kissed him back. Hell, that was *so* not right. Not right in a way that was insanely good. But...still wrong. And his expression now showed how wrong he thought it was too.

"I know who you are," he said. His tone was flat.

"No, you don't," she said, her voice steely again in response to his sudden turnaround. His face was proof of how much he must be regretting what just happened, but she refused to let him see either the way it had rocked her, or the sharp ache it left in her heart. If he'd kissed her as some kind of test, she wouldn't submit to the measurement. "Don't you dare make assumptions about a person you don't even know."

"I'm not *assuming* anything. You're Cin Scott."

Hearing her alter ego's name gave her a jolt of shock, but she revealed none of it. She couldn't decide if that name on his lips sounded like an accusation or a threat, but she lifted her chin. When she spoke, the challenge in her tone was clear: don't mess with me.

"No. Not here, I'm not. Here, I'm Jacinda. I'm me."

He narrowed his eyes, a shadow in the vibrant blue. "You could be."

She didn't stop to ask what the hell he meant. Time to get what she'd come for. She crouched down sideways, ignoring him, and carefully shuffled under the house. Velvet was sitting next to the kayak, so she gathered the kittens up in the blanket, and carried them out as gently as she could.

When she emerged, there was no sign of him. Well, good.

Good.

As she walked back to number ten nursing her bundle of kitteny goodness, with Velvet tagging anxiously along, she tried not to think about the moan that had escaped her as his tongue met hers. She didn't know why he'd play that game—but he'd got the better of her, and he knew it.

It wouldn't happen again.

Chapter Twelve

Forty-eight hours. Two days and two nights. Four high tides and four low, up and down like his mood. The high of the kiss; the low of knowing he'd been, basically, an asshole. The high of recalling her instinctive, welcoming reaction to his lips; the low of imagining what his brother would think of it all.

He tried to work, but kept lapsing into thoughts of black bikinis and red lace panties, her hair soft against his skin, the way her moan echoed the same sound waiting in his own mouth. Then he'd jolt himself out of it, back into the reality of an empty house, a silent summer, an unplayed guitar in the corner, and a history that couldn't be undone.

Once, he'd looked out his bedroom window and seen her sitting on the deck under the shade of a sun umbrella, working on a laptop, a lead snaking up to her earphones. What was she doing? He wondered if she was listening to Wolfmother again. Or writing songs, maybe.

He tried to tear himself away from the window. What did he care? He was only waiting for her to leave. Someone like her couldn't hide out in Sweet Breeze Bay indefinitely. For starters, someone else was going to realize who she was, and then what? Plus, from what he could tell, she was successful, but still in that almost-there zone, tenuous territory that was always wide open to the next up-and-comer. You wouldn't think that kind of career could be left untended for long.

Not that he'd know. His own dreams of a rock star life never drove him on, unlike Ethan, who could totally have pulled it off. Liam might have been the better songwriter—even Ethan had given him that. But even if he'd gotten noticed, by some miraculous kind of luck, his talent would never have taken him as far as Ethan could have flown on the head-turning charisma he was charmed with.

Could have.

He forced himself to step back from the window, turn, and walk out the door, back down the stairs, back to the computer. As he sat down, he felt a twinge in his back that had nothing to do with the twinges he'd been fighting in his groin. His entire body was crying out to move, to release the increasing tightness in his muscles. Clearing the yard the other day had reminded him how he missed the exertion of wielding a hammer and lifting lumber. If he stayed cooped up here, the combined tension of his unworked body and the presence of the girl next door would drive him crazy. How long had he thought he could keep this up, anyway? Something had to change.

Because if it didn't, he knew the temptation to crash through the hedge and do something reckless would be too great.

★

Jacinda hit save again, and closed the laptop with a sigh. Half a draft chapter didn't seem like much of a result for two days of work. If 'work' consisted of bursts of concentration interrupted by Spotify browsing, looking through Nana Mac's family photo albums, and lying on the floor watching Velvet and the kittens, waiting for the first one to open its eyes.

And determinedly *not* thinking about the guy over the fence. No, not at all.

With her sunburn making the beach pretty much off

limits, the farthest she'd been able to go was to the shade of the deck umbrella, and she was starting to get cabin fever. So when Riley called on Friday afternoon, she was ready for a *real* distraction. And Riley had the perfect suggestion.

"Most Friday nights we pull down the shutters and have a girls-only session after closing," she said. "Like a speakeasy, only with leftover cheesecake and wine instead of bootleg whiskey. Sometimes it does get a bit messy though." She laughed. "Anyway, would you like to come tonight? If your sunburn's feeling better, I mean."

"Oh God, I really would, thanks. What time?"

"About ten thirty. We close at ten, so that gives us half an hour to do the last cleaning up. Caro won't leave anything until the morning."

"Ten thirty will be great. See you then."

After Jacinda hung up, she had a moment of hesitation. She'd been bored stuck here in the house while her sunburn settled down, even with the kittens for entertainment. But this anonymity was kind of nice. Once she started going out, she knew there was a chance someone would recognize her, and then everything would probably change. But the lure of cheesecake, and a few drinks with some girly company, was too strong. It sounded like fun—and wasn't that what this break was for?

So at twenty past ten, in the still-warm evening, she sat on the front steps and did up her sandals. There was something in the neighborhood that smelled so good after dark—a lush, tropical fragrance, some kind of plant, she guessed, although she couldn't tell where it was coming from. She paused for a moment with her elbows on her knees, listening to the sound of the ocean and the crickets singing their summer love song. The tall tree ferns in the front yard were silhouetted in the milky moonlight. As she sat and listened, and breathed in the sweet air, a small visitor snuffled into sight—a hedgehog, spiky, quirky, and pointy-nosed. She held her breath as he pottered across the grass, pausing to sniff and rootle in the grass as he went. A few zigzags here and there, and then he was gone, safely into the hydrangeas.

She let out the air she'd been holding in her lungs, and smiled to herself as she stood up.

She couldn't remember the last time she'd walked anywhere alone after dark. You definitely wouldn't do it in LA. Or in Florida, where her mom lived. In fact, she couldn't think of a single place she'd been the last few years, where she would even consider walking alone at night. Maybe nowhere was truly safe, but she felt totally at ease doing it here. The short walk to Clarion Call felt neighborly, even though she was alone. Going past the houses with their windows wide open in the summer warmth, she caught snippets of people's lives: a laugh, the clatter of glasses, the drifting narration from some wildlife documentary. She felt like an observer of the local fauna herself.

Her feet had taken her left out of Tui Street instead of right, so she came onto the main street from the end closer to Clarion Call than to the Kelp and King. She could see a few people hanging around outside the old pub, laughing and joking, and in that moment she knew why her autopilot had taken her the other way. When she went past the pub last time, the ghost of Ethan had lingered there, even though she didn't know he was gone. Now, it was almost too much to look in that direction, knowing he'd never be there again. She wondered if Liam had been in there since he came home. He seemed to be lying even lower than she was.

Now everything was flooding back into her mind, washing away the idyllic vibe she'd felt on her walk. She turned and grabbed the heavy brass knocker on Clarion Call's door, and knocked once, twice, three times, suddenly feeling an urgent need to be inside.

Riley opened the door holding a bottle of red wine, a grin on her face.

"She's here!" she announced to the room, over her shoulder. "Someone find a glass. We can't let her go thirsty, or Nana Mac will come back from wherever she is this week, wanting a damn good explanation."

A chair was found, a wine put in her hand, and

introductions made, and Jacinda felt herself relax again. As well as Riley and Caro, there was Kerry, Stephanie, Jess, and Tina. She vaguely remembered Kerry and Jess from her last Sweet Breeze Bay summer, but the others had moved there more recently. As far as they were all concerned, it seemed, she was Nana Mac's granddaughter, and that alone made her a bit special. And she was happy to bask in her grandmother's reflected glory and goodwill, without the fact of her celebrity (such as it was) getting in the way of a good time with a few nice women.

There were the inevitable questions about where she lived and what she did, but she deflected them with a pre-rehearsed answer. She worked for a medium-sized record label, she said, but no, it was nowhere near as exciting as it sounded, and she just lived in a regular kind of LA neighborhood. Well, regular if you didn't count her neighbors in the fancier houses farther up the hill—like other music biz types, a basketball player, and a celebrity wrestling couple. But that didn't need saying. None of it was actual *lying*, really. Then she avoided any more questions by turning her attention to Jess—obviously the most gregarious one there—and asking her about the amazing necklace she was wearing. And with that, the topic of her American life was closed—for now at least—as they all enthused about Tina's jewelry making and her blossoming online business.

As the conversation flowed from one subject to another, it was obvious that they all knew each other's lives inside out, and Jacinda was happy to listen, drink the very good wine, and let the voices and laughter swirl around her.

"Riley!" Jess said, as a fourth bottle was being opened. "Can't you find something better than this bloody world music?"

Caro looked offended. "Our regulars don't mind this bloody world music," she pointed out.

"It *is* great dining music," Stephanie said, shooting Jess a sideways look. "But maybe something more lively now we're all finished work? It's Friday night, after all."

"I suppose so." Caro nodded to Riley, who went to the

laptop hooked up to the speaker, and selected a new playlist. A top-ten hit came on, and Jess got up, swinging her hips happily to the music.

"That's more like it." She grabbed the nearest person, who happened to be Kerry, and pulled her to her feet. "Come and dance, come on!"

Riley slid into the chair next to Jacinda. "Newly single," she said, waving her wine glass in Jess's direction.

"Oh...that's a shame."

"Not really. He was a dickhead."

Jacinda laughed. "Well, in that case."

"Exactly." Riley raised her glass, and they drank to freedom from dickheads. Then she glanced Jacinda's way. "Are you okay now?" she asked in a low voice. "I know I dropped a bomb on you."

She nodded. "Yeah, I'm okay."

Riley tipped her head as she considered that reply, and Jacinda knew she could see right through her.

"I don't know," she admitted. "Some things just suck."

Riley sighed. "That's the truth."

They watched as Jess and Kerry shimmied around in the space left when the café tables had been pushed against the wall. Then a new song came on, and Jess held up a hand.

"This one! Oh, I love this one." Her face crumpled a little, and she slipped into instant melancholy. "The lyrics, you know."

And she sang along with the words that were as familiar to Jacinda now as her own name.

The hourglass turned at our start
And I keep running but my heart
Won't let me stay ahead of you
Reverberations echo through
All the things I thought I knew
However far I go, one thing stays true...

As Jess sang, only slightly off-key, Jacinda tried to keep her face in neutral. Hourglass Reverb. The song she'd written when she went home that summer, after everything. The song that had been both therapy and confession, and had kick-started her career. The song that had given her band its name. She waited for someone to look at her, knowing, but they were all looking at Jess as she fell into a chair with a dramatic flourish after the first chorus. "Oh, this song always gets me. Always! But especially now…"

Tina reached over and refilled her glass. "You're better off without him, babe. You're too good for him. He always knew it."

"I never liked that song anyway," Kerry said. "Skip to the next one."

Jacinda snorted, then choked on her mouthful of pinot noir. The others looked her way but she shook her head, pointing wordlessly to the glass of wine as she struggled to catch her breath.

"Went down the wrong way," she managed. She didn't add *why* she'd breathed in a lungful of the country's finest. Kerry's words proved at least that there were no suspicions about her other identity, and that was a relief.

With a tap on the laptop, Riley banished Cin Scott from the room, and Jacinda felt herself relax as the girls rallied around Jess, sympathizing and encouraging. The night was hers to enjoy, she had great company, and she was going to make the most of it.

★

By the time they finished up, Jacinda felt like she was one of the gang. The wine had helped, sure, but mostly it was the straightforward, friendly mode that they all operated in. As far as she could tell, there were no unspoken tensions, no veiled comments or rolled eyes behind anyone else's back…just a bunch of girls shaking off the weight of the week, and helping Jess shake off her lousy ex.

Caro had left before midnight, because she was working the next morning. But Riley was taking the Sunday morning shift, so she stayed and partied on with the rest of them. Finally, they all tumbled out the front door just after two in the morning, unsteady on their feet. After farewells and hugs, Riley wobbled off on her bike in the direction of her place, which sat higher up on Bay Road, heading toward the Other Side, and everyone else left on foot. Stephanie and Tina peeled off to their own houses as they walked the quiet streets, giggling and shushing each other occasionally. When they came to the corner of Tui Street, Kerry and Jess offered to walk down with her, but Jacinda shook her head. It only made the world spin slightly. Well, a medium amount. Or maybe, down here in the southern hemisphere, the moon danced in the sky like that every night.

"It'll only take me a minute," she said, gathering herself together. "I can see the front gate from here. You guys keep going."

"Okay, you darling American girl," Kerry said, and gave her a hug, the wine making her effusive. "It was really, really, just so nice to see you, even though I don't think you remembered us."

"Oh, well...I mostly did..." she began, but Jess laughed.

"We don't expect you to remember us," she said. "We weren't in the cool crowd that summer. But we remember you. Who wouldn't remember the girl who appeared out of the blue and snagged Ethan Ward?"

Kerry sighed. "Oh, that guy. Didn't we all just love him? I don't think there was a girl in Sweet Breeze Bay who didn't have a crush on him."

"What kind of magical power did you bring with you, to bewitch him?" Jess asked. "He obviously couldn't live without you after you disappeared like that."

Jacinda's stomach lurched with a sudden pain, and she pressed her fist to her middle. There it was, proof that the old saying was literally true: the truth hurts.

"Jess!" Kerry scolded. "Oh my God. Why would you say something like that?"

Jess looked remorseful, but there was no way to backpedal. "I'm sorry," she said. "I didn't mean...I mean..." She gave up, flustered, her already wine-pink cheeks turning red under the streetlight.

Jacinda felt her fingernails digging into her palms, and her throat tighten.

"That's okay," she said, her voice tense but even. "If that's what people think, then...maybe they're right."

Maybe not as even as she'd hoped.

Kerry and Jess looked at each other, but before they could say anything more, Jacinda stepped back. *Have to get away.*

"Thanks for a great night. I'll see you around."

And she waved, and turned and walked away. Away from Jess's words, away from their remorseful, sympathetic looks...but still in the one place in the world where the truth sat deepest and strongest.

Chapter Thirteen

B y the time she reached the gate at number ten, her tension rising higher with each step, she was so wound up that she couldn't go inside. All she wanted to do was keep walking. There was only one place to go, even though there were memories there too: the beach. She went on past her house, and past the Ward house—in darkness, as she'd expect at two thirty in the morning—and slipped down the narrow beach alley.

When she reached the sand, she bent down and took off her sandals, and left them by the hedge. Even though the city was just on the other side of the peninsula, there was more of the galaxy visible here than she ever saw in LA. She walked in starry moonlight toward the water, feeling the pull of the ocean in her soul.

She stood in the foamy water's edge as the sand washed out from under her heels, letting herself sink deeper one wave at a time. When she was finally about to lose her balance, she stepped forward into the sea. The daytime breeze had died away and the water in front of her was eerily still, but every now and then a swell caught the hem of her dress. She dipped her fingers into the water as she walked out, tempted to pull off the dress and dive in. But it was a delusion to think the sea could wash away her sins. This very place, this ocean, wasn't enough to heal Ethan's pain. Maybe it was only right that she should bear it for him now.

Thinking about him, she felt a prickle on the back of her neck and turned around, spooked. Then she cried out, and pressed a hand to her mouth to stifle the sound.

There was someone on the beach.

But it wasn't Ethan. Of course not.

It was Liam.

She started to wade back in, the frustrating weight of the water slowing each step. The closer she got to the shore, the more she wanted to be on solid ground again. She splashed through the shallows and started up the sand toward him, while he waited. She couldn't see his expression, and she hardly wondered why he was here, in the moonlight, in the middle of the night. Same reason she was, maybe.

When she was just a few feet away, she stopped. Standing in the water, she'd still felt the red-wine haze, but now she was sharply, abruptly sober. The salt-water drops were itchy on her legs, and the three-quarter sleeves of her dress were wet, but she stood still in front of him.

He never had looked much like his brother.

Then again, she'd never seen Ethan look at her the way Liam was now. Deeper, darker, his expression direct but unreadable.

What had she thought he was here for, standing on the beach?

For a moment she felt a chill run down her spine. She really didn't know this guy, or what he was capable of. But she did know how angry he was at her. She looked up and down the beach, but they were alone, just them and the waxing moon. In any other situation this would be romantic. In any other situation where his face wasn't shadowed with disgust.

"I said I was sorry," she said.

When she'd opened her mouth, she'd *intended* the words to sound sorry, but seeing him look at her with that expression, a sort of rebellion had crept into her voice.

"Yeah. I know."

His tone made her mad. *Not an appropriate reaction*, a

little voice in the back of her head said, but she couldn't stop herself. "How sorry do I have to be?"

He took a step nearer, reaching for her arm, and her entire nervous system leapt into high alert. Was he looking so tortured because he was going to kiss her again, which was obviously some special kind of self-inflicted punishment? Or...was it because he was compelled to wring her neck, as unavoidable retribution for her causing Ethan's death? A shot of adrenaline hit her, and she spun around, out of his reach, and made for the alley.

On the third stride she felt an agonizing pain as something small but lethal stabbed into the sole of her foot. As she crumpled to the sand, trying to decide whether it was a scorpion, a snake, or some kind of bitey sand spider, she could see him coming toward her.

He tried to help her up, but she pulled away. "It's just some kind of bite. I don't need any help."

"Don't you?"

She hesitated, clutching her foot. Any poison would be starting to work its way up her leg by now. "Oh, shit. Do you think I should go to the emergency room?"

He bent down and picked something up, then held it up for her to see.

"Yeah, the Barbie doctor will see you now."

Oh, great. She remembered now. *After* she'd already made an idiot of herself. There was nothing poisonous in this country at all—apart from the vibes she was shooting at him as he stood there holding the stupid doll in his hand. She rubbed the bottom of her foot, wiggled her toes, and got up, pulling herself as tall as she could in her bare feet. "It's not a Barbie. It's a Bratz."

He shrugged and handed her the offending toy. "Almost as spiky as you."

"Spiky? This from the guy who didn't want to hear any kind of sorry from me the other day." She narrowed her eyes. "And why are you following me around in the middle of the night, anyway?"

He looked out to sea, where the looming peak of the volcano guarded the bay, and she saw his jaw tense.

"I work at night. I have clients in different time zones."

She looked up and down the beach. "I don't see any clients here."

"They—" He stopped himself. "What I do at night doesn't have anything to do with you."

She raised an eyebrow at his accidental innuendo, and...was he blushing now? There was a surprising satisfaction in seeing him flustered. Thank God he couldn't read her mind, because what she'd been doing at night lately had more than a little to do with *him*. Now was the moment to turn and leave...but some devil on her shoulder drove her on. It wanted payback for the way he'd cut her off when she'd tried to reach out, payback for letting everyone (including her) think Ethan's death was her fault, and payback for the kiss. With that kiss, he'd cut right to a small and vulnerable spot, and, more fool her, she'd let him know it. And feel it, and hear it. But apparently he had a vulnerable spot too.

Before he could say anything else, she let the doll fall to the sand, took a step closer, and reached one hand up to the back of his neck.

He didn't push her away.

Just before she closed her own eyes, she saw the expression in his. Was that how she'd looked, pressed up against the wall of his house? Surprised, hesitant, and...aroused. She squeezed her eyes shut. Payback, that was all.

As their lips met, she took a hold of his jeans at the buckle, and pulled him closer. He made a sound somewhere between anger and defeat, and leaned down to kiss her back, harder and more urgently than she'd bargained for. Her own body responded with treacherous ease, her tongue meeting his, her hips searching for that sweet-hot connection. In the cool, moonlit air, the sudden flare between them felt hot enough to turn the sand to glass at their feet. He buried his hands in her hair, and she let her head tip back as he kissed her, sinking further into an unexpected blur of desire and surrender.

But then one tiny, sane corner of her brain resurfaced,

reminding her of exactly who she was clinging to.

This was not what she set out to do.

She took herself back, breaking their connection with one forceful shove against his chest. Then, without looking at him, she turned and walked away, only stopping to pick up her sandals before heading down the alley and out of sight.

She could play that game too. And when she played, she intended to win.

Chapter Fourteen

The knock came again, loud and insistent, and Liam dragged himself away from the computer. Either someone was ignoring the 'No Soliciting' sign he'd put up, or it was Jacinda. Either way, he wasn't in the mood.

He went out to the entranceway, where two tall, broad-shouldered figures were visible through the frosted glass door. Not Jacinda then. Good. He'd rather let his bad temper rip on some unsuspecting salesmen than have to deal with her again. After she'd left him standing on the beach last night, he'd almost thrown himself into the sea to cool off. Instead, he came back to the house for a hard drink and a cold shower. Sleep hadn't come easy.

Now one of the figures stepped closer and pounded on the door again, and suddenly he knew who it was. He jerked the door open, leaving the visitor with his hand in the air.

"You know there's a doorbell, right?"

Connor's wide grin took Liam straight back to the good years. "I'm not ringing that thing. Are we men, or not?"

"Some of us are," said Dane, balancing two boxes of beer in his arms.

Liam stood back to let them in, laughing. "What the hell are you doing here?"

"That's what we came to ask you," Connor replied as

they went into the living room. He took off his jacket and threw it on the window seat, looking around. In his fitting t-shirt, his muscular frame was a stark contrast to the skinny kid he'd once been.

"Jesus, what happened to you?" Liam asked.

"Don't flatter him," Dane warned, putting the beer on the floor and lowering himself into an armchair. "He already thinks he's God's gift."

Connor shrugged and sat in the window seat. "It's pretty hard to meet girls in Dubai. Have to burn off all that energy somehow." He flexed a bicep, and grinned again.

Liam raised an eyebrow. "Dubai? That's where you ended up?"

"Yeah, for my sins. There's endless work there for engineers, and the money's ridiculous, especially if you start moving into the property development side of things like I have. A few shady characters to watch out for, but you know—if there's big money up for grabs, there'll be big personalities playing the game. Sometimes you step on a few toes." He grinned, apparently unbothered by any toe-stepping he might have done. "Anyway, they pay for me to come home twice a year. So here I am," he added, holding out his hands.

"We heard you were back," Dane said to Liam. "So I decided to come over too. Even though we've been in the same country the last few years."

"Yeah...sorry." He never had replied to Dane's messages way back when. When he'd left the bay with his parents after Ethan's death, he'd also cut himself off from his friends. At the time, he just couldn't deal with any of them, and even though he'd felt increasingly shitty about it over the years, he'd never looked back. But judging by their attitude now, it seemed like he'd been forgiven. "How's Melbourne?" he asked Dane.

"It's fine. I'm not always there, though—I travel a lot, wherever the work takes me."

When they were young, Dane had always talked about being a diver, so Liam had been surprised to hear he'd gone to university instead of doing a dive course. "You did the sport and exercise science degree, right? So what kind of work are you doing?"

"Professional diver. I went through the whole of university and never came up with a better idea."

"Just like you planned. That's cool."

"Yeah. It's mostly commercial maritime stuff though—salvage, checking ships for customs, that kind of thing. The occasional missing person. Haven't gone on any treasure hunts yet."

"Never say never." Liam looked at the two of them. "You two turned out pretty impressive in the end."

"He doesn't think so," said Connor, jerking a thumb in Dane's direction. "He always wanted us to get fit, and now I have, he's totally unimpressed. Can't please some people."

Dane grinned and turned to Liam. "Good to see you haven't withered away in front of your computer screen either."

Liam laughed again. Why had he let these guys slip out of his life? It was surreal in the best way to all be sitting here, falling so easily back into the old ways. The three geeky musketeers—but maybe not so geeky anymore.

"How'd you find out I was here, anyway?" he asked, twisting the top off the bottle Dane handed him.

"Riley told my sister," Connor said. "She said you've been avoiding everyone."

He shrugged. "I've just been busy. You know."

Connor and Dane looked at each other, and he knew they weren't buying it. But Dane nodded. "Web design going well?"

"Yeah. I've got some big clients in the States, and a few in the UK, as well as the Aussie ones. I'm only limited by the hours in the day, really." Or night.

"Maybe you should hire someone," Connor suggested.

He took a slug of beer and shook his head. "Nah. Then it becomes a whole other thing. Right now I'm all care, no responsibility."

"Oh, shit." Connor stood up suddenly. "I left the steaks in the car. Be right back."

"No care, no responsibility," Dane said, and Connor flashed him a middle finger as he went out.

"Some things never change," Liam said, smiling. "Still the absent-minded professor."

Dane laughed. "Yeah. I always thought he'd end up in some ivory tower. Now he's building them instead."

"Would you trust a high-rise he put together?" Liam asked.

He shrugged. "Someone does, because he's making crazy money."

"Can't argue with that."

They clinked their bottles together.

The afternoon rolled into evening as they caught up on the years they'd spent apart. Firing up the barbecue to grill steak and sausages and ribs, Liam wondered if Jacinda would notice the noise over the hedge. If she did, she stayed away, and he slowly relaxed. The collection of empties grew, and the night crept in, until the stars were out and the crickets were singing. Sitting on the steps running down to the lawn, they could have been seventeen again, drinking too much and talking shit. He hadn't realized how much he needed it.

"Let's go have a drink at the double K," Connor said. "Your cover's blown now anyway."

Liam shook his head. He had no intention of ever going to the Kelp and King again—that was Ethan's turf. "No thanks."

"Saturday night though—they'll have a band playing." Connor lifted his eyebrows expectantly.

"It'll be great," Dane said. "We should go, for old times' sake."

"Old times?" He looked at them. "Yeah, I don't think so."

The mood changed abruptly, and there was silence for a minute. Liam rubbed the back of his neck, and Connor picked at the label on his bottle.

Then Dane spoke. "Have you been to see him yet?"

Liam thought about the graveyard on the hill—the uneven rows of headstones, the yew trees left to grow gnarly in the wind, the view over the sea. The sea that had taken his brother.

"No."

Connor leaned forward. "Did you ever...do you know what happened to her?"

He knew who Connor meant, but fixed him with a glare. "Her?"

"Jacinda."

"Why?"

"I just thought..." Noticing Liam's expression, he cleared his throat. "Nothing. Just wondered what happened to her. That was the best summer, until..."

Liam nodded. "Yeah, it was good. Until then."

"All I remember is being at the beach, or being here at your place," Dane said. "Did we ever go home?"

Connor laughed. "I don't think so. Not that my mother was complaining."

"Your mother never complained either," Dane said to Liam. "I don't know how she put up with us."

Liam shrugged. "She used to say she'd rather have us here, than getting into trouble somewhere else. Not that we were allowed to get into trouble, with Dad so high up in the police."

"I never got into any of the trouble I really wanted," Connor said. "Remember Kate? God, I thought she walked on water."

"You were tragic about her," Dane told him.

"No worse than you about her big sister," Connor shot back. "She was never going to look at you. Not when she had that boyfriend at university."

"That asshole." Dane grinned. "We were *all* tragic about girls that summer."

They both glanced at Liam.

"Yeah, I know what you're thinking," he said. "But you were the only ones who knew about that."

He got up and went inside. Maybe more beer would drown that same old ache of wanting. In the kitchen, he paused in front of the open refrigerator. They'd known about his feelings for Jacinda then, because he'd had to tell *someone*. And now, the nearness of her was burning him up again. He went back out and handed each one of them another bottle, then sat down.

"I know where she is," he said in a low voice.

They both stared at him. "Where?" Dane asked.

He pointed toward the hedge, and number ten. "There."

Connor almost choked on his beer. "What?"

"Next door?" Dane asked. "Jacinda?"

"Could you say it a bit louder? Because it'd be great if she heard."

"Shit, sorry." He looked over to the house. "What's she doing here?"

Liam shrugged. "I don't know. Well, she's looking after Nana Mac's cat, and its kittens. But I don't know why she's come all this way just to do that."

"All the way from the States?" Connor asked.

"Yeah."

"Maybe she's on holiday," Dane suggested.

"Maybe."

"Do you know what she does over there? For a job, I mean."

He hesitated. "She's a rock star, I suppose." At the sight of their faces, he nodded. "Yeah, yeah, I know."

"Are you *kidding*?" Connor said. "I have to see." He pulled his phone out of his pocket.

"She doesn't use her own name," Liam told him. "Google 'Cin Scott'. C–I–N."

"Cool name," Dane commented, as he looked over Connor's shoulder.

"Whoa," Connor said, scrolling through the search results. "Look at *that*."

But Dane was frowning. "That's Jacinda? It doesn't look anything like her."

"I know," he said again. He was fighting the urge to knock the phone out of Connor's hand, and the appreciative expression off his face.

"And she's next door?" Connor said. "What are you doing sitting here then, wasting time?"

"She doesn't look like that now," he said. "She's

changed her hair."

Two skeptical faces looked back at him.

"You're an idiot," Connor said. "You should be over there. This is your second chance."

He shook his head. She'd already made an idiot of him—he wasn't going to give her the opportunity again. And he didn't want any kind of chance with her. "No. You know why."

"That was in the past," Dane said. "You're still here. She's still here."

"Don't you remember *anything*? She was his. He's my brother." He stumbled over the words. "He *was* my brother."

Connor's voice was gentle. "You're allowed to be happy, you know."

"Jesus, give it up." He didn't want to see the pity in their eyes. "I am happy." He tipped his bottle back and drained the last dregs of beer.

"We were there," Dane pointed out. "We remember how you felt about her."

"I was a *kid*," he said, a hot tension rising in his chest. "Everything has changed."

"It sure has," said Connor, looking at his phone again.

Liam stood up abruptly, the tension threatening to erupt hotter than the volcano in the bay, but Dane put a firm hand on his arm. Liam didn't miss the warning glance Dane shot Connor, who put the phone back in his pocket.

"We remember how you felt about Ethan too," Dane said, as Connor backed down a step. "But it's not betraying him if you move on."

He shook Dane off, the flare of anger back down to a smolder. "I'm moving on fine. Just not with her."

"Okay, man, that's all good." He looked at his watch, then gestured to Connor. "We'd better hit the road if we want to catch the band."

"Are you sure you don't want to come?" Connor asked.

"Yeah, I'm sure," Liam replied.

They all went back through the house. At the front door, Connor grabbed his hand and pulled him close enough to slap him on the back. "Good to see you, man. I mean that."

"And you." He meant it too.

Dane gave him the same hug, and a smile. "We're here for a few days. See you again?"

For all the years apart, they still knew each other too well to let any bullshit linger. "Yeah, definitely." He paused. "Thanks."

He watched them go down the steps in the dark, like he had so many times in the past. Apparently some things were solid enough to withstand time and distance, and his own bad temper. As he was closing the door, he heard Connor call something from the road.

"Don't be an idiot, remember."

Connor's definition of being an idiot was the exact opposite of his own. He shook his head and went to clean up.

Out on the deck again, he looked up at number ten. The upstairs windows were dark. Maybe she was out enjoying her Saturday night with Riley and the Sweet Breeze girls. Maybe she was downstairs, watching TV or something. Or maybe she was in bed. For a moment, he let his mind go there. Her curves beneath him, her legs around him, her eyes meeting his as he...

He shook the image from his mind, left the empties where they sat, and went to pour himself a whiskey.

Whatever the definition of idiocy, he was falling into it deeper by the minute.

Chapter Fifteen

Jacinda closed the laptop and shut her eyes. She'd worked late enough, and these chapters were turning out even harder to write than she'd thought. She looked at Velvet, snug in her cat bed, surrounded by sleepy kittens, and wished she could shrink down and hide in there with them, warm, purring, and oblivious to the world. Then Velvet looked up, suddenly alert—and a second later, there was a knock at the door.

"Good ears," Jacinda told her, getting up from the sofa. Maybe it was Riley, stopping in after closing at Clarion Call. She wondered if Kerry or Jess had mentioned the incident last night. Jess's blunt, revealing comment still echoed in her head. *He obviously couldn't live without you after you disappeared like that.*

She opened the door, and her heart twisted in her chest. Liam.

"Jacinda."

The rasp in his voice hit her low in the belly. A slow, dangerous burn. Oh, God. She put a hand on her hip. "What?"

"I..." He passed a hand over his face, where stubble darkened his jaw. There was a matching darkness in his eyes, and whiskey sweetness on his breath.

"You what?"

He stood on the threshold, wavering, not meeting her eye. Finally she grabbed his arm and pulled him through the door. "For God's sake, come in."

In the living room, he stood on the rug, looking anywhere but at her, running a hand through his already rumpled hair. The whole rugged, tormented thing was stupidly attractive on him. She stood by the wingback chair and waited, trying not to think about kissing him again, or him kissing her again...feeling that stubble against her skin, running her own hands through his hair. Eventually, he cleared his throat and spoke.

"How's your foot?"

She raised an eyebrow. "Is that what you came to say?"

"No." He looked toward Nana Mac's old-fashioned drinks cabinet in the corner. "Do you have anything to drink?"

"Probably." She went and opened the cabinet. Amongst the sherry and port and brandy, she spotted an almost-full bottle of Jack Daniel's, and grabbed it out. There were heavy, cut crystal glasses on the cabinet's mirror top, so she sloshed a generous helping into two of them. He wasn't the only one who needed it.

He took the glass and emptied it by half in his first sip. She matched him, the liquid hot and bracing as it went down. If he was ready for another round of whatever this was, she was too. Just...thank God he had a shirt on this time.

"What then?" She didn't bother making it sound encouraging.

He shifted his weight. "Connor and Dane came to see me."

"Uh-huh."

"You remember them?"

Where was this going? "Yeah."

"They remember you."

"Okay." Her voice was wary. "And...?"

"They remember that summer."

"Well...so do I. As you know." His cryptic sentences were like pebbles before a rock fall, warning of something bigger on the way. She couldn't stand it anymore. "Just tell me why you came over."

He finished his drink, then took the bottle from the cabinet top and refilled his glass. She held hers out too, and he topped it up. Then he began to talk.

"When Ethan realized you'd gone, he disappeared."

Instantly, her heart started pounding.

"The same night you left. We called him, looked for him, asked around, but no one had seen him. My mother was worried, but I told her he'd be okay."

He closed his eyes for a moment, memories etched into his face.

"Dad said we couldn't report him missing—if he was old enough to go out drinking, he was old enough to get himself home. So she walked the whole of Sweet Breeze Bay, searching, until we convinced her to go home and wait there. He could have gone over to the Other Side, or anywhere. Better if she was there when he came back."

He swallowed the contents of his glass in one go, then set it down. She held her breath, waiting, needing to know but not wanting to hear the words.

"About three in the morning, I went to the only other place I thought he might be. There's a tiny bay around the bottom of Mount Clarion that we always used to go to as kids. It was like our secret place. You can only walk there at low tide, but I swam around. The moon was really bright."

She remembered how she'd looked out at the moon from her window seat on the plane that night. The same moon that hung over Sweet Breeze Bay, and watched as everything fell to pieces.

"There was a bottle of vodka smashed on the rocks. And I found him…washed up."

The beginning of a sound escaped her lips, but she swallowed it back. Nothing she felt now could compare to what that must have been like for Liam, or to the fear that must have overwhelmed Ethan as the sea—once his playground—dragged him down into its cold, churning blackness.

"You brought him home?"

He nodded. "The water was high by then. He was heavy."

The image of Liam struggling through the water, bearing Ethan's body, taking him home, imprinted itself in her mind. She knew then that it would never leave—Ethan's last journey and Liam's moment of horror and loss would be a scar on her heart, forever. But it was so much worse for him.

"I'm so sorry," she whispered.

He nodded again, just once. "I know."

It was the nearest thing to forgiveness she'd had from him, and she held it close. She wanted to hold him close too, find some way to make the unthinkable somehow bearable. But he stood in front of her, unmoving, his gaze fixed on the wall over her shoulder. She bit her lip, and asked the question that had been tormenting her all week.

"It was an accident though, right? He would never..."

"I don't know what was in his mind." Finally, he looked at her, his blue eyes as dark as the deepest ocean. "But yeah...I think it must have been."

At that, something broke inside her, or healed, and the pain and relief welled up. She reached out a tentative hand, not knowing what she was offering, or reaching for, only that the distance between them was too great.

He took one long step and collided into her, the momentum carrying them backward as he crushed her close, her empty glass falling to the floor. With one swift movement he lifted her up, and she wrapped her legs around him. For the first time, their mouths met with equal intention—a blind, urgent need to swamp the past with something here and now, real and hot and overwhelming. Still in the middle of the room, they clung to each other, an island of broken hearts and seeking tongues and rising heat.

When they paused for breath, she slid down to her feet, a blur of emotion, each one fighting with another. Desire and regret. Remorse and hunger. Pain and hope.

"We shouldn't."

But he said nothing. He took her hand and led her to

the stairs, his grip firm and his purpose clear.

She didn't resist.

In the doorway of her bedroom, she hesitated, and he turned back to look at her.

"This room..." she said.

But he pulled her in, and pulled her closer. He took her head in his hands, his fingers tangled in her hair. Reflected in his eyes, she saw the longing of her own heart—connection, comfort...and lust. Each of them was off limits to the other, but their common ground was where need and desire met.

She grasped the hem of his t-shirt and pushed it up, exposing the chest that had distracted her so unexpectedly, and inappropriately. He was sun-kissed and broad and strong, and she lay her hands where they'd wanted to go the first time she saw him again over the gate. He tugged the shirt over his head, and then reached for her blouse. She leaned over slightly to help him pull it off, not bothering to undo the buttons, and when she straightened up his eyes were fixed on her bust. He lowered his head and kissed her neck, his lips traveling steadily lower until he was at her cleavage, breathing her in, losing himself in the lace-clad curves. She threaded her fingers in his hair as his warm mouth roamed the soft skin, one hand cupping each breast, his thumbs finding the hardened buds of her nipples under pale pink satin. As he brushed against them, an answering hot tension intensified between her legs. Suddenly impatient, she reached down, and he stood back to give her room as she undid his belt. Then the button of his jeans. Then the zip. With one determined push, she shoved the jeans down, and he shucked them off and kicked them away. Inside his fitting boxer briefs, the evidence of their game-playing rose large, and hard, and so damn tempting. Her pulse kicked up another notch. Off limits, and out of her mind, nothing but a mess of need. But if he wasn't stopping, she wasn't either.

Now he undid her jeans, his fingers unsteady against her skin. Instead of pulling them down, he lifted her up and tipped her onto the bed, where the moonlight cast strips of pale light through the open blinds. She lifted her hips as he worked the jeans down and tossed them in the corner with his own. He propped himself above her, and she reached up, running her fingertips across his chest, over the rise and fall of his abs, down to the lowest point of his belly. Then she paused, and looked up. He looked right back at her, his eyes heavy and dark, flooding her with desire that she knew she couldn't, wouldn't fight.

"Oh, God. We're in trouble."

At her words, he lowered his head and kissed her, carefully at first, but within a moment the kiss ignited, and the last whispers of hesitation evaporated in her hunger for his mouth. He tried to reach around to her back and undo her bra, but she pushed his fumbling hands away and did it herself, tearing off the lacy constraint. Then she reached down and tugged at her panties, desperate to be rid of everything standing between them. Maybe everything in the real world was standing between them, but right now, here in the midnight glow, was exactly where they were meant to be. Where they needed to be.

When they were both naked, he lay next to her and gathered her into his arms. She pressed against him, tangling her legs with his, and he held her tighter as their lips and tongues said everything they never had with words. She wriggled upward, trying to position herself so that she could slide against him, hungering for that sweet combination of rigid heat and slippery wetness.

"Wait." As he pulled away, a groan of disappointment came from her, and he smiled, just a little. He went to the tangle of jeans on the floor and pulled something from his pocket, then came back to the bed.

"You brought them with you?" she said, propping herself up on her elbow. He looked equal parts guilty and uncertain, and she took the little packets out of his hand. "Three?"

He frowned. "I didn't mean..."

"Yes you did."

She considered the foil squares. While she'd been here, trying not to think about him over there, he must have been doing the same thing. Which was terrible. There was no way either of them should have been thinking any of it. And yet, here they were.

When she looked back at him, his expression was still unsure, and she realized he might be having second thoughts. God, no. Not now. If he left now, she'd die of sudden loneliness and frustrated lust. She gave him a push. "Roll over."

When he obeyed, she straddled his waist, the teasing moisture between her legs dampening his skin. Beneath her, his chest rose and fell as he breathed harder, his lips parted, and she knew he wasn't going anywhere. As he watched, she tore open one of the packets and pulled out the condom. Then she backed up until she was sitting across his thighs. With her own breath coming faster, she held the tip of the condom and rolled the rest of it down the length of him, hot anticipation shooting through her as she realized just what kind of length, and breadth, she was dealing with. Then she leaned forward, her mouth barely brushing his, holding herself oh-so-slightly out of reach.

"I wanted you," he said, his voice husky, the words a painful confession. "Did you know it, back then?"

"I know now," she said, and lowered her hips in one exquisitely deliberate motion. His body arched and his head tipped back, a groan escaping his lips as every inch of him was suddenly, completely inside her. She heard her own answering moan as she began to move, the instinctive rhythm taking over. He matched her movement, pulling her down so that her breasts swept against him with every thrust and return. The ache in her heart was stilled, replaced with an ache to have him deeper, deeper inside her.

Then he flipped her over with a restrained growl, pinning her underneath him, holding still, holding his breath. She tried to grind against him, but he held back.

"Hold still," he said, his voice rough.

But she couldn't. She'd gone beyond holding still, or holding back. With a determined effort, she freed her arms and wrapped her legs around him, lifting her hips and forcing him down into her.

"Fuck. I can't..." he said, and surrendered with a low groan, driving into her once, twice, again and again. She tightened her thighs against his sides and tucked one ankle around the other, desperate to stay close as they moved together. The world narrowed to nothing but skin and heat and the sound of their breath blurring in her ears, and her hands roamed up the sides of his chest, across his shoulders, down his hard biceps, her fingertips savoring every taut muscle. Oh God, this man. Even if this was the one and only time she touched him like this, she'd never again think of him as the teenager she knew back then.

Back then.

For one cold, hard moment, the words froze in her brain, and she was abruptly thrown out of their mutual escape...the sweet, hot deception that neither of them could justify.

He must have felt the change. He slowed, and stopped, and looked right at her. And she couldn't look away. In the hazy bedroom blue of his eyes, she saw the same desire and doubt that was doing battle in her own heart. They held each other's gaze, silent and deep, and in that moment he seemed like the one safe place she never knew existed.

"It's you," he said.

She nodded.

"You," he repeated.

A sudden intensity came into his eyes, and she felt him rise and strengthen inside her. Her body instantly responded, the heat igniting around him again.

"Me."

He caught his breath as she pressed her hips upward, bringing him deeper. Then he dropped his mouth to hers and she opened her lips, letting him in, his hunger quickening her own as his tongue met hers again. Jesus, he was starving, and so was she, and there was only one way to relieve this exquisite desperation. She reached down and pressed a hand on the small of his back, as far down as she could reach, her palm riding their thrusts as they moved together again.

Maybe it was nothing but collusion, or delusion—the wrong thing to do, for the wrong reasons. But something had been lit, and all they could do was let it burn up and burn out. Because it was happening, and there wasn't a single thing she planned to do about it.

There on the bay, in the attic room full of history and regret, she felt a tidal wave rise in her body, from the incandescent point where he was plunging into her, through every nerve and vein and pore, drenching her with an unstoppable heat. With sudden strength, she arched upward, lifting him with her as she came, and they fell to pieces in the same instant, lost and found, abandoned and rescued...made whole, just for a moment.

He collapsed onto her, his breath hot on the side of her neck, the room quiet apart from their unsteady breathing. She put a leg over him, welcoming his weight, not wanting him to pull out and be gone. Not wanting it to be over.

She really was in trouble.

But he levered himself back up, not meeting her eye, and pulled out, carefully taking the condom with him.

"In there," she said, pointing to a trash can by the dresser.

When he came back, he lay down and pulled her close, her back to his chest. He pressed his forehead against the back of her head, burying his face in her hair. She threaded her fingers through his and nestled in, warm in the quiet afterglow.

But after a while, the quiet turned into silence. Too much silence. She listened to his breathing—he wasn't asleep. Maybe he was waiting for her to say something.

"Are you okay?"

"Yeah," he replied. "You?"

Not as good as she'd been five minutes before, and less okay with every awkward second that passed. "I'm fine."

"Good."

Silence resumed.

Oh, shit. What had they done?

"Get some sleep," he said, untangling his fingers and patting her hand.

Patting her hand? She wanted to turn around and slap him in the head in return. Tell him not to fuck her and then fuck *with* her. Force them back to a place of truth.

Then again...maybe that wasn't where they were meant to be after all.

She rolled away slightly, plumped up her pillow, and said goodnight. And waited for sleep to come.

★

An insistent meow broke into her consciousness, and Jacinda opened one eye, just a tiny bit. Velvet, hungry again. Okay. Breakfast.

Then the events of the night before came flooding back. Liam. She turned over, not sure what they'd say to each other in the cold light of day, but instinctively hungry to see him, touch him again.

He wasn't there.

She looked to where their clothes had lain together on the floor. Her jeans were there, crumpled alongside her blouse. His things were gone.

Of course.

If a heart could really sink, this must be what it felt like. She closed her eyes again, and pressed her fingers against her eyelids. It seemed like his second thoughts had shown up after all, only *after* they'd had the best sex she could remember—bare naked in every way, body and soul.

How convenient for him.

How fucking humiliating for her.

She pulled the duvet over her head, embarrassment and anger doing battle as she relived the confronting, redeeming, passionate night. What was it really about, for him? He wanted her, he'd said. Well, he came prepared, and he had her.

Anger won.

Chapter Sixteen

How to be an asshole, in three easy steps.

One, lay all your pain on the most beautiful girl you know.

Two, take her to bed even though you know you shouldn't. Have mind-blowing sex. Don't say any of the things you ought to.

Three, sneak out in the dark when the guilt overwhelms you.

Yeah, easy.

Except for step four: feel like shit. Especially when you wake up with a hard-on heavy-duty enough to power a small city, and you have to do something about it, even though she's all you can see, and you wish she'd get the hell out of your guilt-ridden imagination.

Now Liam stood on the hot sand, his eyes narrowed against the sunshine. The beach was scattered with people enjoying their summer Sunday. Clusters of teenagers, the girls eyeing the boys, the boys eyeing the girls' curves. Dog walkers following their salt-sodden pets, carrying soggy tennis balls. A leathery-skinned old guy who probably swam every day, summer and winter. Kids digging moats that drained as fast as they tipped in buckets of water, while their parents looked on.

All the happy normality made him want to puke.

He dropped his towel and ran four long strides into the breaking waves, then dived under. In the dense, watery silence, he swam as far as he could, and came up way offshore, heaving in a breath. Looking back, the beachy scene made him think of the dioramas they used to make at school—a palm tree here, some scattered sand there, then add a shell or two, and some cut-out people. Right now though, *he* was the cut-out person.

He turned in the water and started to swim parallel to the coast, heading for the rocky inlets and outcrops where Mount Clarion rose out of the ocean. The water was calm, but every now and then a surge of turbulence struck him as a boat passed by farther out. He kept going, slicing mechanically through the water until he reached the spot he was aiming for. At low tide, a tiny, sandy bay was revealed, but now there was nothing but sharp black rocks, studded with limpets and mussels and draped with slippery lengths of seaweed. He let the water carry him in, then grabbed the rocks and hauled himself up, ignoring the stabs to the soles of his feet and the sharp shell edges threatening to cut his hands.

Balancing on the craggy outcrop, he looked at the rocky scene for the first time since that fucked-up night. The breaking sea. Tiny rock pools hiding miniscule sea creatures. Overhanging pohutukawa trees. The green mountain above. Everything just the same as when they were kids.

But nothing had ever been the same, since the summer Jacinda came to Sweet Breeze Bay.

If it wasn't for her, Ethan would still be alive.

Maybe that didn't make it her *fault*, exactly...but it was still the truth.

The other truth was harder to admit. He dragged a hand through his wet hair, swiped the salty droplets from his face.

If it wasn't for him, Ethan might still be alive.

If he'd come here to look for him sooner.

If he hadn't let jealousy get in the way.

If, if, if.

He couldn't make himself go up to the graveyard on the hill. He couldn't go to the Kelp and King. He couldn't touch Ethan's guitar, sitting on its stand in the corner. Hell, he could hardly look at it. But somehow, after everything that went down with Dane and Connor and Jacinda yesterday, this bay had called too strongly.

His gaze swept the rocks around him. The thousand shards of Ethan's vodka bottle would be transformed by the ocean by now, worn smooth by years of moon-driven tides, and the caress of the sand. There was nothing here to show what had happened that night.

Nothing except his screwed-up self.

He took one step back, then dived into the water and swam—away from the bay, but no farther from the past.

★

On top of Mount Clarion, Jacinda stopped and let her backpack drop to the grassy ground. Carefully though—the wine bottles in it would be their reward for making the climb. The breeze tangled her hair and eased the headache she'd had all day, and she breathed deeply, savoring the clean air.

Riley was standing with her hands on her hips, puffing a little. "This view is so worth it."

Jacinda took in the sparkly ocean, the tree-studded suburb of Lancet Bay, and the jumble of city buildings across the harbor. She'd thought about this view so many times over the years, but it was even more beautiful than her imagination had given it credit for. "It's amazing."

"The best place is round the other side," Kerry said, hoisting a cooler bag higher on her hip. "Not so windy."

Tina finally caught up with them. "When did I get so unfit?" She pushed her hair away from her scarlet face. "Bloody hell."

They'd knocked on Jacinda's door just before noon, insisting that she come for a picnic lunch. She hadn't been up long—after catching up on sleep, she'd been having coffee and planning which strip she'd tear off Liam first. But then she'd changed her mind. Screw him. Danielle and Sam would arrive tomorrow, and then she'd hand over kitten duty and hit the road. Might as well try to enjoy her last day.

"Come on," Riley told Tina now. "Almost there."

She groaned, but trudged after them. They walked farther around the curve of the hill until they reached Kerry's favorite spot, overlooking Sweet Breeze Bay. Jacinda scanned the little settlement, laid out like a picture-book town, and found Tui Street with Nana Mac's place and the Wards' house next door. Then she looked down to the foot of the mountain, where the trees ended and the houses began. She could see the rooftops of the oldest remaining dwelling in the bay, an imposing two-story homestead with a big, barnlike utility building to one side, all set on a huge lot. "I always wondered what that old place looks like inside."

"It's been empty for years, just sitting there," Riley said. "The family are all in London now. It really needs restoring, but I don't think they're interested in taking it on."

"That's a shame. It's gorgeous."

Tina pulled a blanket from her bag. "Come on, let's get set up. I'm starving."

They spread the blanket on the grass under a tree, and started unloading the picnic food that Riley had brought from Clarion Call.

"It all looks so good," Tina said, stealing an olive as Riley set the container down.

"I invited Jess," Kerry said, handing Jacinda a wine glass. "But she felt bad about what she said the other night."

Jacinda shrugged. "That's okay." She opened one of the bottles and concentrated on pouring herself a glass.

"Well...it wasn't really." Tina shook her head. "Kerry told us what she said. I'm not a Sweet Breeze native like you guys, but everyone knows about Ethan. Jess was so out of line."

After last night with Liam—and this morning without him—this was the absolute last thing Jacinda felt like talking about. She passed Tina a mini cheese board, hoping to distract her. "What are you working on now? More necklaces?"

But Tina wouldn't be redirected. "Earrings," she replied, layering a wedge of cheese between two crackers before she continued. "That's not what everyone thinks. What Jess said, I mean. There must be something more to it. Why does no one know what happened? Shouldn't there have been a police report or something?"

"Jesus, Tina, you're as bad as Jess," Kerry said.

Jacinda pushed her sunglasses farther up her nose and looked out to sea, the dull pounding in her head starting up again. She took a long sip of wine. And another. Better not to say the things she was thinking.

Tina glanced at her, chastened. "Sorry. I was just wondering."

Riley spoke up. "Let's not talk about it, okay?"

"Okay." Tina put the crackers and cheese in her mouth and chewed morosely.

Jacinda searched around for a new topic. "The kittens are growing."

It was the perfect choice. Riley immediately went gooey.

"Ooh, I want to come and see them."

Kerry nodded. "Me too. Have they opened their eyes yet?"

"Not yet. But it must be soon. I read that they start opening them from about a week old, and they were born on Tuesday. Or maybe Monday night."

"What color are they?" Tina asked.

"Two of them are all black, and one's tabby, and one's kind of a mix-up," Jacinda said. "I guess Velvet's baby daddy was a tabby."

The others laughed, and Jacinda thanked God for the successful change of subject. The conversation went off in other directions, and she put away a couple more glasses of wine. Lucky home was downhill.

Mid afternoon, they started packing up. Jacinda wandered toward the edge of the hill as she folded the blanket, drinking in the view of the sea and beach below.

Riley came over. "Hey...is that Liam?"

The other two joined them, peering down. At the base of the mountain, cut off from the main beach, a man in swim trunks was standing on the rocks. Even from up here they could see the breadth of his shoulders, the cut of his muscular back, and the tattoos running across his golden skin.

"It is," Kerry said.

Tina shaded her eyes and squinted down. "That's Ethan's brother? Wow."

They watched as he ran a hand through his hair, then linked his hands behind his neck and dropped his head, making his muscles flex. At that, Tina said what they were all thinking. "He's hot."

Jacinda couldn't tear her eyes away. Only a few hours before, that body had been in her bed, under her hands, between her legs. Watching him now, she couldn't bring herself to regret that part of it—their aching, desperate collision, unexpected but maybe inevitable from the moment they looked at each other over the gate.

Then he dived into the sea, a perfect arc that hardly left a splash, and started to swim. Was that the bay he and Ethan had played in as kids? The place that took Ethan back, the same night she took herself away? She turned and went back to the tree, and grabbed up her backpack, aware of Riley watching her as the others gathered up their things too.

"Whew," Tina said as they started to head down the hill. "If that's his brother, I'm starting to see why Ethan was so legendary." Kerry frowned at her, but she shrugged as she adjusted her sun hat. "Just saying."

She and Kerry set off, but Riley hung back a little, leaving a gap between them, and Jacinda matched her pace.

"What happened with you two?" Riley asked.

"What?" She stumbled on a loose rock. "Nothing."

"I saw your face. Something happened."

"What are you, psychic?"

"Just wise beyond my years." She laughed, but Jacinda wasn't off the hook. "I always thought he liked you. Tell me I was right."

"Fine." She snatched a leaf from a tree as they went past. "You were right."

"Did he tell you that?"

"Yeah. He told me."

There must have been something in her tone, a hint of something unsaid, because Riley stopped and grabbed her arm. "Wait. He told you, *and?*"

"And nothing."

"And you slept together. I knew it."

She felt her cheeks go hot. "No you didn't." She walked on, and Riley followed, looking satisfied.

"But you did."

Jacinda pinched pieces off the leaf as they went down the track, leaving a trail of green fragments. "Okay, we did. But we shouldn't have. So don't tell anyone, okay?"

"I won't, I promise." She clapped her hands together silently, in repressed glee, loving the secret. "I *told* you I always wondered if he liked you, back then. And I was right. So what are you going to do now? Is this, like, a thing?"

"Oh, it's not a thing. No way." She scrunched up the leafy skeleton and threw it on the ground. "It was definitely a one-off."

Riley looked disappointed. "Damn."

"No, not damn. It's wrong. Ethan died because of me. How sick is it that his brother and I are screwing around, while he's—" She kicked a stick out of the way, and walked faster on the grassy track.

"Stop it," Riley said. "It wasn't because of you. We don't even know how he died, so how can you say that?" Then she paused. "Wait, is that what Liam told you? That it was because of you?"

"Not exactly."

"Not exactly in a good way, or a bad way? Because you guys might have a chance at something here. Think about it. It's not a coincidence that you both decided to come back at the exact same time, after all these years."

"Well, sometimes coincidences suck." She stopped and turned to look at Riley. "If I hadn't come that summer, Ethan would still be alive. There's no way I can have *anything* with his brother, not this summer, or ever. And he doesn't want it either."

"He wanted it enough to sleep with you."

God, she was so determined to put a positive spin on it. "Riley, we both know that doesn't mean anything. It's just sex. And maybe punishment." At Riley's shocked expression, she shrugged, even though she hated saying those words herself. "Whatever it is, it's not right. My cousin Danielle is coming tomorrow, with her son Sam. Once they're settled in, I'm going to go."

"But you just got here!"

"All the easier to leave then."

She pouted. "Well, *I* don't want you to go."

"Oh...thanks. It has been fun hanging out again." That was true. "You'll have to come to LA."

As she said it, she realized that would mean revealing her 'real' life. But that would be okay—she'd just wanted this one undercover summer, to catch her breath, reassess. And it would be fun to show Riley around.

Riley gasped at the suggestion. "Ooh yes! That would be so cool."

They started down the hill again, with Riley talking about all the Californian things she'd like to do. Jacinda nodded and smiled, but her mind was elsewhere. For one moment last night, she'd actually thought about staying. Imagined that the glimpse of wholeness she'd felt in his arms could last. Blame it on the oxytocin, or the pheromones, or the Jack Daniel's, or the phases of the moon. Because from here on, she wasn't trusting her emotions. Not when it came to him.

Chapter Seventeen

Her last night in Sweet Breeze Bay. She'd promised to stop in at Clarion Call tomorrow and say goodbye to Riley, but tonight her only company was the feline kind. She ate a late dinner with Velvet sitting companionably on the chair next to hers, taking a break while the kittens napped.

"You're such a good mama," she told the little cat.

Velvet winked back, but said nothing, watching the steadily shrinking piece of salmon on Jacinda's plate. Jacinda gave her a little piece, and she daintily licked it up, then started to wash herself.

"I might have been a good mama too, you know."

Velvet jumped down and walked away, flicking her tail.

"Fine, whatever." She sighed, and got up to rinse her empty plate and put it in the dishwasher. Then she put on a long, light cardigan over her mini and t-shirt, took a blanket from the hall closet, and grabbed the Jack Daniel's from the coffee table.

One last night. She knew where she wanted to spend it.

She went barefoot down the alley past Liam's place. There was a light on inside, but she was pretty sure that even if he saw her go by, he wouldn't be coming to look for her. He hadn't wanted to see her this morning, after all.

She walked along the beach a little way and picked a

random spot to spread out the blanket. Then she sat down, wrapped the cardigan around herself, and opened the bottle. One last night under the South Pacific moon and stars. One last high tide to fill her up, before she walked away. She'd be back in the real, unreal world of LA soon—but for now, with the bottle in her hand and the warm, salty air in her lungs, she could let herself lose track of time. Whatever had happened between her and Liam last night, she'd move on. Two messed-up people added together could never equal something whole—his dead-of-night exit proved that. They'd each have to figure out their own way to heal from that one distant summer. She leaned back and looked at the star-scattered sky, and tried not to think about him.

"Jacinda?"

A voice interrupted her thoughts—pleasantly Jack-hazy by now—and she twisted around to see who it was. Standing above her were two tall, broad-shouldered men, with familiar faces. She got to her feet, putting the lid back on the bottle.

"Oh my God, look at you. Hi."

"You look great," Dane said, giving her a kiss on the cheek.

She smiled. "Thanks."

Connor shifted the box of beer he was carrying to his other hip and gave her a kiss too. "Good to see you."

"You too," she said. And it was—not just because they'd both grown a foot taller and transformed from slightly nerdy teenagers into seriously handsome men.

"We're going to see Liam," Connor said. "Come with us."

Uh, no. "Thanks, but I won't."

He frowned. "We can't leave you sitting here drinking by yourself. It's unsociable."

She bent down to gather up the blanket. "That's okay, I was just about to go home anyway." She sure as hell wasn't going to explain why she wouldn't go with them. "I have a flight tomorrow."

"All the more reason to enjoy your last night then," Dane said.

Before she could think of an answer, Connor shoved the beer at Dane, then took her free arm and tucked it into his. "Come on. Don't be a snob." And he started to lead her back up the beach, Dane alongside.

"I really don't—" she began as they went down the alley, but Connor interrupted her with a shout.

"Liam," he bellowed, breaking the night-time quiet. "Liam Ward! Get out here."

"Honestly, though," she said, as they drew relentlessly closer to Liam's gate. "It's so nice to see you, but I really should get home."

Connor just grinned. "No way. We don't get to hang out with a superstar every day."

Oh, great. Word was out. "I'm not a superstar."

"You're the closest thing we've ever met," he said.

Dane reached over and unlatched the gate. "Come on. For old times' sake."

"Hey, Liam!" Connor shouted again, propelling her through. "Look what we found on the beach."

Shit. This definitely wasn't part of her plan for the night.

As they reached the bottom of the deck steps, Liam came to the door. When he saw her, his face twisted for a second, but then he grinned and shook his head.

"You guys are a menace."

As he laughed, her morning humiliation washed over her again. His voice had the rough, joking tone that guys only seemed to use with each other, but she'd seen that flash of discomfort as he avoided her eye. Well, good. Let's see how uncomfortable he'd feel with her in his house again.

She laughed too, and started up the steps. "They wouldn't take no for an answer."

He was gripping the sliding door, and for half a second she thought he'd close it in her face. But then he pushed it open and stood back, his unease obvious.

"Surprise," she said as she stepped in. Then she smiled sweetly and stood by as the men shook hands and slapped backs.

"Amazing what you come across on the beach some

nights," Dane told him, gesturing to Jacinda.

"Yeah, amazing," he said, looking directly at her now. "Nice to see you again."

She couldn't help herself. "Is it?"

But he didn't reply, just leaned in to kiss her cheek. She bit the inside of her lip and ignored the flicker of heat that sprang up when the stubble on his jaw grazed her skin. Her eyes closed of their own accord as he stayed there just a millisecond longer than the standard friendly kiss. Was he breathing in...breathing *her* in? She broke away and went to sit on the sofa, her heartbeat skittering.

If Dane and Connor noticed anything off, they didn't let it show. Dane sat next to her, and Connor and Liam took the oversized armchairs opposite. Lit only by lamps, the room was cozy—unlike the vibe running between her and Liam. Bottles of beer were passed around, and she accepted one too, leaving the Jack on the table. No more of the hard stuff for her tonight. She curled her legs up and sipped slowly from her bottle, listening to the jokes and jibes shooting between the others—the years they spent growing up obviously provided a ton of material. She glanced at Ethan's guitar, still standing in the corner. No one mentioned him.

"So what brought you back after all these years, to mingle with the common people?" Connor asked her, tempering the question with a wink.

"Stop it now," she told him.

"Just wondering. It's a long way from the bright lights."

She nodded. "Exactly. I just needed a break. So...can you keep it on the down low? Not tell anyone? I'm trying to keep Cin Scott under the radar for a while."

"Sure," Dane said.

Connor leaned forward. "Your secret's safe with us. It must be full on in that business."

"Thanks. And yeah, some of the stuff that goes on...it's sink or swim."

"I'm not cut out for fame," he said, stretching back lazily in the chair. "Fortune, though...I'm fine with that." He grinned.

"What kind of stuff?" Dane asked her.

Ugh, this wasn't where she wanted the conversation to go. But okay, since he asked. "Like...they want me to take it up a level. You know—be sexier."

Suddenly all three men were looking anywhere but at her, and she tried not to laugh. Well, they had gone there.

"Apparently sex sells," she added, looking at Liam, who kept his eyes fixed on the opposite corner of the room. "You might have heard."

Dane rubbed the back of his neck and concentrated on his beer, clearly sorry he asked.

"That's nuts though," Connor said. "Look at you. How much sexier do you have to be?"

Liam took a swig from his bottle, apparently riveted now by something out the window.

"What about you?" Connor asked him. "You're a sexy guy. Keen to see your name in lights?"

Dane laughed, the tension broken, but Liam shook his head. "Not me."

"You've got some decent talent though," Dane said. "You wrote—"

Liam shut him down with a narrow glare. "No. It wasn't me who had that dream."

There was a sudden silence in the room, and Liam looked at Jacinda. "He would've killed for the chances you've had. For the things you're complaining about. Sounds like a charmed life to me."

"They weren't *chances*," she told him, her blood pressure instantly rising. "I've worked for everything I've achieved."

"Lucky you. Some people never had that opportunity."

"So I should've never done anything ever again? Thrown my own life away?"

He shrugged, not meeting her eye, and took another shot of his beer. She wanted to slap it out of his hand, but she kept her voice steady, and put her drink down on the table. "I didn't even know what had happened. You know that."

Out of the corner of her eye, she saw the other two look at each other, and Dane gestured to Connor.

"Ah…so, we might go, I think," he said, standing up.

"Yeah, better make a move." Connor cleared his throat and stood up too. "It was nice to see you, Jacinda."

She looked at Liam, expecting him to protest, but he didn't try to dissuade them, just got up and went to the door. So she got up too and said goodbye to them both, ignoring Liam as they each kissed her on the cheek. How he managed to have such nice friends was a complete mystery.

"So…we'll see you tomorrow, maybe," Dane told him.

He nodded. "Yeah. Sounds good."

Then they went out, each of them giving him a slap on the arm as they went. Without saying anything, she started to follow them. She'd come in ready to stand her ground, but that was enough. She wasn't going to apologize for her entire life. Not to him. Not after that. And not after last night.

But he grabbed her arm, and slid the door shut.

She shook him off. "What are you doing?"

He stood in front of her, his expression dark and unreadable. "I have no fucking idea."

Then he took her head in his hands, and kissed her.

Chapter Eighteen

"Get the hell away from me."

Hissing the words, she planted her palms on his chest and shoved him, with surprising strength for someone so petite. He took a step back, but said nothing. Seeing her about to walk out the door, his only instinct had been to stop her. And the next instinct after that was to kiss her. Because there was something about angry Jacinda that erased every bit of sense he had. There were spots of color in her cheeks, and fire in her eyes, and all he could think of was the night before, when she'd been alight for a different reason. Now her breasts rose and fell with her rapid breathing, and he couldn't help but look, remembering how it had felt to bury his face in those incredible curves. But she huffed out a breath and pulled her cardigan around herself.

"Nice. You're all class, Liam."

He looked at the ceiling, trying not to think about how she was wearing the same short skirt as the day she got stuck under the house, and whether the red lace panties were underneath. He stuffed his hands into the pockets of his loose cargo shorts, hoping to obscure the growing evidence of his thoughts.

But she wasn't fooled. She looked pointedly at his crotch, then back at him. "This is exactly the kind of shit I left behind in LA."

Unreasonably, given what he'd just said and done (and what he'd done the night before), the idea of anyone trying to take advantage of her suddenly fired him with Neanderthal anger. It might be a charmed life, but yes, he could imagine the kind of sleaziness that went on behind the scenes in that business. And that wasn't him. "I'm not that guy."

She raised a cynical eyebrow. "Really?"

Okay, sneaking out was a shitty move. But up until then, she'd been along for the ride with him, if he remembered right. And hell, did he remember. There was nothing sleazy about the way she'd kissed him, run her hands over him, wrapped herself around him...

"You didn't think I was so bad last night," he said.

She raised herself up. "I wasn't the one who ran out."

Then he remembered all the other stuff. All the reasons why he'd left her there, soft and perfect in the dark, were still true. And there was one more thing he shouldn't forget—she was the one who left first, years ago. *She'd* run out, back to the States, and that was where she should have stayed. For everyone's sake.

"Yeah, that was me," he replied, the words passing out of him before he had time to weigh their impact. "But you ran out on us first."

Her face hardened, and they held each other's eyes, a charge of something dangerous heating up the room.

"You're such an asshole," she told him.

He felt the hard-edged words strike, but didn't let himself flinch. It was better this way. He should never have gone over there last night, full of his father's Glenfiddich, condoms in his pocket, the loneliness of the past loosening his tongue. And he shouldn't have told her that he'd wanted her, all those summers ago—that was something he'd never wanted her to know. *Ever.* But apparently he was as weak as the next man when pinned underneath a luscious, willing woman.

And here was that woman, tiny but tough, calling him on his bullshit. But now, behind the steel, he could see the hurt. And to be hurt, she must have felt something. The possibility sparked a tiny light in his heart—and scared the shit out of him. Getting entangled with the girl who caused Ethan's death? On top of every other reason not to, it would kill his mother.

So yeah, maybe he was an asshole, but it was better to cut it off in the dead of night, than face her in the morning and explain. If she hated him, it took the battle out of his hands. No more fighting with himself about whether, maybe, somehow, she could be his. Because if he hadn't been so self-indulgently obsessed with her that summer, he wouldn't have been secretly pleased that she'd left Ethan. He would have gone looking for his brother earlier. And his family would still be in one piece.

When he didn't reply, she rolled her eyes. "I can't believe I felt sorry for you last night."

"You screwed me out of pity?"

He should care, but in truth, he didn't. That wouldn't have stopped him last night—and not her either, it seemed. With a jolt of arousal, he remembered her wrapping her legs around his waist, pulling him down into her, deep and hard and determined.

She curled her lip. "Well, why did you *screw* me?"

Coming from her beautiful mouth, the word sounded rough and dirty, and he hardened even more. Jesus, he *was* an asshole.

As though she could see it on his face, she looked down at his shorts again. *Busted*. But before she could deliver the inevitable take-down, he stepped blindly forward.

One more kiss, one more taste.

One last screwed-up, desperate grab at what could never be.

But she didn't slap him down. Instead, with a resigned, syrupy 'Oh, God', she seemed to melt in his arms. He seized the moment—no questions, no hesitation. He'd take whatever she was willing to give...which seemed to be more than he expected. As he pulled her closer, her head tipped back, her eyes heavy with surrender and anticipation as they met his.

He still had no fucking idea what he was doing, and he

might be an idiot, but at least he was smart enough not to waste time analyzing this turn of events.

But as he dropped his head to kiss her, something caught his eye over her shoulder—Ethan's guitar on its stand, silently condemning him. Ah, fuck. He turned her around so that his back was to the room, and hers was against the bi-fold doors. Outside was the empty, moon-hushed garden where they'd played as kids, then hung out as teenagers. From innocence to infatuation, then disaster. But inside, here in front of him, was the woman she'd become. Still with the unbelievable breasts, the diamond-blue eyes, and the hourglass curves. But now—even barefoot and unadorned—there was a world-weary edge to her beauty that made her even more compelling.

Connor was right—how could she get any sexier?

Finally, he kissed her. As her lips parted, her fingers dug into his back, and her breasts pressed against him. She angled her hips closer—one deep breath from either of them and she'd be hard up against the erection she'd scorned him for minutes ago. Amazing how things change. After a moment she broke the kiss, but stayed close, holding the back of his t-shirt.

"We are *not* doing this again," she said into his chest, as he hitched up her skirt.

"No."

For once they were agreeing on something.

She twisted slightly, helping the denim rise, and then he could see...not the red panties, but their black lace equivalent. He breathed out a groan and slipped his hand inside them, and she parted her legs slightly, letting him in. Oh, yeah. As his fingers found the small, hot center of her desire, she raised herself up on tiptoe, and slowly, slowly, he started to stroke. A low moan escaped her lips, and she leaned her head back against the glass, her eyes closed.

He had to smile. However mad she was at him, her body was on his side.

As he watched her reaction to his teasing fingers, the lust and waiting and anger and every-damn-thing suddenly coalesced into a rush of primal craving. He fell and pressed his face to her sweet center, lace against his forehead, her scent overtaking him as she threaded her fingers in his hair. Back then, he'd worshipped her from afar. Right now, he was literally on his knees...and he didn't want to be anywhere else.

He eased the panties down, and she stood still, but he could hear her breathing in the quiet room. At seventeen, despite the epic force of his crush, he wouldn't have had a clue what to do with her. But now he did. Now he knew exactly what to do...if she'd let him.

He looked up. "So...we're not doing this?"

"Shut up," she said, her voice husky.

So he did. For half a second, he considered what kind of a view it would be for anyone who wandered into the dark garden. But then her fingers tightened on the back of his head, just the tiniest bit. Message received. He tugged at the black lace and let it fall around her feet, and she kicked the panties away.

He ran his hands around the back of her thighs, and held the place where they curved into the softness of her backside. Jesus, she was all curves and temptation. And right in front of him was the ultimate temptation—the sweet, secret place that she'd let him into the night before. The memory sent him into sudden overdrive, and he surrendered.

She curved toward him as his tongue played against her heat, small, incoherent sounds falling from her lips, each one a benediction. God help him, there was nothing holy about his desire, or the things he wanted to do to her, but right now hers was the only saving he needed. He clutched her bottom and buried his face between her legs, losing and finding himself in her breathy exclamations, her beautiful abandon.

Nothing else existed.

But then he felt her tense, and she put a hand on his shoulder and pushed him back. He looked up, dragging himself back to reality. Then he followed her gaze.

She was looking at the guitar.

Shit. He stood up, pressing his forearm against his lips,

damp with her sweetness. There was no point asking what was wrong. Without meeting his eye, she worked the denim skirt back down over her hips, then picked up the panties and stuffed them in her pocket.

He started to say something, anything, but she silenced him with a look. "Don't."

When he tried again, she shook her head.

"We both know why. It's the same reason you snuck out last night."

Then she turned and opened the door, and went out into the night, leaving him with her lush scent on his face, a colossal hard-on, and a burning urge to smash the goddamn guitar to pieces.

Chapter Nineteen

"Look! They've got blue eyes."

Sam was leaning in, checking each of the little bundles of fluff. The minute he and Danielle had arrived, he'd made a beeline for the kittens, and discovered that two of them had opened their eyes. Now they were taking their first blurry looks at the world, blinking in the morning light. Jacinda smiled as they wobbled around, mewing and trampling on their siblings. With their tiny, softly folded ears and skinny, perky tails, they were ridiculously cute.

"You're the first one to see them with their eyes open," she told Sam, and he swelled with pride.

"Do they have names?"

It hadn't occurred to her to name them—that seemed like Nana Mac's job. But she knew that Nana Mac would give Sam the honor, if she was here.

"Why don't you name them?" she suggested.

"Really? Okay." He tapped his chin, considering. "Maybe a Minecraft name…or Marvel."

"I'm sure you'll come up with something," she said. "But we'll need four."

He peered into the kitteny pile, where the tabby was lying on top of Velvet's head. "Are they boys or girls?"

"Oh…I don't know. I had a peek, but I couldn't really tell."

Hell, she hadn't been a very good cat sitter. Velvet

seemed to know what she was doing, and they all looked healthy, but she'd better take them to the vet for a check-up before she left, and find out who was who. She was one hundred per cent in favor of gender equality, but she didn't want Nana Mac to end up with a female Captain America.

On the other hand, that would be pretty cool.

"Maybe you could help me take them to the vet this afternoon, so we can find out," she said.

Sam nodded, serious. "I can do that."

She left him sitting next to the cat bed, picking up and putting down kittens as he tested out possible names. In the kitchen, Danielle was putting the groceries away.

"He's a cutie," Jacinda said.

Danielle smiled. "Thanks. He's coping really well so far."

"Have you seen much of his dad?" she asked quietly, putting a carton of juice in the fridge.

"Andy? A bit. Sam's used to him being unreliable, so...you know." She shrugged, and looked toward where Sam was sitting, her blue eyes cautious. "I'll tell you later, anyway."

"You don't have to." She didn't want to drag up things that Danielle might not feel like talking about.

"It's fine," she said quietly, tucking a strand of curly hair behind her ear. "I had to start getting over him while we were still together, anyway."

"I'm sorry." She glanced over to Sam, then flicked the kettle on. "Would you like coffee?"

"God, yes. Thanks. We left really early, and we didn't stop on the drive here at all, except at the supermarket in Lancet Bay." She held up a packaged chicken. "Family dinner tonight? We've got a lot to catch up on."

Jacinda spooned instant coffee into mugs. "Actually...now that you're here, I'm going to go. Sam seems like he'll be a great kitten sitter."

"What? You can't go yet," Danielle said. "We only just arrived, and it's been years since we saw each other. Can't you stay one more day, at least?"

"No, I'm sorry, I really have to go. There's a late flight to LA, so..."

Sam's voice came from behind them. "Why do you have to go?"

They turned to see him frowning, his eyebrows furrowed and his cowlick sticking up like a cartoon kid. Danielle pulled him close and rumpled his hair.

"Well, what time is the flight?" she asked Jacinda.

"Uh...just after eleven? I don't actually have a ticket yet." She'd planned to buy one online yesterday morning, but when Riley and the girls arrived, she'd gotten distracted. And then later...distracted again. She batted away the memory of Liam in front of her in his living room, and the way her own knees had buckled when he fell to his.

So yeah, she'd been...waylaid. But if tonight's flight was full, she could kill a night at an airport hotel.

"You *have* to stay," Sam said. "I might need help thinking of names for the kittens."

They both looked at her, expectation heavy in the air. She hesitated. It *would* be kind of rude to leave the minute they arrived. Nana Mac would be disappointed too, when she heard. And even though Jacinda and Danielle were cousins, they didn't really know each other at all. This was quality family time—one thing she'd always wished for.

"Okay. One more night."

"Good." Sam nodded, satisfied. "Now I have to get thinking."

As they watched him go, Jacinda decided not to think about why she hadn't actually gone ahead and bought herself a ticket, even though she was so determined to leave. But she was only delayed a day, that was all. Just one more day.

★

They went in Danielle's car to the vet in Lancet Bay that afternoon, with Velvet and the kittens tucked into a cat carrier. He pronounced them all healthy—three girls and one boy.

133

"Have you got any ideas for names now?" Jacinda asked Sam as they sat down for dinner.

"Maybe. But I wasn't expecting so many girls," Sam said, his face scrunched up.

"Sam!" Danielle said, but she and Jacinda both had to laugh.

"I don't *mind* that they're girls," he said earnestly. "But I was thinking about superhero names, and I don't know many girl ones."

Jacinda and Danielle looked at each other across the table. "Yeah, that's a whole other issue," Jacinda said.

"You'll think of something," Danielle told him, putting a chicken drumstick on his plate.

He nodded. "I'll google it. Mum, can I use your computer?"

"Yes, later," she replied. She passed the dish of broccoli and beans to Jacinda, and Sam held his nose as they went past. "So we heard that you're a bit of a star," she said.

Jacinda shrugged as she took the dish. "Not really."

"Really? What would you call it then?"

"I'm trying not to call it anything at the moment," she said. "I'm kind of...reassessing."

"Mum said you're a ROCK STAR," Sam said, breaking out an imaginary riff on his drumstick. "That's awesome."

She laughed. "Thanks."

"Can you teach me to play guitar?"

"I would, but I didn't bring mine with me. I bet you'd be good at it though." Then she looked at Danielle. "I haven't mentioned anything about it here. Not to anyone. I just needed a break."

She nodded, understanding in her expression. "Got it."

But Sam was listening. "A break from what?"

"Um..." How could she phrase it so a nine-year-old would understand? "Some people want me to do stuff I don't like. Sometimes it doesn't make me happy."

"Ugh, I hate that," he said. "Like when we're at school and we have to do everything the teacher tells us."

"Kind of like that, yeah."

He frowned. "Don't you *like* being a rock star?"

"Mostly. But I'm undercover right now." She looked over one shoulder, then the other, and leaned in. "Don't blow my cover, okay?"

He looked around too, then nodded. "Okay." He mimed zipping his lip, and Jacinda gave him a thumbs-up.

Then she spooned a helping of vegetables onto her plate, and held the dish out in his direction. "Vegetables?"

He made dramatic gagging sounds. "Are you trying to poison me? Yuck!"

Danielle sighed, and Jacinda laughed. "I guess that counts as people wanting you to do something you don't like."

"Ex-*act*-ly." He bit into his drumstick.

Jacinda put the offending dish down at the far end of the table. "I hear you."

Later that night, when he was tucked up in bed, she and Danielle sat on the living room floor with the kittens, drinking wine and reacquainting themselves.

"It's so nice to be away at last," Danielle said.

"You're coping really well," Jacinda said. "Was it a tough break-up?"

She pursed her lips, looking into her glass. "In some ways. The actual process, you know. Finally making the call to end it, and then telling Sam—that was horrible. And then the logistics of dividing everything up, sorting out the house…" She lifted her chin. "But it had to be done."

"Nana Mac said maybe it was for the best?" Jacinda chose her words carefully, just in case she had it wrong. But Danielle nodded.

"Oh God, it totally was. Absolutely. I don't even know why he thought we should get married in the first place. You know how some people are just meant to be?"

"Not personally. But yeah."

"Well, that wasn't us." She gave a short laugh. "I realized pretty early on that we'd made a mistake. And Andy helped me with the realizing, by staying out late as often as he could, and deciding that maybe he wasn't completely over his high school girlfriend after all."

"Oh, shit. Did he cheat on you?"

She shrugged. "Maybe. Probably. He says not, but it's hard to keep secrets in a small place like that. A couple of people came and said something to me, just quietly. But we had Sam by that time, so I couldn't just walk away. I felt like I should try a bit harder, a bit longer."

Jacinda reached out and put a hand on her arm. "I'm sorry. That must have been tough."

"Yeah." She scrunched up her nose. "But now it's done. And it's better for both of us this way. The main thing is to make sure Sam comes through okay."

"You're doing great so far. He's so sweet."

"Yeah, sometimes." She rolled her eyes, but a smile lit up her face. "He's a good kid. I hope he'll make friends here—he needs someone to play with. He had tons of friends at home, and all the cousins too."

"Riley said there are markets this Friday night, on the main street," Jacinda said. "It sounds like everyone goes— maybe he'd meet some kids there."

"Oh, I love night markets. We should definitely go." She nodded. "Now, speaking of cousins, I've got some photos to show you. I can't believe how much you look like our cousin Mandy. And Justine. Hang on, let me find my phone."

As she went to get her bag, she started talking about the family—who was who, and what they were like. The people she talked about were just names to Jacinda, having grown up far from her mother's family, with so few visits back to New Zealand. But then, as they scrolled through the images on the phone, she recognized a few faces. And some of the ones she didn't recognize had a look about them—the family resemblance that she'd never seen until now, apart from in her mom.

"You look like us," Danielle insisted.

"I kind of do. It's weird."

She laughed. "Not weird. Just family."

Jacinda looked at a photo of everyone posing on the farmhouse lawn. Behind them was the wide green countryside, and in front, laughing children were rolling on the grass. It was chaotic and idyllic at the same time.

"Do you think you'll go back there?" she asked Danielle.

"I don't know." She leaned back against the sofa and sighed. "I spent my whole life there, married a guy from down the road, worked in the family business...it feels like it's time for something else."

"I know that feeling." Jacinda's tone was heartfelt.

"Why are *you* going back then?"

She stroked one of the black kittens—the boy—who had set off on a big adventure of his own across the rug. Why *was* she going back? Things with Liam had gotten really complicated, really fast...but after his walkout, maybe it wasn't *her* who should be thinking about leaving. Anyway, she wasn't going to share that story with Danielle. She didn't know anything about the history between Jacinda and the Ward family, and Jacinda would rather it stayed that way.

"There's just a lot going on back there, so..."

"I got the impression that was why you left the States in the first place."

Oops. "Um...it was. I did plan to stay here longer, but..." She let the sentence trail off.

"I can't even imagine what your life is like." Danielle refilled her glass and passed the wine bottle over. "What about guys? You must meet some insanely hot men in your world."

"Yeah. Insane, and hot." She rolled her eyes and tipped the last of the wine into her glass.

"So you're not rushing back for love," Danielle laughed.

She snorted. "No. Other stuff."

Hannah had texted during the day with an update. Todd wasn't home from Austin yet, but he was still negotiating the tour. Lainey Kingsley had been unimpressed about the interview being cancelled again, but Hannah had promised to reschedule as soon as Cin was back—even though Jacinda couldn't say when that would be. She'd been so tempted to tell Hannah about developments with Liam...but she knew Hannah would ask a bunch of questions she had no answer for. Like, how Jacinda felt. What it all meant. And what would happen next. She didn't know. And he'd said it himself—he had no fucking idea what he was doing.

Except he did. He knew exactly what he was doing, and he was very, very good at it. A smoldering heat started up low in her belly as she remembered what an extremely hot complication he was, inked and muscular and hungry. Hungry for her, apparently...at the same time as he hated her for ruining everything.

She sighed and stroked the fuzzy black kitten as he wobbled closer, then picked him up and snuggled him close. He meowed, a tiny squeaky pronunciation that made them both laugh—and then rewarded her by peeing on her shirt.

"Hey!" She set him down carefully, and pulled the damp shirt away from her skin with a grimace. "At least it's warm, I guess."

"Men," Danielle said, laughing again.

"Right? You show a little affection, and that's how they repay you."

Velvet came and picked him up by the scruff of the neck and carried him back to the cat bed, ignoring his protests as she dropped him in with his sisters. Then Jacinda went upstairs and grabbed a clean t-shirt. When she came back, Danielle had opened another bottle of wine, and was looking uncertain. Jacinda sat back down, wondering what was on her mind.

Danielle cleared her throat as she refilled both their glasses. "So I can't even imagine what your 'other stuff' might be, either," she said, getting back to their conversation. "And I know you must be busy. But...is there any way you could stay a while longer? To be honest, I was going to ask for your help. School doesn't start for a few more weeks, and I have to look for a job. I need someone to watch Sam while I go for interviews. Nana Mac said you were here for the summer, so I was kind of hoping..." Her voice faded, and she looked embarrassed to be asking.

Jacinda took a slow sip, thinking. Danielle needed her.

Sam needed her. And Danielle was making a new start, just like she'd done herself a dozen times over.

How could she say no?

"Okay. I'll stay a little longer."

"Thank you! Oh God, that's such a relief." She shuffled over, trying not to spill any wine, and gave Jacinda a one-armed hug, a wayward curl tickling her face. "Thank you, seriously."

Jacinda hugged her back. "You're welcome. It'll be fun."

It would be. If she crossed paths with Liam again, he'd just have to deal with it, like she would. And he knew where the airport was.

Chapter Twenty

A t the sound of a footstep on the deck, Liam tensed over the keyboard. Since the day Jacinda had walked down the alley—and then fallen down in the alley—he'd got into the habit of working at the kitchen table, instead of in the office space upstairs. Not because he was hoping to catch a glimpse of her again. It was just cooler downstairs. That was all.

He squeezed his eyes shut for a second, remembering the way his anger had boiled up on Sunday night, when she'd complained about her life—her seemingly charmed life. The way she'd melted into him, despite the things he'd said. And how something elemental and desperate had swept over him, bringing him to his knees, lost in the Jacinda madness that seemed to be growing stronger the longer she was here. Yesterday had gone by with no sign of her, which hadn't exactly been a surprise. He had no idea where they'd go from here.

Actually, he did. They'd be going nowhere.

Another small sound came from outside, and he listened again, wondering whether to get up and investigate. It was probably one of the huge seagulls that touched down in the yard sometimes, looking for scraps of food around the beachside houses. With a shrug, he went back to work. It was the only thing distracting him at the moment. He'd taken on a volunteer project for a non-profit in California, building a website that would offer support for kids from Mexican families who'd grown up in the States, but whose parents were undocumented immigrants. The kids lived every day with the underlying fear that their parents could be caught and deported. He'd watched as the immigration issue became increasingly fraught, and although he couldn't do much from so far away, it felt good to help in this small way at least.

Then he heard a bump in the living room, and the sound of something falling to the floor. Okay, not a seagull. Instantly, he was on his feet. As he went through the door, he dug deep for his most intimidating, aggressive voice, aiming to get the upper hand by scaring the crap out of the intruder.

"What the fuck are you doing?"

In the corner, a small figure was leaning over Ethan's guitar, where it lay on the ground. The boy spun around, terror on his face.

"I'm sorry!" he squeaked, his eyes round with shock and fear. "I'm sorry, I didn't mean to!"

Liam's heart sank at the realization that he'd scared the crap out of a skinny kid who'd barely come up to his elbow. "Ah, shit. I mean, damn. Sorry, kid."

The boy's eyes darted to the door, then back at Liam. Obviously figuring that he was trapped, he started backing away.

"It's okay, dude," Liam said. "I thought you were a burglar or something."

Trying to look reassuring, he took a step forward, but that seemed to push the kid into full panic mode. With a high-pitched cry, he twisted around and made a break for it, heading around the back of the sofa. But his foot caught on the guitar, still lying on the floor, and he tumbled down, disappearing between the sofa and the bookshelf.

Liam went over and looked down to where he was lying on the ground, one arm over his face as though that would make him invisible. He seemed to be in one piece.

"Are you finished freaking out now?"

One huge blue eye peeked out from behind his arm, but he didn't move.

"Come on man, get up. It's okay."

Slowly, the kid got to his feet, his eyes wary. There was nothing to him—he looked like a collection of twigs flung together with a spiky mess of blond hair tossed on top. And he looked poised to run again. Some kind of damage control was needed.

Liam held out a hand. "So I don't know who you are, but I'm Liam," he said casually.

The kid hesitated, then seemed to gather his courage, and went in for the handshake. "I'm Sam."

His fingers were tiny, and kind of sticky. Liam shook his hand, then leaned against the sofa.

"Sam, huh? Where did you come from?"

His freckled face went red again, but he stayed where he was, still on edge. "Next door."

"Next door...with Jacinda?"

He looked at the boy, studying his features, and for a second he was flung into an alternate reality, where Jacinda had hidden a secret and this scrappy kid was his nephew. Did the numbers add up? He was no good at guessing kids' ages.

"Yes," Sam said. "She's my mum's cousin."

Ah. Okay. He shook his head, forcing himself back to the real world.

"My mum and dad split up, so we've come to stay for a while," Sam continued. Then he frowned. "She said she was going back to America."

Liam stood up again, a sudden tension in his guts. "Really?"

"Yes. Well, except first she said she didn't have a ticket, and then she said she'd only stay one more night, and then Mum told me she was going to stay and help look after me for a while." He grinned, his scare seemingly forgotten. "She's *undercover*."

Liam nodded, smiling, but inside he was reeling. Jesus, he had mental whiplash from being flung in one direction and then the other. She was leaving, she was staying...each one detonated a barrage of conflicting reactions. Trying to ignore the battle going on in his head, he turned and picked up the guitar. Making sure nothing was damaged, he checked the neck and the bridge, then ran a hand over the frets.

"It's a cool guitar," Sam said from behind him.

He set it back on the stand. "It is."

"It's *really* cool. I could see it through the window."

The longing in his tone was obvious, but Liam ignored it. No way was some random kid going to mess with Ethan's guitar. "Uh-huh."

He shifted the stand farther back into the corner, then turned to look at Sam. He was practically vibrating on the spot, as though the guitar was a magnet and he was nothing but a skinny mass of metal filings.

"You know, Sam, it's not a good idea to walk into strange people's houses and start knocking things over."

He went red. "I know." Then he tipped his head to the side. "But you don't look strange."

Liam had to laugh. "We're all strange in our own way. You'll figure that out eventually."

At that, Sam looked perplexed. "Okay…" His eyes went back to the guitar. "So can you show me how to play it?"

"No."

"Please?"

"Seriously, no. This guitar isn't for playing."

His face fell, and Liam sighed. Why had he left the door open? From now on he'd go back to sitting upstairs with the doors closed. Too bad if it was hot.

"Ask Jacinda to teach you. She plays guitar."

Sam's shoulders drooped a little more. "She's *undercover*, remember? She doesn't have her guitar here."

"Go play on the beach then. What are you…eight? You should be outside doing something healthy. Or…I don't know, play on your iPad."

"I'm *nine*. And I don't have an iPad."

Liam pressed his fingers to his forehead. He hadn't come all the way back here to be a goddamn babysitter.

And no one—*no one*—had played this guitar since the night Ethan died.

"And I don't have anyone to play with either," Sam added, in an almost-whisper.

Liam considered the small boy in front of him, currently doing a spectacularly good job of looking tragic. Shit. So his parents had split up, he was new here, and he had no friends. At nine, Liam had all the Sweet Breeze Bay kids to play with...including Jacinda, when she visited. And most of all, he'd had his brother. Playing, fighting, or play-fighting, there had never been a moment of loneliness.

That came later.

"Okay, fine," he said, aware that the gruffness in his voice wasn't from impatience this time. "But just one turn."

Despite the reluctant tone of Liam's agreement, Sam's face was aglow with triumph. "Yesss! Can we play it really LOUD?"

It occurred to Liam that, given how things had turned out, Jacinda might not be thrilled about this arrangement. "You know what, let's just be undercover ourselves," he suggested.

"Cool," Sam said. "Undercover brothers."

He laughed. "Yeah, okay. Whatever." He pushed aside his doubts and went to find an amp. Just one turn wouldn't hurt. After that, the kid was someone else's responsibility.

Chapter Twenty-One

Left shoulder, left arm. Right shoulder, right arm. All the way down her front. Both legs, front and back. Then a couple of pretzel-like twists to get every inch of her back. Jacinda squeezed a last dollop of sunscreen lotion onto her hand and slathered it on her face, then stood back and checked her reflection in the bathroom mirror. She was glossy with sun lotion, strands of hair sticking to her cheeks, but better safe than sorry. At least her tan had started to even out now.

She put a cover-up on over her bikini, gathered up her beach bag, and headed downstairs. As she went into the living room, Danielle came in from outside.

"Have you seen Sam?"

"Not for a while, sorry."

She sighed. "He's the master of disappearing at the wrong time." She went back outside onto the deck and called his name, but there was no sign of him.

Then there was a knock at the door, and Jacinda went to open it. Riley was standing on the top step, with Tina and Kerry behind her. All three of them were wearing swimsuits and cotton cover-ups, flip-flops, and wide-brimmed hats.

"Hi!" Riley said. "Are you ready?"

Jacinda smiled. "Almost. We're just tracking down a

boy who's gone AWOL."

All three of them peered around her, into the house.

"Your cousins, right?" Tina said.

Jacinda stood back to let them in. "Come and meet Danielle. And Sam, if we can find him."

They came through the house, colorful in their beachwear and fragrant with sunscreen, and found Danielle on the deck.

"Would you and Sam like to come to the beach with us?" Jacinda asked her, once everyone was introduced.

"Thanks, but we have to run some errands," she said. "If this kid ever shows up."

She turned and called, "Sam! We're going out!"

"Do you think he went to the beach?" Jacinda asked.

"He'll be in trouble if he did. He's not allowed to go by himself. Plus I told him we weren't going until I put sunscreen on him. He's so pale, he burns in five minutes."

Jacinda knew the dangers of the fierce southern sun all too well. "I hope he hasn't gone far."

Danielle sighed. "He's probably just listening with his man ears."

"Selective deafness?" Riley said.

She laughed. "You got it." Then she yelled out again, putting maximum mother power into her voice. "Sam! Come here please!"

At that exact moment there was a rustling sound, and a section of the hedge suddenly sprang to life. Then Sam burst through into the yard. He stopped suddenly when he saw the team of women apparently waiting for him.

"Sorry, Mum," he said. "I was just visiting Liam. You can get through the hedge just there!"

He looked elated to have discovered—rediscovered— the secret passageway. Jacinda knew Riley was looking at her, waiting for some reaction to Sam's mention of Liam. But she could see Danielle's maternal alarm bells ringing.

"Who's Liam?" she asked him.

"He's...um, the man next door? I went to see him yesterday too."

Danielle frowned. "When did you do that?"

146

"While you were on your computer."

"Sam, we talked about this," she said. "We're not in the country anymore. You can't go off talking to strange people."

"That's what he said. But he's not strange," Sam protested. "He's got a *guitar*."

Jacinda had to laugh. Ownership of a guitar apparently outweighed any stranger danger. But however weird things had become between her and Liam, she knew Sam would be fine with him.

"Liam's all right," she reassured Danielle.

She could feel Riley's eyes on her, but didn't meet her gaze.

"He's more than *all right*," Tina said. "He's hot. Like, oh em gee hot."

"Oh...okay," Danielle said. "Huh. Do you all know him?"

"*Jacinda* does," Riley said.

Jacinda shot her a warning look. "Yes. Well, I did. I mean, I do." Ack, why was she getting in a tangle over a simple question? "His family lived there for years until they moved to Australia. Kerry knows him too," she added, trying to deflect some of the attention.

"He's cool," Sam said as they went inside. "He's got a computer. And *tattoos*."

Between the guitar, the technology, and the ink, Liam had obviously made an impression. She wondered if he'd finally taken Ethan's guitar from its stand, for Sam.

"Did he let you play the guitar?" she asked.

"Yep, yesterday *and* today." He scrunched up his freckled nose. "But we didn't have time to finish today. I had to come back here." He sent his mother a reproachful glare.

"Come on, let's get ready to go," Danielle said, ignoring it. "But no more disappearing. Okay?"

He exhaled a gust of frustration and resignation. "O-*kay*. But can I go over there again?"

"Maybe. But I want to meet him first, and make sure you're not bothering him. Little pest."

She grabbed him and rumpled his hair, and he shrieked and ducked out of her embrace. As he scampered off, Danielle shook her head. "Poor kid. He needs some friends."

"He'll meet some other kids before long," Kerry said. "They're all out and about this time of year. And you should come to the night markets. Everyone's friendly."

"Yes," Riley agreed, with exaggerated enthusiasm. "We're very *friendly* here." She gave Jacinda a tiny, surreptitious pinch, making her jump.

"Ahh!" she exclaimed. When the others looked at her, curious, she said, "I mean, ah, yes, that's so true. And once he starts school he'll be fine."

"I hope so," Danielle said. "Anyway, we'd better get going. It was nice to meet you all."

After they said their goodbyes, Jacinda whispered to Riley, "Thanks a lot."

She just laughed. "It was too good. But your secret's safe with me."

Thank God she didn't know there was even more to the secret now, Jacinda thought. And she herded them all out the door before Riley was tempted to say anything else.

★

It was nice to go down the alley in a gang of girls. The chat and laughter seemed to form a defensive bubble as they went past Liam's gate and onto the sand. Riley gave her a curious look, but she shrugged. It wasn't like she was expecting him to rush out and...whatever. After their last encounter, she had even less clue what was going on in his head. Well, apart from the dirty stuff. And what was wrong with her? The way her resolve had instantly disintegrated, leaving her standing in his living room, her panties on the floor, breathless and senseless as he...

She cut the thought off. None of it was doing them any good. Better to leave the mess where it was, tangled and grubby, and walk away—which she'd do as soon as

Danielle was ready. She was applying for jobs already, so it wouldn't be long. It was already Wednesday, and if they'd been able to avoid each other since Sunday night, there was no reason that couldn't continue until she left. Even if Sam was visiting him.

They turned left and went along the beach to a spot where the spreading branches of a pohutukawa tree reached out from someone's front yard, casting dappled shade on the hot sand. They spread blankets half in and half out of the shade—catering for the sun lovers and the shade shelterers—and settled in.

"No Jess today?" Jacinda asked.

Kerry shook her head. "No, she said she was busy."

Jacinda hadn't seen Jess since the night she'd blurted out what everyone was thinking. What would she say if she knew what had happened between her and Liam since then? Well, she wouldn't be finding out, anyway.

She pulled a twig out from under her beach towel and lay down again. "I thought you'd all be at work."

"It's January," Tina said. "Everyone's on holiday."

"Not me," Riley said. "I have to be back at Clarion Call by four. But I'm not letting this day go to waste." She waved an arm at the blue, blue sky. "Stephanie's going to meet us here."

After half an hour or so Stephanie found them there, still lazing and chatting.

"Is no one swimming?" she asked, plunking down her beach bag. She was wearing an athletic-looking swimsuit, black and sleek and sporty, and her hair was pulled up into a high ponytail.

Tina lifted her head from her arms. "We only just got here."

"Come on. The water's so warm."

Riley sighed. "I'll go. And you can come too." She poked Tina, who protested and inched away. "We've been here ages. And you said you wanted to do more swimming this summer."

"Oh, fine." She got up, brushing sand off her elbows. "Come on, Jacinda. If I have to, you do too."

They left Kerry reading her book, and headed toward the water. Stephanie ran ahead, looking ready for an Olympic outing, and was in the water and away before they reached the foamy edge.

Then Riley nudged Jacinda. "Look," she whispered.

Jacinda looked. Three figures were coming out of the water a little way along. Three tall, buff, masculine figures. She quickly looked away, but out of the corner of her eye, she saw them starting to come nearer, Liam lagging behind.

"Oh, God." She walked faster, splashing through the shallows. "Let's just swim."

But Tina had stopped to watch them coming. "That's him, right?" she stage-whispered. "And he has *friends*."

It was no good—Riley had come to a halt now. With a sigh, Jacinda stopped and waited too.

The men reached them, and they stood in two clusters, boys and girls, two teams of three facing off.

Well, one on each team was determinedly *not* facing off—she and Liam, making sure their eyes didn't meet. But the others were smiling at each other, Connor and Dane surreptitiously taking in the girls in their bikinis, Riley and Tina ever-so-slightly flushed as they looked at the muscular, swim-trunk clad men in front of them. The water rose and fell around their strong thighs, and salty droplets glistened on their tanned skin. Jacinda tried not to look too, but she couldn't deny it—the three of them were ridiculously hot.

"Hi ladies," Connor said, straight into charm mode.

They all knew Riley, from years before, and they exchanged hellos, duly remarking on how long it had been. But Tina was a Sweet Breeze Bay newbie.

"Hey," she said. "I don't think we've met."

Connor grinned. "I'm Connor," he said, putting a hand on his broad chest. "And this is Dane, and Liam."

"Great to meet you." Tina took her time shaking hands, sweeping her gaze over each guy as he had his turn. "What are you guys doing?"

Dane swiped a hand through his dripping hair. "Swimming."

Tina sent him a dimpled smile. "Yeah, I can see that."

Liam had been quiet, but now he cleared his throat. The other two looked at him, and Jacinda could see the silent message he was sending—*let's go.*

Dane turned to the girls. "We'd better keep moving. It was nice to see you."

"It *was*," Tina said.

"See you around," Connor replied.

The women all said goodbye. Liam said nothing, only made a noncommittal sound, and started wading in to shore. Connor and Dane followed.

Jacinda immediately turned and set off into deeper water. The top half of her body had soaked up the heat of the sun, and chills went through her as she edged into the ocean, slightly sideways. Hot and cold...just like Liam.

Tina was inching in beside her, holding her arms high, but still watching over her shoulder as the men headed away up the beach. "Holy hell," she said. "Hot in triplicate. And your Liam is even better close up."

"He's not my Liam. But...yeah. I know."

She knew it all too well, because she'd been way too close.

Sucking in a huge breath, she dived under. Her body reacted with instant, global goose bumps, but she stayed under, letting the shock clear her senses and her head. Why should she be surprised that he wouldn't look at her? Two nights before, she'd been on the verge of going way too far again. Correction, she *had* gone way too far. And when she'd pushed him away, and he'd looked up at her with those dark eyes, his desire had shot through her like an arrow. But desire was its own animal, wild and unthinking, and they didn't have to let it loose. They *shouldn't* let it loose.

Then something brushed against her leg and she freaked out, struggling upward, twisting as she tried to get away. Surfacing, she dragged in a breath and grabbed at her ankle, scrabbling to get rid of whatever it was. And her hand closed on a tangled, leathery length of seaweed, pushing against her on the incoming tide.

Seaweed. Okay. All right. Just seaweed. Wiping

seawater from her face, she made herself breathe more slowly as she paddled to stay at the surface. She focused on the shore, letting the squawking seagulls and warm breeze and laughing beachgoers gradually override the momentary panic.

Then she noticed something. Connor and Dane were gone, but Liam had stopped by the alley and was looking back at her. For a moment they held each other's gaze, across sea and sand. She squinted in the bright sunlight, trying to see more clearly...was that a smile that passed briefly over his face? Then he spun around and disappeared down the alley.

She turned and tossed the seaweed into the air, watching as it settled back down into the water, where it belonged.

This ocean had secrets. And so did they. His careful, unexpected smile lingered in her mind, an offering from the shore to the ocean, where she was working to stay afloat.

Maybe not everything dark and tangled was bad. Maybe, if you brought it into the light, it could look like a different kind of animal after all.

Chapter Twenty-Two

The pixels weren't cooperating.

Liam squinted at the screen, then pressed his hand to his eyes. Forget the website, he was brutally pixelated himself today. Last night's session with Dane and Connor had snuck into the wee small hours. They'd come back from the beach, ordered pizza, and hung out, just talking and drinking, still making up for all the years apart. A light summer rain had started falling when the sun went down, so they'd shifted inside and got dangerously comfortable in the living room. They avoided the topics that had caused them trouble last time, and smashed through who knew how many beers, and the best part of a bottle of tequila. It had been a great night. And now...he was feeling downright shady. He hadn't blown through this much alcohol in a week for years—maybe it was lucky they were only visiting.

He leaned back in the chair and blew out a slow breath, trying not to aggravate the dull ache that sat deep between his temples. The clock in the top corner of his screen showed the time: ten fifteen. Jesus, why was he even up? Almost without realizing it, he'd started keeping more conventional hours over the last few days. Something about the sea air, maybe, more fresh and clear than the Australian atmosphere ever was. Or maybe, despite trying to keep his head down, he'd been forced into it by the interruptions to his routine. His non-routine, that is.

The universe must have been listening in, because right then, the doorbell rang. He rolled his eyes as usual at the musical extravaganza, but it was accompanied by a hit of nostalgia. His mother had always loved this house, and it was full of little touches she'd added over the years. It had been weird spending time here without her—he kept expecting to hear her singing in the kitchen, or find her working in the garden, wearing one of her battered floppy hats. His father had always put in long hours at work as a career cop, eventually climbing in the ranks to district commander, and the garden was her distraction and her joy. But once they left New Zealand, after Ethan died, she never gardened again. Liam knew it wasn't just because of the Australian snakes and spiders.

He closed the HTML tag (not strictly necessary for that one, but the neatness satisfied him), saved his progress, and went to the front door. When he opened it, he found Sam, smiling on the doorstep with a tall, slender woman. Her eyes were the same wide blue as Sam's, and they had matching freckles.

"Hi, I'm Danielle," she said. "Sam's mother."

"Oh, hi." He scratched his head, dragging his brain up out of the hangover swamp he'd been immersed in. Then he remembered his manners, and held out his hand.

"I'm Liam."

She shook firmly, and smiled. "Yeah, I heard."

"Oh, right. Hi Sam," he added.

The kid grinned. "Hi."

"I'm sorry to bother you," she said. "But Sam told us he'd visited with you, so I wanted to introduce myself."

He nodded. "It's nice to meet you."

Should he invite them in? He hesitated, thinking of the client in London who'd be waking up in a few hours, expecting to have a first look at his new website. It needed to be finished, hangover or not. Luckily, his hesitation seemed to be enough of a hint.

"We won't keep you," she said. "But we did have

something to ask. A favor."

"Okaaay…" He knew he should try to sound more encouraging, but agreeing to a favor in advance wasn't going to happen.

"It's…" She stopped, then tried again. "Sam is so keen to play guitar. Would you be willing to teach him?"

He frowned. He'd let Sam play the guitar that first time because he felt sorry for him. Then yesterday, there was no way to *not* let him—he'd turned up on the deck in the morning, bright-eyed and expectant, his face lit up like it was Christmas. But lessons? He hadn't bargained on that development. And getting more involved with Jacinda's family didn't seem like a good idea. He remembered how he'd had to stop on the sand yesterday afternoon, for just one more look, and even though he tried to fight it, the sight of her in the water had made him smile in appreciation. With her hair slicked back and the salty water glistening on her skin, she looked incredible. But there was nothing encouraging about the way she'd frowned back at him.

"Please?" Sam said, jolting him out of his thoughts.

He looked at Danielle and shook his head. "I don't really play these days, so…"

"I'd pay you, of course," she said quickly. "I wouldn't ask you to give up your time for nothing."

Sam was pressing his lips together, obviously trying not to say anything, but his fingers on both hands were tightly crossed.

"We're new here, as you know, so Sam doesn't have any friends yet," she added, putting her hand on Sam's head and smoothing his wayward hair. Her nails were bitten short. "His dad and I are separated, so…" Her voice tailed off.

Ah, shit. How could he argue with that? He sighed.

"I don't want you to pay me."

Sam's eyes widened. "So you'll teach me?"

"Okay. Sure."

"Can we have a lesson now?" Sam asked. "Please?"

They were both looking at him so damn hopefully. His head ached.

"Yeah, okay."

"That's fantastic!" Danielle said. "I'll leave you to it. Just send him back when you're done. And thank you." Above Sam's head, she sent him a look of such gratitude that he felt like a complete shit for even thinking about trying to get out of it.

"No worries."

"I'll see myself out," she told them. "Have fun!"

Sam was already taking Ethan's guitar from the stand again, and getting settled on a chair. The instrument was almost as big as him, but he wrestled it into position. Then he looked up, and the pure joy in his face tweaked something in Liam's heart.

Maybe that client could wait after all.

★

Jacinda looked up from her spot on the floor, surrounded by kittens, as Danielle came into the living room. "Where's Sam?" she asked, closing her laptop.

"I left him there playing guitar with Liam. He's going to give him some lessons. How nice is that?"

"Very nice." And surprising. From what she could tell, Ethan's guitar never left its stand, and Liam wouldn't play anything himself. But Sam had walked in and shaken things up, just like that. Interesting.

Danielle sat down in the wingback chair, and reached down to tickle a wandering kitten. "I know Tina said he was hot, but wow."

"Oh, well...yeah." She shrugged.

"No, seriously though." Danielle fanned herself. "He's *gorgeous*."

Jacinda nodded. "Everyone thinks so."

"He's single, right?"

"Yup. Single." She stroked one of the girl kittens.

"Huh." Danielle's grin was wicked. "Interesting."

Jacinda forced herself to smile. That stirring pang of jealousy in her chest had no right to be there. Danielle had been through a miserable time. If she wanted to find love again, good luck to her. There was no reason she and Liam shouldn't be perfect together. No reason at all.

The smile made her face hurt.

Then her phone rang from the table, making her jump.

"I'll go make coffee," Danielle said, getting up. "Want one?"

"Yes, please."

Something stronger would be even better. But she grabbed her phone, and smiled for real when she saw the name on the screen: Hannah.

"Hey, you."

"Hey! How are you doing?" Her friend's voice was an anchor on the line, a sweet reminder that even in a storm-tossed world, she always had something to hold on to.

"I'm okay."

"How are you feeling about everything? Is it okay with Liam now?"

Last time they talked, Jacinda remembered, she'd only just found out about Ethan. But that was before the recklessly sexy stuff that had complicated things even more. "Uh...it's a bit up and down, I guess. But I'm not seeing much of him now."

She didn't add that she'd previously seen a *lot* of him. Like, most of him, from up very close. And she'd liked it, way too much. She closed her eyes, remembering his hard body under her hands, the gravel in his voice when he said he wanted her, the unbearable bliss of feeling him slide inside her. Then she shook her head. Why was she so weak when it came to him, the one person who should be completely off limits, when she was so strong in other ways? Maybe it was the change from regular lanky teenager to full-grown hotness that had thrown her. Like they'd each just stepped out of the room, and stepped back in to see each other transformed.

And his transformation had been spectacular.

Now Hannah's voice interrupted her thoughts. "That's probably for the best. And the kittens, and your cousins?"

She forced herself to focus. "All good. It's really nice to

spend time with Danielle and Sam. And we have four kittens—three girls and a boy, two black, one tabby, and one mix-up. Sam named the boy Titan, but he couldn't think of anything for the girls. So we went with the textile theme, like Velvet, and called them Suede, Taffeta and Paisley."

"Naw, cute. You have to send a photo." Then she hesitated. "So...Todd's going nuts wanting to know where you are."

"Ugh, sorry. Did you tell him?"

"No. I promised I wouldn't. But he's heard from Greg about the tour. He has a proposal for you."

"Really? Wow, after the last time I saw him, I thought..."

"Yeah, me too." Hannah laughed. "You're lucky Todd's a fast talker."

She snorted. "He is that."

"So you're looking at an eighteen-city tour, including two stops in Canada."

"Really? That's more than I expected."

Hannah paused. "There's just one thing..."

"What?"

"It's...you'd actually be the support act."

"Oh." Well, she was surprised to have any kind of tour at all, after the incident with Greg. Playing support might be okay, if it was for someone good. "Who for?"

Hannah cleared her throat. "Eli Tyler."

Her mouth fell open. Well played, Greg, you cunning bastard. "Great," she said. "That's payback for you."

"Cin, I know it's not ideal. But maybe you should do it. It's still a good opportunity. Eli is really huge now, and if he's willing to have you..."

"If he's willing to have me? You're joking, right?"

"But what's the alternative? Are you going to throw everything away? You've worked too hard for that."

"Greg and Eli. Those two stand for every freaking thing I hate about this business. You know that."

"Eli's not that bad—"

"Hannah, stop. You *know* how that went down. I'm not

going to be his backup act. Todd will have to figure something else out."

She sighed. "Well, maybe you should tell him. I'm not exactly in the mood to talk to him myself."

A red flag went up in Jacinda's mind. "Why, what's going on?"

"It's nothing. I'm just sick of being a music biz widow, you know. Even when he's in LA, he's hardly around."

"Is he there now?"

"I thought so. But he went to a gig last night, and I fell asleep before he got home. When I woke up, he'd sent a message to say he'd decided to drive straight out to Palm Springs afterward. Apparently he had some meetings there this morning."

Jacinda checked the time. It would be mid-afternoon in California. "That stinks. Has he been in touch today?"

"Yeah, to say he'll probably be back tomorrow. At least I know he's not dead in a ditch somewhere, I guess."

Hearing the sadness in her words, Jacinda felt like killing him herself. "I'm sorry, hon. He's lucky to have you, he should be treating you better."

"It's okay," she said, obviously forcing optimism into her voice. "He's trying to build something here. It'll be worth it for all of us in the end."

"You're right," Jacinda said, but she wasn't convinced either.

"So promise me you'll think about the tour, okay? Even though that was a shitty thing Eli did. I know you really liked him—"

She made a dismissive sound. "I didn't."

Hannah's voice was soft. "I know you did. But now he's seriously big league, and you might as well use *him* this time around." She paused to let her point sink in. "Just think about it."

As usual, she was making sense. "How did you get to be so right all the time? It's so goddamn annoying."

"You love me for it. Does that mean you'll think about it?"

"No. It means I'll think about thinking about it."

Hannah laughed. "That's good enough."

"Now go do something fun. And kick that man's ass for me when he gets home."

"With pleasure," she replied, with enthusiasm.

It was good to hear her sounding a little less despondent as they ended the call. Jacinda sat for a moment, watching the kittens clamber over each other in their bed, then went to get the coffee Danielle had left for her in the kitchen. How would it look if she played support for Eli? When it happened, their breakup had been all over the news in the US. But only those on the inside knew the truth—as soon as Eli's management gave the word, he'd traded up to a leggy starlet six years her junior. Only Hannah knew how much she'd liked him, and how stunned she'd been to discover his pretense. Apparently he was as good at acting as he was at singing.

Meh. She didn't believe in love stories anyway.

She stirred sugar into the coffee, sweet for bitter, and took a sip.

She'd think about it.

Chapter Twenty-Three

D anielle stood in front of the hallway mirror and turned from side to side, frowning. Her curly hair was smoothed into a ponytail, and in her well-tailored gray suit—brand new, she said—Jacinda thought she looked exactly like the capable PA the advertising agency had described in their ad.

"You look great," Jacinda said. "They'd be lucky to have you."

She tugged down her jacket and breathed out. "Thanks. New starts, right?"

"Exactly."

"Ugh." She stuck out her tongue. "I feel sick."

Jacinda laughed. "Go. You'll slay them. Plus you look totally hot in that little suit."

She stood a bit taller in her heels. "I wasn't aiming for hot, but actually, that helps."

"Mum, you're hot," Sam said, giggling.

She poked him in the ribs. "Okay, that's inappropriate, but thank you." Then she turned to Jacinda. "Let me know if you have any problems. My phone will be on vibrate."

"We'll be fine. Good luck!"

They waved her off from the top of the steps, then went back inside. Immediately, Sam turned to her.

"Jacinda," he said. "Let's go over to Liam's place."

She frowned. "Your mom didn't mention going over. The only plan I heard was to go to the markets tonight. And didn't you already have your lesson this morning?"

He shuffled his feet. "Yes. But he doesn't mind! And I want to show you the song he taught me."

"Me? Oh no, I don't think so."

"Please?" he said, all puppy eyes and tippy-toed enthusiasm. "You don't have your guitar here. And I'm already really good at this song. Like, really, *really* good."

Oh, hell. That face. She was in no hurry to see Liam again, but how could she resist? "All right. But if he's busy, we're not staying."

"Okay."

Before the second syllable, he was heading out the French doors to the back yard, aiming for the hedge. But she called him back.

"I'm too big to go through there now."

"Oh, yeah," he said. "I forgot. We'll have to go the long way."

She smiled at him. "Yeah. It sucks being a grown-up sometimes."

If they were small enough, maybe she and Liam could have solved their current problems over cookies and juice boxes in the leafy hedge. But those days were long gone.

Sam led the way through the Wards' front gate and along the side of the house, bypassing the front door. She involuntarily tugged down her skirt as they went past the small access door where she'd gotten stuck that day. Then they went up onto the deck, Jacinda trailing behind just a little. The doors were open, but there was no sign of Liam.

Sam wasn't deterred. "Liam! *Li*-am!" he yelled, loud enough to send birds fluttering from the trees nearby. "We're *here*!"

"Did you tell him I was coming?" Jacinda whispered.

He shrugged as they went inside, uninvited. "No."

Before she could answer, Liam appeared from the kitchen. When he saw her he tensed for a moment, but then he grinned at Sam.

"Hey, buddy."

Sam glowed. "Liam, this is Jacinda. Remember I said she plays guitar too?"

"Yeah, I remember." He held out a hand, playing along. "Hi, Jacinda."

"Hi, Liam."

His hand enfolded hers, and she matched his grip as Sam looked on, beaming. Nothing to see here. Everything just fine. As they shook hands, she tried not to think about the last time she was in this room—her panties on the floor, Liam on his knees, her hands in his hair...

She let go of his hand.

"Can I play the song for her?" Sam asked, blessedly oblivious.

"Oh." Liam glanced at her, then away. "We haven't had many lessons. Don't you want to practice a bit more before you play it for someone else?"

"No. I'm ready now."

The way he said it, there was no way a reasonable person could argue. She waited to see if Liam was feeling reasonable today.

Finally, he nodded. "Okay, then. Sure. Go for it."

He went to sit down, rubbing the back of his neck. Jacinda looked away as his bicep flexed, the intricate tattoo accentuating the rising muscle. Damn it, computer geeks were supposed to be scrawny. He was totally cheating. She found a seat—not next to Liam—and concentrated on Sam.

But when Sam took Ethan's guitar from its stand and plugged in the lead, she glanced across at Liam. She was still amazed that he was letting someone play it. Mind you, she was learning that Sam on a mission was an unstoppable force—obviously Liam was no match for his determination either.

"Let's check the tuning first," Liam said, and Sam passed him the guitar.

As he tested each string, Sam tipped his head to the side, listening carefully. "It's fine, I think?"

Liam nodded. "Yeah, sounds good to me too. It's all yours."

He passed the guitar back to Sam, who got himself

organized on the chair, sitting the instrument on his lap just so.

"What about you?" he said to Liam. "I can't play it by myself."

For a moment, Liam hesitated, and Jacinda thought maybe he'd refuse. But then he stood up. "Okay, I'll just get the other guitar. Hang on."

"He plays the tune, and I play the chords," Sam explained for Jacinda while they waited for him to come back. "We're a *duo*."

She smiled. "That's cool."

"Yeah."

He adjusted his position in the big chair, then put his fingers back on the strings ex-act-ly where they'd been before. Her heart ached at his earnest sweetness, his innocent enthusiasm for the music, and his pleasure in being 'cool'. If only it could last.

Then Liam came back in, carrying an old acoustic guitar. She remembered when he was sweet and innocent too. How things change.

He sat down in the chair next to Sam's. "Okay, ready?"

Sam sat up even straighter. "Ready."

Then they started to play.

Sam strummed carefully, his tongue sticking out as he concentrated. Liam played the melody and sang, patiently matching Sam's uneven rhythm. And her heart practically stopped in her chest as the sweetly melancholy tune and heartfelt words she'd labored over years before filled the room.

> *The hourglass turned at our start*
> *And I keep running but my heart*
> *Won't let me stay ahead of you…*

Hourglass Reverb. Her song.

As he sang, Liam stayed focused on Sam, encouraging him through a tricky chord change, nodding when he strummed in time. And she tried to keep watching Sam too, but her eyes kept returning to Liam. The lyrics fell from his lips without hesitation, and the slight rasp in his voice gave the words a gritty, aching edge, sexier than her version. His long fingers effortlessly picked out the notes, and he even threw in some improvisations of his own. He'd played this song before, enough times to be not just proficient, but expert. And now he was letting her see, knowing that she'd know it. He'd sat over here by himself and played her song—repeated the notes until they were perfect, sung her words over and again in that gravelly voice...

When they finished, she was silent for a few seconds.

Then she smiled at Sam.

"That was awesome. I mean really, seriously good. You're going to be an amazing guitarist."

"Do you know that song?" Sam asked her, mischief in his grin.

She played along. "Well, it *is* kind of familiar..."

"It's yours!"

He cracked up, the whole thing hilarious, and she had to laugh too.

"That was a *total* surprise," she told him. "I loved it."

"Thanks! I want to show Mum next."

"You should. She'd be really impressed."

He nodded, and went back to strumming, working on the tricky chord change that had tripped him up during the song.

Finally, she looked at Liam. "You made it sound pretty great."

He shrugged, messing with the tuning pegs on his guitar. "Thanks."

"Interesting choice," she added.

His deep blue eyes were on her now. "I know the girl who wrote it."

"Oh, okay." Her pulse kicked up a notch. "Is she a friend, or...?"

"I don't know," he said, holding her gaze.

She ran with it. "Hmm. What does she think about you?"

"I don't know," he repeated, with the smallest lift of an eyebrow.

That was her cue—the moment to suggest what this girl

might be thinking, or feeling, about him. She considered him from across the coffee table. She knew what she *thought* about him. He was smart, and kind (as evidence, Sam played on, only slightly mangling her song). He had a dirty-sexy singing voice. His habit of showing up shirtless was more than justified by the body it revealed, his tattoos were ridiculously hot, and even in a whiskey-laced hurry he was good in bed. And other places. She felt her cheeks heat at the memory. All of that was straightforward, unarguable fact. But how she *felt* about him? That, she didn't know.

And anyway, she wasn't allowed to feel anything about him. They might have been thrown together again *this* summer, but that other summer overrode everything else. Sometimes the past shouldn't be left behind.

So she said nothing.

He took a breath, as though he was about to say something himself, and she waited.

But then Sam played a wonky chord, and let rip with a curse. "Bloody hell!"

They both looked over as he flung his head back and groaned in dramatic frustration.

"Sam!" She tried not to laugh, and Liam stifled a chuckle.

Sam went pink. "Sorry. Everyone swears on the farm."

She smiled. "Well, you can play like a rock star, but if you start talking like one too we'll be in major trouble."

Liam leaned on his guitar, and looked at her. "And I'm in enough trouble already," he said quietly.

For the briefest moment, they looked at each other, and the current that ran between them jolted her senses into overdrive. But enough had to be enough. She was done with all the backward and forward. With Sam on the scene, she'd probably be seeing more of Liam until she left, but there'd be no more blurred lines. He might like the idea of fooling around—she did too, God help her—but she knew where the bottom line was. It was where Ethan's ghost stood. Liam had made that much clear himself.

"So I'm going to be around a while longer," she said. "Danielle needs me to help look after Sam."

"Yeah, I heard," he said.

She tipped her head toward Sam, who was laboring over the song again, chewing his bottom lip as he concentrated. "You have a fan there."

"Oh, I don't know." He shrugged, but she could see the thought pleased him.

"So maybe we can make it okay? For him?"

He nodded. "For him. Sure."

"Good."

She turned to Sam, and clapped as he finished up with a totally rock star windmill arm, and a shout of *Oh yeah*. Then he stood up and bowed, and Liam joined in the applause.

She laughed. "Woo-hoo! Nice!"

They'd make it okay for him.

Being okay for themselves was a whole other thing.

Chapter Twenty-Four

Well, it was official. He'd been shutting himself away too much.

As they hit Fife Street and merged with the night market crowd, Liam felt a cloud of discomfort settle over him. Connor and Dane had talked him into coming, with promises of great street food and good music. Everyone would be there, they'd said. *Everyone.*

That should have been enough to make him stay home.

But he didn't.

As they walked past stands selling handcrafts and fresh vegetables and homemade pickles, he was aware of people noticing him—the long-lost, last remaining Ward brother, home at last. Shit. He was tempted to turn around and walk straight back home again, to escape the curious glances and whispered comments. But Connor and Dane had a spring in their step, saying hi and waving to old friends and acquaintances, trading the occasional smart quip. They'd both been able to fit right back into the bay, as though they'd never been away.

Connor noticed that he'd fallen behind. "Come on, man," he said. "Keep up."

"I am," he muttered. But he picked up his pace.

They found Connor's little sister Penny, talking to Riley Dawson by a stall selling honey products.

"Hi, Liam," Penny said. "Haven't seen you in *forever*."

"Yeah..." He didn't know what else to say. Instead, he looked at the pots of lotions and creams on the stand. What the hell was royal jelly, anyway?

But she persevered. "How *are* you?"

Her tone expressed unspoken sympathy for his loss, and an acknowledgement of his years of absence. But he wasn't about to go there.

"Fine, thanks," he said casually, and looked away again, hoping that would satisfy her. The weight behind her question made small talk seem extra small. But then he noticed that everyone was looking at him, waiting. He cleared his throat. "How are *you*?" he added belatedly.

But he didn't hear her answer, because at that moment, Jacinda arrived, her cheeks pink and her hair tousled. All the air caught in his chest. *Don't stare.* But she was so freaking beautiful. He'd only seen her that morning, when she came over with Sam, but the shock of her beauty caught him off guard all over again. Her eyes were bright, her tan had evened out, and the little red sundress she'd changed into emphasized all the glory of her curves. These southern latitudes seemed to suit her.

"Sorry I'm late," she said breathlessly to Riley, hitching her bag on her shoulder. "My friend Hannah called while I was getting ready." Then she noticed him, and her face changed. "Oh."

"Hi," he said. And now he was glad he'd come...even if she wasn't.

"Hi," she replied. Then she seemed to remember that everyone was there, and added a polite smile.

"I thought you'd forgotten!" Riley said to her.

He wondered if Riley knew what had happened between them. Didn't women tell their friends everything? He glanced at Riley, but she was giving nothing away. Maybe she and Jacinda weren't at that stage yet.

"No, Hannah just needed to talk." She pressed a hand to her stomach and looked in the direction of the food trucks parked down the street. "I'm starving."

Riley nodded. "Me too. But I want to show you Tina's

stand first, with her jewelry, then we can eat." She waved around at the group. "See you guys later."

"I'll come too," Penny said. She poked Connor in the ribs. "Bye, Poophead."

He messed up her hair. "Bye, Stinkface."

Listening to the old nicknames, Liam was instantly a teenager again. Apparently some things would always be the same in Sweet Breeze Bay. He tried not to watch the women go, but one glimpse of Jacinda's hips swinging in the red dress as she walked away, and he was captivated. The teenage him threatened to rise up again, horny and inappropriate. He swung around before she turned and caught him looking.

"Come on, Poophead," he said to Connor. "I'll buy you a beer."

"I'll buy *you* a beer if you swear never to call me that again," he replied.

Dane laughed. "I'll buy you both a beer. Go find us a seat."

In the tree-lined park between Tony and Marie's and the corner store, a stage had been set up at the far end. It seemed to be an open mike event, with performers coming and going, their music spilling from the park into the street, threading between the stalls and floating into the fading evening sky. They found seats at one of the picnic tables under the trees. Liam sat with his back to the street, where the table was partly hidden behind a tree trunk, cutting himself off from any curious passers-by. He breathed with relief. That was better.

Soon Dane came back with the beer. "It's five o'clock somewhere," he said, plunking the tall plastic glasses down on the table. "And that place is here."

As they drank and talked, shooting the warm evening breeze, they listened to the performances on the stage. Some were good, and some decidedly average. When a deeply serious man got up, sporting a complicated beard, and announced he was a slam poet, Connor snorted.

"That's my cue. I'll get the next round." He extricated his long legs from under the table, and strode off to find more beer.

As the evening set in, the fairy lights grew brighter in the trees, and the stage lit up too. From his spot behind the tree, Liam tried not to keep looking back to the street, checking for Jacinda. Catching himself for the umpteenth time, he forced his attention back to whatever they were talking about. It turned out to be Dane's close call with the bends on his last diving assignment.

"There are two parts to it," he was saying. "Decompression sickness and arterial gas embolism."

Connor shook his head. "That's serious shit."

"Is that the same as astronauts?" Liam asked. "I read that they get something similar."

Then he felt a tap on his arm, and looked to see Sam standing next to him.

"Oh, hey Sam. How's it going?"

He grinned. "Good."

"These are my friends Dane and Connor."

"Are you guys talking about *astronauts*?" His eyes were wide, as though he couldn't believe adults would talk about something so awesome.

"Amongst other things," Dane said. "Good to meet you, Sam."

There were firm handshakes all round. Then Sam bit his lip, and looked at Liam. Something was obviously coming. He gulped in a breath, his freckled face anxious.

"Liam...can we play our song on stage?"

Liam blinked. "No. Not tonight." He'd had enough surreptitious attention, heard enough whispered comments, endured enough loaded questions about how he was. He wasn't going to get up on stage in front of everyone, like a sideshow from the past.

Sam bounced on his toes. "Please, though? Look, there are guitars up there already. We just have to play."

"Sorry, Sam, I'm not up for it." He hated himself for refusing, but there was no way he'd draw even more attention to himself. He felt Dane and Connor looking at him, but knew they'd understand. Hoped they would.

Sam put his hands together like he was praying, his face

still hopeful. "Pleeeease?"

Jesus, this was torture. But before he could reply, Danielle was there, putting an arm around Sam.

"Come on bud, tonight's not the night. Another time."

She tried to turn him away, but he wouldn't be placated. His eyes started to brim, and his face was red with longing and frustration as he looked at Liam. "But it would be so cool!" he said, trying one last time.

Then Liam heard Jacinda's voice behind them. "I'll play with you, Sam."

They all turned to where she was standing.

"I didn't know you were there," Liam said.

"I know," she replied. "Come on Sam, let's do it."

"Oh, *yeah*," Sam exclaimed, pumping a fist in victory. Then something occurred to him. "Can you remember the notes?"

Liam could see her stifle a smile. "I can. But remember..." She lowered her voice. "I'm undercover. Don't give me away, okay? Tonight I'm just your band member."

Sam nodded, and gave an exaggerated wink. "Got it."

"Thank you," Danielle said to her, over the top of Sam's head, and Liam could hear the gratitude in her voice. Jacinda just nodded, and both women glanced at him before they walked away, Sam dashing ahead to the stage. He took a slug of his drink. Well, it was what it was. He'd promised nothing more than a few guitar lessons.

And to make it okay for Sam.

He rubbed the back of his neck. Damn.

Then again, they'd *both* promised that. So it was only fair that Jacinda should take a turn on this one. For all his secret practicing of her song, she'd do a better job singing it than he would, anyway.

"We'd better watch this one," Dane said.

So they left their drinks on the table, and went closer to get a better view. Standing on the grass, Liam watched as Danielle gave Sam a good luck kiss, then he and Jacinda went up onto the stage together. Probably no one would realize it was her. And if they did, well...how long had she

172

expected to stay incognito, anyway? New Zealand might be the end of the earth—literally—but the country wasn't completely cut off from everything. She wasn't well known here, like she seemed to be in the States, but that one song had been popular. So even if he kept her identity quiet, and Dane and Connor did too, and whoever else knew, someone would figure it out soon enough. Maybe Riley knew already, in which case it would probably be common knowledge before long. He shook off the tension that had crept across his shoulders. She knew what she was doing.

On stage, Sam got settled on a stool, his skinny legs dangling. Jacinda swiftly shortened the guitar strap to the right length and settled the guitar around Sam's body, then adjusted the mike stand in front of him. When everything was just so, she said something to him, and he nodded. Then she winked at him, and he winked back, before she took her place on a stool alongside but slightly behind him, giving him the spotlight. He beamed out to the audience, not looking even slightly nervous.

Jacinda didn't seem nervous either. But she turned slightly to the side, toward Sam, and let her dark hair fall across her face. Then she counted him in, and they began. The first notes of Hourglass Reverb lifted into the night air.

Even though she was singing extra slowly, to match Sam's pace on the guitar, the song was unmistakable. And there was no doubting her voice—that sweet, clear tone with an edge of something darker, catching occasionally in a way that also caught at the listener's heart. As she sang, the market-goers became increasingly focused on the stage, and Liam noticed more and more people drawing closer, until he was standing in a crowd.

"Wow, she's good," someone said, in an American accent.

He tore his attention from the stage to see who had spoken. A woman with striking green eyes and dark hair was standing next to him.

"Really good," she added, speaking directly to him this time.

"She is," he agreed. Then he returned his gaze to the

two figures under the stage lights. One in particular. The raw purity of Jacinda's voice was rolling through him, working its magic, churning up memories and feelings better left tamped down.

The woman laughed. "Weird to come all this way and see an American up on stage."

Did she have to talk through the whole thing? He kept his eyes on Jacinda. "Yeah, it must be."

"Does she play here often?"

He grit his teeth. "I don't know. I live in Australia."

"Oh. Okay."

She turned away, and for a moment he wondered if he'd offended her. He looked at her profile, noticing the small diamond stud in her nose, but couldn't read anything in the expression on her delicate features.

Then he noticed something else. Was that recognition on the faces of the people around him, as they listened to Jacinda sing? There were whispers and pointing, and here and there, a phone held up to take a photo. The tightness gripped his shoulders again. Had she blown her own cover?

"That kid is the *cutest*," the American woman said, holding up her phone too.

Sam was grinning out at the audience, clearly relishing the moment. Every now and then, enthusiasm got in the way of accuracy, but he recovered and found his chord again. Not once did the glow leave his face.

"He should have his own show," she added, reaching a little higher with the phone.

"He probably will, one day," Liam replied. "He's determined enough."

She turned to him, still holding her phone up. "Oops, sorry." She lowered it again, then smiled. "Yeah, I'd watch him on TV."

He nodded. Maybe all the enthusiasm was for Sam, showman of the night, and the secret of Jacinda's other identity was safe for now.

When the song finished, she stayed seated, but Sam leapt awkwardly down from the stool. With the guitar almost as big as him getting in the way, he treated the audience to a series of extravagant bows and waves. And they loved it, cheering and clapping. He was a hit.

Liam clapped along with everyone else, but his eyes were fixed on Jacinda. She was smiling quietly, staying in the background. Then she put her guitar on the stand and snuck offstage, giving Sam his moment.

"I had no idea she could sing like that!"

This time, the accent was not American, but New Zealand. Liam looked to his side, and instead of the American woman, it was Riley standing next to him, looking incredulous.

"She's amazing! She sounded just like the song." She shook her head. "She said she had a boring job with a record company, but they should totally sign her."

He nodded, giving nothing away. "They should."

So Riley didn't know Jacinda's big secret. And if she hadn't guessed, even after seeing that performance, maybe no one else had either. Which would mean he was off the hook...in one respect, anyway.

Chapter Twenty-Five

A summer Saturday. A perfect beach. Warm sun. Wide blue sky. Sea breeze. And yet there was hardly anyone there. Jacinda looked up and down the golden curve of sand. Sun umbrellas were dotted here and there, and there was a scattering of people walking and swimming. Where else in the world could you be minutes from a big city, and still have this much of paradise to yourself?

She propped herself on her elbows and watched as Sam worked busily on the sand, creating roads and castles and a row of feather and twig palm trees.

The roads and celebrity castles and palms of LA seemed a million miles away, rather than six or seven thousand. When Hannah had called the night before, asking if she'd made a decision about playing support for Tyler, it had been a shock to realize that the world was still out there, waiting for her to rejoin it.

"You said you'd think about it," Hannah had reminded her.

"I said I'd *think* about thinking about it."

Hannah snorted. "Okay, so have you thought about thinking about it?"

The truth was, she hadn't really. Because from the moment Hannah told her about the offer, she knew she didn't want to do it. And wasn't that what this trip was all about? Like she'd said to Sam, there were too many people wanting her to do stuff that didn't make her happy. At this point, she didn't care if it seemed selfish—she wanted to play by her own rules. And despite the problem of the boy next door, the longer she was here, the less inclined she felt to return to her old life.

Now Sam set off down to the water to fill his bucket again, and she turned to Danielle.

"This is really nice."

"It is. We weren't anywhere near a beach on the farm, so Sam's loving it."

"Did he meet any kids last night at the markets?"

"Some." Then she laughed. "Anyway, I think pretty much everyone knows who he is now."

Jacinda nodded. "He was so fearless. It was amazing."

"I know. I should be more like him. I'm all in knots waiting to hear about this job."

"Did they say when they'd let you know?"

"Middle of the week." She grimaced. "I really want it, you know? But I have to keep applying for other things too."

The tension on her face was obvious, even behind her sunglasses, and Jacinda remembered what was at stake. A fresh start for her and Sam, building something new, far from family and friends. Moving on from her marriage. And proving something to herself, too.

"They'd be idiots not to hire you. But if they *are* idiots, you don't want to work for them anyway. The right job is out there somewhere."

Danielle bit her lip. "I guess."

"Try to relax and enjoy the weekend."

"I am relaxing." She gave a forced, toothy grin.

"*Relax*. Or else."

Danielle laughed. "Yes ma'am." She lay back on her beach towel and pulled her hat over her face.

Then Sam came barreling toward them, water sloshing from the bucket. He dropped it by his building site and came over.

"Mum, what's the time?" he asked Danielle anxiously.

She sat up, pushing the hat back. "Ugh, I don't know. Why?"

"I just…want to know."

"Just a sec." She dug in her beach bag to find her phone, then lifted her sunglasses to peer at the screen. "Twenty-five past ten."

He nodded. "Okay."

"Why?" she asked, but he was jigging on the spot.

"I need to pee."

She groaned. "Seriously? You just went before we left the house."

He looked over his shoulder, toward the alley. "Maybe I drank too much juice at breakfast."

"I'll take him back to the house," Jacinda said, getting up before Danielle moved. "You're *relaxing*, remember?"

"Okay." She sank back again. "Thanks."

Jacinda pulled her cover-up on over her bikini and took the house key from her beach bag, while Sam waited, jogging and hopping. When she was ready, he shot ahead. But as they turned into the alley, his jiggles suddenly disappeared, and Jacinda watched as he started walking with purpose. Something was up.

"Sam. Did you really need to go?"

He giggled, apparently unbothered by being busted. "Nope."

"Why are we going home then?"

"We're not going home. Liam said he had work to do, but he'd be finished at about half past ten. I want him to come to the beach with us."

Now she wished she'd let Danielle take him after all.

"You asked him already?"

"Yep, last night."

They paused at the gate. "And he said yes?"

"He said maybe." He reached over, scrabbling for the latch. "Come on, let's go get him." He finally got the latch undone and pushed the gate open.

She hesitated.

"*Come* on," he said impatiently, obviously itching to go.

She looked at the eager pup of a boy in front of her.

They'd agreed to make it okay for him. They'd both promised—even if Liam obviously wasn't as committed to it as she was, judging by his refusal to play last night. But she'd stick with her promise—not for Liam's sake, but for Sam's.

"You go get him," she said. "I'll wait here."

"Okay," he said, and took off at a run, bounding up the steps like a mountain goat and disappearing into the house without stopping to knock.

She had to laugh as she stepped back and leaned against the fence. She bet this wasn't how Liam had imagined spending his time back in the bay. Come to think of it, she didn't know what he'd planned to do with his time, other than sit in the house attached to his computer. If the rest of them hadn't turned up and thrown a spanner in the works—Dane, Connor, Sam, and herself too—he'd probably be permanently indoors. By rights, he should be all gangly and pale, like a plant growing in the dark.

But he wasn't. He definitely wasn't.

She jumped as she heard footsteps coming down the steps.

"He's coming!" Sam announced redundantly, as Liam followed behind.

She was glad of the camouflage her sunglasses provided, because she couldn't look away. Just like the night before, when he'd unexpectedly been at the night markets, instead of doing his hermit thing at home. Thank God Riley had whisked her off to look at jewelry, and then to eat, because she'd gone there to hang out with the girls and have fun, not to do battle with her own wayward desires. Now he was wearing board shorts and a dark blue sleeveless t-shirt that revealed the muscular breadth of his shoulders, and the substantial cut of his arms. She found herself tugging down the hem of her cover-up, and cursed inwardly at his effect on her. Maybe that sun stroke had permanently addled her brain. Actually, that might explain her moments of madness. Then she noticed what he *wasn't* wearing.

"Where's your hat?" she asked him. "The sun is brutal here, you know."

He considered her for a moment, and she waited to see how he'd react to having his own words shot back at him. But he just flipped his beach towel over his shoulder.

"Maybe I'm not planning to stay long enough to need one."

They looked at each other, and Jacinda got the distinct feeling he was testing her. But before she could reply, Sam piped up.

"You can stay as long as you want. I want to show you how I do a forward roll in the water."

Liam smiled down at him. "Great. Let's go then."

They walked back to the spot where Danielle was waiting, Sam talking all the while about the need to tuck your chin into your chest, and the exact best position for your arms. Liam listened carefully, nodding and making all the right comments. Jacinda lagged behind slightly, trying to concentrate on the green slopes of Rangitoto rising from the sparkling water in the distance, instead of the man in front of her.

When they got there, Danielle sat up and took off her sunglasses. "Oh, Sam. You can't keep bothering Liam all the time. He has work to do."

Sam stood straighter. "I'm not *bothering* him. He's my friend."

She shook her head. "I'm sure he has better ways to spend his Saturday than going to the beach with us."

"Not really, actually," Liam said, dropping his towel on the sand. "And I was ready for a swim."

"Oh." Danielle said. "Well...okay then."

"Awesome," Sam said. "I'm ready too."

"Right." With one smooth movement, Liam took hold of his shirt at the bottom, lifted it up and over his head, then let it fall by his towel.

Jacinda swallowed. The effect of the shirtlessness didn't seem to diminish, no matter how many times she saw it. And she didn't miss the way Danielle's eyes swept down his body, then back up again, before she looked away. It was exactly what her own eyes had done as he came down the steps. And did again now.

Sam had been looking too, but for a different reason. Now he tugged at his snug-fitting rash shirt. "Mum, do I *have* to wear this?"

"Yes."

Her tone was final, and he sighed, obviously figuring he wouldn't win that fight. "Okay. Let's go, Liam."

They headed down toward the water, Sam looking like a sudden gust might blow him away compared to Liam's strapping height.

"Wow," Danielle said. She looked at Jacinda, a smile playing on her lips. "I suppose he's not *such* bad company. What do you think?"

She was trying her hardest not to think anything at all. "I think he's a big show-off."

"I bet *something's* big," Danielle said in a wicked tone, sticking out her tongue as she watched Liam walk away with Sam.

Jacinda laughed along with her, but the territorial pang that hit her took her by surprise. "Keeping it classy, huh?" she said lightly, ignoring the twist in her stomach. "We must be related."

"Well, I *am* a woman on the rebound. And you know what they say about us..." She grinned. Then her phone rang somewhere in the depths of her bag. "It's probably Mum," she said, reaching in and digging around. "She can't go more than a day without talking to every one of her kids."

Her words sent a wave of guilt through Jacinda. Tomorrow it would be two weeks since she arrived, and she'd only called her mom twice. They usually talked regularly, and somehow, it helped keep Trina on the level. Phone contact seemed to be enough—when they spent too much time together in person, Jacinda couldn't do anything right, and soon Trina would start stressing and fretting and becoming more anxious rather than less. Maybe that was why she'd chosen to live in Florida, far from Jacinda in LA...although she claimed it was because the climate suited her better than any other place in America. Then again, she'd know, given how many places she'd dragged Jacinda to in the years before they sort-of settled in

Pleasanton. And despite it all, during those years they'd gotten closer than a lot of mothers and daughters ever did. Jacinda made a mental note to call her again soon.

Danielle finally pulled out her phone, but it had stopped ringing. "Damn, I missed it," she said. Then she looked at the screen, and emitted a strangled squeak. "It was *them*."

Jacinda craned to look. "Them?"

"The job. The...oh, God. Why are they calling on a Saturday? Is that good? Or bad?"

"Um...good, probably?"

She threw everything into her bag, still clutching the phone, then got to her feet and hauled up her towel, scattering sand over Jacinda. "Sorry, I have to...I have to call them back. Oh, God." She bunched the towel under her arm and looked out to where Sam and Liam were bobbing in the water. "Can you...?"

"Yes, of course. I'll keep an eye on Sam. Go. Stay calm."

"I'm calm. *Very* calm."

As she hurried away in the direction of home, she looked anything but.

Jacinda smiled, then settled in to watch Sam. And if Sam's friend Liam was in close proximity, she supposed she'd have to watch him too...

After a few minutes, she noticed Sam waving to her, beckoning her into the water. She got up and shaded her eyes, trying to see what he was getting at. His waving intensified, so she went down to the water's edge.

"I want to show you my forward roll," he yelled.

"Okay," she yelled back.

He shook his head. "You have to come in!"

Damn. Feeling self-conscious, she took off her cover-up and sunglasses, and tossed them back up on the beach, on the dry sand. Then she waded into the sea, sucking in a breath each time the water hit a new, sensitive part of her body. By the time she reached them, it was too deep to stand. "Why are you so far out?"

"I need more room, otherwise I hit the bottom," Sam said.

"Okay, well, show me then," she said, doing a slow doggy paddle to keep afloat, acutely aware of Liam just a few feet away.

He took a giant breath, and went under. At the exact same moment, the wake from a boat came through, knocking her off-guard and washing salty water into her mouth. As she gasped and coughed, Sam emerged again, grinning like a cartoon fish.

"Did you see me?"

She wiped water from her face. "I'm sorry, Sam. I missed it."

He frowned. "I'll do it again. Make sure you see me this time."

Liam spoke up. "I'll hold you steady."

For a second, she thought he was talking to Sam. Then she realized they were both looking at her.

"Good idea," Sam said. "Tell me when you're ready."

Liam came over. He was so tall that the water only came just over his shoulders, and he picked her up easily, holding her against him so that she had no choice but to put her legs around his hips.

"You could have lifted me up the other way," she told him.

"I know." Something that could have been amusement flickered on his face. "Are you watching Sam or not?"

"Yes," she huffed. "I am."

He turned sideways so she could see. "We're ready," he called to Sam.

She tried not to think about the warmth of his body in the water, his steady strength, and the way her legs were wrapped around him, just like they'd been that one night in her bed...

Sam tucked in his chin, positioned his arms just so, and executed a perfect somersault in the water.

"Did you see?" he asked, tipping his head to get the water out of his ears.

"I did," she called back. "It was amazing."

He was suddenly distracted by something on the beach. "Mum's back," he said. "I'm going to see if she has anything to eat." And he was gone, powering through the shallows and toward his mother in search of food.

"Okay, he's gone," Jacinda said to Liam. She wriggled slightly, signaling that he could release her. "You can let me go now."

"I know," he said again. But he didn't let her go.

"We're finished here," she told him. But she didn't let go either.

His arms were under her bottom, holding her up, and her arms were around his neck. His body was hard and strong between her thighs, and even though her breasts were pressed up against him, he didn't look down. He looked at her. All at once there was just the ocean, and the sky, and the deep, dark blue of his eyes. She was seventeen again, with a boy, at the beach, with a look in his eye.

Except she wasn't. And the boy was a man, and the look in his eye was something more than his brother's lust and mischief. It was a question, and a promise.

"We're finished," she repeated, her voice suddenly unsteady.

He held her gaze, and her heart raced in her chest as he spoke.

"Are we?"

Chapter Twenty-Six

At that moment, a trio of stand-up paddleboarders skimmed past a few feet away, shouting to each other across the water. She twisted in his grasp, and he let her go, then watched as she kicked off and swam for shore. Shit. Why had he even said that?

He set off after her. When she reached the shallows, she stood up, and the water sluiced off her, running down her body, over those delicious curves, and down her legs. The droplets left behind caught and reflected the sunlight, each one a jewel on her golden skin. She ran a hand through her hair, pushing it off her face, and the dark strands fell around her shoulders. As she stopped on the sand and bent to pick up her things, he specifically did not look. Did *not* sneak a glance at a certain part of her anatomy.

Well, only for the briefest moment.

They walked silently up the beach to where they'd left their things. Danielle was there, her face aglow. She passed Jacinda her towel. "Guess what? I got the job!"

Jacinda clapped her hands. "That's awesome, congratulations!"

"I'm so *happy*." She shimmied on the sand. "Seriously, I can't believe it."

"Congratulations," Liam said, blotting himself dry with his own towel.

"When do you start?" Jacinda asked. "Soon?"

"The week after next," Danielle replied. "Which is when Sam starts school. It's perfect."

Listening to them talk, something suddenly occurred to him. If Danielle had a job, and Sam was starting school, they wouldn't need Jacinda's help anymore. And they would both be there to look after the kittens until Nana Mac came back.

Which would mean she had no reason to stay.

No reason at all.

"It *is* perfect," she said to Danielle. "I'm so happy for you."

He glanced at her. She was looking thoughtful. Probably planning her exit already. Well, good. Easier for all of them. He could carry on with his life—wherever he ended up—and she could get back to enjoying the career Ethan never had. It was all good. *All* good.

He scrubbed his hair dry with violent force. Maybe that would shake the stupidity out of his head.

As he lowered the towel again, he couldn't help noticing that both women had their eyes on his body. They both averted their gaze quickly, but it was too late. With a certain sense of satisfaction, he took his time pulling his top back on. His board shorts would drip dry in no time.

As Jacinda dried herself and put her cover-up back on, he looked around for Sam, and saw him farther down the beach talking to a couple of kids. A woman stood with them.

"Did Sam find some friends?" he asked Danielle.

She laughed. "They recognized him from last night at the markets, and came to talk to him. Such a celebrity. They're going to have a play date, and I'll have coffee with their mum." She slipped her feet back into her flip-flops. "Catch you guys later."

She went to join Sam and his new friends, and they all started down the beach.

"Looks like he ditched me," Liam commented, watching them go.

Jacinda put her sunglasses back on. "Yup. You'll have

to play with the grown-ups again."

Automatically, he replied, "That's overrated."

"Really?" she said, and started walking away.

And just like that, all the playing they'd done was suddenly front and center in his mind again. *That* kind of playing was definitely not overrated. He followed after her, catching up within a few strides.

As they headed for the alley, she was silent. What was she thinking? Should he say something about that moment in the ocean? What did *he* think about it, come to that? Lately he'd been blurting out things without thinking...before he even knew he thought them at all.

The silence was doing his head in, so he grabbed onto a safe topic.

"Great about Danielle's job," he said.

She nodded. "Really good."

He glanced sideways, but her eyes were hidden by her sunglasses, and her expression was giving nothing away.

"I guess you'll be going, then?" he asked, not sure what he wanted her answer to be. But...was that a slight trip, a break in her stride as she heard his question?

"Yeah, I guess," she said. "They won't need me anymore, so..."

Okay. Maybe it was just the uneven sand. Not a stumble at the thought of leaving. It was only him who'd tripped up on the idea.

They went down the alley and came to his gate, but she kept walking right past. And all he wanted to do was reach out and stop her. He scrambled for something to say.

"Would you...uh...like a drink?"

She paused, then turned back around. As she looked at him, inscrutable behind her sunglasses, he felt his fist tighten around his towel, and his breath stop in his chest. Why would she want to come in for a drink? They were finished, she'd said in the water, and he knew what she meant. If there'd been a flicker of confusion in her eyes as she looked at him, it was only because he wouldn't let her go, like a total prick.

He was excelling at that lately.

But then she shrugged. "Okay."

"Oh." He wasn't expecting that. "Okay, great."

They went through the gate and up onto the deck. He had no clue what he was doing, only that he wanted her around. He wasn't going to ask himself why. Make conversation, he told himself. Be pleasant. He unlocked the side door and stood back to let her in. "That was really nice what you did for Sam last night."

"Yeah." She kicked off her sandy flip-flops, then stepped inside. As they went into the kitchen, she put her sunglasses on her head and added, "On the other hand, you were a dick."

He flinched. "Well...it turned out okay."

"No thanks to you."

Ouch. That was rugged. He took two tall glasses from the cupboard and set them on the counter, then turned to her.

"I had my reasons."

She made a skeptical sound. "What? To disappoint a little boy?"

"No." He leaned against the counter, noting the hard edge in her eyes. "If you really want to know—and maybe you don't, but I'm going to tell you anyway—it's because I didn't want to be up there in front of everyone. This is the first time I've been back since..." The words wouldn't come, but judging by the look on her face, she knew what he meant. "Since then. And I didn't want to go up and stand in front of everyone, like a goddamn sideshow. It was bad enough fending off their loaded questions and their sympathy one by one."

He paused. Her brows were knit, and she was worrying the edge of her lip. Maybe he was getting his point across. "I think you know about wanting privacy, right?" he added.

"Oh." She looked down. "Right."

"Yeah."

They stood just a few feet apart. The only sound in the room was the slight hum of the fridge.

Then she crinkled her nose. "Sorry."

"Yeah," he said again. But this time, it came out softer.

She looked up at him, the hardness gone from her face. Her hair was drying all wavy, and there was a smudge of sand on her cheek. The front of her translucent cover-up was slightly damp in the two spots over the triangles of her bikini top. She was tousled, salty, and, God help him, completely stunning.

Forcing himself to focus, he picked up the glasses and walked around her to fill them from the water dispenser in the fridge door. Even after being in the ocean, her fragrance lingered around her. The ice clattered into the glasses, jarring in the quiet. Then he filled them with water, and handed one to her. As she took it, their fingers briefly touched, and she avoided his eye.

"Sam did look like he was having the time of his life," he said, as she took a sip.

A smile crossed her face. "He did."

"Born for the stage," he said, putting his glass down. "Like someone else I know."

Satisfaction hit him as he watched her cheeks flush pink.

"Pfft, whatever," she said.

He laughed. "Yeah, whatever. Because that's what grown-ups say."

She shoved his arm. "Shut up."

"You shut up." He reached out with one hand and squeezed her waist, making her squeak and lurch away, giggling, and water sloshed from her glass and slopped onto the floor.

"Oops," she said, looking down.

Without warning or thought, he gathered her up and pulled her close. Her laughter stopped on one sharp intake of breath, and she leaned the top part of her body away. The bottom half, though, remained pressed firmly against him. He took the glass from her hand and put it on the countertop, his eyes never leaving hers.

Suddenly, their pre-teen antics had morphed into something decidedly adult.

Leaning back, she had exposed the soft skin of her décolletage and throat, and it was too much to resist. He lowered his head to her neck and let his lips fall there once, twice, over and over again, describing a random, teasing pattern. When his tongue brushed her throat, there was a salt-tang on her skin, and a tiny hum of pleasure escaped her. He felt the tension melt from her body, her hips arch toward him just a little more. He knew she must be able to feel him hardening against her.

He looked up, checking her reaction.

"Why are you doing this?" she asked, her eyes heavy with something that could only be desire. She didn't move.

"Why are *you?*" he countered, still holding her.

"I don't know. Because you are." She laughed, a short, disbelieving sound, as though she knew her answer made no sense. Then she shook her head. "We were finished with all this."

At that moment, he was sure she'd pull away, probably get mad again, and maybe storm out of his house. Then again, she didn't seem to be the storming type. Her style was more the decisive, quiet exit.

But instead of delivering a rapid rebuke, she deliberately ran one hand up each side of his body, under the cotton of his sleeveless t-shirt, letting her fingers trail slowly across his skin. He held his breath, telling himself not to hurry anything, but when she pressed closer, draping her arms over his shoulders, he felt the familiar tide of lust rush in.

"Bloody hell," he said, touching his forehead against the top of her head. "This is trouble."

She laughed. "You sound kinda fancy when you say bloody hell in that accent."

"That's one thing I'm definitely not," he said, abruptly lifting her up and setting her on the counter. She sat there for a moment, then put her arms around his neck and wrapped her legs around his hips. He took a step back, holding her tightly against him as he stood between the counter and the kitchen table. And then her lips were on his, and her hair was falling around them both, and he staggered slightly, the swell of desire making him unsteady. He stepped forward quickly to balance himself—clearly, dropping her on the floor would be a mood-killer. But just when he was about to breathe in relief, she exclaimed in surprise and arched forward, as ice suddenly burst from the dispenser in the fridge behind her, rattling into the tray and scattering on the floor.

"Oh, my God," she said, laughing. "That gave me a hell of a fright."

"Shit, sorry," he said. He stepped away from the fridge, but immediately stood on an ice cube, and his foot went out from under him. She gasped, clinging onto him, and adrenaline hit as he tried to keep his footing while holding her at the same time. After a moment of complete panic, he managed to regain his balance. Heart pounding, he turned and set her on the table.

She let go of him and released a long breath. "I thought we really *were* in trouble then."

"Yeah." His heart was still thundering in his chest. "Not the sort of trouble I was hoping for. Sorry."

She laughed again. "That was pure slapstick." Then she paused, and tipped her head. "What *kind* of trouble were you hoping for?"

The provocative tone in her voice was unmistakable. He suppressed a grin. "The grown-up kind of trouble."

She pursed her lips, a teasing thoughtfulness coming over her face as she thrummed her fingers on his chest. "Like...being audited?"

"Not quite," he said.

She grasped his shirt and pulled him closer. "Not paying the gas bill?"

"No."

She wound her legs around him, her roaming hands setting his skin on fire everywhere they touched.

"Overdue library books?"

He shook his head. "Not even close." The words came out raspy, and he caught her fleeting, knowing smile. Then she pouted.

"I've run out of ideas. You'll have to give me a hint."

"Okay." He reached under the filmy cover-up she was wearing, and pulled on the strings securing one side of her bikini bottoms, letting them fall away undone. She didn't move, so he repeated the trick on the other side. She sat perfectly still, watching, then looked him in the eye.

"Speeding ticket?"

He would have laughed at her fake cluelessness, but undoing her bikini strings had started to undo him, too. "You're not getting any warmer," he managed.

She wriggled deliberately on the table, her voice breathy as she replied, "Actually, I am."

Looking down, he could see through the fine fabric that the front of her bikini had fallen down between the top of her thighs, where his hands were resting. All at once, electricity seemed to buzz in the tips of his fingers. Without saying a word, she squirmed again, so that his hands shifted higher on her legs, toward the 'v' that hid the sweetest place he'd ever been. He could take a hint too. He slipped one hand between her legs, and she parted them for him. In slow, unhurried movements, he gently, deliberately dipped one finger deeper...then another...letting her wetness slick his fingers, feeling his own body respond as he watched her reaction. It was insanely hot seeing her expression shift from teasing to abandoned, her eyelids heavy and her lips parted, her breath gradually coming faster and shallower. He took his time, playing in deliberate, teasing strokes, and when he finally reached the small, concentrated point of her desire she sucked in her breath, a sudden tension in her body. But it was the good sort of tension. The low, hungry sound she made proved that. He smiled, ready to show her exactly what his kind of trouble was made of.

But before he could take her any further, she took a hold of the front of his board shorts, determinedly working them down just enough to let him free. With a groan of anticipation, she slid forward on the table until he was pressing right against her, on the very verge of sliding into her hot, wet sweetness.

Then he realized—he didn't have any protection nearby. He held her steady, just out of the danger zone. Because with her hard up against him, irresistibly luscious and eager, it definitely was a danger zone.

"We have to stop," he told her.

When he stepped back an inch or two, she moaned, her frustration echoing his own. For a moment he drank in the sight of her there on the table, her hair wild and her cheeks flushed, her legs apart...and there was only one thing to do.

He ran his hands up her legs again, pushing the cover-up out of the way. She glanced at the window, obviously suddenly remembering where they were, so he reached over and adjusted the wooden blinds. "No one can see now."

Finally, he could do what he'd hungered for when she stood before him in the living room that night. He dropped his head between her legs, and she leaned back on the table, breathing out a low sigh of surrender as her sunglasses fell from her hair. Almost in disbelief, he took his chance, immersing himself in her heady essence, losing himself in the woman who had been his dream and his downfall, his teenage crush and now his adult obsession.

Within what seemed like barely a minute, he felt her arch abruptly under his tongue, and she exploded into an orgasm. One 'oh' after another escaped her as her hips lifted off the table, her fingers digging into his shoulders, and he rode her wave, keeping up his pace, burning with his own acute need. Finally, sated, she took hold of his head and pushed it away. Then she struggled upright and grabbed onto him, pulling him close and burying her face in his neck. He held her tightly in return, his breath coming unevenly. Her chest rose and fell in time with his own as she clutched the back of his shirt.

"Oh my God," she said into his ear. There was a wobble in her voice.

He stood up straighter and adjusted his board shorts. "You okay?"

"Yeah. Just...my God." She blew out a breath against his neck, and he could feel her shake her head.

"Come on." He lifted her from the table and lowered her to the floor, then took her hand. "We can do better than this."

He went to kiss her, but she laughed, her cheeks flushed, and ducked away. He swiped one hand over his lips, still damp from her bliss, and tugged gently on her hand with the other. He had no idea if she'd go with him, or turn and walk out, like she had that night in the living room. To stack the odds in his favor, he brazenly picked up her bikini bottoms and put them in his pocket. Then he turned to go, still amazed that any of it had happened.

And she followed.

Chapter Twenty-Seven

L iam's hand was firm around hers as he led her up the stairs. Which was lucky, because her legs were ridiculously weak—probably because she'd gone from zero to sixty in a crazily short time. In his room, she sank gratefully onto the bed, and he shuffled her across, tucking a pillow under her head. Then he grabbed a blanket from the end of the bed, and pulled it up over them. It wasn't cold, but it felt good to snuggle in.

"That was...unexpected," she said.

"Yeah." He studied her face. "Bad unexpected, or good unexpected?"

"Couldn't you tell?"

He laughed, and she felt her cheeks get even hotter.

"Good unexpected, then," he said. "And fast."

"*So* freaking good," she admitted, her voice a little husky.

"I enjoyed it myself," he said, and she could have sworn he looked proud. Typical man. Although he had every right to be pleased with himself, after that. It felt like the entire area between her belly button and her knees was still humming. She forced herself to think straight.

"Except we're not supposed to be doing any of this," she added. "Remember? We're just making it okay for Sam, until I go."

He looked away, hesitating, then back again.

"Right," he said, his tone casual. "But he's not here. So I thought I'd make it okay for you instead." He shrugged. "And it *seemed* like that was okay."

"You can stop fishing for compliments now," she told him.

But he just grinned, and tucked the blanket around her.

She looked around his room, which didn't seem to have changed at all since that summer. Then, with a jolt, it occurred to her that Ethan's room was just down the corridor. Was it still exactly as he left it, too? She shook the thought away. Because nothing was the same as it had been then...not the important stuff, anyway.

She noticed a worn blue notebook on the nightstand next to the bed, and reached for it, curious. But Liam stretched over her and put his hand on it, and lifted it away.

"What's that?" she asked.

"Just...notes," he said. "Nothing really."

She watched as he put it in the nightstand drawer. "Hidden depths, huh?"

"Don't get carried away," he told her dryly, and she laughed.

He turned back to lie close to her again, his head propped on his hand, watching her like he was waiting to see what she'd do next. She had no idea—she didn't even know why she'd agreed to come in for a drink in the first place. Especially when she'd known the drink was just an excuse.

Or maybe she did know why, even if she wouldn't admit it to herself.

And...it hadn't turned out *so* bad.

Because he wasn't just muscle-flexing, guitar-playing, clever-tongued eye candy. Much as she liked all those things—a lot, apparently—he was more than that. She had to acknowledge the way he shouldered life's painful complications, and his need to do the right thing, even as he frustrated the hell out of her. Despite what he'd just said, there was an intriguing depth to him, a loyalty and moral compass that was very obviously doing battle with their mutual desire. She was feeling the same kind of conflict herself—the push and pull of an unexpected, off-limits attraction—but for him, the stakes were even higher. She wished she could read his mind, figure out how he could swing from practically cursing her name, to lavishing her with the hottest kind of attention. And she still didn't know why he was even here, back in the bay, at all.

"So...why did you come back, after all this time?" she asked.

He tangled his fingers in the strands of hair that trailed over her shoulder. "I don't know," he said. "It just felt like everything reached critical mass, you know? I have this friend, Grant...he builds houses, and I help him out a few times a week. Keeps me from seizing up in front of the computer. I go to the gym, too, but manual labor works out the knots better than anything. In your body and your mind."

She nodded, running a finger over the curve of his bicep. "That explains the muscles on a confirmed computer geek."

"Yeah." He smiled. "Anyway, we'd just finished building a house for Grant's brother and his family. And we were all there, having a few drinks to celebrate. And I realized..." He stopped, rubbing the edge of his jaw, where a dark whisker shadow was starting to show.

"What did you realize?"

He cleared his throat. "That everyone was moving on. All around me. Moving forward."

"And you weren't?"

"No. Not really."

She rested her palm on his chest, and he covered it with his hand. Underneath his shirt, she could feel the reverberation of his heartbeat, steady and regular, keeping on.

"So I came back here to...restart," he said.

"Like your computer."

"Yeah." He laughed. "I think some of my coding got messed up."

She frowned. "I'm sorry."

"I'll live." He waved a dismissive hand. "What about you, though? How's your coding?"

That was kind of a complicated question. "I don't know. I think I'm rewriting it at the moment. Trying to decide what the next lines will be."

"When you go home."

He said it matter-of-factly, as though he was totally fine with it. Which was perfectly okay with her. She swallowed, but it didn't lessen the lump in her throat. She crossed her ankles and pressed her thighs together, trying to stifle the lingering heat where his mouth had been.

He was totally fine. She was perfectly okay.

"I might have a tour to do." She shrugged. "Still figuring out the details."

She could be cool about it too. No need to tell him the tour would be opening for a guy who'd dumped her and moved on with someone younger, prettier, and thinner.

But then he was running his hand along the ridge of her thigh, following the curve under the cover-up she was still wearing, over her bare hip and into the dip of her waist. Then back down her leg. Then back up and over the curve.

"I love that," he said, in an appreciative tone.

"The tour?" she asked. But she knew what he meant. Under his hand, her skin was alive, her nerves humming, waiting for the next place he'd touch her.

That place started up a slow, hot burn of anticipation all over again.

The space between them was suddenly taut with expectation.

"Not the tour," he said. And he tugged at her cover-up. She wriggled out of it, with his help, and then he reached behind her and undid the strings of her bikini top. When she took it off, her breasts spilled free, and she was entirely naked beside him.

"It was dark last time," he said, his voice heavy with wonder and desire.

"Now you see me," she said simply.

He nodded. "I do see you, Jacinda Prescott. I see you. That's who you are."

At that moment, she remembered their exchange after he rescued her from under the house, and told her that he knew she was Cin Scott.

No, she'd said. *Not here, I'm not. Here, I'm Jacinda. I'm me.*

You could be, he'd said.

And now she was. Why had it taken his company, his touch, to bring her back to herself? He resented her, hated what she'd done. And yet...he was caressing her with a tenderness that could only be genuine.

And, he was still fully clothed.

She quit the self-analysis, and focused on the one thing she knew. There was a tall, dark, and stinkin' hot man in bed with her, and she was wasting time.

"Who *I* am, is a woman in need of action," she told him, pointedly grabbing the front of his tank. "And *you* are a man who's overdressed."

He raised one eyebrow. "Am I?"

She worked her way closer, pressing her breasts against him, feeling the heat of his body through the cotton shirt. Then she dragged it upward, and he pulled it over his head. She smiled as he threw the shirt somewhere off the bed, and ran her hands over his broad, sculpted chest, warm as though he was still standing in the sun. Shirtless again. And so completely lickable. But still overdressed.

She tucked one finger into the waistband of his board shorts, but he was way ahead of her. He shucked them off, and then they were gone from the bed too, and she was suddenly on her back, looking up at him. He leaned down and planted a kiss on her exposed throat, sending a shiver through her body.

"Now I'm not overdressed," he said. "And you're going to get your action."

She laughed, but that one kiss had already set her senses alight. "Well, you sure know how to talk to a lady."

"It's not about the talking," he replied, his expression suddenly dangerous. "It's about the doing."

And then he was doing all the things she'd thought about over in her bedroom at number ten, all the nights since that first time, intensified by the night she'd walked away drenched with her need for him, her panties in her pocket. If he'd guessed what she was thinking and doing in her room in the dark, while he was lying in this room, not even a stone's throw away...

His long, elegant fingers were playing across her skin, leaving a trail of blazing sensation. His lips followed, stoking the fires, and she held her breath as he went lower, nearer, closer...and then he was between her legs again, his mouth working the same perfect, dirty magic. As she breathed faster, her body given over to wanton heat and craving, he slipped his fingers inside her, and she moved involuntarily against his hand, matching his rhythm, feeling the rise of something deep and desperate.

"Oh, God," she ground out, not wanting him to stop, but wanting something else even more. She pulled at his arms, wrapping her legs around him and urging him up. "I want...I..."

He pulled away and dragged open the nightstand drawer, and reached in for a condom. With lightning speed, he had it unwrapped and on, and was back in the exact same spot, oh so ready.

"I like your style," she teased.

But he didn't laugh, or shoot back a smart retort. Instead, he looked right at her, straight and level. "I like *you*."

In that moment, with the afternoon sun lighting the room, his words counted for more than any grand declaration of love. Something shifted in her heart...a crack in the ice, or the break of a wave. Just like he'd seen her, she saw him too—a decent man watching the world move on while he carried his painful past with whatever grace he could. Sometimes struggling, sometimes failing. She didn't know if what they were doing counted as a failure, but she wanted to give him something to hold on to. Wanted to be the one he could escape to.

"I like you too," she whispered. Because she did.

At that, he kissed her, gently at first, then growing more insistent, and she parted her own lips, their mutual confession igniting the kiss into something inflammatory and revealing, any last reticence or resistance gone up in flames. She tangled her legs in his, grinding close, acutely aware of the heat of his tongue, and his rock hard desire against her. She shifted and twisted, hungry for the one thing she needed right now, angling closer to the exact right position to take, and give, what she wanted so badly.

But then he paused, unbearably near and yet so far away. "Seems like maybe we're not finished after all."

She writhed underneath him, trying, trying, trying to get nearer. "Cancel what I just said. I don't like you at all."

He grinned. "Yeah, obviously." Then, very slowly, he slid inside her, so easily, but just a little, just enough to bring a moan of pleasure and frustration from her mouth. She lifted her hips, only wanting more of him, overflowing with need and lust and not caring that he knew it.

"Like me yet?" he asked.

"No," she replied, arching beneath him, forgetting everything but his body under her hands and the desperate need to have him inside her. "Yes."

The word came out half plea, half demand, and he relented, sinking into her, finally filling her completely, and her head tipped back as sensation overwhelmed her. All the longing and teasing collided in a rush of urgent, ravenous heat, and instantly they were moving together, their rhythm rapidly becoming faster, deeper, more determined. A tiny corner of her brain knew she should slow down, that it would be over too soon, but her body had its own momentum, in tune with his, and there was no putting the brakes on now. She gave in to her own impulses, and his, abandoning any last thought or reasoning, letting them both ride the irresistible, exhilarating wave. Finally, with one last thrust, he came apart, and she felt herself tip over the edge along with him, pulsing around him, the stars bright behind her eyelids, only half hearing the raw, incoherent sounds coming from her own mouth, and from his too.

When they finally came down, back to a blurry, smoldering reality, she was only aware of how tightly they were holding each other, of their hot, damp skin, and the occasional jolt where they were still joined. If the world could be condensed to just this, it would be enough. She closed her eyes again, burying her face in the side of his neck, where his pulse was still pounding. But then he raised himself off her a little, and they looked at each other. And in his eyes, she saw the bare emotion of the moment—his undisguised need and turmoil, and something that looked so real and heartfelt, her own heart tilted in her chest. He touched her cheek, her nose, her lips, as though he was committing every inch of her face to memory, then kissed her fiercely. And she kissed him back.

It was sexy, and strange, and sweet. Never in all these years had she expected to be in this situation with him. Never even thought about it. But now that she was…she liked it. A lot.

"You're not so bad, Liam Ward," she told him, faking a surprised voice, her blood still rushing in her veins. "Not. So. Bad."

But instead of coming back with a smart reply, or a compliment in return, he froze.

"Not so bad," he repeated, his voice strangely dull, considering what they'd just done.

She dropped the act, a twist of foreboding starting in her belly. "That's what I said."

But he suddenly rolled off her and pulled away, putting space between them. She raised herself on one elbow, trying to catch his eye, but he wouldn't look at her as he went over to the trash can, then came back. As he pounded his pillow into shape and lay down, she only just heard him mutter, "Except I am."

Surely he wasn't serious. "Well then, we must both be," she replied, the twist turning into a knot.

"Maybe you're right," he said. "Because we shouldn't be here."

No. Not this. She felt rebellion rise from somewhere. "Can't we try to be happy?" She nudged him. "Don't we deserve that?"

He didn't say anything, and she felt anger creeping in. No way was she letting him back out on her again without explanation. They'd had a glimpse of something hopeful, and all she wanted was to cling onto it, like a life preserver in a wide, stormy sea. She couldn't, wouldn't, be one of his failures.

"Even if we don't deserve it, we have to decide," she said. "Either we're doing this, or we're not." The words were a gamble she had to take.

But he stared at her in the shuttered light, his eyes so deep blue they were almost black. "We'd better not then."

She tried to breathe away the jagged feeling in her ribcage. "If you want it that way."

It was time to go. She couldn't bear to get all attached like this, and then have him pull out with an attack of the guilts. She was only just keeping her own under control. And she couldn't go any further down this path, and then lose him. Those depths of his were turning out to be over her head. She started to search around under the blanket for her bikini.

But he took hold of her chin, making her look at him. "I *don't* want it that way," he said.

His voice was hard and sharp, the sound of someone who'd been through hell and hadn't yet made it out the other side. But the words made a foolish hope flicker in her heart.

"What *do* you want then?" she asked sharply. "Because until today, it seemed like I was the last thing you wanted, even when you had me."

One corner of his mouth twisted upward, in a dark half-smile, and he shook his head. "Do you know why I didn't go looking for Ethan?"

"You said your dad wanted you to wait for him at home."

"He was wrong. I could have gone. I should have. But I didn't, because..." He closed his eyes for a moment. When he opened them again, the pain she saw in them made her heart twist. "Because I was secretly pleased you'd left him. Because I was jealous." He ran a hand through his hair, his gaze fixed on the ceiling. "Because...I was in love with you."

She could hardly drag in a breath. He'd already confessed

to wanting her, but love? She'd always known that Ethan hadn't felt that way—and she'd never lamented the absence of the 'L' word, because it was obvious from the start. They'd been a fling. A summer fling, on the edge of adulthood. Love hadn't come into it.

She looked at Liam. He was still staring upward, his jaw tense, his brows darkening his face. "If I hadn't been so fucking wrapped up in myself, so wrapped up in my *brother's* girlfriend..." He stopped, then blew out a breath. "He'd still be alive."

Her chest was one giant knot of conflicting emotions. "You were in love with me?"

He passed a hand over his face. "Yes," he said, in a resigned voice.

She didn't even know where to start processing what he'd said. Because of his feelings for her, he hadn't gone looking for Ethan until it was too late. He was still carrying the blame for his brother's death, and guilt about his feelings for her. All of it still real and raw.

And he'd been in love with her.

"Ethan was never in love with me," she said. "He was only playing around."

At her words, Liam flinched. She knew it was all kinds of weird to be talking about his brother like this, when they were in bed together, after everything they'd done. But she had to say it.

"If it hadn't been for the baby, it all would've been so simple. Ethan would have gone to university in Sydney, and I guess I would have missed him for a while. But I would have stayed and finished school on the Other Side, and then gone home to the States again. And we both would've moved on."

"But that wasn't what happened," he said, his voice flat.

"No. But it's not your fault." She wanted to shake him. "You can't spend your life second-guessing and blaming yourself."

"Yeah, sounds easy when you say it," he said, the bitterness obvious in his voice. "Try living it for a while. For ten years."

She let the barbs lie where they fell. "I can see why you'd hate me now." She paused for a minute, figuring out exactly what she wanted to say. "I'll walk away if that's the right thing to do. But even without me in the picture...Ethan wouldn't want you to live like this."

At that, he exhaled a heavy breath. "Ah, fuck." He blinked, and pressed a hand to his forehead. "I don't hate you."

"Sometimes it seems like you do." She frowned. "And then you have a temporary change of heart."

He rolled toward her and took her face in his hands, threading his fingers in her hair. The intensity she saw in the deep blue of his eyes sent a shiver down her back.

"Just before," he said, in a low voice. "You asked what I want."

She nodded. "Do you even know?"

"I do." His gaze didn't waver as he answered. "I want to know if we can make it okay for us, too."

Chapter Twenty-Eight

Jacinda let herself in the front door, hoping no one was home, and she could sneak upstairs and have a shower. But the minute she closed the door behind her, she heard Danielle call her name.

She went into the living room. Danielle and Riley were sitting on the floor, each holding a kitten. The two of them looked up when she came in, and their faces said it all. She was busted.

She played innocent anyway. "Oh, hi Riley."

"Don't 'hi' me," she replied, grinning. "Where have *you* been?"

She tried to smooth her hair. "Uh...I was helping Liam with...a project."

"Would you care to tell us about this impromptu 'project'?" Riley asked, making air quotes. "Does it involve biology? Human anatomy?"

Jacinda made a face. "You know I'm pleading the fifth, with a child in the house." Then she looked around. "Where's Sam?"

"Still at his play date," Danielle said. "They asked him to stay for dinner. So, back to your project..."

"Was it a *big* project?" Riley asked, holding her hands apart, and she and Danielle giggled like schoolgirls.

"Very funny, you two." She dropped her beach bag on

the floor and sank into the wingback chair.

"I *knew* it wasn't a one-off," Riley said, her voice rich with smug satisfaction. "I *knew* it."

Jacinda looked at Danielle. "I suppose Riley told you what happened with him before."

"Yes. But even if she hadn't, your little moment in the ocean was a pretty gigantic clue. I might have been distracted by my job news, but I'm not blind. Why did you let me go on about him before, if you've got a thing happening?"

She shrugged. "Because we don't have a thing happening." Apart from the thing they did in his kitchen. And the things they did upstairs. And all the other things they did before that...

"Well, you should," Danielle said. "He's all kinds of hot."

She shook her head, but her mind was still reeling after his crisis and confession. Could they make something work between them? It was such a huge leap from the place they were when she arrived—two people divided by blame and remorse and regret, a rift that seemed wider than the ocean between their countries. And his long-held guilt had burrowed down into him, creating a barrier that would take more than one conversation to break down.

She'd had no answer to his question, beyond 'maybe'. Because so much of it was up to him, and the ghosts of the past. And in truth, she was afraid that if she let herself get closer, he'd pivot again, leaving her adrift. So she'd left him there, not running out in the dark, but with a goodbye, and kisses, and the excuse that she'd promised to make dinner for Danielle and Sam tonight...along with the truth that she just needed some space to think.

"We can't really," she said now, in answer to her cousin. "I mean, we shouldn't, but..."

"Why not?" Danielle asked, reminding Jacinda that she didn't know anything about what had happened here that long-ago summer.

But before she could say anything, Riley spoke up.

"Seriously, you two should give it a shot. I've seen the way he looks at you."

"If it's anything like the way he was looking at her today, I agree," Danielle said.

Jacinda scooped up the black girl kitten, Suede, and cuddled her close. The little creature immediately nestled into her neck, purring. Despite her small size, the sound was loud in Jacinda's ear, and comforting.

She looked at the two women in front of her. Now they both knew about her 'thing' with Liam, whatever the hell it was. Or wasn't. Or could be. Meanwhile, Danielle knew about her career as Cin Scott, but not about her history with Ethan. And Riley knew about the history with Ethan, but not about Cin. And neither of them knew about the baby, who had thrown everything into chaos and then disappeared, leaving Jacinda half heartbroken, half relieved, and entirely messed up. Suddenly, she felt exhausted, carrying her secrets around. Did she really need to hide anything from these women?

"I'll tell you why not," she said to Danielle. "Because one summer, years ago...I was involved with his brother Ethan."

Danielle pursed her lips thoughtfully. "Hmm. I guess that would be a bit awkward. But hasn't the brother met someone else by now?"

"No..."

"Really? Well, ancient history and all that." Then she looked from Riley to Jacinda, obviously realizing they both knew something she didn't. "Don't say he's still in love with you, or something."

"It's a bit more complicated than that. He's actually..." The word stuck in her throat. It was so blunt. So final. "He's dead."

Danielle gasped. "Oh, my God. I'm so sorry. Were you seeing each other when it happened?"

"Uh...not really."

She looked at Riley, who nodded encouragement. But what would she think once she knew the whole story?

"It was after Jacinda left," Riley told Danielle. "And no one even knows how it happened. He was like the star of our town, everyone loved him. He was one of those guys, you know—talented and smart and super handsome. The whole package."

The guilt clenched around Jacinda's heart again. She hadn't only taken him away from his family—the whole town had lost a shining star.

Danielle shook her head. "How awful."

"Yeah." Riley paused for a moment. "Although…not to speak ill of the dead or anything, but he did have a massive ego." Then she winced. "Sorry, Jacinda."

Jacinda waved a hand. "That's okay." But Riley's words had taken her by surprise—that was the first time she'd heard anyone say something less than glowing about Ethan. "I know he wasn't perfect. None of us are," she added.

"So…you broke up before it happened?" Danielle asked.

'Broke up' wasn't exactly the way to describe it. Or maybe it was. "I had just gone back to the States. I didn't even know he'd died until I came back this time."

"No one told you? Not even Nana Mac?"

"No one. I wasn't in touch with anyone else, so…"

"Bloody hell, that must have been a shock."

Jacinda looked at Riley, who sent back a sympathetic look. "Yeah."

Danielle frowned. "But…why does that mean you and Liam can't be together? I mean, I can see it might feel weird at first, but there'd be nothing wrong with it, really."

"She's right, you know," Riley chimed in.

Jacinda stroked Suede, her mind working overtime. If the Wards had kept the secret all this time, did she have the right to break it? And did she have the stomach to tell her own secret? People already seemed to think she had caused Ethan's death—maybe Riley and Danielle would hear the full details of what happened, and be convinced of it.

Or maybe not.

Either way, the need to talk about it was too great to resist.

"You know how I said it was a bit more complicated?" she said. "This is why."

As they listened, she told them the story, starting with the romance between her and Ethan, for Danielle's sake. Then the pregnancy test. Then the anxious, uncertain moment she told Ethan the news, and his whiplash reaction. Her decision to go home to her mom—even though her mom had problems of her own—and the loss of the baby. And finally, her return to the bay, and Liam's heartbreaking revelations. Listening to the story of him finding Ethan's body, bearing his brother home through the water, their faces were pale with shock.

"That must have been horrific." Riley wiped an eye with the side of her hand. "No wonder he seems kind of...dark."

"He doesn't always, though," Danielle said. "He's lovely with Sam."

"He is," Jacinda agreed. "You know, it's amazing that he let Sam play Ethan's guitar. No one's played that since he died."

"Really? Oh, God. That's just..." She shook her head wordlessly.

"I know." Jacinda blinked, feeling the dampness in her own eyes. "All of it. Can you see why he blames me?"

"But it's not your fault," Danielle said. "And that's pretty mean of him. Especially as you lost the baby. I'm really sorry about that."

"Me too," Riley said. "I can't even imagine."

"Thanks." She bit her lip. "But the thing is, even if Ethan didn't do it intentionally, because of me...it sort of *is* because of me."

"No, it's not," Riley exclaimed. "And if that's what Liam's saying, then I'm going to go over there and set him straight. Don't you let him convince you that you're to blame." At Jacinda's dubious look, she persevered. "Promise me."

Jacinda had to smile at the thought of small, sweet-faced Riley charging next door and tearing into gruff, six-foot-something Liam. But then she sighed.

"What makes it even more of a mess, though...he said he didn't go looking for Ethan earlier, because he was glad

I'd left him. Because..." She hesitated, not a hundred per cent sure if she wanted to share this detail. "Because he liked me himself. And he thinks that if he'd gone looking in time...things would have turned out differently. So he blames himself, too."

"Ohhh." Riley pursed her lips. "That *is* complicated."

Danielle nodded in agreement and sympathy. "It is."

Then Jacinda remembered something. "Don't tell anyone about the way Ethan died, okay? I don't know why the Wards went to so much trouble to keep it quiet, but I don't want to be the one who reveals their secret."

"Liam was actually the one who did that," Riley pointed out. "By telling you."

"I don't know if he'd agree. Especially when I already screwed up so badly."

"I think you did exactly what you could at the time," Danielle said. "I'm sorry you had to go through all that." She came over and gave Jacinda a hug. "And anyway, he wouldn't be sleeping with you if he really does blame you for what happened." Her tone implied that was self-evident.

Jacinda made an unconvinced sound. She wouldn't even try to explain the heated, needy way they'd flung themselves at each other that first night, desperate for comfort, and the ups and downs since. The way he'd desired and despised her at the same time. The way he filled the hole in her heart one minute, and tore it deeper the next.

"I guess," she said.

Danielle nodded, satisfied. "Okay, then. Now I'm going to get a bottle of wine."

"Good call," Riley said. While Danielle went to the kitchen, she added, "And I agree with Danielle. We talked about this before, up on Mount Clarion—it wasn't your fault. I think you and Ethan were both kids, trying to deal with something huge. And Liam too. I'm sorry things happened the way they did."

"Thanks." She forced herself to smile. Maybe they were right. At least they'd been able to see both sides of the whole sad story.

Danielle came back with three glasses tucked between the fingers of one hand, and a bottle in the other. Once the glasses were filled and handed out, Riley leaned forward.

"Changing the subject now...I actually came to tell you how amazing you were last night, playing with Sam. I had no idea you could sing like that! I told Liam that the record company you work for should totally sign you."

Danielle glanced at Jacinda, obviously waiting to see if she would confess her Cin Scott secret.

Well, it seemed to be a night for truth-telling. "Actually, I have a confession about that too," she said.

But before she could say anything more, Riley slapped her hands on her knees, sending startled kittens skittering away. "I knew it! Everyone was wondering, after that performance. You sounded way too much like the real thing." She laughed with glee. "Because you *are* the real thing! I'm *so* coming to visit you now, and you can show me your celebrity lifestyle. How did you even think you could keep a secret like that, Cin Scott?"

Danielle was smiling, and Riley's unbridled enthusiasm made Jacinda laugh. She shrugged. "I didn't know if I could. I just wanted a break from that version of myself. I'm not some kind of mega-celebrity—not at all—but there's a constant pressure. Especially that whole thing about selling yourself based on how sexy you are, not on the music."

They both nodded, understanding. "That sucks," Riley said.

"Yeah." Jacinda sighed. "I don't know if it's worse now I'm getting older, because they think I'm turning into some old hag, so they're putting more pressure on. Or maybe I'm just getting less tolerant. The thing that finally made me walk away was an A&R guy hitting on me. He'd tried it before, a ton of times, but this time it was the complete come-on, including the hard-on." She shuddered.

"Oh, yuck," Danielle said. "Did you lay a complaint?"

"No...but maybe I will. God knows how many other girls he's treated like that. Or gone even further." Now she felt even worse about it—by not saying anything, was she giving him a free pass to do it to others?

"You'll know what to do when you get back," Riley said. "Don't take any shit from some power-crazed old sleaze."

Jacinda smiled. "I won't."

"By the way, no one could accuse you of being an old hag," Riley added. "I mean, *no one.*"

"Well...thanks," she said, smiling. Then something occurred to her. "If everyone was wondering, why did no one mention it?"

Riley laughed. "You're in New Zealand now. We don't fling ourselves at famous people. We're completely backward in coming forward. Especially in the bay."

"Well, I love you for it."

"And we love you, Jacinda Prescott, secret celebrity."

It was a nice sentiment, but there was just one problem. "Even though I killed Sweet Breeze Bay's favorite son?"

"Okay, stop. You didn't." Riley sat forward, shaking her head emphatically. "Don't even *think* that anymore. You can't carry it with you for the rest of your life. And if Liam wants you to, then he doesn't deserve you."

She thought back to the words he'd said as he held her close. *I want to know if we can make it okay for us, too.*

"Well, you know...I think maybe he's starting to see things differently," she said. And the thought was suddenly so freeing, so full of hope, that anything seemed possible. Even a love story.

Chapter Twenty-Nine

Today, the beach was full. Sun umbrellas sprouted like exotic flowers along the curve of the bay, and brightly colored beach towels were laid out in clusters on the hot, golden sand, topped with sunbathers. But even though the beach was the busiest she'd ever seen it, with locals and visitors all there for the annual 'Big Dig' fundraiser, there was still more than enough space for everyone. Still room to breathe.

The kids had been working on sand castles and sculptures down on the firmer sand, hoping to win one of the prizes on offer. Now the judges had been through, and Jacinda stood next to Sam's creation, trying to figure it out.

"Guess," he said again.

"Uh…is it a…dragon?"

He frowned at her. "No. Dragons have wings."

"Oh right, of course. Sorry. I wasn't even thinking."

He seemed to be placated. "Okay, guess again then."

"Let's see. Well, it has some very cool sort of spiky parts…" She walked around to the other side. She was maintaining a thoughtful façade, but inside her mind was racing. She remembered someone telling her that you should never try to guess what a child's artwork represents, because a wrong guess is a blow to their creative self-esteem. Better to ask an open-ended question, and let them define their own art. But now Sam was totally putting her on the spot. She tapped a finger on her lips. "Is it a...chameleon?"

"What?" He groaned. "No. A chameleon has a long, *curly* tail. And googly eyes."

"Oh yeah...I forgot about that."

Apparently, she was a disaster at this. Then, suddenly, she realized that Liam had come to stand beside her. All at once she was self-conscious in her bikini, her hair still dripping down her back from the swim she'd just had.

"I didn't know you'd be here today," she said, looking up at him. And there it was, a heat in her cheeks that she couldn't put down to the afternoon sun.

"Yeah, I noticed you didn't invite me." His tone was deadpan, but she saw a whisper of a smile come and go on his face. "Everything okay here?"

She didn't miss the way he emphasized the *okay*. She'd left him on a maybe the night before, but one look at him and she was veering straight toward yes. And judging by the way he rested his hand ever so lightly on the small of her back as he asked the question, he was doing better than a maybe too.

"So far, so good," she replied.

Behind him, she could see Riley and Danielle back on the beach blankets, both sending her a not-so-subtle thumbs up. She turned away, praying he wouldn't see.

"Not *very* good," Sam piped up.

"Actually, I do need help," she said, grateful for the diversion. "Seems like my biology skills are substandard."

"They are," Sam said, shaking his head.

Liam took his hand back and rubbed his chin, considering the slightly blobby creature in front of him. "So we've ruled out dragon and chameleon, is that right?"

Sam nodded.

"Hmm...the arms and legs are pretty small compared to the body...does it swim?"

Another nod from Sam, this time with growing excitement.

"And the spiky bits by its head...okay, I think I know."

He paused for a moment, letting the tension build. "Is it an axolotl?"

Sam flung his hands in the air. "Yes! Axolotl! The judge didn't know either, but I thought *you* would. I should have been in the finals, at least."

"You were robbed," Liam said, and Sam nodded in agreement.

Jacinda smiled to herself. The hero-worship was still going strong.

Then an announcement blared out from a loudspeaker, making them turn and listen. "The big dig is starting now. All children please report to the big dig zone."

Sam grabbed up his spade. "I'm definitely going to win something in *this* one."

"Don't forget to take Izzy with you," Danielle called to him.

Jacinda watched as Nadia pulled Izzy's hat down firmly and gave her a spade, and the little girl raced over to Sam. Then the two of them headed to the marked-off area where, for a couple of dollars, they could dig for a token with a number on it, and swap it for a prize. Sam had already checked out the prize table, and was determined to win the big one—a handheld gaming device.

As Jacinda and Liam went back to where everyone was sitting on beach blankets and towels, Nadia was saying, "She wants to win a doll. She's still sad about losing her favorite one on the beach."

"Oh, no," Danielle replied. "We'll keep an eye out for it."

Nadia laughed, jigging baby Oliver on her lap. "Don't look too hard. I wasn't a fan. Not convinced about the extreme eyeliner and the super short skirt."

Jacinda knew exactly which doll they were talking about. She wasn't much of a fan either, not after her late-night freak-out on the sand. Liam glanced at her as he sat down, amusement in his eyes. Did he remember the way she'd kissed him that night? She'd intended to torment him right back, like when he'd kissed her hard up against the house, and she'd had no idea if he was testing her, or punishing her, or proving some kind of point. But all she'd done with her own kiss was stoke the off-limits fire he'd started so easily.

As though reading her mind, he pulled off his t-shirt.

Oh, no. Oh, *yes*. She sat down on one of the blankets, at a safe distance. Any closer, and she'd be flinging herself at him, and then the whole town would know she'd gone from one brother to another. She frowned. It sounded so terrible put like that. She concentrated on listening to Danielle and Nadia chatting instead.

All the gang was there, boys on one side, girls on the other, like a pre-teen disco. Dane and Connor were sitting with Liam, and Tina, Kerry, and Riley were on beach towels close by. Stephanie had taken her mom shopping in the city for the day, and Jess was working at the Kelp and King, apparently. Jacinda hadn't seen her since the night at Clarion Call, and that uncomfortable moment afterward, under the street light.

Danielle and Nadia were the most organized—as mothers always seemed to be—with blankets, umbrellas, and cooler bags full of snacks and drinks. Connor was eating a kid-sized packet of rice crackers, laughing at something Kerry was saying. When Penny arrived and saw him plucking mini crackers from the tiny packet, she snorted.

"Where's your juice box, little brother?"

Nadia reached into her cooler bag and tossed one in their direction, and Connor caught it with one hand, grinning. Then he tipped his head at Penny. "I'm not sharing, Stinkface."

She stuck out her tongue. "I don't want your boy germs anyway."

He slurped the juice in one go, then crushed the box in a he-man parody, purposefully flexing his bicep. "You'd be lucky to have any of our mighty *man* germs."

"Pfft." She rolled her eyes, chuckling. "I'm going for a swim. Anyone else coming?"

The guys went with her, Liam included, but the women stayed on the sand, chatting and soaking up the sun. Nadia passed Oliver to Jacinda, so that she could go and check on Izzy. And as she watched Liam walk away toward the ocean, his broad back muscular and tan, Jacinda was glad she had an excuse to stay behind—she didn't trust herself to be in the water with him again. She turned her attention to entertaining Oliver.

As the swimmers returned, Nadia came back with Sam and Izzy, who were both triumphant. Izzy was proudly carrying a new doll, and although Sam hadn't scored the big prize, he'd come away with a book about coding for kids. He went straight over and showed it to Liam, and they fell into conversation about Scratch and Java and Objective-C. Jacinda listened in, noticing the way Liam talked to Sam as though he was an equal, encouraging him without being patronizing.

Then Dane looked at his watch, the kind of high-tech, waterproof timepiece that divers wore. "Who's coming to the Kelp and King?"

Connor shook water from his hair. "Me."

Tina, Riley and Kerry got up too, but Liam stayed put, the sun glistening on his damp skin.

"Liam, you coming, mate?" Connor asked him.

He shook his head. "No thanks. Got some weekend work to do."

"Oh, are you working on a *project?*" Riley asked loudly.

Even though no one else got the jibe, Jacinda felt herself blush.

For a moment, he looked puzzled at Riley's very pointed enquiry. Then he nodded. "Yeah. A volunteer project for a non-profit, supporting the kids of immigrants in the States."

"Oh," she said again, but this time she sounded impressed instead of sarcastic. "Well, that's cool. Jacinda? You coming?"

Jacinda bit her lip. Did he really plan to work? She glanced at him, but he was giving nothing away as he pulled his t-shirt back on. "Uh…I'd better not come either," she said to Riley. "I have to work on that thing I was telling you about."

"Oh right," Riley replied with a grin. "The *thing*." And her eyes went to Liam.

Thank God everyone was busy picking up their belongings and getting ready to go. "No, you know—the chapters. The book."

"Riiight. The book."

Jacinda waved her away. It was pointless to argue...especially when, in truth, she was secretly hoping to do absolutely no work at all. She'd said she needed space to think, but seeing him again today, the last thing she wanted was space. Or thinking. All she could think about was the doing.

With little ones in tow, Danielle and Nadia couldn't go to the pub, so they gave in to the kids' pleas to go to the playground. The others decided to head to the double K via the beach and the surf club.

After a round of goodbyes—and with so many knowing glances headed their way, she guessed they must be totally failing at keeping their secret—Jacinda looked at Liam. Now it was just the two of them.

"Back to work then," she said with faux gusto as they turned and went in the opposite direction from everyone else, back toward their houses.

He took her beach bag and slung it over his shoulder. "Apparently." As they crossed the sand, he stepped deliberately closer, bumping his arm against hers. "You know, I do have some tasks that require a co-worker."

"Oh, really? What kind of tasks would these be?"

He shrugged, but his grin said it all. "This and that."

She tapped her chin, pretending to consider it. "What's the remuneration like?"

"It's kind of a profit share system. I know you're still thinking about things...but I'd make sure you ended up with more rewards overall."

He'd already proved his commitment to making sure she came out ahead on 'rewards'. She flashed back to that moment on the kitchen table, when she'd known nothing but his tongue and her burning, spiraling need, and then the overwhelming, shuddering peak and release under his mouth. The memory sent a dart of desire through her.

Yes. She wanted more of *those* rewards.

She stepped over a castle-shaped bucket abandoned on the sand. "Let's negotiate."

He kept his business voice on, but the corners of his lips curved upward, just for a moment. "Sounds like a deal in the making."

"Could be." She was more than ready to cut a deal with this guy—but his reaction yesterday was still fresh in her mind. "I'm not interested in making either of us feel bad again, though."

He adjusted his sunglasses, suddenly looking uncomfortable. "I did actually listen to what you said, before you left me there all alone."

"Really?" she said. "I thought you were just looking at my boobs."

He laughed out loud. "That too."

It felt good to make him laugh.

As they left the sand, something caught her eye farther down the beach, and she paused. A woman with long, dark hair was making her way slowly along, winding between the sand castles. She looked vaguely familiar, but from this distance it was hard to see her properly, especially as she was wearing a wide-brimmed hat and oversized sunglasses.

"You coming?" Liam asked, waiting just inside the alley.

She turned to answer. "Yeah."

Before she followed him, she looked back one more time, but couldn't spot the woman again. She shaded her eyes and squinted into the sun, trying to see better. Whoever it was had gone.

Then she looked to where Liam was waiting for her, all tall, dark, and beachy, and a flutter of anticipation started in her belly. She had some rewards to collect.

Chapter Thirty

They went up onto the deck, and he unlocked the door and pushed it open for her to go through. Inside, he hung the key on a hook just inside the kitchen. Then he turned to her, hesitant all of a sudden.

"Uh…do you need anything?"

She glanced at the table, the scene of her most wanton climax ever. "No thanks." Then she thought about it again. "Actually…yes."

He'd followed her gaze, and now he smiled, the memory obviously fresh in his mind too. "And where would you like it?"

She felt a heat flush her cheeks, because honestly, looking at his sun-kissed skin, and his strong arms, and the tempting curve of his lips, she'd like it right here, right now. He came and stood in front of her, just out of reach, and she felt an arrow of need shoot through her.

"Would you like it here?" he asked. She bit her lip, and he nodded. "I see."

It hadn't taken long for her to give herself away.

"Here works for me." He took a step forward, and she could feel his body heat.

She found her voice. "I thought we were negotiating," she pointed out.

"Right," he said. "I forgot. So okay, *maybe* here."

Then he took her hand and led her through the living room to the bottom of the stairs. In one smooth movement, he reached down and grasped the hem of her cover-up, and pulled it up and over her head. Her arms went up of their own accord, letting the fine garment come free, and he draped it over his shoulder.

"Or, would you like it here?" he said again, his voice slow and curious, as though he had no idea, even though she knew full well he understood the desire rising in her body. He trailed his fingers down the side of her neck, across her throat, and over the exposed swell of her breast in her bikini. Then he bent and followed the same path with his lips, letting his tongue run across her skin.

"Maybe," she replied casually, while her nipples betrayed her by hardening inside her bikini top, and the heat grew between her legs.

"Hmm," he said thoughtfully. "Okay."

He went behind her and rested one hand low on her back, encouraging her forward up the stairs. "After you."

He let her go a couple of steps ahead before following, and she was acutely aware that he had an unimpeded view of her bikini-clad butt, right at eye level. She swung her hips just a little more, and smiled when she heard his appreciative murmur. She kept on going.

"The good thing about working from home is that you can do it anywhere," he said in a conversational tone as they went up. Then she felt him take hold of her hips, stopping her in her tracks and turning her around as he came to the step right below hers. He reached up easily to where her bikini strings were tied behind her neck, and deftly undid them. The top slipped down, coming to rest around her hips. She held her breasts in her own hands, feeling the heat in them, and an unmistakable fire leapt higher, low in her belly.

"So...would you like it here?" he asked, still playing the game, but there was a pleasing rasp in his voice. And as she teased him, taking her own nipples between her fingers and thumbs, feeling them harden even more, she saw a telltale daze come into his eyes.

222

There on the stairs, she decided to call his bluff. She slipped a hand into his board shorts and wrapped her fingers around him, satisfied to hear his deep rumble of desire. Slowly at first, she moved her hand, then bolder, faster, and then she pushed the shorts out of the way with her other hand so that he was free of the fabric. He propped himself against the wall over her shoulder with one hand, and cupped her breast with the other, letting his thumb circle the hard bud of her exposed nipple. All the while he looked right at her, knowing in his eyes, and her breathing sped up in sync with his, the heat growing between her own legs, until she was wet and hot and so, so needy.

Then he lowered his head and kissed her, hard and hungry, and she was against the wall, pinned by his bulk and the force of his desire. She only managed to keep the rhythm of her hand going for a few moments before she lost all coordination. She slowed and stopped, lost in the tumult of hot breath and delving tongues and the urgent need to feel him closer, closer, not in her hand but inside her, and the sound she made against his mouth was a raw call that only he could answer.

At that, he stepped back, and she saw the equivalent animal hunger in his own eyes.

"Come on," he said, his voice ragged. And he pulled her along the hallway into his room, where he tossed her cover-up away, and rapidly undid the other bikini strings, letting the top fall from her hips to the floor.

With a hot exhalation, he gazed down at her breasts.

"Just looking at my boobs again?" She couldn't resist the jibe.

But he shook his head. "Not looking. Revering."

She laughed. "You're crazy."

"Not as crazy as I want to make you," he replied, tugging down her bikini bottoms.

And when he tipped her onto the bed, pausing only to cover himself before plunging deep inside her, she did feel a kind of crazy overtake her. But it was the kind of unstoppable, elemental madness that she had no intention of fighting.

Afterward, she lay with one arm flung across her forehead, her pose accentuating her luscious curves, her breath slowly steadying again.

"Well," she said. "I believe this negotiation is complete."

"We definitely came to an agreement," he agreed, letting his hand rest against the damp curls between her legs. He might be spent for now, but he didn't want to let go.

Her lips curled into a sultry smile, and she peeked at him from under her arm. "I think I came to an agreement twice, actually."

"Very good," he said appreciatively. Jesus, she was sexy. "By the way, there's nothing wrong with your biology skills."

She laughed, bringing her arm down and curving her hand on the side of his neck. "Likewise," she said. "That was very...rewarding."

He lay slow kisses along the line of her collar bone, down into the dip between her breasts. "Didn't I tell you you'd come out ahead?"

"Mm-hmm," she said, her eyes still half closed. Then she cupped her breasts, offering them up to his mouth. He trailed his lips over the soft skin, kissing here and there, circling one nipple with his tongue, then the other, each one hardening even more under his mouth. He felt himself twitch and stir again in response to her own reaction. God help him, she was a walking aphrodisiac.

"I could just stay right here," she murmured into his hair.

He looked up at her, drinking in her rosy, post-orgasm beauty, her blue eyes shining above high cheekbones. She could stay in his bed as long as she wanted.

"Sounds good to me," he said. But her words had triggered a question in his mind. "You know, I never asked why you left LA. Why now?"

She shifted underneath him, so he rolled over onto his

side on the mattress, taking her with him. She tangled her legs in his, staying close.

"It was in the back of my mind for a while," she said. "But I always had commitments that stopped me from leaving. And then something happened, and I was like, that's it. I'm out."

"What happened?"

She sighed. "It's the usual boring story."

"I want to hear it."

The story she told made him see red. When she finished, he shook his head, feeling his pulse pound in his temple. "If I ever meet that fucker..."

Her eyes widened at the sudden venom in his voice, and he stopped. He wasn't joking...but she didn't need to know that.

She shrugged. "Anyway, I'm basically elderly, compared to the girls he keeps threatening me with."

He put his face close to hers, squinting as he pretended to examine her. "You look pretty damn good for an old-timer."

"Yeah, yeah." She put her palm against his forehead and pushed him away, trying not to laugh. "Okay, maybe that's a slight exaggeration," she admitted. "I know you think I should be grateful."

"I don't think you should be grateful for pricks like that."

She frowned. "Just for other things."

Shit. Apparently she hadn't forgotten the way he'd ripped into her that night, in front of Dane and Connor. He grimaced. "No. That was me being a prick too. I know you've worked hard."

"Really? You're giving me credit now?"

"I googled you," he said, twiddling his fingers as though they were on a keyboard, and was relieved to see her laugh.

"No secrets, huh?"

"Apart from the big one. Yourself." He cupped the side of her face, caressing her cheek with his thumb, and her eyes fluttered closed for a moment. Then she put her hand on top of his, and looked at him.

"Riley seems to think that particular secret might be out, after Friday night. But it's just like...I'm giving Cin Scott a vacation. Sometimes I think maybe I'm not cut out for that life, even though I always thought I wanted it."

He sat up a little more. "You *are* cut out for it."

"How do you know?"

He twiddled his fingers again. "All the proof is on Google."

"So basically, you've been stalking me on the internet."

"Yep." He grinned. He'd go right ahead and admit it. "And in real life."

"You perv."

He pretended to leer at her, and she made a fist, aiming for his chin. Lightning fast, he grabbed her hand, held it tight, and leaned in to kiss her. When they came up for air, her cheeks were satisfyingly flushed.

"Speaking of perving, you don't spend nearly enough time with your shirt off." Her hands traveled down his chest, then lower, tracing the lines of the abs he'd sweated to achieve. Thank God for house-building and gym-going. As she went lower, he held his breath, but she stopped, one eyebrow raised.

Tease.

"Thank you for your feedback," he said, working to maintain his best customer service voice. "I'll take that into consideration."

"Good," she replied. "Because you're not too bad for an old-timer either."

He grabbed her waist on each side, and she reacted instantly, twisting away with a little scream of laughter. And then they were kissing again, and their hands were on each other, and there was nothing to think about except her skin, her scent, her softness, and the way she hungrily met his seeking mouth.

When everything settled down again, he was struck with a depressing thought: he would really, really miss her when she was gone. But then, she'd said she might be touring—maybe she'd come back to the South Pacific for that.

226

"So what's the deal with your tour?" he asked, one hand still roaming over her warm, smooth skin.

She frowned at the seemingly random question. "Just the States, and maybe a couple of shows in Canada. It would be opening for a guy who plays sort of Southern rock, mixed with country." She shrugged. "He's a pretty big deal, so..." She let the sentence trail off, twisting a strand of hair in her fingers.

He got it. She had plans. Things to do. She wasn't going to sit around here at the ass end of the earth forever, no matter how pretty it was, no matter how much he wished things were different. But there was something off in her tone.

"You don't sound very excited about it."

"Yeah, well...it's a long story." She pressed her lips together.

Something in her expression gave him a sudden certainty. "You were involved with him." It was a statement of fact, not a question. When she abruptly looked away, he knew he was right.

"No," she said, suddenly fascinated by his old Star Wars alarm clock on the bedside table.

Shit. Not only was she leaving, she was leaving to go on the road with a guy she used to date. Great. He felt a swell of jealousy creeping through him.

But then he looked down at her—irresistible curves, dark hair sweeping across her soft skin, and remembered. She was here now. She was here in his bed, despite all the things he'd said and done. Despite their past. Or maybe because of their past.

He reached for her, putting every other thought aside. "It's none of my business," he said, even though it was killing him to think of her with some 'big deal'. It made him crazy to think of her with anyone else. His brother included...but somehow, he'd found himself starting to come to terms with that.

She turned back to him. "It's been ten years," she said. "You must have been with plenty of girls."

This was *not* the direction he wanted the conversation to

take. There'd been other women, sure, most of them nice, some of them pretty great. But not one of them had compelled him the way Jacinda did. Only she inspired this kind of sweet torment, consuming his thoughts during the day, and keeping him awake at night. And now he wanted her with him *all* night.

"None of them were you," he said, gathering her close and kissing her forehead. Then he threaded his hands in her hair and pulled back so that he could see her bright blue eyes. "Stay the night," he said.

"Well...if we're in your bed I guess you won't be running out on me."

Her voice was teasing, but he didn't miss the point. He'd take that burn like a man, if it meant she was staying. "I'm not running anywhere."

He loaded the words with all the meaning he couldn't say aloud. And judging by the flash of recognition and warmth in her eyes, she didn't miss it.

"Okay," she said finally. "I'll text Danielle so she doesn't worry."

Relief ran though him. If this was as okay as it got, he should be grateful himself. Even if he wanted more—and he always wanted more when it came to her, even when he shouldn't—these short weeks would have to tide him over. Maybe forever.

He banished the thought, and focused on the woman right in front of him, right now. It was enough that they had a chance now. And if she fell for him the way he'd fallen for her—long ago—then maybe everything else would fall into place too.

"So we're okay," he said, as though it was a signed-and-sealed sure thing. At this point, the alternative was unthinkable.

"We're...complicated," she replied, her face serious, and a sudden doubt and fear lurched in his guts.

Then she smiled.

"But I think we could be more than okay."

Chapter Thirty-One

Morning was her new favorite time of day. With her leg flung over his, and a hand on his broad chest, Jacinda looked at the man next to her in bed—his hair thoroughly pillow-rumpled, five o'clock shadow carried over to ten fifteen, the way he was watching her right back, with those amused, oh-so-blue bedroom eyes. Not to mention all the ridiculously hot things he'd just done...and done the night before. He made it easy to forget all the drag and drama of the outside world, and even their complicated history seemed like just that—history. If only every day could start this way.

As if reading her mind, Liam said, "I could do this every morning."

"I could do it *twice* every morning," she said.

He lifted his head and looked at her. "Oh, really?"

"Really." She ran a hand down his arm, then over the plane of his stomach. "Could you?"

He feigned indignation. "Do you doubt me?"

She paused, hearing a sound from downstairs. "Is that someone at the door?"

He listened, then shrugged. "Probably Sam. He's always turning up during the day at random times. Or it could be Connor and Dane—they refuse to use the doorbell. I'll go and see."

He got out of bed, but seeing him standing there, carved and golden, she knelt up and took hold of his arms. One more touch before he left. One more helping of warm skin to tide her over. She leaned forward just enough that her breasts brushed against his torso, then matched the delicate touch with her lips, letting her tongue graze along the slightly salty skin on his chest. They'd been in too much of a hurry to think about showering when they came back from the beach yesterday. He let out a low groan, and she smiled as she felt him start to harden once more against her belly. Got him.

He bent down and buried his face in her neck. "You are a bad, bad girl," he said into her ear, his breath hot. "And I fully intend to lay you down and prove I can do it twice. With variations."

She shivered as he kissed the sensitive spot under her ear. Then he stood up straight again, and tapped the tip of her nose. "But there's a kid on the loose to deal with first."

"Or two big kids."

He laughed. "Yeah. Either way, I'll be right back."

"You'd better." She feigned a pout.

He grinned, running his hands down her back and cupping her bottom. "Oh, I will, I promise. See?"

She looked down. That promise was pressing hard against her, taut and eager all over again. She laughed, and resisted the temptation to play. Magnificent though it was, he couldn't go and open the front door with that leading the way.

"I do see." She put her hands behind her back. "And hurry, because I have some variations of my own to suggest."

"I'm *very* open to suggestions."

He let her go, still grinning, and she reached to put the pillows back in place so she could lie down while she waited.

But then his grin froze and disappeared, replaced with an expression of shock. With lightning speed, he grabbed her and pulled her back in front of him, hiding his now rapidly deflating hard-on. In turn, she scrabbled for the sheet, trying to cover her bare bottom. Her instant thought was that Sam had let himself in and wandered up the stairs, and seen something wildly inappropriate for a nine-year-old. But then someone spoke—and it wasn't Sam.

"Liam?"

She looked over her shoulder, her heart pounding, and instantly wanted to die.

Liam's mother was standing in the doorway.

"Oh, shit," she whispered, her face blazing hot as she knelt in front of his nakedness, wishing she was invisible, waiting for the older woman to make a hasty exit.

But instead of turning away, like any normal person would, his mother just stood there staring at them blankly, her mouth a silent, stupefied O.

As she clutched the sheet to her butt, Jacinda waited for Liam to say something. To take some kind of action. But he seemed as paralyzed as his mother. She looked desperately around for his clothes, and saw his board shorts and t-shirt lying on the floor at his mother's feet. And the tip of her shoe was on the edge of Jacinda's bikini top. Oh, God. She looked away.

Finally, his mother spoke.

"Is this...Jacinda?"

He abruptly let go of her, as though he'd suddenly realized she had leprosy, and found his voice. "Go downstairs, Mum. I'll be there in a minute."

She started to go, but turned back. "I can't believe you would do this. I just can't believe it." Then she wheeled around and disappeared.

Still kneeling in front of him, Jacinda let out a breath that turned into a slightly hysterical laugh. "Oh, my God. I thought it was Sam." She pulled the sheet fully around her, feeling the need to be covered up. "What a nightmare."

But there was no laughter from Liam, hysterical or otherwise. His face was grim as he went to the closet and pulled out fresh clothes. "You'd better get dressed," he told her, pulling on underwear, then jeans.

"Sure. Yes." She got up and collected her bikini top from the floor, then looked around for her cover-up, and found it down the side of the nightstand.

He said nothing, rapidly doing up his belt and putting on a t-shirt.

"Are you okay?" she asked him.

Obviously, this was pretty much everyone's worst-case scenario—the only thing worse would have been his mother walking in on them forty-five minutes before, when he'd had his head between her legs, rendering her helpless with lust. Or half an hour ago, when she was reciprocating the pleasure. Or just fifteen minutes earlier, when her legs were wrapped around him, her hands pinned to the bed as he sank into her again and again, looking into her eyes as she rose to another toe-curling, body-shaking orgasm. Now, that seemed like forever ago. She was in a state of shock herself, and it must be even worse when it was your own parent catching you unawares.

But still...it wouldn't kill him to say *something*.

She waited, holding her things in a bundle in front of her, but he just pointed to where her bikini bottoms lay on the floor. He didn't pick them up for her. And then she remembered how he'd let her go, like she'd scalded him, when his mother realized it was her.

"They won't give you cooties, you know," she snapped, reaching down and grabbing them up.

He frowned. "I'd better go."

The words also said, *You'd better go*.

"Fine," she said.

She turned her back on him, and started to get dressed. Behind her, she could hear him leave the room.

"Fine," she muttered to herself, fumbling with the bikini string, then dragging her cover-up over her head. "Go to mama."

And then a wave of guilt washed over her, because that mama only had one child left.

She sat on the edge of the bed and pressed her fingers to her forehead. Great. The first time she saw Liam's mother again—Ethan's mother—and this was how it went down. What kind of damage control was Liam doing down there? The poor woman must be in even more shock than they were. She sure as hell wouldn't want to see Jacinda again now, fresh from her remaining son's bed.

As quietly as she could, she crept down the stairs. The sound of muffled voices was coming from the living room.

She couldn't help it. She stopped and listened, holding her breath. Mrs. Ward's voice was agonized.

"Liam, I can't even...can you even imagine what this is like for me?"

"I'm sorry you had to see that," he started to say calmly, but she interrupted him.

"Sorry I had to *see* it? But not sorry you did it?"

He murmured something Jacinda couldn't make out. Which kind of sorry was he?

But his mother continued, the pitch of her voice getting higher. "Don't you *remember* what happened? Did you forget everything?"

"No," he replied emphatically. Then there was silence for a moment, before he spoke again. "Actually, yes. I did forget. And I'm sorry..."

At that, her heart seized in her chest, and she knew where she stood. She'd heard enough. Apparently he wasn't seeing things differently after all—except for when he thought he could get some action. No different from all the men who'd looked at her over the years and seen nothing but boobs and possibility. Nice.

With the sound of their voices behind her, she grabbed up her beach bag from where she'd left it at the bottom of the stairs, went along to the laundry room, and silently let herself out the side door. Once again, it was time to make an exit from their lives.

★

Home...or the closest thing to it. Safety, at least. Jacinda closed the front door behind her and leaned against it, her eyes scrunched shut. From heaven to complete horror, without warning. She shuddered, trying to shake off the lingering feeling of being exposed—in more ways than one.

And the way Liam had given in, the moment his mother turned up, without a word in their defense. Didn't take much for him to change his mind about the whole thing.

Danielle looked up as she came into the living room.

"All that *work* took a long time," she said, grinning. Then her face changed as she registered that something wasn't right. "What happened?"

Jacinda stood in the middle of the room, thrown completely off center. "Something just…"

"What is it?" Danielle stood up. "Are you okay?"

She looked around. "Is Sam here?" She was very glad it hadn't been him at the bedroom door, but his wasn't something he needed to be in on either.

"No. He's gone back to the beach with his new friends."

"That's good." She managed a smile.

"What, then? You're making me worry."

She went over and collapsed on the couch, tipping her head back. "Liam's mom."

"She's in Australia, right? Has something happened to her? Is she sick?"

Jacinda snorted, then looked back at Danielle. "Yeah…I think she just had a heart attack."

Confusion passed across Danielle's face. "A heart attack?"

"Pretty much at the same time I had mine. Which was the moment I saw her standing in the doorway, looking at me and Liam in bed."

Danielle's eyes widened suddenly, and she clapped a hand over her mouth. "No."

"Yes. And it was just as much fun as it sounds."

"Oh, my God. Were you in the middle of…?"

"No, she just missed it. But she saw enough." She pressed her hands to her face. If she'd thought it would be hard to face his mom before, this took it to a whole new level of impossibility.

Danielle's eyes were still like saucers. "So what happened?"

"I grabbed the sheet and covered myself up, but Liam was standing up by the bed, and I was in front of him, so I couldn't move. And his mom...I kept waiting for her to spin around and leave, but it was like she couldn't tear her eyes away. It might not have been cardiac arrest, but she definitely found it arresting."

At that, Danielle laughed. Then she shook her head. "Sorry, I just...the picture in my mind..."

Jacinda smiled too, but a sigh came with it. "I know. It would be hilarious if it wasn't so fucked up. We were this close to thinking we had something that could work...and then his mother walked in and saw him betraying her with the woman responsible for her other son's death. And that was it."

Danielle started to protest, but Jacinda held up her hand.

"I know what you're going to say, but it is what it is. Fault, blame, whatever. We were carrying way too much baggage to make it work anyway."

"Are you sure? You guys seemed so into each other."

His words echoed in her head. *I'm not running anywhere.* He'd sounded like he meant it. But she already knew how people could say things they didn't mean. Or just plain change their minds under pressure.

"I'm sure," she said. "Now I'm going to have something to eat, and then a shower, and then a nap. It was a long night, and now..." She blew out a breath and waved her hand, unable to sum up her current state of mind.

"Good plan," Danielle said. "I'll run interference down here if anyone turns up looking for you."

Jacinda picked up her beach bag. Suddenly, she was exhausted. "Thanks, but I doubt there'll be any need. None of the Ward family will be in a hurry to see me ever again."

Chapter Thirty-Two

The bar was sticky under his elbows, and the music sucked, but Liam wasn't going anywhere. He lifted his hand, and the bartender came over straight away. It wasn't like there were any other customers to serve. While he waited for his next whiskey, he looked around. Mid afternoon on a summer Monday, and it was quiet in the Kelp and King—the dark wooden booths deserted, every other bar stool empty, the sound system playing generic classic rock to no one but himself and the bartender. Thank God. He wasn't in the mood for company.

He wasn't in the mood to be *here*, either—a place so tied up with Ethan, he'd refused to step foot inside until now. But he desperately needed a drink, and there was nothing left at home. And he wasn't about to buy something and take it back there, with his mother in the throes of Shakespearean tragedy about what had happened that morning.

He'd tried to reason with her, tried to explain, but she was beyond listening.

Like he didn't feel shitty enough about it. The expression on her face as she realized that not only was she seeing him in bed with a woman, but that woman was Jacinda...

It was burned into his brain, along with the memory of her pain when he brought Ethan home.

Fuck.

He emptied the glass, and from her spot in the corner, the bartender raised her eyebrows. He resisted saying something smart, and pointed to the Jim Beam sitting behind the bar.

"Can you just give me the bottle?" He'd already made a decent dent in it—might as well save her the trouble of going backward and forward.

She brought it over. "Bad day, huh?"

"It must be if I'm in here," he replied.

She considered him. "You're Liam, right?"

"For my sins." Which seemed to be accumulating. At least she didn't say 'Ethan's brother'. He poured himself another shot.

"You're Ethan's brother," she said, on cue.

The look on his face must have been as black as his mood, because she held her hands up in front of her. "Sorry."

"Yeah, okay." He didn't ask her name.

Then the bell rang over the door, and she left him alone, presumably to serve whoever was coming in. He didn't turn around. There was literally no one he wanted to talk to right now. He downed the shot. He wasn't quite numb yet, but he was getting there.

He stood up and reached over the bar, grabbing more ice from the tub on the other side. Then he refilled his glass, leaving the lid off the Jim Beam. No point pretending he wasn't going to have more.

A minute later, someone spoke.

"Oh, hey," she said. "Imagine seeing you here."

Recognizing the voice—and the accent—he turned. Just along the bar, the American woman from the night markets was sitting on a stool, some kind of fizzy drink in front of her. She smiled encouragingly at him, obviously waiting for a response.

Right. Because he really needed someone to pester him with inane questions right now. He raised his hand briefly. "Hey."

She picked up her drink and came closer, slipping onto the stool next to him. "How's it going?"

How did she think it was going? He waited a moment before answering. "It's Monday lunchtime and I'm sitting in a bar by myself, halfway through a bottle of Jim Beam. You be the judge."

She checked the bottle. "Looks more like a third of the way to me."

He picked it up, and poured until his glass was brimming. Then he put the bottle back on the bar with a thud. "Half."

She laughed. "You're closer." Then she raised her own glass. "Cheers."

He looked at his drink. One move and it would spill everywhere. Shit. He considered leaning down like a four-year-old and slurping from where it sat, but even in this I-don't-give-a-fuck mood, he wasn't going to make a fool of himself in front of whoever this woman was.

He picked up the glass carefully, leaned forward, and took enough of a sip to lower the level half an inch. Then he grabbed a napkin from the nearby holder and wiped the spillage from his fingers.

"So what's up?" she asked.

He shrugged. "Long story."

"I'm only killing time until I go to the airport," she said. "Heading back to the States tonight. But I always have time for a story. I live for them, actually." When he didn't reply, she tipped her head. "It's a woman, right?"

"No." His voice echoed in the empty bar, unexpectedly loud, and he slugged back another gulp of bourbon. "No," he repeated, more quietly.

She tutted. "Love. What a fuck-up it is."

He barked out a laugh. "You got one thing right." Then he looked at her more closely. "What are you, an agony aunt or something?"

She grinned, then gestured to the bottle of Jim Beam, her eyebrows raised in a question. He nodded, and she filled her empty glass. "Or something." Then she added, "I've been there myself, so..."

In one smooth movement, she swallowed the contents of her glass. As it went down, she scrunched up her nose, and he noticed the tiny diamond again. Then she poured herself a refill, and held it up, rebellion in her green eyes. "To love. It can get fucked."

"Okay, *that* I can drink to," he said. And they tipped their glasses back.

Then she splashed a little more into her glass, and refilled his to the top. He didn't say anything. He wasn't looking for company, but at least she was marginally less irritating than he'd expected.

By the time the bottle was heading for empty, he was vaguely aware that he'd actually been talking more than her. Maybe inane questions were just the distraction he needed.

"So you're Australian?" she asked now.

"Shit, no." He frowned, and squinted disapprovingly at her. Or maybe just to get her in focus. "That's like asking a Canadian if they're American."

"Sorry. I thought you said—"

He waved a hand. "That's okay. I'm from here. I've just been away a really long time."

"Really? Why would anyone leave this place? It's like heaven."

He rolled his eyes. "There's no such thing."

But he was wrong. He remembered the one place that was heaven—holding Jacinda close, bare skin against bare skin, each of them remembering and forgetting in the other's arms.

When his mother asked if he'd forgotten everything, his first reaction was to deny it. How could he forget the worst thing that had ever happened to him, to his family? Then he'd thought about it again...and apologized in advance for the truth he was about to tell her, hoping she'd understand. Forgetting some of the pain was the only way he'd ever move forward. But it didn't mean forgetting his brother. And despite her involvement in the events of that summer—or maybe because of it—Jacinda was the only respite he'd found from the memories and feelings that hung over him, crushing him a little more every day. Coming back to the bay had been an attempt to look them in the eye and face them down. Deal with them, and let them go. Jacinda understood.

But now he'd have to find another way to forget. And he'd be doing himself a favor if he forgot about *her* too. Forgot her soft, inviting curves, and her fighting spirit, and the sweet relief of her forgiveness. The way she'd looked up at him the first time they made love, cautious and reckless at the same time. Her willingness to take another chance on him, even though he didn't deserve it.

Now he knew he couldn't stay here, even once she was gone. He'd just have to go back to Australia, and move on. And she'd move on too. The bright lights of her showbiz life would leave him in the shadows again, just another guy who'd wanted her. He could only imagine how many of them she came across, nothing but greedy lust and lurking hard-ons.

He pressed his fist to his chest.

"I know," the woman next to him said. "It goes a long way back, right?"

He looked at her. One of them was swaying slightly, and he suspected it was him. She smiled gently, her eyes fixed on him. And suddenly he found himself telling her things he'd never told anyone. Like some anonymous comment on a website, he spilled the truth to this stranger. Maybe if she took it with her, away across the ocean, it would leave him cleansed and empty. Like throwing up after a hard night on the town. Better out than in.

In the still-empty bar, he told her about his brother—the incomparable Ethan, destined for everything, but gone before he had a chance at any of it. And, without uttering Jacinda's name, he told her about the girl Ethan had fallen for—who'd come from far away, and left disaster in her wake. The baby, the ocean, the broken vodka bottle, and the guilt of knowing it could have been different. And then the girl's return. Not as a girl, but a woman, with a whole other life. A woman he wanted, and shouldn't want...a woman he blamed, and couldn't blame. A woman who was everything he dreamed of, and more than he deserved. And, just to make it worse, she was right next door.

The American woman listened wordlessly, letting him spill his guts, void his heart.

When he was finished, he ran his hand over his face. "You said it right. It's a fuck-up."

She nodded. "It's messy, alright. Life's like that."

They sat for a moment in silence, watching the bartender quietly set clean glasses on the mirrored shelves behind the bar, the light reflecting and blurring in his hazy vision. She was taking her time to arrange the glasses perfectly in line, the exact same distance between each one. He fought the urge to go back there and smash them all out of place.

Then the woman beside him pulled out her phone and looked at the time. "Shit, I'd better go. Good luck with everything though."

Like an emotional one-night stand, he knew she'd be leaving. But it had been weirdly cathartic. So he nodded, ignoring the way the room tilted a few degrees off vertical. "Yeah. You too."

She slipped off the barstool and walked steadily to the door, and left without a backward glance.

"Who was that?" the bartender asked, as the door closed behind her. "She was in here yesterday too."

He shrugged. "Some American on her way home." He looked at his shimmering reflection in the mirror glass on the back wall, behind the bottles of tequila and vodka and Southern Comfort. So much for soft focus—even blurry, he looked like shit.

The bartender was texting on her phone, her bottom lip caught between her teeth. He held up a fifty-dollar note, and waved it to get her attention.

She looked over, and her frown deepened. "Sorry, I won't be a sec."

"S'alright." He threw it on the bar. "Keep the change."

Then he headed unevenly for the door.

His mother would be even less impressed with him when he turned up drunk, but too bad. Shakespearean tragedy always needed a villain, or a wayward son. Right now, he was playing both.

Chapter Thirty-Three

S tanding in the shower, the morning's events crowded Jacinda's head, small snippets of blissful moments drowned out by the ones that followed. Liam's face as he saw his mom...his mom's face as she saw Jacinda. The overheard conversation that made his allegiance clear. Could she blame him, really? If it came down to family, or her, what choice did he have? Between the two of them, they had enough guilt to sink a ship...and if he didn't want to sink his own family all over again, she could hardly condemn him for that.

Even though it hurt.

She groaned and got out, wishing only for the oblivion of sleep as she gave her hair a quick rub, squeezing the excess water out, then wrapped the towel around herself. Then she heard her phone ringing down the hall in her bedroom. She opened the bathroom door and went along to grab it.

Hannah. Thank God. "I'm so glad you called," she said, in place of 'hello'.

"Oh," Hannah said. "Hi."

"I mean, I'm always glad to talk to you, you know that." She shut the door and sat on the edge of her bed. "But especially now."

"Really? Why?"

She groaned. "You won't believe what happened."

"Is it something bad? Tell me."

"So..." A cold drip ran down her back. "Liam's mom walked in on us in bed this morning."

"Wait—you're sleeping with Liam?"

"I *was*. Not anymore." She sketched out what had happened over the last couple of weeks, finishing with the conversation she'd overheard between Liam and his mom.

"Well, that stinks," Hannah said. "But last I heard, you guys were arguing, and you were avoiding him, not sleeping together. Is it serious?"

She hesitated. Was it serious? "It seemed like it was heading that way. Maybe." She let out a frustrated groan. "I don't know...what do you think?"

"I think sometimes love is just right, no matter how long it's been. And sometimes it's *shit*."

Alarm bells went off in Jacinda's head. Hannah almost never swore, especially with such violence in her tone.

"What's happened?" she asked. "Is everything alright?"

"Depends on your definition of alright." Then she laughed, a harsh sound that sent a spike of worry into Jacinda's chest.

"You don't sound alright at all. What's going on?"

"Remember how I said Todd was Austin a while ago, checking out new talent?"

"Yes."

"He was checking it out *really* closely. Checking *her* out. And then he had to check her out again in Palm Springs."

The hard, bitter edge to her voice was something Jacinda had never heard before. "Do you mean...?"

"Yeah. He's been screwing around."

She sat up, suddenly knocked out of her own pity party. "Oh God, Han. I'm so sorry. Here I was going on and on about my drama..."

"It's okay."

"It's not okay. I want to kill him." This was what she'd always worried about—that having fallen for Hannah, Todd wouldn't see it through. Immersed in an ego-driven, unforgiving business, always looking for the next big thing, surrounded by people who'd do anything to succeed...his scrappy, risk-taking personality was his ticket to professional success, but made him a shitty husband. "How did you find out?"

"The woman called and told me. Said I should know what kind of man I'm married to. She was pissed because he ditched her when none of the labels showed any interest in her. Nice, huh? And he didn't deny it, so..." She fell silent.

"Jesus. I'm so sorry. What are you going to do?"

"I don't know. I mean, I do know one thing—I'm not staying with him." She sighed. "At least we don't have kids to complicate things."

Jacinda bit her lip. "There is one complication though. Me."

"Yeah, I did think of that." She managed a laugh. "Who's going to get custody?"

"Well, I can't stay with him either. If it comes down to choosing between my best friend and my manager, it's no choice at all. We'll just have to figure something out."

"Thank you. But...just don't make any decisions now, okay?" Hannah replied, assuming a businesslike tone that wasn't completely convincing. "He's getting this tour sorted for you. Eli has a one-off show at the Greek coming up, and he's going to announce the tour then. If you're on board, he'll want you to play a couple of songs."

"Okay."

"Okay what? About staying with Todd or doing the tour? Because I want you to do the tour. And I want you to do it the way *you* want to."

Jacinda thought about it. If Danielle had found a job, she didn't need anyone to watch Sam while she went for interviews. The kittens were taken care of, and Sam had friends his own age to play with. No one here needed her anymore. Not even the guy next door. It was time to get on with her real life. And Hannah was right—she'd do it her own way from here on, like she'd planned. Whatever she decided her own way would be.

"Both," she said to Hannah. "And I'll come back now.

You've always been in my corner, all the way through. Now it's my turn to be there for you. Come and stay with me for a while."

Hannah made a sound somewhere between a laugh and a sob. "That would be really good."

"Okay. I'll check out the flights and let you know when I'm arriving."

"Don't rush," Hannah said. "I'm fine." But the quaver in her words said otherwise.

"You will be. We'll make sure of it." She switched to her best menacing voice. "Todd, on the other hand..."

This time, it was definitely a laugh. Jacinda smiled, but her heart was breaking for her friend. "Love you."

"Love you too," Hannah replied.

When they hung up, Jacinda pulled her damp hair into a ponytail, and tugged on yoga pants and an old Green Day t-shirt. She and Hannah went back a long way, and had so much in common, they were like sisters. The kind that didn't fight. No way was she staying with Todd after he did that to her best friend. Some men didn't know what they had until it was gone. And some women didn't need those men anyway.

★

Downstairs, she found Sam out on the deck, herding kittens.

"Look!" he said. "They're outside!" He laughed as he diverted one away from the edge.

Jacinda bent down to stroke Velvet, who was keeping a close eye on her little family. "They're growing up." Then curiosity got the better of her. "Are you...going to see Liam today?"

"I went over already, but there was just a lady there. She said he was out." He trailed a long piece of twine along the deck, trying to get the kittens to chase it, but they were still too little. "I'll go back later. I can't miss a lesson. Liam says we're doing A minor next. He's good at that one."

"Sounds good," she told him. Even though he had his

own friends now, he was obviously still dedicated to his guitar lessons, and to Liam. "Where's your mom?"

He shrugged, engrossed in teasing Suede with the twine. "I don't know."

She left him there and went back inside to look for Danielle, to talk to her about going back to LA. She found her in the kitchen, rolling dough into little balls.

"What are you making?"

"Snickerdoodles. Sam loves them." She scooped another chunk of dough out of the bowl. "I thought you were going to bed."

"I was, but Hannah phoned. She's got some...stuff going on too."

"Oh, is she okay?"

But before Jacinda could reply, someone knocked at the door. She looked over her shoulder, anxiety suddenly stirring behind her ribs. Surely he wouldn't leave his mom to come and see her, after the morning's trauma.

Danielle blew a strand of hair off her face. "Could you see who it is? My hands are all sticky and snickerdoodley." She held them up.

"Uh...okay."

"It's probably the grocery delivery," she added, seeing Jacinda's hesitant face. "Totally worth paying extra to have it come to your door."

She breathed out. "Definitely. I hate going to the grocery store."

She straightened her slightly crumpled t-shirt, and went through to the entranceway. At this point, the world could take her as it found her. And the delivery guy had probably seen worse anyway.

She opened the door, wondering if Danielle had ordered ice cream.

Lainey Kingsley was standing on the porch.

Chapter Thirty-Four

L ainey's eyes flicked down and back up again, obviously taking in Jacinda's yoga pants, faded Green Day t-shirt, and makeup-free face.

"Did I catch you at a bad time?" she asked.

The concern in her voice was entirely fake.

"No." Feeling the height disadvantage, Jacinda stood a little taller. Lainey was famous for her persistence—she'd broken some of the biggest music industry stories for Meltdown, the magazine she worked for—but coming all the way to New Zealand was ridiculous. Jacinda could only wish she was newsworthy enough to be worth the trip. She held her chin higher. "Actually, yes. I'm busy. Can't it wait until I get back to LA?"

Lainey tipped her head, the light catching the diamond in her nose. "You look so different. Almost different enough that no one would recognize you." Then she smiled. "Almost."

Jacinda gritted her teeth. *Don't bite. Don't give her anything to write about.* "You're just the same though," she replied.

Lainey's gaze was level. "Yep, same old, same old, still just doing my job."

She decided not to ask why the hell Lainey had endured a twelve-hour flight just to pursue a delayed interview with her. But now she knew who the figure on the beach had been—Lainey, apparently doing her job.

"I'm sure," Jacinda replied. "Well, as you can see, I'm not doing *my* job right now, but Hannah will let you know when I'm back in LA."

With a thin smile, she wondered whether closing the door was worth the risk of an even more negative article next time round. But then she noticed Jess coming through the gate toward the front steps.

"Jacinda," she called as she approached. "Someone's—" She stopped as Lainey turned and stepped out from behind the clematis that hid one side of the porch. "Oh."

"Hi," Lainey said to her. "Finished work?"

"No, actually," Jess said. "And I thought you were on your way to the airport."

She shrugged. "Change of plans."

Jacinda looked from one of them to the other. "What's going on?"

"Some interesting things have come to light," Lainey said. "I'm here to see if you'd like to comment on a story."

Oh, shit. Maybe there was a reason why her nemesis had endured that flight after all. "What story?"

"The story about you and Ethan and the baby. And Liam."

Jacinda's stomach dropped. Her deepest secrets, in the hands of none other than Lainey Kingsley. How the hell did she find out? Her pulse racing, she looked at Jess, who shook her head.

"My source is very reliable," Lainey added. "But I'd like your perspective, for balance."

Source? She mentally counted up the people who knew the full story. It was a short list—Danielle, Riley, and, as of only a few minutes ago, Hannah. And Liam.

Obviously, it wasn't Hannah. And Danielle or Riley would have told her if someone had been asking questions.

Liam, though…what would he have done?

Lainey was watching. "So, would you like to comment?"

Looking down, she could see that Lainey was holding

her phone in her hand. She'd bet money it was recording their conversation. *Don't bite.* "There's nothing to comment on."

"Is that what you want me to run with?" Lainey raised an eyebrow. "Because you know people will fill in the blanks."

Inside, Jacinda was a tornado, but on the outside, she maintained a poker face, and a steady voice. "People will believe what suits them, whether a story is true or false. I have no comment."

"Well, okay," Lainey said, putting her phone in her pocket. "But don't say I didn't give you the chance."

When Jacinda didn't reply, she shrugged and went down the steps, bypassed Jess on the path, and went out the gate. Jess came up and stood next to Jacinda, and they watched as she got into a rental car and drove away.

When the car turned the corner, Jacinda grabbed onto the porch railing, her heart pounding, her mind going a million miles an hour.

"So she's a reporter," Jess said.

"Yeah. And she's really good at it. Unfortunately."

"I'm sorry I didn't get here before her," Jess said. "I was stuck at work, and I didn't have your number, so I was texting Riley, but she didn't reply." Her words were tumbling over each other. "Finally a friend of mine came in for a drink, so I basically shoved her behind the bar and came over."

"That's okay. It's not your fault," Jacinda replied. She was still trying to think whose fault it *was*. "Let's go inside."

"Will this ruin your career?" Jess said as they went in.

Jacinda stopped and looked at her. "My career?"

"Yeah. Everyone knows you have an alter ego. A *famous* alter ego."

"Everyone?"

"Pretty much. After you got up and sang, it wasn't too hard to figure out. Even with the hair."

"Oh." So Riley was right. Everyone did know.

"Which I really like, by the way," Jess added. "The blonde was a bit overdone."

For a second, Jacinda was almost offended. Then she screwed up her nose. "You know what? I thought so too."

They went into the living room, and Jacinda collapsed on the couch, trying to process the day's latest surprise. None of them had been good.

Danielle came in. "Was it not the groceries? I need milk for my coffee." Then she noticed Jess. "Oh, hi. I'm Danielle."

"Hi, nice to meet you," Jess replied. "I'm Jess."

"It wasn't the groceries," Jacinda said. "It was a reporter wanting me to comment on the story she's running. About Ethan and Liam and me...and everything."

Danielle's mouth dropped open. "How did she find you? And how did she get the story in the first place?"

Jacinda looked at Jess. "Maybe you know about that?"

Jess nodded. "I was working the bar at the double K today. And Liam came in."

With a sinking feeling, Jacinda knew she'd found the source. But something else had her attention too. "Liam went to the Kelp and King?" He'd said he would never go there—that it was Ethan's turf. But today, he went...after the drama with his mom.

"Yeah," Jess said. "And he just about drank us out of Jim Beam."

"And Lainey came in?"

"She made a beeline for him. At first I just thought she was interested in him. I mean, even all unshaven and disheveled, and half-lit, he's so hot."

Danielle looked at Jacinda, but she just gave a wry smile. It was true.

"When you're behind the bar, it's kind of like you're invisible, so people talk like you're not even there," Jess continued. "Mostly just the usual bullshit, you know. But something didn't seem right with their conversation. Like she was trying to get him to trust her, cozying up to him so he'd tell her stuff." She frowned. "And then he did. He never said your name, but obviously she knew who he meant."

Jacinda pressed her fingers to her forehead, rising anger

offsetting her sinking heart. She'd never been less happy to be right. She should never have gotten tangled up with him—this was what happened when you let lust override everything else. Faced with his mother's condemnation, he'd obviously gone full circle, back to the resentment, blame, and guilt they'd started with. And she couldn't condemn him for protecting his family, if it came down to her or them...but it was beyond shitty of him to spill everything out to a *reporter*.

Jess looked at her. "What happened with you guys? He was a mess."

She couldn't decide if him being a mess was a consolation or not. Probably not. "His mom found us in bed together and freaked out. I guess he couldn't handle it, on top of everything else."

Jess gasped. "That's horrific. I would *die*."

"What are you going to do?" Danielle asked.

"Do?" She waved the question away. "Brace myself, I guess. Hope it blows over quickly. People go nuts over stuff like this."

Now that her career was possibly heading for even shakier ground, she realized something. It was one thing to step away for a while, or think about making changes that would be unpopular with her label, and maybe with some of the fans she had. Even to consider walking away entirely, as her own decision. It was completely different to imagine it being snatched away by thin-lipped moralists and keyboard warriors, who'd revel in tearing her down for her youthful missteps.

"I shouldn't have come back here," she added. "I just wanted a break, to figure out how do things on my own terms. But you know, maybe that's just naïve. Once you put yourself out there, it's like everyone owns a little piece of you."

"Not here," Jess said. "Here you're just you."

Her words resonated in Jacinda's weary heart, an echo of what Liam had said. *You could be.* She could be herself, here in the bay. And she had been, just for a short time, with him. That glimpse of herself would have to be enough to sustain her back in her real, unreal life, a seed that she'd grow into something true and strong.

As if to confirm it, Danielle spoke. "You're right," she said to Jess. Then she turned to Jacinda. "It's a shame you can't stay forever...but we know you have a life to get on with."

Jess nodded, and Jacinda let out a breath. This had been an insane day. "Things come in threes, right?" she said. "Today it's been Liam's mom, my asshole manager betraying my best friend, and now Lainey Kingsley on my doorstep with probably the scoop of her year."

"Your manager?" Danielle asked.

"He and Hannah are married. But he's been cheating on her."

"Bloody hell." She shook her head. "It never rains..."

"Apparently." Then she sat up. "I need to get back to her," she said. "Can you manage without me?"

"Yes," Danielle said. "I've got the job, and now Sam has friends he could stay with if necessary. And Nadia said she'd help out if I need anything."

"That's great," Jacinda said. "You're on your way."

Danielle smiled. "I think so. And now you can get on your way too. Even though we'd rather have you here."

"Thanks." She looked at Jess. "And thank you too."

"I don't need thanks," she said. "After what I said that night..." Her cheeks reddened.

"Don't worry about it," Jacinda said. "You were only saying what everyone thought."

And what the rest of the world will probably think now.

"But I can't let this bring everything to a halt," she added, standing up. "I have things to do."

Chapter Thirty-Five

S he'd said her goodbyes. To Riley, who'd arrived in a flap just in time, and to Jess. And to Velvet and the kittens, with a smooch for each of them. Sam had arrived home, so Nadia came over with Izzy and Oliver to babysit, leaving Danielle free to drive her to the airport.

"But Jacinda, when are you coming back?" Sam asked as they said goodbye.

"One day. But not for a while." She hugged him tight. "Rock on, okay?"

"I *will*," he said confidently. "Liam has more chords to teach me."

"That's cool," she said. And meant it. Things might have gone to shit with Liam for her, but no one should get between a kid and his music. She and Liam both knew that.

Now she paused for a moment at the gate, and looked back at Nana Mac's house. It still felt like home, maybe even more than her place in Los Feliz. It was the place she'd hit her lowest point, but also the place she'd risen from.

In a strange way, the events of this trip had brought her two selves together. Jacinda Prescott and Cin Scott didn't have to be facing different directions. They could stand together, moving forward. And here, in the little wooden house on Tui Street, was the place to leave her memories of Ethan and the baby. She wouldn't forget—not at all—but maybe now she could let the past rest a little easier. She looked along to the Ward house. Maybe if she was gone, Liam and his mom could do the same. She'd leave without a word, just like he'd done that first night, leaving her to discover his absence. Like he'd said then, it was better this way.

She squeezed her eyes shut for a moment, defying the emotions that spiraled up in a rush, a sudden squall of anger, disappointment, and what-ifs. She was going back to LA to make sure Hannah was okay, and goddamn it, she'd be okay too. And so would Liam, eventually. In truth, she was only getting in the way of his healing, muddying things up again, stirring up memories and guilt every time they were together. They couldn't be okay together, but individually, they had a chance.

Then she took one last breath of the fragrant, salt-kissed Sweet Breeze Bay air, and got into the car.

★

As Liam went into the living room, three faces turned to look at him. Connor and Dane were perched awkwardly on the couch, each holding a cup of coffee. And his mother didn't look much happier than when he'd left a few hours before.

"Liam," she said, getting up. "Where have you *been?*"

"At the double K," he said.

He saw Dane and Connor exchange glances. Yeah, I went there, he wanted to say. What of it?

"After everything that happened, you left me here to go and get drunk," his mother said, disgust in her tone.

"I'm not drunk." Then he rethought it. "Okay, maybe I am. But I never needed a drink more than I did today."

She huffed. "So irresponsible."

"What happened?" Connor asked, looking from Liam to his mother, and back again.

So she hadn't told them. No surprise there.

"Great story," he said. "Mum came upstairs this

morning and found me and Jacinda..."

When it came to it, he couldn't say the words. Not with his mother standing there. But judging by the expressions on his friends' faces, he didn't need to.

"Holy shit," Connor said.

Dane's eyes were wide, but he held his tongue.

Liam nodded. "Yep. It was awesome."

His mother looked infuriated, probably at both his revelation and his sarcastic tone. "Was there any need to tell them that?" she said.

"Would you rather say nothing?" he asked her. "Would you rather keep everything a secret, like we've had to do for the last ten years?"

She blinked, color rushing to her cheeks. "That's enough."

But he couldn't stop himself. More than a decade's worth of frustration and guilt and secrecy was coming to the boil, and he had to take the lid off, no matter who else was here.

"What was the point of running like that?" he asked her. "We could have stayed. We could have rebuilt our lives, with our friends around us."

Dane stood up. "Uh...we actually just came to say goodbye. Maybe we'd better leave you to it."

But no one paid any attention. He sat down again.

"You *know* what the point was," Liam's mom replied.

"Yeah, for the sake of Dad's job. I know the drill. But for what? It was just an everyday tragedy. There was nothing illegal about what happened."

As he said it, he saw something change in her face.

"What?" he said, a sharp alert slicing through the bourbon fog. "What aren't you telling me?"

"I never wanted to keep you in the dark." With a deep sigh, she sat down too, clenching her hands on her lap. Then she looked at him. "The coroner's report found drugs in his system."

He frowned. "What kind of drugs?"

"Ecstasy. That's why we kept it secret. Your father had to pull strings to have the report suppressed."

Liam swayed on his feet. Even the dead have secrets. The dead, and their parents.

"Oh, shit," Dane muttered.

Everyone looked at him, and he shifted in his seat.

"Do you know something about it?" Liam asked.

He winced. "Not specifically."

"Generally, then." His tone suggested that Dane would be wise to volunteer the information himself.

"My brother, Blake," Dane said. "He lives in Singapore now. But…he used to deal."

"I didn't know that," Connor said.

"Me neither, until after he left the country. I went to visit him a few years ago, when I had a diving contract over there, and he told me. He's a straight-up family man now." He looked at Liam's mother. "I'm sorry, Carol."

She hesitated for a moment, then shook her head. "We don't know if Ethan got it from him," she said. "But I'm glad he's put it behind him."

Liam felt something niggling at him, a sort of karmic dissonance.

"Wait a second," he said to her. "You forgive Dane's brother for probably selling Ethan the drugs that could have tipped him over the edge, but you're still blaming Jacinda?"

She had no reply to that. He watched, feeling deadly calm, as she pursed her lips, denial all over her face.

"You know I'm in love with her," he said. The words were confession and accusation, aimed squarely at his mother.

"I knew it!" Connor exclaimed, but Dane shushed him.

Liam waited for her to reply—for the inevitable anger and resentment.

Instead, she burst into tears. "I never wanted to take you away from here," she sobbed. "But we realized that if it came out that your father had the report suppressed, he'd never work on the force again, in any country. It was better to slip away and quietly make a new start. And anyway, I couldn't keep looking at that ocean every single day, lying in bed at night listening to the never-ending waves, remembering. Night and day, day in and day out…"

"Ah, shit." Liam hesitated for a moment. Then he went over and sat next to her, and awkwardly gathered her in for a hug. She leaned her head against him, weeping as he patted her back, and soon the front of his t-shirt was damp.

"And now she's back," she said into his chest, her voice somewhere between incredulous and bitter. "And you're *sleeping* with her..."

At that, he let her go.

"I love her," he said, low and uncompromising.

"You *think* you do," she said. "But you're just caught up in her looks, the way Ethan was. How could you do that to the memory of your brother?"

And she started to cry again, her face crumpled and her shoulders shaking.

This is your mother, he told himself, as rage ran through his veins. She's still grieving. Fists clenched, he thought about Jacinda. Thought about the guilt. Thought about everything they'd acknowledged and worked through, to give themselves a chance at finding love and closure. She was beautiful, but she was so much more than that.

He stood up and looked at Connor and Dane, still sitting in silence with their coffees, which were no doubt cold by now. "When are you leaving?" he asked them.

"Not until the morning," Dane said. "But we both have early flights."

He glanced at his mother, who was still caught up in her anger and tears. "Can you stay here with her for a while, make sure she's okay? There's something I need to do."

"No worries," Connor said.

"Go get her," Dane added quietly.

He nodded. That was exactly what he intended to do.

★

He peered over Danielle's shoulder, hardly registering the words she'd spoken.

"Liam, she's not here," she repeated.

"But I need to talk to her."

She rolled her eyes. "You had all day to do that. And now you can't. She's gone."

The truth in her words stung, but he forced himself to stay focused. "What time is her flight?"

"Six thirty."

He looked at his watch, calculating the drive to the airport at this time of day, heading into rush hour.

But she shook her head. "She will have gone through customs by the time you get there."

Still standing on the doorstep, he took out his phone and hit Jacinda's name. It went straight to answerphone, a robotic male voice inviting him to leave a message. With a groan, he ended the call and stuffed the phone back in his pocket.

"Turned off?" Danielle asked.

"Yeah." He ran a hand through his hair, cursing his own stupidity. What was that Connor had said about being an idiot? "I totally screwed up."

She snorted. "It's not all about you, you know. She's had a terrible day all round. Her friend Hannah is having a crisis in LA. And a reporter turned up here, asking her about Ethan, and you." She narrowed her eyes. "Any idea how that came about?"

A sick jolt went through his guts. "A reporter?"

"Her name's Lainey Kingsley. Apparently you know her. American? Went to the double K today?"

He tipped backward. The American woman. She'd stood next to him at the night markets, and seen how he couldn't tear his eyes away from Jacinda on stage. She'd sat next to him at the pub, while he'd indulged in his own misery, and listened to his story. He'd fallen for her fake sympathy, and given everything away—including the fact that they were neighbors. Then he'd walked home, bourbon-laced and unthinking, probably with the reporter on his tail. He'd led a reporter right to her door.

And now Jacinda would have to pay for his fuck-up.

As the implications sank in, Danielle was watching him.

"So yeah," she said. "You totally screwed up."

Chapter Thirty-Six

The airplane icon moved slowly but steadily, tracking across the screen set into the seat in front of her. Jacinda ran a finger over the blue expanse of the Pacific, from the small islands of New Zealand at bottom left, to where the States loomed on the right. The distance was greater than pixels on a screen, or miles across an ocean. It was the distance between the future she'd almost had, and the future that awaited her in reality.

She sighed and leaned back, looking out the window to where daylight was fading on the horizon. It was going to be a long flight, especially knowing what she'd find at the other end. At least she hadn't gotten on board and discovered Lainey Kingsley sitting across the aisle.

And there was one thing she could do to pass the time. She pulled out her laptop and set it on the tray table in front of her. She'd been struggling with the chapters she was supposed to write for the book, but now she knew what to write. It wasn't what they'd asked for, exactly—but it would be the most honest advice she could give any young woman starting out. She opened the document, and started over.

★

After dragging through customs at LA airport, Jacinda put on a baseball cap, pulled the brim down low over her sunglasses, and stepped out into arrivals. In almost any other city, walking out in sunglasses would make you more conspicuous, not less. But this was LA—she'd be just one of many.

Hannah had replied to her text before she left, promising that a car would be there for her, and saying that the driver would be looking for a passenger called Shelley Breeze. Jacinda had laughed at her clever choice of name, and hoped like hell that Ms. Breeze would get out undetected. Now she looked at the line-up of drivers holding signs, searching for her own.

Just as she caught sight of it, she heard someone shout her name. But not Ms. Breeze, and not Jacinda Prescott.

"Cin! Cin Scott!"

She veered toward her driver like a fox dodging hounds, but there was no escape. Within a moment she was being jostled by reporters, flashes going off around her as bystanders gawped at the commotion.

"Is it true?" one of them asked, thrusting a mike in front of her. "Did your teenage lover commit suicide when you left him?"

"Why are you sleeping with his brother now?" another called, trying to elbow closer.

She put her head down and silently plowed on, her heart going like a jackhammer in her chest as they milled around her. When she reached the driver, he took her suitcase in one hand and put the other arm around her, shielding her from the onslaught.

"Come with me," he said.

And she did. He was tall and strong, and tucked close against him, she was sheltered from the physical danger. But he couldn't protect her from the questions that kept flying, each one tearing her more apart.

"What do you have to say to your fans?"

"What about the baby?"

"Did you have an abortion?"

With the paparazzi swarming around, they made it to

the car, and the driver helped her in. She breathed out with relief as the door slammed shut, and the shouting was suddenly muffled. The car pulled away from the curb, leaving the melee behind. Then, behind the tinted windows, shut off from the driver's seat, she leaned back, rested her head against the seat, and let herself cry. Just one time. For everything that might have been, but never was. And never would be.

Then, as they hit the freeway, she sat up straight, blew her nose, and got out her phone to call Hannah and let her know they were on the way. Now, she'd have to be strong.

When they arrived to collect Hannah, she was waiting by the front door with her bags packed. Jacinda went up the steps and pulled her into a fierce hug.

"I'm so sorry about Todd," she told her. "That shithead."

A tiny laugh erupted from her friend. "Yeah. And I'm sorry about Liam."

They took a step back, and smiled at each other. God, it was good to see Hannah again—but the guarded pain in her eyes was obvious. Jacinda shook her head. "Men."

"Right?" Hannah threw up her hands. "And the moral of this story is, we're better off without them."

"They don't deserve us."

"Ex-*actly*," Hannah agreed.

"Yeah. We don't need them."

Then the driver came and picked up Hannah's bags, easily lifting all three at once and carrying them down to the car. They watched him go.

"Apart from the ones who carry our bags, maybe," Jacinda clarified, as he effortlessly hoisted them into the trunk.

Hannah laughed. "I missed you."

"Ditto." She tipped her head toward the front door. "Is he home?"

"No. He's been spending most of his time at the office."

Jacinda took her hand. "And you won't be here when he gets back. Let's get out of here."

★

Jacinda pushed the last morsel of apple pie around her plate as Hannah concentrated on the screen, thoughtfully sipping from her wine glass as she read. Finally, she put the glass down and looked at Jacinda across the table.

"This isn't what you signed up to write," she said, gesturing to the laptop.

Jacinda bit her lip. "I know." God, she hadn't realized how nerve-wracking it would be having someone else read your writing.

But then Hannah smiled. "This is way *better* than what you signed up to write."

"Really? Thanks." She grinned. "I couldn't find a way into it originally, but once I started thinking about that, it seemed like the only way to go. I wrote it all on the flight back."

She'd kind of stuck to the brief—two chapters offering advice to female singers and musicians wanting to get started and move ahead in the industry. It just wasn't the kind of uplifting, jazz-hands tone the publisher had in mind. Nothing was sugar-coated—but it was empowering. With clear-eyed honesty, she'd set out the pitfalls alongside the pluses, encouraging young women to stand up for themselves, and others.

Which reminded her of something.

"By the way, I'm going to talk to Mitchell about Greg," she said.

Hannah made an O with her lips. "Really?"

Mitchell Dunn was the head of Altitude Records. Jacinda hadn't spent a lot of time with him, but she knew he wasn't a man to be toyed with. She didn't know how he'd react to being told straight up about Greg's misdemeanors...but she'd find out soon enough.

"Yeah." She frowned. "I don't know how many other women he might have treated that way. I *have* to say something."

"I'll back you all the way," Hannah said. "You know that."

"Thanks."

"Whatever happens," Hannah added, an indirect acknowledgement that things might not go smoothly.

Jacinda blew her friend a kiss from the other side of the table. She didn't mention the other question—whether Todd would also back her all the way, even though he knew what had been going on. If he wasn't her manager anymore—which she and Hannah had yet to decide on—he'd be more likely to take Greg's side than hers, for the sake of his other acts. Time would tell.

She stood up. "Come on, let's go sit in the comfy seats."

"Oh, I'm ready for that," Hannah said, patting her stomach.

It had been a night of ups and downs. Hannah had told her about the phone call, and how Todd had come home to find her waiting with the bitter truth—and not denied it. Recounting that night, she was stoic, and Jacinda could tell she was determined to be strong and professional. The three of them were tied together in business just as much as by friendship, or marriage. Untangling the three threads of their triangle might not be easy, especially if Todd decided to play hard ball. Jacinda had seen him do that often enough on her behalf—and she wouldn't put it past him to do it now.

After that, they'd gone online to see how far the story about Jacinda's South Pacific summers—then and now—had spread. The answer was, pretty much everywhere. And sure enough, people were filling in the blanks, the comment sections full of speculation, fake facts, and the kind of gleeful meanness that spread like a rash online. Here and there, people commented in her defense, but they were definitely outnumbered.

Jacinda had sat back, chewing her thumbnail as she tried not to react. She was used to being in the public eye, and criticism was nothing new. But this made her feel so...*exposed*. She hadn't even got to grips with it all herself—with the new, fragile relationship between her and Liam, and the past that both divided and connected them—before it was splashed all over the internet. She wondered if her father was reading it, nodding as it confirmed his long-held opinion of her. And, she realized, she'd better call her mom. This was the last thing she needed.

Thanks a lot, Liam. And Lainey.

She sighed as she scrolled through the comments section of yet another click-baity website, below the picture of Liam at the night markets, and herself under siege at the airport. "I guess we knew this would happen."

"We did, unfortunately," Hannah said. "But people will move on to the next scandal before long."

"I hope so."

"I know so," she said firmly, shifting the laptop away. "Don't read any more. We'll deal with it tomorrow."

So they'd quit Google and talked some more about everything that had happened while they were apart, shed tears over things gone badly, and laughed through those tears as they settled back into the warmth of their friendship.

Thank God for women friends, Jacinda thought now as they cleared the dessert from the table, leaving the dishes for later. She'd been lucky enough to make some in Sweet Breeze Bay too. What would they all be doing right now? She looked at the clock on the microwave. It was getting late here, so it would be early evening there now, but the next day. It was weird to think of them all there, getting on with things in the future.

For a moment, she let herself wonder if Liam was getting on with things. If he was reading everything online, trying to hold it together, like she was. And if he was feeling guilty about being the one who handed Lainey her scoop.

Part of her hoped so.

The other part of her missed him so much it hurt.

Hannah went past, carrying the bottle of wine. "I call dibs on the corner."

They both sprang into action, aiming for the corner of the couch that was undoubtedly the best seat in the house. There was a table alongside for drinks and snacks, it was closest to the kitchen (and thus the fridge), and it had a premium view out to the lights of LA.

They were almost there, with Hannah slightly ahead, when Jacinda heard her phone ring, and looked over her shoulder. Her hesitation cost her the seat.

"That doesn't count," she said, as she went to see who was calling. "I call a do-over."

She'd switched back to her American phone. After checking with Danielle, she'd left her little New Zealand one with Sam, and the memory of his face when she gave it to him still made her laugh. She smiled as she picked up the phone and saw it was a New Zealand number calling. Maybe Sam had his new SIM card and was calling to let her know.

"Hello?" she said.

There was a brief silence, then Liam said, "Hi."

Shock knocked the words out of her, and she felt her cheeks flush with heat. Taken aback, she looked at Hannah, sitting in the coveted corner spot.

"Who is it?" Hannah whispered.

She pointed at the phone, and silently mouthed, "It's him."

Hannah's eyes widened in surprise, and Jacinda nodded.

"Are you there?" Liam said, his voice uncertain.

She cleared her throat. "Yeah. I'm here."

And she waited to hear what he had to say.

Chapter Thirty-Seven

The distance in her voice reflected every one of the miles between them, and then some. Sitting on the edge of his bed, Liam hesitated. Now that he'd called, everything he wanted to say caught in his chest, like that first time he saw her again over the gate. It seemed like the more important the moment, the less eloquent he became.

"How did you get my number?" she asked, when he didn't reply immediately.

"Riley gave it to me," he said.

She made a sound that could have been resignation or irritation. "Of course. Always looking on the bright side."

He wasn't sure if the bright side meant something good in this case. Right now, it was bloody hard to see any bright side at all. "So, uh...have you been online since you got back?"

"To see all the stories about myself? With all the details *you* gave Lainey Kingsley? If I hadn't, the paparazzi pack waiting for me at the airport would have given me a clue."

He'd seen the pictures—Jacinda shielding her face, sheltering in the lee of some huge minder, as reporters swarmed around. "I'm really sorry—"

"Listen, you didn't have to throw me under the bus," she said, cutting him off. "I would've gone anyway."

"What? I didn't want you to go."

"Sure. That's why you let me walk away after your mom turned up, without defending me. That's why you apologized to her for forgetting everything."

"You heard that?"

"I did. And that's fine. For one thing, it made it really easy to come home when Hannah needed me."

He wanted to reach down the line and shake her. For once, the words came freely. "If you'd listened a bit longer, you would have heard the *rest* of what I said. That I was sorry because I knew she'd find it hard to hear, but being with you is the only way I've *ever* been able to forget. The only reprieve from the fucking albatross of guilt around my neck." He paused. "Which is now two albatrosses."

"Well, good," she said. "Because for everything I might have done wrong all those years ago, I didn't deserve this. After everything we—"

He couldn't stand it. "I *never* intended to hurt you. I had no idea she was a reporter. I'd been drinking, and it just...overflowed."

She snorted. "You know 'I was drunk' doesn't actually cut it as an excuse."

"No, it doesn't. But my own mother had just seen me with a full-scale hard-on, and a naked woman. And given that the woman was you, and the fallout was spectacular, I needed a goddamn drink. If you hadn't left the country without saying anything, I could have explained."

It was hot in his room, but he could feel the chill on the line. Shit. This apology wasn't coming out as...apologetic as he'd planned.

"It doesn't matter now," she said, her words stiff and careful. "I've got fallout to deal with here too, thanks to you. It's better if we just make a clean break. Like you planned when you snuck out that night."

The reminder stabbed in his already aching chest. "If I could take back either of those shitty mistakes, I would. You know that."

"I know," she said. "But I'm not going to come between you and your family yet again."

"The remnants of my family have nothing to do with

you and me."

She was quiet for what felt like a long while. Then she said, "We both know that's not true."

He let out a frustrated breath, and dragged a hand through his hair. She might be right, but he wasn't going to give her the point. Right now, it seemed like his family was even more fractured than before. His father had called from Australia, enraged that Liam had dragged them "through the mud". Liam had aimed a reciprocal anger down the line. If his father hadn't been so determined to suppress the truth—unnecessarily, in Liam's opinion—they could have stayed in the bay, surrounded by friends, and maybe found some kind of healing over time. Instead, they'd walked away from everything they knew, and their broken hearts had never begun to mend. Then he remembered what Jacinda didn't know.

"There's something you should know," he said. "I found out that Ethan had ecstasy in his system when he died."

He heard her intake of breath. "Really? I never..."

"Yeah. None of us would have picked it either. The thing is, I don't think he ever felt as invincible as he wanted us to believe. Maybe he just needed to feel it that day."

There was a heavy silence at her end. "I'm sorry I made him feel that way," she said quietly.

"Don't be. He had a lot going on. He'd been a local hero for...I don't know, forever. I think the thought of going to Sydney and starting from nothing was more daunting than he'd admit. Then your news, and finding out you'd left..."

She made a small, pained sound.

"I'm not aiming that at you," he said. "I think all he meant to do was escape for a few hours with a bottle of vodka and an uncomplicated high. Get away from things...just hang out somewhere secret and look at the moon. But...it went wrong. And when he found out about the coroner's report, my dad pulled strings to get it suppressed because he was afraid it would mess with his chances of promotion. Even when he started out as a cop on the street, he always wanted the next step up, and the next. By then, he had a shot at making it to the top job in the country."

"But you left anyway," she said.

"From what Mum told me, he ended up more worried that people would find out he'd played the system. And she found it too hard living by this ocean..." He left the sentence unfinished.

"Oh, God." She hesitated, then asked, "Is she okay?"

He sighed. "She's angry with me. Luckily Lainey didn't find out those extra details, but having the story all over the internet...and you and me...it's brought everything to the surface again. But then, she's been angry with everything for a long time. All these years."

"I get that. Which is why me leaving was the best thing."

"No, it wasn't. I didn't want you to leave. I wanted you to stay. And I never expected to want that. All these years, for me, thinking about you made me feel worse—the guilt of letting myself fall for you then, when you were with Ethan, and then the way those feelings wouldn't go away, even after everything that happened."

As he spoke, he expected her to interrupt and shut him down, but she didn't. So he kept talking. He had nothing to lose now. Maybe, somehow, he'd find the right words to make her understand. And maybe they had no chance of a future together—but he wanted her to admit her feelings too. He wanted it to be real, to know that what they'd shared wasn't just a desperate need to smother their memories with sex and denial.

"But *being* with you..." he said. "It was like I could breathe again. That summer turned into a nightmare. But this summer, it felt like we had a chance at something new." When she didn't reply, he added. "I think you felt it too. We weren't just drowning out the past with lust and body heat. We had something. We *have* something."

"Maybe..." she said slowly, and that one word held all his hopes. Two syllables of possibility, where his future could veer in a new direction.

"But we always knew this was trouble," she continued. "We knew we should stay away from each other. The past never really goes away, especially a past like ours—it would always get in the way. And I'm not going to come between you and your mom—you're all she has. She needs you. And you need your family."

He could feel her slipping away from him. "What about you, though?" he asked urgently. "What do *you* need?"

"I need to move on, and that's what I'm doing. And so should you."

The finality in her voice was matched with a gentleness that made his heart sink.

"So I'm going to hang up now," she said softly.

And then she did.

Chapter Thirty-Eight

As he sat on the bed, his head in his hands, he heard footsteps coming up the stairs. Then his mother looked around the door frame.

"Who was on the phone?" she asked.

Not for a moment did he consider lying, or using the all-purpose 'No one'.

Anyway, judging by her demeanor, she'd already guessed.

"Jacinda," he said. "In LA."

Distaste flashed across her face. "Why is she calling you?"

"She didn't call me. I called her."

She pursed her lips. "Don't be childish."

"There's nothing childish about it." He stood up. "Who called who matters. I called *her* because I knew she would never have called me. Because I owed her an apology, for a whole lot of things. Because she's worth fighting for."

"And what did she have to say?"

"She told me to move on," he said. "And that's exactly what we all need to do."

His mom stepped back as he went through the doorway and headed along the hallway. Move on, Jacinda had said. And she was right. Something had to give—and for better or worse, he was going to push it to the edge, and over. He could hear his mother following behind him but he didn't stop, just powered down the stairs and into the living room. He grabbed up Ethan's guitar, and the amp, and started for the front door.

"What are you doing?" she asked, the indignation on her face suddenly replaced with trepidation.

"Something we should have done long ago," he said. "But it's not too late."

"What's going on?" she cried. "Did she tell you to do this?"

At that, he stopped in his tracks and turned to look at her. "No, she didn't. In fact, she told me we shouldn't see each other again, because she didn't want to come between you and me."

His mother blinked in surprise, pulling her chin back.

"That's right. She was thinking about *you*."

He turned and went out the front door, banging it on its hinges, leaving her standing there with a disbelieving expression. As he went out the gate and turned left, the skateboard boys were rolling down the sidewalk.

"Cool guitar, bro," one of them called.

He raised his eyebrows and nodded in agreement, but kept moving. "Thanks."

At number ten's gate, he stopped, and his mother caught up.

"Why are you doing this to me?" she asked, pressing her hand to her chest.

He looked at the woman who'd been there for him and Ethan through everything. Who'd cared for them and cared about them, encouraged their dreams and reprimanded them for their misdeeds, and done the work of two parents while their dad put in endless shifts at work. Who'd sat alongside through hours of homework, made a thousand school lunches, put up with loud music and rowdy teenagers, hosted parties, fed hordes of their friends, and always had faith that they were destined for greater things than she could even imagine.

She'd loved them both equally, but now seemed to miss one of them more than she loved the other. Nothing he'd done had made up for Ethan's loss, and he knew he never could. But, like some kind of on-the-fly intervention, he knew what he had to do now.

"Mum," he said, as gently as he could. "It's not about you. It's about finding some kind of peace, for all of us. It's about letting ourselves forget in one way, but still remembering all the important stuff."

She eyed the guitar. "And how are we supposed to do that?"

"One step at a time," he said. "Come on."

He led the way along the path and up the steps, and knocked on the door. After a moment, Danielle answered.

"Oh," she said, the corners of her mouth turning down. "It's you."

Given their last encounter, after Jacinda's departure, he'd been prepared for this. But he knew he had one ally in the house.

On cue, Sam came to the door.

"Liam!" he said. "Sorry I didn't come to my lesson yesterday. Mum wouldn't let me." He sent her a dark glare.

"That's okay. You have to do what your mum says, right?" He turned to the side, making room. "This is *my* mum, Carol."

Danielle stepped forward, ignoring Liam as she held out her hand. "Nice to meet you. I'm Danielle."

His mum took her hand, looking flustered. "You too."

"And I'm Sam," Sam informed her. Then he looked at Ethan's guitar. "Are we having a lesson now?"

"No. Well, maybe. I forgot the leads, though. And I actually came for a different reason." He put the amp down, and stood the guitar in front of him as he addressed Sam. "You're an enthusiast, and that counts for a lot in music. And in life. You'll never get to meet him, but my brother was a lot like you are now. I think you could be as good a guitarist as he was. He's not here to use his guitar anymore, so I want you to have it."

Sam's mouth fell open. His freckled cheeks were suddenly pink, his big eyes even huger than usual. "Me?" he squeaked.

Liam glanced at his mother, standing next to him. Her mouth had also fallen open, but in contrast to Sam, she did *not* look beside herself with happiness. He watched as the frown line between her brows deepened, and then her lips pressed into a thin line.

Before she could say anything, he took her hand. It sat rigid in his, and he knew the same tension was gripping her whole body. It had been there since the night Ethan died, inhabiting her like a ghost.

"She didn't see your amazing performance on Friday night," he continued. "But my mum knows that boys and guitars belong together, like Marmite on toast. So now this one is yours."

With one hand, he passed Sam the guitar. With the other, he grasped his mother's hand more firmly, as both comfort and warning. She didn't say anything.

Sam took the instrument reverently, his expression rapturous. He held it up for Danielle. "Mum...look," he said, awe in his voice. When he looked back at Liam, it was obvious that his eyes were bright with tears.

"This is the best thing that's *ever* happened," he said. "*Ev*-er."

"Don't forget your manners," Danielle told him. And her eyes were shining too.

"Thank you, Liam!" Sam said, breaking into a grin. "This is *so cool!*"

Then he sat down right there on the doorstep, his skinny legs sticking out in front of him, and started playing.

Danielle laughed, wiping a finger under each eye. "Thank you," she said to Liam. "For everything." Then she turned to Carol. "He's been amazing with Sam. I don't know what we would have done without him."

Both women looked at him. In his mother's eyes, he saw something unexpected—pride. Then a tear slipped down her cheek, and her hand finally closed around his in return. He squeezed back, relieved that she was still with him. But with that gentle pressure, something seemed to break in her. All at once, she collapsed into tears. There on the porch of number ten, within a stone's throw of the ocean, all her pent-up anguish and loss and memories seemed to escape in an unstoppable flood of great, gulping sobs. She buried her face in her hands, and her shoulders heaved. Without hesitation, Liam gathered her in, and this time there was nothing awkward about the hug.

"I—I'm s—sorry," she sobbed.

"It's alright," he said, letting her cry, letting the past flow over them both.

At their feet, Sam gaped at the sight of a grown-up—a mom, even—weeping like a child. Liam saw Danielle put her hand on Sam's head, silently letting him know that it was okay, and also to keep quiet. All three of them waited, giving Carol the time she needed.

After a while, her sobs began to settle, and she lifted her head and wiped her eyes.

"I really am sorry," she said, as Danielle handed her a tissue.

"Don't even think about it," she replied. "Truly."

Carol gave her nose a resounding blow. "Thank you."

"Do you think...would you like to come in?" Danielle offered gently, gesturing inside. "We have tea and snickerdoodles."

Sam looked up at Liam. "Will you give me a lesson now?" His mind was obviously back on the important stuff.

"Sure," Liam said, in reply to both of them. "If that's okay with my mum." He turned to her, unsure if she was up to it.

"Yes, that's okay," she said. "In fact, that would be nice." Then she smiled at him, and despite her teary eyes and red nose, there was a lightness in her face that he hadn't seen for a long, long time. "And I think that will be your second lesson for the day," she added.

Sam got to his feet. "You were going to teach me A minor," he reminded Liam.

Liam gave his mom's hand one last squeeze. "I was," he said. "But that'll cost an extra snickerdoodle."

"We have *heaps*," Sam said. "I bet Mum will let you have an extra one."

He looked hopefully at Danielle, and she nodded. "You

know, I think there might be enough. Come on in."

On the verge of following his mom through the door, Liam hesitated, and she looked back. "What about Dad?" he asked.

She dabbed her nose with the tissue, and shook her head. "He's tried to be a hero all his life. But sooner or later, we all need rescuing...as I realized just now. I'll take care of him."

And she went with Sam into the house, leaving Liam on the doorstep.

Sooner or later, we all need rescuing. He'd been rescued himself, but his rescuer didn't think she had a place in his life. He didn't know if she wanted to be convinced otherwise—or if he even had a place in hers—but he had to find out, one way or another.

Chapter Thirty-Nine

Mitchell Dunn had the corner office to beat all corner offices. Big enough to swing not just a cat but an elephant, with a luxurious expanse of pale, plush carpet, a selection of mid-century and antique furnishings clearly put together by an interior decorator, and a view that stretched from the city to the hills.

Jacinda sat in one of the huge leather armchairs on the other side of his desk, and looked at that view as she waited for him to finish his phone call. Her feet barely touched the floor, and she wondered if the choice of enormous chairs was deliberate—there was no better way to get the advantage in business, or in life, than to make others feel small.

She wasn't going to feel small though. Greg had tried that often enough, and it was exactly what she was here to stand up against—not just for herself, but for anyone else in his orbit. After a night's sleep to recover from the flight, this was her first stop.

Mitchell finished up his call and tossed his phone onto the expansive mahogany desk. "We've been following your story online," he said, getting straight to business. "Obviously it needs to be addressed."

It was the first time she'd seen him one on one, without A&R people or assistants—and actually, *he* was smaller than she remembered. She took off the baseball cap she'd worn on the drive there, and ran her fingers through her hair. It had grown since her home haircut, but the natural color starting to show at the roots was pretty much the same as the brown she'd used to cover her faux blonde.

"Yeah, Greg called last night," she said. She didn't add that she'd ignored his call. And his next call. And the one after that.

"You're looking...different," Mitchell said. "Are you seeing Heather this week, now you're back?"

"No," she said. "I hadn't planned to."

She knew what he was getting at—as the stylist who worked with most of the label's artists, Heather would throw a fit if she knew that Jacinda had put a box color in her hair. Not to mention her lack of makeup. But, for better or worse, she'd given up hiding behind layers of Mac or Lancôme. A little piece of that barefoot Sweet Breeze Bay girl had come home with her.

"Oh." His eyes swept her from head to toe, communicating his thoughts without a word needed. "And what does Todd think about this new look?"

"It seems likely that Todd and I will be parting company." She didn't offer any more details. That was between Hannah and her husband. Soon to be *ex*-husband.

Mitchell raised an eyebrow. "I see. But I hear you're on board for Eli's tour?"

She still wasn't thrilled about Todd and Greg coming up with that, but in the end she'd agreed with Hannah that she shouldn't throw away the opportunity—not until she was sure about what she wanted to do next. If nothing else, it would be the perfect way to test her new look with an audience, and try out some new material. Plus, she needed something to keep her busy. Something to stop her mind from wandering back across the seas, to a complicated man, in a small bay, in a faraway country.

She nodded. "Yes, we're getting together tonight with his team to start planning."

"You and Greg?"

She paused for a moment. "That's why I'm here. There's a

problem with Greg. He's been acting inappropriately for a long time...and after my last show, he went too far."

She was ready to elaborate, but Mitchell sighed.

"You're not the first person to mention this."

"You *knew*?"

He leaned back in his chair, peaking his fingers together. "You know this business well enough by now. Greg gets things done. He plays the game. Do you think you would have come this far without him?"

A hot point of anger concentrated in her chest as his words sank in. "Well, I'm not playing his game anymore. If the label still wants me after the fallout from Lainey's interview—"

"Oh, we still want you," he said, interrupting her. "In fact, we think you just upped your currency."

She frowned. "In what way?"

"You just got a whole lot more interesting," he said. "And we want to capitalize on that. We want you out there doing press and kicking ass."

She shook her head. "That's pretty much the opposite of what I want to do."

"Cin." His mouth twisted into a smile. "In this world, everything plays into your brand. It's entertainment. And right now, people are extra entertained by your scandal. It's tragedy, sex, and drama, all the stuff that keeps people engaged. Once you put yourself out there, the personal is always public. And your 'personal' just got a whole lot sexier."

She forced herself to take a breath before she answered. "I'm not using my personal life—and someone else's personal life—to build my brand. There are real people involved here. Real people I actually give a damn about. And I'm not making my 'brand' sexier." She made air quotes around the hated word. "And Greg is a deal breaker. If we can't find a solution, then..."

"Then what?" His tone dared her to say it.

"Then I'm out." She stood up, calm as the water in Sweet Breeze Bay on a still night, despite the fact that she'd just put everything on the line, in the hands of the most powerful man at Altitude Records. But she had no regrets. She'd already considered walking away, and if it came to that, she'd have options. She didn't know exactly what they might be, right now…but one way or another, she'd make it work.

"I'll have to think about that," Mitchell said, not getting up.

"Okay," she replied evenly. "You know where to find me."

And she went out, leaving the door open behind her.

Chapter Forty

Saturday night in LA, and the Greek was jumping. From her spot in the wings, Jacinda watched Eli Tyler blast through one hit song, and then another, filling the cool night air with music. Every one of the red seats was occupied by an enthusiastic fan, all of them now on their feet. In the hills behind, the scrappy trees were awash with colored lights, and the audience was lit with screens and camera flashes. For Eli's fans, this one-off night was an event to capture and share, something they could brag about and sigh over for a long time to come.

There were bigger venues he could have chosen—probably three times as many people would fit at the Hollywood Bowl—but she knew it wasn't about that. With its storied past, the Greek was the perfect place for an exclusive showcase. Drawing on the Greek's history, and becoming part of it, was worth more than any head count.

Although she still had mixed feelings about signing on for the tour, she'd met with Eli and his team that first time determined to follow through. Until she heard otherwise from Mitchell or Greg, she'd just have to assume she still had a label.

Eli had raised an eyebrow at her new look, then grinned. "Notoriety suits you."

She'd scanned her brain for a smart come-back, then

decided to go with gracious instead. "Thanks."

"I didn't know you had such a racy past, Cin Scott," he said. "Then again, maybe the name should have given it away."

"I'm going back to Jacinda now," she said. "And you didn't know a lot of things about me." She gave him a level stare that held the weight of their own past. "Just like I didn't know things about *you*."

He tipped his worn cowboy hat. "Touché."

For a few moments, they'd looked at each other, measuring the challenge of what might lie ahead. Being on the road condensed everything into an intensity greater than everyday life, and they had more baggage than the road cases and guitar bags they'd be traveling with. Then he shook his head.

"I have the feeling I missed out on something, not getting to know you properly," he said. "For what it's worth, I was a jackass."

She cupped one ear. "I'm sorry, you were what?"

"A jackass," he repeated. "Totally."

She smothered a smile. "Yeah, you were."

He held out his hand. "Looking forward to working with you, Jacinda Prescott."

"You too, Eli Tyler." She took his hand, and they shook on it. And with her hand in his, she felt no remnant of their history. No anger or resentment, no attraction—just the possibilities of what lay ahead.

"Even if *you* should be opening for *me*," she added.

He laughed. "One day, I bet."

But she didn't care. She was starting over, in her own way, and whatever happened would happen. She'd shocked Hannah by saying that maybe this would be her last tour, before backtracking—the last thing her friend needed was to think she might lose her job as well as her marriage. And Jacinda could only wait and see what would happen with Altitude, too. But she knew that nothing was guaranteed, and she'd do what her heart told her was right.

Since then, she'd done one thing she knew was right—she'd left Todd, and Hannah had stepped in to look after things in the meantime. And despite Mitchell's request, she hadn't done any press—especially not that postponed interview with Lainey Kingsley. She was waiting until after this show, and Eli's announcement, so there was something other than her Sweet Breeze Bay scandal to talk about.

She'd successfully avoided talking about it, even if she couldn't stop thinking about it. But...if she kept on keeping busy, those thoughts might start to fade away.

That was the plan, anyway. No luck so far.

Now, as the lead guitarist launched into a solo, Eli glanced Jacinda's way, and gave her a wink. She had to smile. His charm hadn't lessened at all—if anything, it was increasing as he matured, the years (and his growing collection of ink) adding a rugged, knowing edge to his looks that only made him more attractive. His screaming fans obviously thought so too.

Mitchell came up behind her. "He's a showman," he said, tucking his hands into the pockets of his designer jeans.

She watched as Eli tipped back his signature cowboy hat with a cavalier grin, and kicked into the chorus again. "Yeah, he is."

They stood side by side for a couple of minutes, watching the performance. Then Mitchell spoke, keeping his eyes on the stage.

"So, Greg has decided to take a job in a different part of the organization."

She felt her eyes widen, but didn't look away from the stage. "Really?"

He nodded. "He and I agreed that a more behind-the-scenes opportunity would suit him better. Something less...hands-on."

After their meeting, she'd fully expected Mitchell to do absolutely nothing about Greg. But he'd gone ahead and assigned her a different A&R person, who hadn't pushed back when she'd stood firm about not taking things sexier. She'd been waiting to hear what, if anything, would be done about Greg, and had talked to Hannah about what to do next herself. She hadn't expected this.

"I had a word with our legal team," Mitchell continued. "You were right. He's been pushing it. Putting us in a potentially untenable situation. Something had to be done."

Translation: Mitchell was avoiding a law suit. She glanced sideways at him, but his face was impassive. She might wish he'd taken action for nobler reasons, but at least something had been done.

"Well, I hope he can make a success of his new role," she said.

As Mitchell nodded in agreement, she resolved to keep her ear to the ground.

Then Eli gave her a nod, and they heard him introduce her to the crowd. Feeling the familiar butterflies in her stomach, and the adrenaline start to race in her blood, she adjusted the strap on her old Gibson. It was a bit battered now, a few of the edges knocked off...but the heart of it was the same, the sound still true.

Kind of like her.

"Break a leg," Mitchell told her.

Then she walked out onto the stage...with no idea how she'd be received.

Eli greeted her with a kiss on each cheek, sending a message to the audience, the cameras, the world—they were on the same stage, and everything was great. Then he took her hand and held it up, the gesture of a champion, imbuing her with a little of his own magic.

"Jacinda Prescott!" he announced, as though she'd already triumphed in some mighty challenge, and the audience roared with approval.

She waved to her mom, who was standing with Hannah in the front row, and then held her hand out to the crowd. So far, so good. Off stage, she'd always been quiet, diffident about attention (particularly the unwelcome sexual kind). But on stage, in front of people waiting to be entertained, she always felt transformed, revolutionized—and now she remembered that high all over again. Their anticipation was palpable, charging her with a buzz better than anything available over the counter or in a back alley. In a way, she was standing before them as someone completely different.

New hair, a new look, and a new strength. And a new name. Cin Scott was no more—not forgotten, but put to rest along with the other parts of her past.

The things that had made her what she was, but couldn't be part of her life now.

The people.

Liam.

For the briefest moment, she closed her eyes. Part of her brain was hardwired on New Zealand time now, and she knew without calculating that if it was nine at night here, it was just hitting evening there. A summer Sunday, the sand still warm, the tide on its way in or out, the ocean hiding one less secret now. She opened her eyes again and looked up to the winter sky, refusing to mourn the lack of stars...the lack of him.

She raised her chin. No one said moving on would be easy. She was different, but the music was always there. And the people were here, waiting, row after row of expectant faces, waiting to see what this new version of her would bring. She had no idea if they would go along with her on this new path, or if this path was even the one for her—but she was setting off anyway.

She nodded behind her to Eli's band, and struck the first chord of Hourglass Reverb. She had a ton of other material to choose from, and after everything that had just happened, she'd intended to pick something else. But for this night, Eli had asked her to play that one. Now, at the sound of the familiar song, a cheer went up from the crowd, and she knew it had been the right choice.

Just as it always did once she started to sing, something cut loose. Some indefinable switch flipped in her mind, and she was herself again, set free, everything else forgotten under the stage lights. For a few minutes, the world narrowed to music and melody, the power and precision of the band behind her, the audience singing along with her heartfelt lyrics. Tonight, after everything that had happened in the bay this summer, the words had an extra, bittersweet resonance.

It was relief and bliss, satisfaction and emotion, rolled

into one heady package.

But as she started into the last chorus, the band in full swing, a murmur of something rippled sharply through the audience. All at once, she knew she'd lost them somehow, their attention no longer on the music. Instead of moving as one in time to the beat, they were scattered, distracted, pointing...

She faltered, the Gibson suddenly heavy on its strap, and turned to see what they were looking at.

A man was standing on the stage, with Eli's guitar. But although he was tall and handsome, like Eli, it wasn't him.

Her breath caught in her chest, and she stopped singing.

It was Liam.

Chapter Forty-One

As he walked toward the front of the stage, Liam kept his eyes focused on Jacinda. When he'd asked Hannah to help him make this happen, he hadn't factored in the possibility of gut-wrenching stage fright adding to his nerves. He'd never been on stage in front of fifty people, let alone five thousand or more, not to mention the robotic cameras trained on the stage. He concentrated on Jacinda's face—currently frozen somewhere between confused and shocked—and on not tripping over the lead attached to Eli's guitar as it trailed alongside him.

It didn't help that she seemed to be backing away, one hand over her mouth, the other clutching the neck of her guitar. But after a couple of steps, she bumped into the other guitarist, and came to a halt. The band stopped playing. She looked around at them, questioning, but they all just grinned. She had no idea that they were in on it too.

He came all the way to the front of the stage, a few feet from where she was standing. To his right, thousands of people waited and wondered in a hum of curiosity, obviously poised to complain at the interruption, but unsure what was going on. Here and there, a phone was held up, recording the moment. He swallowed.

Breathe.

Breathe.

The bass player came over and handed him a microphone, and Jacinda's eyes grew even wider. She took a step toward him.

Realizing something was up, the roaming camera guy who'd been taking close-up shots for the big screens on each side came nearer. Liam ignored him, zeroing in on the woman in front of him—smart, talented, beautiful…and off-limits.

Or not.

He'd thought about her constantly since she left.

Regretted leaving her standing naked in his room, her beachwear clasped to her chest.

Regretted the staggering stupidity of drunkenly offloading his pain and secrets onto the stranger who'd turned out to be Lainey Kingsley.

Regretted that he couldn't prove to her, in that phone call, that they could overcome anything standing in their way—the pain of the past, or the uncertainty of the future.

The only thing left to do was come and find her, and lay it all on the line. Because if he didn't, he'd regret that too. And he was done with regrets.

Here on stage, in her natural habitat, she was even more beautiful than he remembered.

He held the microphone tight, and smiled at her. "Hey."

"Hi," she replied cautiously, and her headset mic picked up the word and broadcast it out across the crowd.

"Hi!" some smartass yelled back, and a few others echoed the greeting, causing a ripple of laughter.

"Which brother are you?" someone else bellowed.

Jacinda flinched, and Liam looked out to the audience. Shit. This crowd could either help him, or totally undermine him, and make everything a hundred times worse. He squinted a little, trying to make out the faces beyond the first few rows. Hopefully they'd take pity on him. He turned back to Jacinda.

"You look amazing," he told her.

A volley of wolf whistles came from all sides, and she frowned.

Damn. That was the wrong thing to say. He couldn't help that he was blindsided by her beauty, even if she refused to be defined by her looks. And he knew how much more there was to her. Standing in front of her, he started again, without preamble.

"Jacinda...I screwed up. And I'd give anything to undo that. I'm sorry."

"He's sorry," a woman in the front row called out.

"He's hot," her friend yelled, and there was an eruption of catcalls and whoops from the women in the audience.

He felt his face heat up, and swiped his forearm across his brow. Jesus, it was warm under these lights.

Jacinda ignored the women and stood silently, watching him. With tousled hair and black eyeliner, holding a battered black electric guitar, she looked every inch the rebel—a woman doing things on her own terms. She'd planned a life for herself, without him. It was entirely possible that she didn't want to be convinced of anything different.

"I know our past is messy—" he began.

"We *all* know that," someone shouted from the audience.

Jacinda looked toward the voice, her brows knit, then back to him. "We do," she said. "Even our recent past."

With a sick feeling, he realized that putting her on the spot could completely backfire. But there was no going back from here. He looked out to the audience, now dotted with phones held high. Obviously, this was going to be on the internet, so he'd better make it good—good enough to knock his previous screw-up off the front page of every entertainment site out there.

Good enough that Jacinda would give him a chance.

Holding the bridge of the guitar, he forged on.

"I know our past is messy," he repeated. "*And* our recent past, which is my fault. But the rest of it was no one's fault. Ethan made his choice, and I carried it with me for years. And then it became your burden too. I never wanted that to happen."

She pressed the back of her hand to her cheek, her eyes

bright under the lights, but stayed silent. He didn't care about the audience now, or the band members standing nearby, or Eli Tyler watching from the wings, or the camera guy sliding ever closer. There was only her.

"But you and I are still here," he said. "We have our lives ahead of us. And when I look at my life without you—" The thought was a lump in his throat, and all he could do was shake his head, his eloquence gone. "If you'll let me, I'll do whatever it takes to make it up to you," he said, plain and true. "And maybe one day you'll forgive me."

Inevitably, someone yelled from the darkness, "Forgive him!"

"I'll forgive him for you," offered a woman's voice, triggering a wave of laughter. "Send him out here!"

"Put him out of his misery," advised someone from down the back.

The audience was restless, and so was he.

Jacinda remained silent, a line of doubt etched between her brows. He wanted to go and kiss the line away, along with all the complications and sadness, until her beautiful face was lit up in a smile again. Instead, he waited.

Finally, she spoke, her voice uncertain. "Your family, though…"

"They know I'm here," he said. "And we're figuring it out."

She tipped her head sideways, disbelieving. "Really? Your mom? Because that's important."

She glanced out to the audience, and he followed her gaze to where her mother was standing in the front row, looking back at her daughter. As Trina put a hand to her heart and smiled at Jacinda, he thought about his mother, now back in Australia doing damage control. After the visit to Sam and Danielle, fortified by snickerdoodles, they'd gone home and talked…and talked…until they found the beginning of an understanding that had been missing for so long. He hoped he could eventually do the same with his father—who was probably still apoplectic about having family secrets spilled online. But he'd be damned if he'd let either of his parents stand in the way of this.

"It's a work in progress," he said. "But you were right. We have to move on. And I want to move on with you."

"Oh..."

She worried the corner of her lip, maybe processing what he'd said. Seeing the doubt still in her eyes, he reached for his last piece of ammunition. From his back pocket, he pulled out his old blue notebook, full of lyrics.

"Open it to the marked page," he said, handing it to her.

From the way she looked at him, her brow furrowed, he knew she remembered it from the day she found it on his nightstand. She took it, and opened it to the page he'd folded down. He watched as her eyes ran over his handwritten lines, and then she looked up at him.

"This is the song. From the beach."

He nodded. He'd never forget that night by the fire, playing backup on the old acoustic guitar, listening as his own lyrics came from Ethan's mouth. Watching Jacinda's face soften and her eyes grow dreamy as the words entangled her heart. Sitting there, gutted, as she and Ethan walked away from the circle of light and warmth, leaving him dark and cold with jealousy. Because even then, he knew what he felt for her was true and right, even if it seemed wrong. And it was more than the careless summer fling Ethan was having.

Now, years later and half a world away, she stood holding the words in her hands, along with his heart—proving him right.

"But...this is *your* notebook...your writing," she said.

"Yeah." He waited for her to join up the dots.

"*You* wrote these lyrics?"

"I did," he replied. "I wrote them for you. They say everything I never could back then. Everything real I felt about you, even if I shouldn't have." He paused. "And everything real I feel now."

He watched as emotions rolled across her face, like the sunshine and shadow of a spring sky. "But they're so beautiful," she whispered, and the words fluttered from the speakers into the crisp, charged night air, where the audience stood riveted by the scene unfolding in front of them.

"Like you," he said.

A collective 'oh' went up from the crowd, in time with Jacinda's own. Maybe he *did* have a chance. He'd crossed an ocean for this—to claim back his words, and claim her heart.

He adjusted the guitar, took a breath, and started to play.

Chapter Forty-Two

J acinda had come on stage ready for whatever the night threw at her—but Liam wasn't one of the possibilities she'd imagined. She listened to him sing, captivated and disbelieving, and in that moment, everything shrank to him. His hands on the guitar, his ocean-blue eyes on her, his intentions clear.

She was standing on a stage in Los Angeles, but she was on a beach under South Pacific stars.

She was twenty-seven, and she was seventeen.

She was lost, and she was found.

As he sang, the words touched her like they did the first time...except it was different. The two of them were different. Everything was different.

> *The earth turned true and brought you here*
> *Your stars in my eyes, a galaxy near*
> *The moon and tide in quiet awe*
> *My waiting arms still wanting more*
> *Where oceans break, my heart goes too*
> *The only thing I want is you*

Once, those words had led her to a decision that changed everything. To a guy who was charming, and handsome, a high school hero who didn't love her. But she hadn't loved him either—they were only kids, venturing into an adult world that held challenges they couldn't have anticipated.

Now, though…she was a grown-up, and so was Liam. Both battle-scarred, but unbeaten. They'd been on opposite sides, but when they suspended hostilities it had been the hottest, sweetest truce in history.

She hadn't thought a permanent peace was possible…but after that phone call, he'd come all this way to persuade her otherwise. Taken the risk of widening the rift in his family. Acknowledged his screw-up—in front of thousands of people—and asked her for a chance.

Maybe it was possible.

Maybe they weren't on opposite sides after all.

She watched him sing, the simple melody carrying his lyrics on that dirty-sexy voice she'd had no idea he possessed. To her left, the audience was now a hundred per cent with him, the rectangular fairy lights of their phones setting the slanted seating of the Greek aglow. When the last note of the unnamed song echoed into the sky, they went crazy, clapping and cheering. But the sound seemed to wash over him as he held her gaze, focused only on her. His feet were planted squarely on the stage, the guitar resting low and easy against his body, but she could see the tension in his jaw, and the intensity in his eyes. He looked a little weary—maybe jetlagged from the flight—but he carried the edge of tiredness and a five o'clock shadow with a rugged sexiness. She wondered how much sleep he'd had over the last days, while she'd been rehearsing, fending off requests to do press, and trying not to think about him every minute of the goddamn day. Every minute of the day, until he turned up here in her world—the world he'd once resented her for being part of.

Her heart was pounding.

He waited.

The audience waited.

Just as she opened her mouth to speak, a shout came from the seats. "Kiss him!"

"Kiss him!" yelled another voice, and then another, and then all five thousand plus voices were raised in a repeating chant of "Kiss him, kiss him."

She felt her cheeks flame, because that was exactly what she wanted to do.

He grinned, but turned toward the front of the stage and held out his hands, palms downward, trying to hush them. Finally, they settled down, and she spoke.

"So you wrote that song for me," she said.

He nodded. "I did. For my sins."

"I like it. A lot."

"That was the plan."

She remembered the beach, the bonfire, and the flickering flames. Two brothers, both talented, smart, and handsome. One with a self-assured exterior hiding his very human vulnerability. The other always in the background, with a quiet strength he'd been forced to draw on for all the years since. She was suddenly struck with regrets for everything that had happened—her past decisions, one on top of the other, that had built toward the ending she never saw coming.

"I wish I could change things," she said. "I wish I could go back and do it differently."

"I know." There was understanding in his eyes. "The past never really goes away, especially one like ours. But everything we do from here on, in the future, is making a *new* past. And I want to make it with you."

He made it sound so simple, like explaining time travel without the pesky paradox. And when he said it, she believed him. Right now, if he gave her some explanation for why yawns were contagious, or what was outside the universe, she would totally get it.

"So...can we make it okay?" he asked. "For us?"

It was the question that had pushed them forward, and the stumbling block that had tripped them up. And now, it was the sixty-four-thousand-dollar question that would decide their future...and their future past. And the answer was easy.

She nodded. "I think maybe we can."

But he shook his head. "I heard a maybe from you before, and that didn't turn out so well. I came a really long way, you know. And there's *no* leg room in economy. I'm going to need a better answer than that."

She laughed, looking up at him. "I think we've both come a long way." And instead of an ocean away, he was within arm's reach. She wanted him closer. A *lot* closer. "My answer is yes."

And suddenly he didn't look tired at all. He looked like a light had gone on inside, sending hope and possibility into the darkest corners.

"Can you just kiss him now?" someone yelled.

It was the best idea she'd heard in forever. She stepped forward, and he stepped forward to meet her, two wanderers each rescuing the other. But as they collided, their guitars clashed together, sending a sudden, discordant noise blaring through the speakers, and a roar of complaint went up from the audience.

"Sorry," she said, to them, and to Liam, and to the band. "Sorry!"

She pulled off her headset and unhooked the transmitter from the back of her waistband, and passed them to a roadie who'd raced onstage. As she unplugged the lead and pushed her guitar around to her back, Liam lifted Eli's guitar off, and the roadie took it too.

Then Liam looked steadily at her, and she knew what he must be seeing. Her cheeks flushed, her eyes bright. What he couldn't see was how her heart was sending a happy, anticipatory heat through her whole body.

Or maybe he could.

What had she told herself? Nothing was guaranteed. She'd do what her heart told her was right. And what she'd once thought was wrong—what they'd both thought was wrong—had turned out to be totally, completely right.

"So...can you just kiss me now?" he asked, echoing the fan's question.

And she did.

She stepped forward again, then stood on tiptoe under the lights, put her arms around his neck, and pressed her lips to his. He took her head in his hands, tangling his fingers in her hair, and she felt the tension leave him, as though all the complication and confrontation and remorse had finally found a release.

It was the simplest kiss, under a spotlight with nothing to hide.

It was escape, but not running away. Redemption, but not regret. Moving on without forgetting. Desire without doubt.

It was just them.

And a cameraman.

And five thousand enthusiastic onlookers.

As the audience applauded and hooted, finally getting the satisfaction of a happy ending, the band started playing again. She heard Eli say, "Jacinda Prescott, ladies and gentlemen!" before he launched into yet another hit song, and the camera guy turned away from them to focus on the performance.

She pulled Liam offstage, half kissing, half laughing, until they were safely in the wings. He gathered her into his arms, and she pressed herself against him. He was sweet surety in a messy world, the safe place she she'd visited, but never thought she could stay.

"I'm glad you came all this way," she said, over the music. "But you still have a bit farther to go."

"Really?" He raised an eyebrow. "How far?"

"All the way," she replied, pulling him even closer. "*All* the way."

A slow grin spread across his face. "I'm in."

"In trouble?"

"The best kind," he replied. Then he put a hand against her cheek, letting his thumb brush the corner of her lips. "So...remember how I said I was in love with you, back then?"

She nodded. "Yes."

"W*as* isn't exactly the right word."

She started to reply, but he kissed the words away, an unspoken signal that he didn't want her to say anything she wasn't ready for. When they parted, she looked at him for a moment, and smiled. Then she silently took his hand, and led him away from the stage area, toward the stairs that led to her dressing room.

This man, with his own grown-up kind of trouble, was welcome in there any time.

Epilogue

High on the grassy peak of Mount Clarion, Jacinda stopped and breathed in the warm evening air, taking in the sea, the softening sky, and the offshore islands scattered across the water of the gulf. Up above, the moon curved in an indigo sky, and the first stars were just starting to shine. This view was still worth the climb.

After a year of commuting, she'd been in the bay two weeks. Sometimes at night, she'd wake up and listen to the waves, their quiet rush and return reminding her of what was precious in life, and so easily lost. Those nights, all she had to do was roll over, or reach out a hand, and find the warm, strong body of Liam next to her.

And then he'd wake up too…and neither of them would go back to sleep for a long while.

"I can see my house from here," she said to him now, as he came nearer in the dusky light. "And your house."

He stood close behind her, putting his arms around her waist. "And *our* house."

She leaned into him, feeling his warmth against her back. "I like the way that sounds."

"Me too," he said, lifting her hair and dropping a kiss on the side of her neck.

They looked down to the old Sweet Breeze Bay homestead, nestled at the very end of the beach where

Mount Clarion rose up from the coast. It was getting darker by the minute, but they could see people sitting on picnic blankets on the lawn, where they'd celebrated Christmas Eve day in the sunshine with friends and family. Friends and family who still lingered there—even though Jacinda and Liam had snuck away from their new home.

She smiled. "You know it's bad form to run out on your own party."

"They had us all day," he said. "And I wanted you to myself for a while. It's not my fault they wouldn't go home."

She laughed. "It was a really good day."

Everyone had relaxed on the lawn with drinks and snacks, enjoying the sun and the view straight out to the ocean. Velvet's kitten Suede—now a bold, black cat—picked her way across the blankets, stopping occasionally to be petted and check plates for any interesting tidbits. At the end of the garden, there was a small drop directly down to the beach, where Sam and his friends competed to see who could make the most spectacular leap onto the sand. Beyond them was the high tide of a blue, blue sea.

Under supervision from Liam's dad, Liam and Dane had manned the barbecue, managing the serious task of grilling steaks, sausages, and four of the most enormous crayfish Jacinda had ever seen. Connor had started out helping, but gotten distracted. Jacinda had watched him bring Hannah a drink, saying something to her with a grin. Hannah played with her blonde hair as she replied, blushing prettily, and Jacinda smiled to herself. The Sweet Breeze Bay magic must be working if Hannah was finally willing to be charmed by someone—she'd hadn't even thought about dating yet. It had been a rollercoaster year, as she wavered between kicking Todd to the curb—as Jacinda had—and being swayed by his declarations of repentance and devotion. Even though he'd brought it on himself, unfortunately proving Jacinda's fears true, it seemed like he wouldn't let Hannah go without a fight.

After lunch, they'd had Nana Mac's homemade pavlova—a New Zealand meringue dessert—with strawberries and ice cream. And later, those who weren't too lazy had gone for a swim. Even her mom had joined in.

After a few days vacationing in the bay, Trina had started to relax, as Jacinda had hoped she might, slowly letting go of her anxieties like peeling off layers on a warm day. It had been especially nice to see her and Liam's mom getting along. Jacinda didn't think Trina would ever return to live here—she was too settled in Florida—but she hoped the visit would wash away some of the lingering memories, and let her enjoy her childhood home again.

"I hope there'll be lots more good days," Liam said now.

"Oh, I think there will be," she replied, turning in his arms to look at him. A slight breeze ruffled his hair, and she put one hand around the back of his neck, loving the feel of him against her. "It's going to be amazing."

After all the teasing from Danielle and Riley about 'projects', she had Liam really had started working on something—a retreat center for anyone needing a break from entertainment industry overload. It had been a serious investment to buy the homestead and renovate it to the standard expected by the pampered but weary artists they hoped to host. But although it had been left to quietly deteriorate for years, it was basically sound, as well as charming—a little piece of Sweet Breeze Bay history. And the end result was worth it—with the beachy but luxurious accommodation in the outbuilding now in the last stages of renovation, they were nearly ready for guests. They'd included a small recording studio at the side of the main building, with equipment good enough for professional use. And she and Liam had reserved the best rooms for themselves a self-contained suite upstairs, with a wide deck looking all the way from Mount Clarion across the curve of the bay.

The whole thing had turned into a team effort. Riley and Caro were ready to help with catering for guests, and now Hannah had come to stay for a while, helping to take care of the thousand and one things needed to get set up. Jacinda was pleased her friend had accepted the offer—it was doing her good to get away from LA for a while. After working as Jacinda's manager, Hannah had been offered a job managing a new band signed with Altitude Records, starting in the new year, and she was thinking about taking it.

Eli had already visited, checking out the almost-finished facilities for a possible retreat with his team in the new year. After he and Liam colluded to surprise her at the Greek, with Hannah's help, the two men had struck up an unexpected friendship. The tour had been extended, and Liam had joined them for a while on the road. The whole thing had been weird at first, but eventually she'd even gotten quite fond of Eli herself...since forgiving him for being a self-confessed jackass.

"It's already amazing," Liam said, the sudden intensity of his voice matched by the midnight blue of his eyes in the almost-dark. "But...are you still sure about your decision?"

After the tour, equal parts fun and frustration, and a lot of thinking, she'd made the call to step away from the spotlight...mostly. She'd kept her Los Feliz loft, and cut a great songwriting deal that meant she could work between the bay and LA, still creating the music she loved, without the scrutiny she'd come to hate. In the end, it had been the easiest decision ever. It was what her heart told her was right...not because of Liam, but for herself.

"I'm totally sure," she replied. "And now I get to have my cake and eat it too."

She gave him a teasing squeeze, waiting for the smart reply that would surely come. But then his phone dinged with a message, and he reached into his pocket for it, still holding her against him.

"Sorry," he said, as he typed a one-handed reply, just out of her view. "Just a second."

Then he put the phone away, and looked back at her.

"I'm glad you're sure," he said. "Because there's just one more decision you need to make."

She frowned. "Really? What?"

He didn't answer. Instead, he took her by the shoulders and turned her around.

And she drew in a sudden breath.

Far below on the sand, in the space between the sea and their new home, was an enormous heart of golden lights. In the waning light, she could only just see that each light was being held by one of their friends or family. She looked back at him, wondering and waiting.

"A lot can change in one year," he said, his eyes fixed on hers. "But one thing will never change—the way I feel about you. No matter where in the world we are, summer or winter, good days and bad days. And we've had a few of each." Then he reached for her hands. "I came back to the bay last summer looking for something—closure, I guess. I never expected to find you."

She thought back to the shock of that moment over the gate, when she'd first seen him again. And then that other shock, seeing him on stage at the Greek. "I never expected you, either."

"I know," he replied. "But you saved me. We faced the past and made it okay. We remembered what was important—*who* was important—and found a way to move on, just like you said. Even though there were times when it seemed impossible."

She squeezed his hands. "And you gave me the clarity to remember what was important to me, too. You gave me a place to call home. A place to be me."

He nodded. "The bay is that kind of place."

But she shook her head, just a little. "I didn't mean the bay. I meant you."

"Oh." A softness came into his eyes then, and he leaned down to kiss her, tender and real. Then he pulled away again, and cleared his throat. "So, I have to ask you something."

"Okay."

The hesitation in her voice was from nerves, not negativity, but she saw a sudden doubt overtake him.

"Shit, I haven't done any of this right," he said. "And I didn't get you a ring yet," he added quickly, "because I know you like to make your own choices, and I wanted you to have the perfect one. But now I'm thinking I should have..."

She couldn't help laughing at his sudden, endearing jitters. "I think you just gave the game away."

He groaned. "Wait, I'm supposed to—" He started to get down on one knee, but she grabbed him and pulled him back up.

"No," she said. "I can't kiss you if you're down there."

So he stood tall again, straight and true in front of her, and took her hands again. "I just love you," he said. "And I want to ask if you'll marry me."

She looked up at him. This man, once conflicted and complicated, had brought a simple peace into her own life. Not to mention a sweet, hot, uncomplicated lust. And love. She glanced down at the heart on the sand, glowing just like her own. The lights shifted slightly as though the people holding them were impatient, the lights blurring and moving...or maybe that was the sudden dampness in her eyes. She looked back to Liam, and saw a restrained impatience in his own eyes. From lost to found. From far away to home. From wrong to a very unexpected right.

"I love you too," she said. "But I think you know that. And I think you already know what my answer is. Even without a ring."

He breathed out with a laugh, and only then she realized that he'd been holding his breath. He scooped her up and spun her around on the hillside, under the South Pacific moon and stars that had seen their every high and low. She pressed her face into his neck and hung on, laughing.

Then he suddenly put her down. "Wait. I have to text them."

She watched as he typed a single word—YES—and sent the message. Then they looked down to the beach and laughed again, as all at once, the heart broke apart, the lights racing madly around on the sand, a wild zigzag of celebration under the stars.

Then he pulled her hard against him and kissed her, as though it was their first kiss and their last, the proof of their triumph against doubt and secrets and an unforgiving world. And she kissed him back, because she knew they'd always honor how they began, and remember what they meant to each other now.

One distant summer had started something...and the next had changed everything. And now, all their future summers stretched ahead, uncharted but full of possibility.

She couldn't wait.

Acknowledgements

Every book is the book of a writer's heart, but this one is kind of special—a little bit of home, a little bit of elsewhere, and a lot of escapism, all rolled into a sweet, hot, and beachy story that was tons of fun to write.

Thank you to everyone who helped me bring it to life:

My editorial readers LaVerne, Lissa, Lauren, and Paula, for your insights, encouragement, and enthusiasm.

The Unicorn girls, for all things American.

Jackie, Sherilee, and Nicki, my fellow runaway writers, for road trips, real talk, and things to look forward to.

Adam, for your unwavering certainty…and for being sweet, hot, and beachy too.

And to all the readers who've bought my books, left reviews, shared with friends, and sent me messages—thank you for coming with me on this adventure!

About the Author

Serena Clarke writes escapist romantic fiction set all over the world. Readers have described her books as engaging page-turners, with sigh-worthy happy endings that will leave you smiling.

Her own story? She's lived in thirty-nine houses, in seven cities, in four countries. She's been a riding instructor, edited a medical journal, worked at a London law firm, and taught English as a second language to wayward teenagers. And now she's found her own happy ending—living near the beach in beautiful New Zealand with her family, writing the kind of feel-good books she loves to read. She hopes you'll love them too!

Find her online at www.serenaclarke.com.

Also by Serena Clarke

Where We Began
A North So True
The Same But Different
All Over the Place